BEST I NEVER HAD

BEST I NEVER HAD

A ROMANCE NOVEL

JEANNIE CHOE

LN
♡P

To anyone who has ever been told they're "too much."
Take your too much and change the world.
And to my girls.
For New York City, late-night karaoke sessions, and endless boba runs.

note to the reader

This book contains themes and subject matter that some may find triggering. For more information, please visit www.jeanniechoeauthor.com for a list of content warnings prior to reading.

Furthermore, triggers are not listed here to avoid spoilers in consideration for those that would like such information to be left out.

BEST I NEVER HAD

1

Natalia

past - senior year

I FIDGET in my seat as the hard stool underneath me grows uncomfortable. The classroom, decorated with various atomic models and a poster of a sad animated cell holding a phone with the words "no cell phones" in block letters, starts to slowly fill with students. One by one, they take their spots as our teacher, Mr. Khan, points to the assigned places on his seating chart.

"Okay, class. You're going to grab your microscopes from the cabinets. The slides for the cells are sitting on each of your tables for you and your assigned lab partners." Mr. Khan's voice rings through the classroom now that everyone has settled into their seats. I notice Hayden Marshall to my right eyeing the slides sitting between us as we play a silent game of who's-going-to-get-our-microscope before I start to stand.

"I'll get it." His low voice rings calmly.

I tilt my head up, meeting his eyes while making sure to smile, not wanting to come off as rude or unfriendly. His eyes, light with the tie-dye effect of olive and copper, look down at me as the wavy locks of his hair curl along his forehead and earlobes. His hands are tucked into

1

Jeannie Choe

the kangaroo pockets of his black hoodie, slightly faded, showing its comfort and use, with the sleeves rolled up to his elbows. I swivel back onto my rusty stool, turning to face the black surface of our lab table.

Why did I decide to take AP Bio? A class that I have no use for, will probably pass with a mediocre B, and will cause me unnecessary stress the entirety of my senior year. And now, I've been officially assigned Hayden as my lab partner.

Hayden Marshall. The jock whose interest in science shouldn't have extended beyond learning which starch source was most efficient in fermenting beer or exactly what about the female anatomy attracts their sexual counterparts. Yet here he was, ready to differentiate squamous cells and basal cells.

I watch from my periphery as Hayden stalks back with one hand gripping the arm of the microscope and the other supporting the base. He slides the microscope across the counter, the rounded tip of his thumb brushing against the tabletop, before unraveling the thick cord and plugging it in.

"I'm Hayden, by the way," he offers, his voice cool and collected as he steps half a step back, enough room for me to fill the space he was occupying in front of the microscope. Almost as if his plan is to follow my lead, his unfamiliarity in a lab setting showing through the cautious hesitance in his body language.

I don't offer my name. Instead, I nod as I flick on the light source and position the first of our slides over the mechanical stage.

"You're Natalia?"

"Nat," I answer too quickly, pulling away from the eyepiece long enough to correct him.

"Nat," he repeats.

Considering we've been going to the same schools since we were in eighth grade, it's unbelievable that this is the first real interaction we've ever had. Maybe it's the fact that our social circles run differently or that it's obvious even to us that we would get along as well as oil and water. But the reasoning behind why we're lab partners isn't some cosmic alignment or a sudden realization that we'll make the best of friends. It's simply the most original order of sequence known to mankind: the alphabet. When our last names come right after the other, Marquez and Marshall, it was only a matter of time before we were brought together in a way that wasn't our yearbook pictures sitting side by side.

I flick my pencil against the eyepiece, a hollow *clink-clink* filling the awkward silence between us. "That's simple squamous."

He steps in front of the microscope. His tan arm brushes against my shoulder as I lean away. I start filling out the worksheet that was passed around at the start of class while I wait for his observation of the slide. He nods as he pulls away and removes the slide for the next one with a scowl on his face that lingers between frustration and determination.

The rest of the class continues. I correct Hayden when he mistakenly identifies a pseudostratified columnar epithelium as a simple columnar, something Mr. Khan warned us of. He asks multiple times where in our text these epithelial cells can be found after finding that he had been going over the wrong chapter in our reading assignment.

After we've placed our equipment back to the correct spots, with Mr. Khan hovering over us like a hawk to make sure we handle everything with care, we hook our backpacks onto our shoulders and watch as the rest of class files out of the room.

Hayden turns to face me with his index finger scratching the small plane of smooth skin in front of his ear. "I swear, I'm not some dumb jock that's hoping to skate along on my lab partner's good graces," he says apologetically. I look up at him, his height stretching toward the porous tile ceiling, as he waits for me to say something, anything.

"It's fine," I say, sounding too timid.

"Yeah," he answers. "I'll be more prepared for the next class."

I give a sympathetic nod while realizing maybe this perception of Hayden Marshall that I've had over the years is completely wrong. Maybe those superficial titles like "jock" or "flirt" I mentally assigned to him are inaccurate in describing the Hayden Marshall standing in front of me now.

"I really don't mind until you catch up to the current chapter."

He smiles at me. "Thanks."

present – eight years later

I've always wanted a puppy. Growing up, my sisters, Carmen and Lucy, and I begged our parents for a dog, but they never budged. Responsibilities and whatnot. So whenever I see one, their furry tails wagging side to side and ears perked up in overzealous excitement, I find it hard to ignore them. As a result, I always give in, even if the owner is a stranger. Just a light scratch behind the ears, allowing a warm lick into the palm of my hand, or sometimes, if the moment allows, reducing myself to baby talk.

But right now, as the fluffy ball of eagerness begs for my attention, I'm left dumbfounded. Gobsmacked, befuddled, flabbergasted. All of the adjectives I can scour from my brain to define the effect of this bombshell that's been dropped in front of me. So instead, I watch blankly as the owner, an elderly woman with a full head of silver hair, tugs at the dog's bright-yellow collar as she gently coaxes it to follow along. Both dog and owner scurry off into the busy sidewalk, oblivious to the numbing shock coursing through my limbs.

"Sorry, Nat." Lucy's voice rings through the dull city sounds. "I probably should have waited till we got back to your place to tell you."

Matteo's getting married.

He's getting married. He's getting married.

I whisper a faint "it's fine" through my lips, but the words feel weak. And rough. Like it's been finely grated against the rough side of sandpaper before trickling through my lips. I continue to walk, my steps slow and sluggish. I don't need to look to my side to know that Lucy is watching me to make sure I don't pass out or do something absolutely crazy like run into traffic.

Her warm, comforting hand smooths against my chenille-covered forearm. "Nat, I really am sorry."

She's not sorry that she told me. Not anymore. She's sorry that the man I loved—*still* love—has moved on. The same man who decided I wasn't the one that he wanted to spend the rest of his life with and found someone else to share that future with instead. That my mending heart is no longer healing but has returned to a state of defeat, all within a matter of minutes and a few words.

"Matteo doesn't know what he wants," she offers, a small sigh of frustration blowing through her nose from her repressed anger toward my ex-lover. "Even Mom said so. He's just hurt, and this woman is the next best thing he was able to find."

But that isn't true. Because *he* broke it off. *He* was the one who told me he couldn't do this anymore. Us, planning a future, deciding if we wanted to venture down a path where we vowed to love each other in sickness and in health. It was all too much for him.

My heart clenches. It actually squeezes just the tiniest bit before I remind myself how far I've come since our breakup. How the nights spent wallowing in my sorrow as I cried myself to sleep wearing a dress shirt that belonged to Matteo was for something instead of having to circle back to how it felt when the heartbreak was freshest. My teeth gnaw on my lower lip, and my gaze zeros in on the cracked sidewalk before Lucy takes my hand in hers and squeezes it.

"Come on, Nat. Let's get some lunch, and we'll stock up on some goodies for tonight."

I smirk, unable to hold back my smile as Lucy leans her head against mine. "And by goodies, you mean liquor?"

She shrugs with a sly smile. "I mean, if that's what works for you."

I envy her at this moment. Twenty-five with a heart that hasn't yet been splintered in two by heartbreak. Her normally dark hair, now light with the magic of bleach and toner, is perfectly coiffed and held together in a gold claw clip. After a six-hour flight from Seattle that included a one-hour layover in Minneapolis, she looks flawless. Her casual wear clings to her slender body, and her makeup looks smooth and untouched. As if it were done by a professional, not by herself using a small compact and her meal tray on the last leg of her flight into JFK.

When I look at myself in comparison, I look exactly how I feel: tired and rejected. Like I've been living in the same clothes for a week instead of the full day I've been relaxing in my fuzzy sweatsuit set. And my dark hair, untouched by the same magic Lucy paid an arm and a leg for, is barely being held together by the worn-out elastic I stretched out to fit all of my long, full hair in.

We continue, sidestepping a man with an adult ferret on a leash, which elicits a double take from Lucy, as we finally arrive at our destination. My stomach turns with the reminder that it's lunchtime and this will be my first meal of the day. Our entrance into the small sandwich shop is announced with the twinge of the copper bell hanging at the top of the doorframe. Muffled pop music plays over the single speaker mounted next to the convex security mirror as a lone fluorescent light flickers in the opposite corner of the cramped store.

"They have a really good BLT here. Or if you're not in the mood, their pastrami is good too," I inform Lucy. "What do you want?"

Her nose scrunches as she considers her options. "I think I'll just have the grilled chicken salad. With the vinaigrette dressing."

"Just a salad?"

She nods, her forlorn eyes leaning toward the glass display case holding a large assortment of cakes and other pastries.

"At least split a brownie with me," I request, coaxing her to give in to her obvious desire for a treat.

Her mouth twists to one side in a half smile. "Fine," she caves. "I'm on vacation after all."

I turn to the cashier, place our order, and pay.

"So who else is coming tonight?" Lucy asks as we step away from the register to the long pick-up counter.

I stare at her blankly, slightly confused by her question. The last time I spoke with her, on speakerphone with Carmen in the same room, we agreed on a welcome party for Lucy in the small apartment Carmen and I share but discussed no further than the fact that we would have plenty of alcohol and that Carmen would be managing the playlist. "I don't know."

"What do you mean?"

"I didn't invite anyone," I elaborate.

"What?!" She crosses her arms and lightly huffs, annoyed that our night may be limited to the three of us, plus Carmen's boyfriend, David. "So it's just the four of us?" Her bottom lip juts out, pouting like a child. And I can't help but notice the light stomp of her right foot, a habit that she hasn't grown out of since she learned it got her what she wanted at the age of four.

"David might have some friends he can invite," I finally offer when the furrow in her brow doesn't relent. "We can ask Carmen when she gets home."

"Are they cute?" she inquires a little too eagerly. When I look at her with an expression that borders judgment, she smiles coyly. "What?"

"Nothing," I answer, teasingly rolling my eyes at her. "I just didn't know you were looking to meet someone while you were here."

"Nat, I am not looking to *meet* anyone. But a girl can have a little harmless fun on vacation."

The cashier standing a couple of feet away raises his brows as he overhears our conversation before placing our order on the pick-up counter and calling out our number. We take our lunch placed neatly in a brown paper bag, along with the large brownie that I can't stop thinking about, and head toward the doors.

I smile at Lucy. I'm glad that she's visiting for the weekend, even if she brought with her the grim news of my ex's relationship status strapped onto her carry-on. The last time I saw her was over the holidays, when Matteo and I were still together, and I can't believe how much I miss spending time with her. I miss having *Twilight* marathons on our squishy living room sofa back home or lying on my childhood bedroom floor, as hers was always scattered with wrinkled clothes and dirt-covered sneakers, while we listened to the latest One Direction album.

The sad look of rejection that was on my face is now fully replaced by an eager, hopeful smile as I look at Lucy over my shoulder. "Are you excited for this mini vacay away from school?" I ask.

Her nod is vigorous, excited with the anticipation of getting drunk off whatever hard liquor we have access to. "I really needed this trip. School has been horrendous. Why I thought grad school was a good idea is beyond me."

A light laugh slips through my lips as we open the door, and I crash into a cardboard box held up at eye level. "Oof!"

The box nearly drops to the floor before the person carrying it manages to balance it with their knee. I smile apologetically, consciously keeping my eyes zoned in on the floor while rubbing the spot on my chest where the hard corner of the box poked me. I turn my body sideways, awkwardly squeezing through the narrow opening between the box and the doorframe.

"Natalia?"

My gaze shifts up, following the edges of the wide box gripped by large hands that look tan not only by the sun but by genetics as well. When I get to the stranger's face, there's something oddly familiar. Tall, dark-haired, and eyes that light up through a smile that's all teeth and dimples.

My brow furrows as I finally place the stranger to a point in my mind that I've long left behind but never fully forgot about.

"Hayden?"

I spent a lot of my senior year at Coolidge View High worrying about trivial things. Like making sure my grades were good enough to land me an acceptance letter to NYU, passing my driver's test after failing twice my junior year (it's not *my* fault the stop sign was strategically placed behind a tree branch!), and begging my mom to buy me a pair of Doc Martens when everyone else wore ballet flats and knee-high pirate boots.

But I also had my Advanced Placement Biology class and Hayden Marshall. While our brains worked through the various stages of cell division, our hearts were poured onto that contaminated black tabletop, and we were able to forget for the entirety of fifth period that we came from two different social pods.

"Hayden Marshall!" The loud, high-pitched squeal of excitement isn't coming from me. It's coming from Lucy. "Nat! It's Hayden!"

I nod, eyeing her as if I hadn't already acknowledged his presence when he crashed into me.

"What are you doing here?" Hayden asks, directing his question to me while shifting the box from one arm to the other.

"I'm visiting for the weekend," Lucy answers.

"It's...Lucy, right?" he says, his eyes narrowing as he tries to place her.

"Duh, silly!"

Hayden smiles politely, then looks back at me. "Do you live in the city?"

"Um, yeah," I answer, still a little shocked that I've run into a Coolidge View High alumnus hundreds of miles from home. "Just around the corner. You?"

"I live in Brooklyn. I'm just here making a delivery." He holds up the box. "The restaurant I work for does deliveries for their desserts." He tilts his head in the direction of the glass display I was just ogling.

My eyes widen. "So I have *you* to thank for those brownies?"

He laughs. "Among other things." He shifts the box again. "Hey, listen. Let me get this inside. Don't go anywhere."

I nod and look over at Lucy, who's grinning from ear to ear.

"Nat, it's Hayden Marshall!" she whispers sharply as soon as he's out of earshot.

"Yes, we've established that," I whisper back, giving her a look of disapproval. *Geez*, you'd think we just ran into one of the Ryans. Gosling or Reynolds, of course. Now *those* men are worthy of this level of raucous excitement.

"He is so hot!" she exclaims, smiling eagerly while ignoring the sarcasm in my tone.

"Lucy!"

"What?" she defends herself. "He is."

I stay silent, neither agreeing nor disagreeing with her. Our heads turn toward the inside of the store, both observantly watching as Hayden hands over the large box to an employee while smiling and nodding a quick exchange.

One of the best things about being an adult well past the legal drinking age is that your past self starts to blur. Those cringe worthy memories as a teen start to fade and become replaced by new ones of adjusting to being an adult in the real world. But sometimes, those memories come back to you in human form. In my case, through Hayden Marshall.

He's no longer dressed in his black Adidas hoodie, faded jeans, and Jack Purcells. Instead, he's wearing an open chef's jacket with a yellow bandanna loosely tied around his neck. His hair is tousled, long enough for it to be called shaggy and somehow evident that he doesn't usually wear it as long as it is now.

"Tell me you didn't have a crush on him in high school," Lucy deadpans, expecting the obvious: that everyone in our high school, not just the ones in my and Hayden's graduating class, thought he was attractive. "I'm going to invite him tonight."

My head swerves to face her. "What? Why?"

"You said it yourself, it'll most likely be just you, me, and Carmen. It'll be fun!"

Before I can change her mind, Hayden reappears. He smiles at me and Lucy through the scattered water spots staining the glass door as he pushes it open to greet us once again.

"So, you moved all the way to New York City," he says, his smile curving up as he looks at me.

"Yeah," I answer with a timid voice. "I've been here since college."

"Wow, that long?" He whistles. "I moved here from Chicago just before the summer. I'm still getting used to the city."

"It takes time." I smile sincerely.

"So," Lucy interrupts, "we're having a party tonight. Would you like to come?"

"Oh…"

"You don't have to," I add.

"But it would mean a lot if you did," Lucy adds, side-eyeing me with a glare. "I'm only here for a couple of days."

"Yeah, I'd love to," Hayden answers with a smile.

"Are you sure?" I ask. Lucy not so discreetly nudges my side.

"Yeah," Hayden affirms sincerely. "I don't really know anyone in the city, so it would be nice to be around a familiar face." His smile deepens, his eyes leaving Lucy's to linger on me for a bit longer. I tilt my head to the side when I smile back, remembering how comfortable I used to be around him. Poking fun at his quirks and casually making jokes that led to learning a language of sarcasm only he and I seemed to understand.

Lucy clasps her hands in front of her. "Great! It'll probably start around…ten?" She looks at me for confirmation, and I nod. "And if you have any cute friends, they're welcome to come too."

I suppress an impulsive eye roll as Hayden reaches into his pocket and pulls out his phone. He unlocks the screen and hands it to me. "Here, put in your number."

"Oh yeah. Sure," I say. I take his phone and do as I'm told, Lucy's eyes practically glued on Hayden as he patiently waits for me.

Hayden looks down at his phone screen once it's back in his hands. His hair hangs loosely across his forehead as he punches his fingers along the keyboard before a *swish* noise emits from his phone. My phone pings from my back pocket.

"That's me."

I slide my phone out of my pocket and see a row of ten digits lighting up the screen with a new message. "So we'll see you tonight?" I ask, smiling up at him.

"Yep. I'll be there."

Lucy smiles proudly at me with her chin tilted upward and lips pursed together in silent approval.

"See you tonight!" Lucy exclaims as she lightly shoves me in the direction of my apartment. "Come on," she says in a hushed tone even though Hayden is out of earshot. "I have to look extra sexy tonight."

2

Hayden

senior year

"IF YOU DON'T MIND, can I label the cell samples today?"

I gesture toward the cutouts of the cartoon-style images of cells. Carefully drawn by Mr. Khan, each print is cut out into two-inch by two-inch pieces of paper with no indication of it being a skin cell, a bone cell, or a muscle cell. Natalia peers up at me with dark eyes that look like they belong to a sweet, timid puppy dog.

"Sure," Natalia answers a little nervously, though she appears less skeptical than last week when I worked through our lab assignment like a bumbling idiot. I spent the weekend reading through this week's chapter ahead of time. If not to prove that I know what I'm doing, then at least for the sake of my steady grade point average.

"Thanks."

We both sit on our stools, with Natalia having to take a small hop before somewhat awkwardly climbing onto the seats that are too high. I can feel her eyes on me as she silently studies which images my hand lands on and where I place it to correspond with the correct labels. My brow furrows as I reconsider my offer to take over the assignment while wondering if maybe I looked over the wrong chapters at home once again.

From my periphery, I can see Natalia's hand where she has a pencil twirling between her index and middle finger. She's sitting close enough that I get a whiff of the subtle vanilla scent lingering around her. It's not the cheap, artificial kind of vanilla. It's more like the kind of sweetness that's warm and inviting. It reminds me of how my entire house smells when my mom bakes a fresh batch of her oatmeal chocolate chip cookies, wrapping me in comfort and affection. That's what Natalia smells like. Like coming to a warm home after a long day at school in the dead of winter where everything bites from the coldness.

"You know, I remember you from Mrs. Knight's class," I say abruptly in an attempt to break the silence between us.

When she tears her eyes away from the laser focus she had on the cell images, she looks surprised. As if there's no explanation as to why I would remember her. Even though we've been going to the same schools since we were thirteen, passing by each other in the hallways, and always managing to see each other's faces throughout every school year since.

"US History? At Madison?"

"Yeah," I confirm. "Eighth grade, third period."

I turn away from the counter, facing her completely as she tilts her head. She has her hair curled today, different from when she had it straightened last week, and the curls bounce as they drape over her shoulder. A breadth of a smile starts to appear as her eyes widen, the first time I've seen her face show anything but timid insecurity. I didn't notice before, most likely because I've never paid attention to the way her smile lights up her whole face, but the tip of her nose dips for a second when she does.

"I remember you always coming in with a mustard-colored backpack that had an angry penguin hanging from the zipper."

"Badtz Maru," she says quietly.

"I'm sorry?"

"That's the name of the penguin."

"Oh." I chuckle lightly, turning back to our assignment, determined to prove to her that I'm not some average jock who skates through classes based on my field position on the varsity football team. I actually want to do well in this class.

"I didn't think you knew who I was."

"I know who you are."

Her smile grows even wider, and her eyes light up in a way that makes me think that maybe there's more to Natalia Marquez than what's on the outside.

past

"Everything go okay with the delivery?"

Uncle Pat greets me as soon as I walk into Pour Toujours, his restaurant and where I've been a sous chef for the past four and a half months. I don't usually make pastry deliveries, so he walked me through each sandwich shop and coffee house that I had to stop by for our weekly orders.

"Uh, yeah." I bite back the smile that creeps onto my face, thinking about how I ran into Natalia Marquez just a couple of hours ago.

"Andy will be back next week, so you shouldn't have to continue these deliveries," he explains apologetically, referring to our usual delivery man who was out with the flu. Pat leans back in the dining chair he's sitting in, situated behind a clothed table nearest to the hostess counter. A tall glass of soda water with a lime wedge floating on the top along with a spread of menus and napkin cloth samples sit in front of him.

I wave him off. "It's fine. I really don't mind."

I turn to walk into the kitchen to prepare for our dinner rush. But Pat clears his throat, his usual signal that there's more to the conversation he wants to add. Sure enough, when I look at him, his solemn expression confirms it.

"I talked to your dad this morning."

I nod, my eyes narrowing on the menu between his fingers as his thumb runs over the neat calligraphy print on the high-end paper stock.

"He just wanted to say hi and make sure you were doing okay."

I purse my lips together, forming a judgmental smirk. "The phone rings both ways, Pat."

"He knows," he says with an understanding tone.

"He can talk to me when I call Mom," I add for good measure.

"Hey," he yields, avoiding taking sides, "I'm just the messenger. I already get heat for hiring my favorite nephew."

I shake my head with a quick eye roll, knowing that I'm his *only* nephew. "I'm going to get back into the kitchen." I tap two fingers on the tabletop, a dull, rhythmic thud signaling the end of our conversation.

"Yep," he answers with a gruff nod.

I sigh, the frustration blowing out through my exhale as I realize that this, my strained relationship with my dad, isn't my uncle's fault. He and my mom are the ones who are caught in the middle, trying to mediate a rift that started with a blowout. One that ended with my dad accidentally flinging candied yams onto my mom's holiday-themed tablecloth trimmed with fall leaves, right next to the uncarved turkey and steaming pile of stuffing. Uncle Pat was there to witness the whole argument. Right up until I stormed out and my dad stood with his fist pounded into the dining table.

I wish things were easier. I wish my entire past didn't revolve around my dad's idea of what my future should look like. I felt ashamed for choosing to go against the grain, opting for a career he once called "home economics" instead of becoming this idea of the perfect son along with the profession he deemed appropriate. Something that forced me into a straitjacket of a suit every day while surrounded by men in the same attire, all proving themselves through power struggles and measuring sticks.

I let out a deep sigh as I stalk toward the kitchen, walking through the almost empty dining room, and get hit in the face with heavy steam and the hot sizzle of oil hitting pans. I ready myself for our dinner rush, positioning a worn washcloth at my waist and washing my hands, just as the lingering thoughts of my dad and my career choices that drew the rift between us are interrupted by the clanging of plate to metal.

"*Who left the lamb out?!*"

Every movement in the kitchen stops. Spoons stirring in pots, knives hitting plastic board surfaces. Even the in and out of traffic between the swinging doors all comes to a halt. Everything is at a standstill as our head chef, Augustus DuPont, demands answers.

"I asked who left out the *fucking* lamb!"

With every member of the kitchen staff frozen in place, Pat rushes in to handle yet another anger-filled blowout from Chef DuPont.

"Chef, what's going on?"

"I asked who the fuck left the lamb out when it was supposed to be put in the walk-in right off the truck."

Pat sighs. His hands come up in an attempt to calm Chef DuPont. "It's fine. I'll get someone to move it."

Chef DuPont turns to Pat, his face coming inches away from him as his finger points at Pat's chest. "I can't work with an incompetent team like this. I'm tired of it!"

I watch from the assembly line, stacking a pile of clean plates, as Chef DuPont's face grows redder and redder.

"Gus, it's not a big deal," Pat explains, attempting to smooth down his anger. "The delivery came in less than twenty minutes ago. I know because I signed for it. The meat hasn't gone bad."

Chef DuPont throws his towel against Pat's chest and storms off. He purposely knocks over a saucepan sitting on the corner of the countertop as he rounds toward the back exit. Pat turns to the rest of the kitchen staff that seems to breathe a sigh of relief with Chef DuPont's exit.

"Okay, people. Let's keep things going. We have a busy dinner ahead of us," he calls over the length of the kitchen. He then turns to me. "Hayden, can you take this to the walk-in? And make sure there isn't anything else that was missed from the delivery?"

"Sure."

"Thanks." Pat sighs as he walks away, his shoulders hunched with stress and worry.

I pick up the plastic crates carrying the slabs of lamb chops, all neatly stacked with times and dates stamped along the cellophane covering, and walk them toward the walk-in on the other side of the kitchen. I avoid Chef DuPont as he stalks back into the kitchen. He mutters profanities under his breath as he works his way through the sous vide station to package and seal filets of monkfish for their water bath.

I spend the rest of my shift watchful of Chef DuPont's where-abouts, trying to minimize contact with him while working through our nightly dinner rush. I plate dishes carefully and sear the prepared lamb chops to perfection, despite Chef DuPont's rage over proper oil temperatures, until my shift is over late into the night.

"I'll see you tomorrow, Pat." I peer into Pat's office as he waves at me without looking up from his desk. I wave a quick goodbye to a couple of servers at the hostess station before I walk out the door. Once outside in the early fall air, I look down at my phone to a new message from Natalia.

Natalia: We moved the party to 11 but feel free to show up whenever.

Her message is followed by her address, along with a reminder that I don't have to bring any "cute friends" as Lucy requested.

Me: Sounds good. I'll see you later.

There are a few memories that I've held on to since my time at Coolidge View High. Football practice and our homecoming games usually take front and center. Spending my lunch trying to stuff as much as I could into my Subway sandwich with disgusting junk food choices like Cheetos, ramen noodles, and gummy worms comes in a close second. But another constant memory I have is the fifty-five minutes I spent in AP Bio with Natalia Marquez as my lab partner senior year. Before that class, we'd never spoken a word to each other. We were just two fish in the sea of Coolidge View High students. But in the small bubble that formed around our lab table surrounded by the pungent odor of formalin and fragile beakers, we were two ends of a magnet, the opposite poles coming together for a single hour to talk about everything and nothing.

Natalia, much like all the minute details of high school, unexpectedly made an imprint on me. When I think of her, I think of home. Like what it felt like to stop by the local Wendy's for a Frosty on Thursdays after school. Or the comfort I had going to Five Guys to stuff my face with burgers and shelled peanuts with the rest of the football team. It also reminds me that during one of the last years of our adolescence, before the both of us entered adulthood, Natalia was the most constant and real presence in my life. Someone who I had a hard time saying goodbye to when the last days of school finally approached.

When I walk through the front door of my apartment, I find my roommate, Dexter, sprawled along the couch with his phone held in the air.

"Hey," he calls, lacking any form of energy.

"Do you have any plans tonight?"

"I'll probably get off this couch at some point." He exhales loudly, groaning as he sits up from his too comfortable position. "And walk over to Pepper Thai for some food. You?"

"I got invited to a party."

His brows perk with interest. "A party? By who?"

"I ran into this girl I went to high school with," I say softly, still unbelieving that the encounter happened at all.

"Is she cute?"

I ignore his question. "You want to go?"

"Sure," he says with a casual shrug while tossing his phone onto our cluttered coffee table.

"We'll leave in about an hour," I say before I walk into my room.

I strip from the grease-infused jacket and the stiff polyester pants, tossing them into my hamper before stepping into my shower stall. The scent of coq au vin and chocolate soufflé dissipates into the stream of hot water as I lather cedar-scented body wash into my hands and wash away the remnants of the day from my body.

As the heat melts the tense muscles in my neck and shoulders, the expectancy of seeing Natalia starts to grow in small flutters.

Suddenly, senior year feels like an entirely different time. I know both myself and Natalia aren't the same kids we were back then, but the need to revert back to being those imperfect seventeen-year-olds fills me. As if I can swipe the last eight years of my life and somehow transport back to that small classroom with Natalia by my side.

I don't have very many friends, only a handful that I've made since my arrival to the city this year. Dexter is one of the oldest friends that I have. We met during our freshman year in college when we were assigned as roommates that first year before I never returned. But there's no friendship like the one I had with Natalia, all of it revolving around memories, secrets, and inside jokes. Like how if I were to reference "Starbucks lovers," Natalia would smile at the vivid image of our guidance counselor, Mrs. Geiss, incorrectly singing along to the very Taylor Swift song during a pep rally before spirit week. Or how if I were to say "mind the gap," we would both think of Mr. Walton, with his fake British accent, bellowing at every student that ran through the threshold of each classroom more than ten seconds after the bell rang to announce each tardy arrival.

Showered and in the gradual process of air drying, I wrap a towel around my waist and search my closet for something to wear. I find that more than half of it is filled with chef's jackets and the same uncomfortable polyester pants I wear every day, just in different variations of gray and black. Once I settle on a casual dress shirt with the sleeves rolled up and worn jeans, I walk into the living room to find Dexter dressed in an outfit almost identical to mine.

"Well, one of us has to change," Dexter jokes.

3

Natalia

senior year

THE PETRI DISHES clink on the counter with our samples freshly smeared on the agar plate, waiting to be grown into disgusting blobs of bacteria. We start stacking our plates, gently securing the lids and flipping them upside down like we were instructed to by Mr. Khan.

"So you already applied to NYU?"

I nod, my finger twirling around the tip of my fishtail braid draped over my shoulder.

"That's great. Good luck."

Hayden's voice carries something else besides the standard well wishes. Something like a small twinge of disappointment that can only come from an undecided future as we both stand at the gateway to adulthood, a cap and gown in our hands as we dive headfirst. Or maybe that's just how I feel about our future, no matter how prepared I think I may be.

"What about you?"

He looks at me, his brows raised as he waits for me to elaborate.

"College? Have you applied anywhere?"

"Penn State 'cause that's where my dad wants me to go. And I put in an application to Ohio U as a backup."

"To play football?"

It's a question, but it's more of an assumption. One that I don't expect him to deny with his obvious love for the sport. He shakes his head, and his fingers curl into a loose fist on the table before he turns to face me.

"I don't know."

"You don't know if you want to play football?"

"I don't know if I even want to go to college."

"It's okay not to know," I offer with an encouraging smile. "We're only seventeen. We have at least seven and a half more years of mistakes before we finally know what we're actually doing with our lives."

His entire body turns to face me, his movements suddenly urgent. "But have you ever felt like if you were ever given the chance to find out what you wanted to do, it would change everything for you? Like you just need that door to open up so you can finally discover what you're destined for?"

No, I haven't, I think. Doors have always been open for me. Mainly because my parents don't set limits when it comes to my, and my sisters', future. Every opportunity I've wanted to venture into has been laid out for me to test the waters and see if the path I want to take is one I really want to dip my toes in.

"Do you feel like you know what you're destined for?"

He shrugs, the urgency gone and replaced with the same uncertainty he had when I asked him what colleges he applied to. "It doesn't even really matter," he says, trying to hide his somber mood with disinterest.

"Why not?"

"Because whatever my dad wants, whatever he wants me to major in or whatever college he wants me to go to, that'll be my life." He sighs, the indifference seeping through his voice along with the blank look of resentment in his eyes. His fingers toy with the petri dishes, sliding them around before I place my hand on his, signaling him to stop before he pushes one off the edge of the table. He quirks a brow at me and pulls his hand away just as I tuck my hand back under my thigh.

"So if he wants you to go to clown college and major in balloon animal design, you're going to do that?" I ask, unable to hide the sarcasm as I wait for him to deny it. But he doesn't.

"That's what it looks like."

I study his features for a minute. I notice the tic of his jaw and the furrow of his brow causing a shadow to cast over his features. He tucks his head down toward his chest as he stuffs his hands into the pockets of his hoodie.

"For the record, you would look absolutely ridiculous in an orange fro wig and a red ball nose," I say, my poor attempt to lighten the mood. "Not to mention those obnoxiously large feet. Like, who are they kidding?"

But it works, because he smirks, his amused eyes looking at me as he pulls his gaze away from his lap.

present

Lucy and I are pushing my love seat and coffee table against the wall to make more floor space for our party. Our tiny kitchen table is filled to the brim with bottles of hard liquor. Party-sized bags of chips and red Solo cups are stacked in a neat pile, waiting to be filled with various alcoholic concoctions.

As soon as we both slump on the soft cushions, our muscles tired from the unfamiliar laborious work, I hear the door click open to find a tired and frizzy-haired Carmen peek through the door in her wrinkled, royal blue medical scrubs.

"Carmen!" Lucy runs to greet Carmen with a warm hug, leaving me sprawled on the couch.

Lucy arrived in front of our building this afternoon, a yellow cab carrying her and her two suitcases for a three-night stay when I was the only one home. This is only the fourth time she's seen Carmen since she graduated college and moved to Seattle three years ago, making the trek to the opposite coast before finally pursuing her graduate degree. The distance, plus Carmen's demanding schedule at the hospital, has made it near impossible for the three of us to be in the same time zone.

Carmen squeals as her tired eyes light up, holding our baby sister tight to her chest and smiling warmly over Lucy's shoulder.

"I missed you!" Lucy squeals.

"I missed you too, baby girl." She reaches up to ruffle up Lucy's hair, making her recoil and flinch.

"Ugh! You guys have to stop treating me like a baby!"

"But you are a baby, *baby*," I tease, moving a bottle of Ketel One from the table to the freezer.

"Says the person that's literally eleven months and four days older than me," she teases with a scrunched expression and her tongue poking out.

Carmen sets her bulky lunch cooler on the kitchen counter before she does a once-over on Lucy. "You lost weight," Carmen states matter-of-factly, regaining Lucy's attention.

"I know." She smiles, proud that she's withering away. "I started this no carb diet after Labor Day, and it's doing wonders for my summer body."

"Summer isn't until next year."

"So?" Lucy counters. "It doesn't hurt to start now."

Carmen rolls her eyes. "You should be glad that Mom doesn't see you looking like this. She'd have a fit."

Lucy waves her hand at her. "I look amazing though!"

"So what are the final plans for tonight?" Carmen asks, settling into a stool tucked under our mini breakfast bar.

"Natty said that you were going to ask your super hot and super sweet boyfriend if he had any friends he could invite tonight."

"I said that David *might* have some friends he could invite," I correct her from the small pantry and reappear with a roll of paper towels in my hand.

"So?" Lucy says to Carmen, oozing excitement.

"I'll ask him," Carmen answers with a small surrendering smile.

"Yay!" She hops, her hands clapping in front of her. "By the way, I put my luggage in your room. I figured since you have the California King, you wouldn't mind sharing. Plus, Natty kicks in her sleep."

"At least I don't snore!" I call, walking into my room to get ready while letting my two sisters catch up.

I spend the next hour running a tornado through the bathroom, pulling out all of my makeup and hair care products while distracting myself from facing the reality of Matteo's new relationship status. Just as I'm running a straight iron through my hair, I meet eyes with Carmen behind me. She's leaning up against the doorjamb to the entrance of the bathroom dressed in fitted jeans and a thin gray cashmere sweater as she watches me with her arms folded in front of her. Before she says anything, I know she already knows.

"You want to talk about it?"

I play dumb. "About what?"

Her brows rise, telling me not to play her a fool. She took Lucy into her room to let her unpack while they caught up, so I know she already told Carmen everything.

I put down the flat iron and unplug it before sighing and turning to face her. "There's nothing to talk about."

"So…you're completely okay with the fact that the man who broke your heart after four years of your life has moved on and is *engaged* to a woman barely six months after you broke up?"

I visibly wince, eyes closed and forehead cinched. "You don't have to paint it so vividly."

Lucy only knew the details after a phone call with my mom, when she accidentally spilled the details from her own conversation with Matteo's mom. They grew close over the course of our relationship, even referring to each other as their in-laws. When we broke up, I don't know who took it harder: me or our moms.

"Apparently, Mom's invited to the wedding?"

I scoff. "That's nice of Matteo."

Carmen steps up to my side and slinks her arm around my shoulders, leaning her head against mine. "You know you deserve better, right?"

I smile weakly at her through our reflection. "Maybe someday I'll believe that."

Carmen is the big sister that everyone wants. With there being an entire decade gap between us, she's never treated me or Lucy as if we were a burden. She loves me and Lucy with a passion. The kind of love that carries the responsibilities of being the first child but without the resentment of those responsibilities. Mainly because my parents never placed the weight of being the eldest on her shoulders. They've always accepted whatever she's able to give and never made her feel guilty for it. It's probably why she's such a good doctor. Her compassion doesn't come with conditions. It's one of the reasons her boyfriend loves her so much, almost as much as I do.

When Matteo and I broke up, I showed up at her door, a suitcase in hand and tears running down my cheeks. She welcomed me, clearing out her spare bedroom and telling me that I could move in. No questions asked. She watched as I picked up the pieces of my broken heart for the last six months, each day getting a little better at an excruciatingly slow rate. With the news I got today, I feel like I've reverted back to square one.

She slumps onto the closed toilet seat, drawing her knees up as she keeps a watchful eye on me. "Oh, by the way," she says. "Starting next week, they want me to work the night shift."

I drop the makeup brush in my hand and cross the narrow hallway to my room. "For how long?"

"Indefinitely," she answers, following my steps out of the bathroom.

I'm at my closet, searching for the outfit I already planned out for tonight, when I swerve my head around to face her. "What! Why?"

I've hated when she works nights on the few occasions she's had to work a double shift. It means I'll spend a lot of nights alone, and being in an apartment that still feels slightly foreign to me, I'm not happy about it.

"There's no one else. The senior specialist suddenly decided to retire, so I'm going to fill in until they find a replacement." She crosses the length of my room and perches at the edge of my bed.

I harrumph, not even trying to hide my disapproval.

"I know," she answers. "David isn't too happy about it either."

"Can I maybe come with you?" I plead. "I promise I'll only take up a small bed, and I won't even ask for snacks. Just that you check in on me every once in a while."

"Carmen!" We both turn our heads toward my open door, Lucy's shrill cry demanding Carmen's attention.

She stands and places a hand on my shoulder. "Nat, you'll be fine," she says with a reassuring voice, trying to soothe down the slight frown on my lips before she walks away and leaves me to mentally prepare for the loneliness I'll have to sit through in an empty apartment for the coming weeks. Or maybe even months.

I huff as I get dressed, thankful that I already planned on what to wear since our doorbell is starting to ring nonstop.

The black pleather pants and matching corset I decided on cling to me, lining my curves and exposing a small sliver of my abdomen. My dark hair, shiny and pin-straight, billows down my bare shoulders as I apply a fresh layer of cherry-red lipstick in front of my floor-length mirror.

When I walk into the living room, I see Lucy, who's dressed in an emerald-green silk dress barely covering her the way a medium-sized terry cloth towel would, pouring a drink for David. Carmen is going over a playlist on her phone with music playing over our Bluetooth speakers as a man, who I assume is one of David's friends, hovers over her to approve of her music choices. I wave a quick greeting to David before the doorbell rings yet again.

When I hurry toward the door, I find Hayden on the other side.

There was an assembly during our senior year. It was during the sweltering heat of September and our principal, Mr. Walton, decided to start the school year with a bang by introducing all the teachers, counselors, and other essential staff, including a sophomore wearing a yellow-beaked falcon costume. Along with the staff, the entire varsity football roster joined them in the gymnasium. And when Hayden entered, the crowd went wild. He jogged across the shiny wooden floor, waving toward the pullout bleachers with a wide smile on his face as a dimple pressed into one side of his cheek. His chest puffed proudly as he stood tall, the large number eight on the center of his long torso on display for all of our peers. Meeting the end of the line, he stood along with the rest of his teammates, winking at the cheerleaders and fake punching other jersey-clad football players, basking in every glory day that high school had to offer him on a silver platter.

When I see Hayden now, dark, messy hair that curls at the roots only to flick outwards at the base of his neck and the same hazel eyes flecked with chocolatey specks around the pupils, I feel like I've been transported back to that gymnasium. How the smell of pubescent body odor and Victoria's Secret's Very Sexy Now body mist will always remind me of the look on Hayden's face when we met eyes for a fleeting second across the sea of students.

"Hayden!" I greet him. He's wearing a crooked smile, widened to expose his teeth, with eyes that light up when my own smile spreads across my face.

Seeing him, the warm sense of familiarity giving me the assurance that he isn't just another acquaintance I'll have to struggle through small talk with, brings a sense of calm I didn't expect. The same calm that washes over me when he envelops me in a gentle bear hug.

Once Hayden pulls back, he steps aside to reveal a second guest beside him. "This is Dexter."

Dexter steps forward, taking my extended hand. "Hi, nice to meet you," he says with a voice that's low and raspy in a sultry kind of way.

"Hi. I'm Natalia." I wave them in, opening the door wider for them to enter.

Lucy comes bounding. She hugs Hayden, pulling him down to her while hanging on to his neck as he wraps a hand around her shoulder.

"Come in!" she squeals. "I'm making drinks."

Hayden steps in, and Dexter follows. I close the door and walk into the kitchen to gather the rest of the chips and chicken wings that David brought with him.

Our small apartment begins to fill with people, followed by the low rumble of chatter and peppy music. People that I assume David invited, along with some friends of Carmen, mostly fellow doctors that don't mind letting a little loose on tequila shots, which Lucy is passing around right about now, are scattered around in clusters. I didn't even know Carmen invited any of her colleagues, but some look as if they're coming off a long shift, dressed in the similar rumpled scrubs that Carmen comes home in.

I stay back, sipping on the vodka and cranberry drink I mixed together in an attempt to let the thoughts of Matteo drift away from me. When all I can see is the image of him sitting on our cream-colored couch that we purchased at Crate and Barrel, telling me he couldn't handle the pressures that his mom and I were putting on him to settle down and get married, I need air.

I step out onto the fire escape from Carmen's bedroom, bypassing a few scattered guests leisurely chatting over bottles of beer and glasses of wine on Carmen's bedroom floor. I lean against the cold metal railing as I look down four stories onto the sidewalk, where I watch people passing by in hurried steps. The vodka is making its way into my bloodstream, warming me and finally fuzzing the memories of Matteo, when my thoughts are interrupted.

"Got room for one more out here?"

When I turn, I see Hayden climbing out of the window to the fire escape. His large body is barely able to squeeze through the frame.

"Sure," I say, scooting to the left to make room for him. He has a half-empty beer bottle in his fingers, loosely holding the neck as he sidles up to me.

"Getting a little crowded in there for you?" he asks, pointing his thumb into my packed apartment.

"Something like that," I answer softly. I tilt back the rest of my drink, the vodka that settled to the bottom of the cup burning as it trickles down my throat.

A slightly embarrassing silence lingers between us, Hayden filling it with a light tap of his nails against his beer bottle.

"So, do you still talk to anyone from high school?" Hayden asks, his shoulders slightly hunched and elbows braced against the railing as his posture mirrors mine.

I shrug, coming off more awkward than the blasé nonchalance I was going for. "Not really. The occasional congratulations or happy birthday on social media. That's about it." I turn my head toward him. Our eyes meet for a second before we both look away.

"Yeah, me too. Not much to keep up with now that we're all so busy with our own lives." He pauses to swig his beer. "Mmm," he exclaims through his pursed lips as if suddenly remembering a bit of detail that I should be aware of. "Jenny Chen married my cousin. I guess they took a class together at Ohio State and started dating after. They just had a baby last year."

My brows rise. "*Jenny*, Jenny?" I insinuate, knowing the exact Jenny he's talking about. The same Jenny that he had an on and off relationship with throughout most of our senior year, the two oftentimes blowing up in an argument in the crowded hallways.

"Yeah, yeah," he answers with a defeated eye roll. "No need to rub it in."

"I guess she kept it in the family," I comment. He shakes his head as he moves closer to me and bumps his shoulder into mine.

"Oh!" I gasp, suddenly remembering my own hint of gossip as we share more news from our graduating class. "I heard Tina and Ben got married." I grin, my smile turning sly, then amused, hoping he'll remember what the couple was famous for in high school.

"Didn't they hook up in the back of a car? And everyone saw?"

I nod a little too enthusiastically. "Mm-hmm."

"Wow," he answers softly as both of us take a small trip down memory lane to when the rumors spilled through the halls about the back seat hook-up that everyone was talking about, teachers included. "Well, good for them."

I scoff, remembering another detail about Tina that's left a sour taste in my mouth since senior year. "Yeah," I say bitterly.

"No? They should burn in hell?"

"Let's just say Tina wasn't the nicest person to be around," I say, not wanting to go into further detail about my buried hostility toward Tina and other members of her clique.

"Ben wasn't that great either," he offers. "The only thing he was good for was a joint and asking random people for a ride to the shadiest parts of town."

"Hmm," I hum.

With Hayden talking about high school and seeing him now as an adult beside me, I can't believe how far we've come since those days in biology class. I thought I would only remember him as the playful, silly seventeen-year-old who managed to make our hour spent in Mr. Khan's class fun. But looking at him now, I can't help but notice how much he's grown out of the teenage skin I was so accustomed to. He towers over me by more than a foot, and his shoulders and back have spread wider, bigger. When I avert my gaze, my eyes trail over the exposed area below his elbow where his tanned skin, noticeable even in the dark, flexes with each movement, somehow further reminding me that he's a man now.

"It feels like just yesterday, doesn't it?" he asks a little wistfully as he stares off into the open space in front of him. "Like high school was just last Wednesday, and now we're almost thirty."

I gawk. "Okay, Mr. Dramatic. We're barely twenty-six. Thirty is still light years away."

He chuckles. "So what have you been up to since those wonderful memories at Coolidge View High?" he jokes, lightening the mood.

"Nothing really," I answer sincerely.

"Nothing?" he repeats my answer. "Nothing interesting has happened to you in the eight years since our graduation?"

My mind flashes back to Matteo, something I *really* don't want to talk about tonight. "I mean, there isn't much. I've just been living in the city since we graduated, and I work for a tech company downtown. That's basically my life."

"Wow, that's it, huh?"

I poke his side with my elbow. "You don't have to make my life seem so boring."

"I'm sure you've got something exciting going on that you're just keeping from me."

I frown, thinking how far from the truth his assumption is and that this party is the most exciting thing to happen to me in years. And I'm not even enjoying it that much. "There really isn't much going on with me," I say softly, more to myself than to Hayden.

"Okay, then," he says, tapping my arm with the back of his hand in an encouraging, supportive sort of way. "Tell me one exciting thing that happened to you this week. You gotta give me something."

"Hmm." My lips purse together while I consider his answer. "My coworker brought me these amazing lemon tarts from this French bistro off Broadway in the Tribeca area. And I haven't been able to think of anything else since."

"Pour Toujours?"

My eyes widen as my hand grips his forearm. "Yes! You've been there?"

"I work there," he confesses.

I gasp. "Hayden, if you don't tell me that you're lying right this second, I'm going to have to prematurely apologize for the fact that you will never get rid of me."

He laughs, the sound echoing off the opposite walls of the apartment building facing ours.

"So you're, like, a cook there?" I ask, my hand still gripping his arm.

"A chef," he corrects. Not to be rude, just to inform me of the accurate terminology in his line of work. "Actually, I'm the sous chef. Basically, I'm second in command."

He brings the narrow opening of his beer to his lips, glugging the amber-yellow ale as he watches me over the bottle. I drop my hand back to my side, suddenly realizing that it's been resting on his bare skin this whole time.

"How did you become a sous chef?" My body turns to face him, our arms no longer grazing against each other.

He does the same, gnawing on his lower lip while studying the label peeling off his beer bottle as if deciding to remove it completely or leave it alone.

"It's a long story," he says to the bottle with an air of hesitance, indicating that the problem with the story isn't that it's long but difficult to tell.

"We have all night."

He smirks before letting out a long, drawn-out sigh. "I spent a year at Penn State to study finance, and I quit school after that year."

"What did you do?"

"I went to France. Studied the art of *le French cuisine* in Montpellier."

"Wow," I respond, genuinely impressed with the journey his life has taken.

"Anyway, after about a year and a half, I came back and moved to Chicago, where I worked at a restaurant for five years before my uncle offered me a job at Pour Toujours, so I accepted."

"Wow," I say again, this time as more of an acknowledging whisper. "That sounds pretty impressive. Maybe we should have started with your story first so I could've made up a more exciting version of mine."

"It's really not that exciting," he assures. "A lot of burn marks and getting yelled at."

I clear my throat. "So you've only been here for, like, four, five months?"

He nods, swallowing the rest of his drink. "It's been a bit of an adjustment. Hasn't really felt like home yet."

"I felt like that at first too," I agree. "Kind of like a fish out of water. But I'm sure you'll have no problem adjusting and meeting new people." I playfully nudge him, poking the hard muscle of his forearm with my index finger.

A small smile lifts one side of his mouth while his eyes linger on the warm spot of skin that I just pressed, revealing the dimple that I've always remembered is there. The same one that only appears with certain smiles. Like the one he has on his face right now, not full but curved upward in one corner. "What's that supposed to mean?"

I smirk. "Just that if you're anything like you were in high school, gaining the attention of those around you shouldn't be that difficult."

"You make me sound a little arrogant. Like I *like* being the center of attention."

"Come on, Hayden. You were a pretty big deal on the football team. Even I know that. *And* you were the prom king to top it off." I side-eye him with a smile that carries the knowledge full of the lasting details of "hot guy" gossip that seemed to center around Hayden and the other guys on the football team. But the funny thing is, even though he played the popular guy role at school, that facade was only surface deep. It's as if there are two sides of Hayden that I remember. The one that sat by me in biology class and the one that I watched from afar in the hallways.

"Runner-up prom king," he says, as if correcting this minor inaccuracy lessens the status he held. "Meaning I wasn't popular enough to win."

I roll my eyes, bringing my hands up in fake surrender with a sarcastically obvious *my bad* plastered on my forehead. He smiles shyly, his face lowered to the ground as he stuffs a hand into his pocket.

"It still gets a little lonely sometimes," he claims, his gaze loosely settled on the railing in front of him before he looks up at me. "Those *Final Destination* marathons start to become all too real after watching them alone so many times with no one to tell me that it's just a movie. I start to come up with a hundred different scenarios on how *I* would go."

"Nothing can be worse than getting smashed by a large tree trunk," I comment.

"I don't know. I'm thinking getting burned to death in a tanning bed is worse."

"Oh, so *that's* how you get your skin that nice golden color. Here I was thinking you won the genetics jackpot."

He chuckles, and his brows lift along with that amused smile before the corner of his eyes crinkle.

I tilt my head toward him and realize that as Hayden's eyes stay fixed on mine, we're both two lonely souls in the city of millions. And it seems like some big cosmic alignment that we're here, hundreds of miles from home and almost a decade since our last goodbyes. Kismet really does work in mysterious ways.

"Well, you have me now," I finally offer. "If you ever need a friend, I'm here."

4

Hayden

senior year

"YO, you guys want to go to Five Guys after practice?" Toby bellows across the row of tables that holds about ninety percent of the varsity football team.

My head perks up at the mention of burgers and fries. As usual, I'm still hungry even after the footlong I devoured fifteen minutes ago.

"I'm down."

Other members of the team and some of their girlfriends chime in, nodding along their agreement to stuff our faces with greasy fast food after what is sure to be a grueling practice.

As I'm finishing the chocolate chip cookie that came with my sandwich, I notice Natalia walking through the cafeteria with her thumbs hooked through the straps of her backpack held close to her body. Her hair is blown out, crimped into deep waves that I know she took time to style. She runs her fingers through it, shifting it to one side, and the soft angle of her jawline tilts upward, exposing her slender neck. Her steps come to a halt as she rounds a table, a small group of her friends already seated and sharing a large bag of chips that looks odd in a crowded school cafeteria. She sees me watching her and when I wave, she gives a small smile before turning back to her friends and reaching for a chip.

"You talk to Natalia Marquez?" Toby asks as he watches the whole exchange.

"We have AP Bio together. She's my lab partner."

"You're taking AP Bio?! Who knew our hunky wide receiver was sexy and smart!"

I scoff, releasing a *pshh* sound. "Shut up, Tobe."

He punches my arm, and I punch him back before I catch another glimpse of Natalia looking back in my direction.

"Hi." I turn my head to see Jenny Chen saunter up to my seat on the cafeteria table where my feet are resting on the long bench. It's still technically summer, but the warm weather is gradually easing itself into hibernation, causing the cooler winds to make us wrap our sweaters a little tighter. But Jenny manages to stick to her short shorts as long as she can, trying to keep herself warm with the hoodie she found in the back seat of my RAV4 rather than switching her wardrobe to something more practical. She settles herself in between my knees, her hands braced on my thighs as she gives a soft, seductive squeeze.

"I missed you earlier after third period," she croons into my ear. She purposefully grazes her cheek against mine before pulling away, looking at me with hooded eyes.

My smile curves into a crooked smirk. "Sorry," I say. "I had to talk to Madame Martin before class."

"That's okay," she says, her voice low and drawn out. "Maybe you can make it up to me. My house later?"

"I have practice. And the guys wanted to make a Five Guys run, but sure, maybe after."

She turns her face to her right, her hands outstretching to Tina Alves as she offers Jenny an opened bag of gummy bears. When I look back up toward where Natalia's sitting, I see she's looking at me again. I look away when Jenny tugs on my arm to wrap it around her waist, pulling my attention toward her and away from this pull that has me using an extra ounce of mind power to not look at Natalia yet again.

present

I'm finishing the last of my drink, eyeing Natalia and reminiscing about our shared memories of high school in silence. Her hand crosses her chest, and her fingers grip the opposite shoulder as she looks at me with her chin resting on the back of her hand. My eyes linger on her hand, watching her fingers trace over the smooth lines that connect her neck and shoulder before my gaze trails up to the small silver hoop earrings pierced through her earlobe.

Everything about her looks so soft and comforting. Even bound in the leather that runs the length of her legs and the tight top that wraps around her torso, all of it in a color that's usually associated with death, she looks warm.

I've never seen that in a woman. Dressed up while looking as if she's dressed down. Looking like she took the time to look nice while making it seem effortless. I can almost imagine her looking just as comfortable and easygoing in stained pajama pants and a T-shirt two sizes too big for her.

We're interrupted by a high-pitched squeal from inside the apartment. We both turn to find Lucy leaning against the bottom sill of the window. Her hands are gripping the sides of the frame as she looks at us with glazed eyes and a hysterical giggle that makes her shoulders bounce.

"Natty! Carmen and David said they'd do tequila shots with me but only if you do too!" And then she disappears, filtering back into the crowded apartment with her hands in the air, waving in sync to the music.

"Ladies first," I say, my hand extended toward the window in a slight bow.

"Come on. Let's get this over with," she groans.

"It's tequila, Marquez. Not a root canal."

"Says you, Mr. I-Can-Drink-You-Under-The-Table-Any-Day."

"One shot, Nat." I hold up a finger to emphasize the count.

She bends her body into a perpendicular angle, her hair falling like a loose curtain around her. Her cleavage rises upward when she leans forward, making me avert my eyes as she slides back into the apartment. "And that's one tequila shot closer to me hugging the toilet all night."

I cringe.

"Yeah, doesn't sound very pretty now, does it?"

She's inside now, with the opening of the window dividing the space between us. She reaches through it and tugs at my arm as I follow suit, curling my body inward to fit through the small opening.

I didn't realize how many people filled Natalia's small apartment or when the night shifted from a small gathering of friends to a full-on party. People are filling every corner, leaning against the walls, speaking over the music, and careless to the noise complaint that will most likely come within the hour.

Natalia leads the way, weaving around people and avoiding a splash of beer that misses her feet, hitting the wood floor instead. She turns and looks at me over her shoulder as she watches me struggle to maneuver myself through the crowd. She reaches for my hand, and her delicate fingers grip my thumb. Her hand doesn't move to cling to my whole hand. Instead, it stays there, wrapped around my thumb as she tugs it gently, making my hand look large and awkward in contrast to her small one as I follow her lead.

I watch as she peers at me over the bare skin of her shoulder, her long dark hair billowing behind her as I catch a peek of the red lipstick painted on her full lips. I smirk lightly when her smile spreads into a wide grin.

How did this happen? When did we grow up? A familiar pang hits my chest as in between the vision of Natalia standing in front of me, I catch glimpses of her at seventeen. Her hair always styled in different ways while her feet were bound into the clunky boots of her Doc Martens. I can't believe it's been eight years, our graduation procession with us in our navy-blue cap and gown misting away into nothing but a fond memory. We're actual adults now, settled into a stage of our lives where we have real responsibilities.

After squeezing through the crowd, we arrive at a small table lined with small shot glasses filled to the brim with a clear liquid I can bet my next check isn't water. Dexter stands at one end, eyeing the row of perfectly lined up liquor as if it were a slab of red meat. He looks up and grins widely at me. His eyes are glazed over, with the flush of redness filling his cheeks and neck. Lucy stands next to him, her face hovering over his ear as she whispers something before they break into a fit of giggles.

Lucy has a shot glass already in her hand, carefully lifting it and handing it to me first and then a second one to Natalia. Natalia eyes hers, her eyes widening as she suppresses a nervous gulp. Around us, more people have gathered, claiming their own glasses as they raise it into the air. A man, who I was introduced to as Natalia's sister's boyfriend and whose name I can't quite remember over the chaos, speaks over the voices.

"I just want to say," he starts, "thank you for gracing us with your presence this weekend, Lucy. I hope you visit us more often."

Everyone cheers, bringing their glasses up in the small circle, barely clinking as they hurriedly toss the contents to the back of their throat. With my glass empty, I grimace, biting down on the juicy, citrusy lime that was passed around before I look at Natalia. Her glass is still in front of her, full and teetering to the edges. She wasn't kidding when she said she can't hold her liquor. Without a second thought, I take it from her and toss it back, chasing my already consumed tequila with another one.

Her mouth gapes as the corners lifts into a smile. No one noticed that she didn't take her shot as everyone else is consumed in the bitter after taste that usually lingers into a violent shiver, no matter how accustomed one is to the taste of tequila. I discreetly hand the glass back to her and wink.

She laughs as she brings the back of her hand to her mouth and turns to face the other way. When she does, her cheek comes close to my arm. Not enough to touch but enough to let me know that this is our little secret. I peer down at her. Her twinkling eyes curve as she suppresses her laugh.

"Thanks, Marshall," she says through her smile.

"Anytime," I answer.

5

Natalia

senior year

"CAN you take me to the bookstore after school today?"

I look at Lucy. Her shoulder is leaned up against the locker neighboring mine as I rub lotion into my hands. She extends her left hand toward me, silently requesting a small dollop.

"Sure," I answer, squeezing a pea-sized amount of the coconut vanilla cream onto her hand and tossing it back in my locker before slamming it shut. "Is there something you were looking for?"

She shrugs. "Just wanted to look around."

"Can I come?" our friend, Yuri, asks from my side as she pops an Ice Breakers mint in her mouth. "There's this Victorian romance book I've been wanting to get."

"Is it like the last one you read? Something about a duchess and the stable boy?" I ask, poking fun at her love for romance novels that revolve around steamy sex scenes and forbidden love interests. Her most recent one included a particularly sexy romp where the main characters were caught in a rainstorm and stuck in a secluded stable.

"Doth thou accept my most treasured declarations of love," Lucy calls dramatically with a fist clutched to her chest, making us all break out into laughter.

"I'll see you guys later," Yuri calls before walking off to her fifth period class. Lucy and I wave at her as I turn to see Hayden across the hallway. His back is up against a wall, and Jenny Chen is pushed up against his chest. Their faces are less than an inch away from each other with smiles that cut into their cheeks and reach all the way up to their ears. Just as I'm about to look away, I see their tongues tangle together.

I look back at Lucy, shaking the image of the intense PDA I just witnessed. "Carmen emailed me about this book she thought I might like. Maybe I'll find it while we're there," I say.

Lucy's gaze follows where I was looking, where Jenny now has her arms up around Hayden's neck, and his hands are roaming down her waist, traveling further south.

"She's so lucky," Lucy croons wistfully.

I chortle, rolling my eyes as I turn to walk in the opposite direction. "Yeah," I say sarcastically. "So lucky."

Lucy nods a lazy goodbye as we separate, her walking into her English class and me right into bio where I'll have to sit next to Hayden for an hour and wonder what it is about him that Lucy has deemed Jenny such a "lucky girl."

I'm already reaching into my binder for our homework assignment when Hayden finally saunters in with a lazy smile plastered on his face.

"Hey, Marquez," he says with a relaxed edge to his voice as he slides into his seat.

"Marquez?" I question. "I didn't know we were on a last name basis."

"Are you kidding?" he responds, the disbelief creasing his brow and deepening the curve in the corner of his mouth. "You're the only one that knows how dirty the inside of my mouth is."

I cringe, mentally recalling a recent assignment when we had to swab our own soggy saliva onto agar plates for bacterial and fungal growth. "Don't remind me."

He chuckles, nudging my shoulder with a fist as Mr. Khan powers up the projector, calling our attention to the front of the class.

present

By Monday morning, my hangover still hasn't abated. The multiple tequila shots Lucy forced down my throat, ones that Hayden couldn't intercept, with my sister's hip attached to my side as she grew drunker and clingier, have a lot to do with it. The lingering nausea, along with a dull headache, remind me that I'm no longer in my early twenties when I can bounce back after a night of binge drinking as quickly as it takes me to pop two Advil. Still, as I watch Lucy shove her belongings into her matching lavender-colored suitcases, I can't regret the weekend that we had.

"Text me when you land," I instruct. "I'll be at work, but call my office if you need anything in the meantime."

She heaves her suitcase, the smaller of the two, and hoists it into the trunk of the yellow cab with ease. "I will."

She looks significantly peppier and brighter than I do. The day before, while Carmen and I stayed in bed well into the late morning, Lucy was already up, exploring the city and bringing us a tray of coffee and turkey BLTs by lunchtime.

We embrace in a tight hug. My arms cling to her as I say goodbye, knowing that the following months we're going to spend apart will only remind me that my baby sister is an independent adult before we unwillingly separate.

"Bye, baby girl," I tease, bracing my hand against the open car door.

She rolls her eyes and slides into the back seat as I close the door behind her. "Bye, Natty," she calls from the open window.

I watch as the cab drives off, and she pokes her head out the window to wave back at me. The cab disappears into the sea of traffic and busy New Yorkers on their daily commute.

After my own twenty-minute pedestrian commute, I walk into the building that houses my office, riding the elevator as it climbs up the high rise to the thirty-sixth floor. Dern Tech Solutions has been in the business of software design and computer hardware manufacturing for eight years. I came on board as a product manager with nothing more than a communications degree, learning the field of tech as I worked closely with our marketing department. I've grown comfortable in the field, learning to keep up with the fast-paced digital age that consists of tablets and computer apps. It's a job that's kept me busy when my life revolved around building a life together with Matteo. One that I had no idea would crumble so quickly when I broached the subject of a future.

"Good morning, *mi amor*!" a cheerful voice calls as I place my laptop bag on my desk chair.

I turn to see José, a member of our marketing department who has literally become my work husband, standing too energetically for a Monday morning at the doorway to my office.

"Good morning," I say quietly, the nausea resurfacing as the scent of José's onion bagel permeates through the wax packaging in his hand.

"Uh-oh," he says, noticing the greenish-gray undertone of my complexion. "Fun weekend?"

"It was fun until Saturday morning and I remembered that I'm not twenty-two anymore."

He laughs, oblivious to my aversion to his breakfast and peeling back the crunchy sounding wrapping in front of me. "How about we go out for lunch today? My treat."

"Sure." I settle behind my desk and hear my Slack message ding on my desktop as soon as I power it on. I roll my eyes and look at José. "Mark is already messaging me, and it isn't even nine a.m."

He shakes his head. "Which means I probably have a message waiting for me too."

José's wide mouth clamps onto his bagel, and he inhales almost half of it as he turns to walk away. I type a response to Mark's message asking me if I'll be attending this afternoon's meeting with the marketing department, José's department. I smirk as I see José's name pop up in the group chat window.

Before I know it, I'm elbow deep into our meeting's agenda and responding to three days' worth of emails from Mark. A heavy pile built up in my inbox, as I took the day off on Friday for Lucy's arrival. Mark working through most weekends, this past weekend obviously not the exception, doesn't help either.

I'm responding to an email from one of our software engineers about a new iOS program and the compatibility for our users when José knocks on my glass door.

"You ready?"

My eyes squint, looking at the clock on my monitor and finding that it's already close to one o'clock. And as if on cue, my stomach rumbles softly.

"Yeah," I say, reaching for my wallet and locking my computer. We walk out of the office in silence, falling in step with others on their way out for their lunch break. "Where did you want to go?" I ask when we approach the elevator.

"I've been craving a really good fish taco since last week," he says, followed by a quick, thoughtful hum.

"Las Tres Vientos?" I suggest as the elevator arrives at our floor. My mouth starts to water thinking about the creamy flan coated in the gooey syrup and savory sweetness I always order after a steamy plate of fajitas.

"Oh yes!" José answers excitedly.

There's a pep in our steps as we walk out into the afternoon sun. The late summer air is warm but breezy and fresh, and I'm so relieved. It looks like the days of having to carry around an extra stick of deodorant in my purse can be tucked away until next year.

"Ah, I feel like I can finally breathe," José comments, whipping out a pair of sunglasses. "That summer humidity was doing horrors to my skin."

"I think we can stop bugging Jason to sneak us into the Soho House now. I'm pretty sure I got my money's worth on that neon orange bikini from Saks," I add, referring to our lazy weekend pool days when

José's boyfriend, Jason, snagged us guest passes to the rooftop pool at the Soho House.

"I think we can get in one more pool day before the weather gets too chilly," José says. "I got these new swim trunks, four inch inseam. It's so hot. Pink with palm leaves all over it. Jason's going to see what he's got when he sees all the man candy eyeing me."

I laugh and José tosses his head back, making a show of flipping an imaginary tail of hair over his shoulder.

On our way to Las Tres Vientos, we pass by Pour Toujours. I smile to myself, remembering my run-in with Hayden and our trip down memory lane at the party. Before Friday, I had nudged away the memory of our friendship, something that felt personalized and was meant for only us two during the short year that filled our senior year. And now here I am, peering into the storefront of his workplace, hoping to catch a glimpse of him. It's as if we were always meant to be a part of each other's lives, and time or distance is irrelevant in the matter.

José is talking animatedly about his Saturday morning with Jason searching for vintage furniture during their trip to Newport, Rhode Island over the weekend. I laugh when he tells the story about how Jason was approached by a woman, pixie blond hair and visibly in her fifties, making a pass at him when José stepped away to get gelato.

"Natalia!"

Both José and I turn at the sound of my name to see Hayden halfway out of Pour Toujours before he lets go of the open door and bounds toward me.

"Are you on your lunch break?" He stands with one hand braced on his hip and the other cupping the back of his neck.

I nod. "Yeah, we were having a hankering for some Mexican food," I answer, tilting my head in the direction we're headed. "This is José," I say, gesturing toward José as they shake hands and smile. "José, this is Hayden," I add as José's eyes bounce between me and Hayden.

"I didn't get a chance to thank you on Friday night," Hayden says, turning to face me. "Dex and I had fun. I hope Lucy wasn't feeling too hungover the next morning."

I smile, remembering Lucy's intoxicated haze as she slumped on the couch once the crowd dwindled back down to just the Marquez girls, as David started endearingly calling us, and David.

"She handled it better than I did." I laugh. "She left this morning."

His head shifts into a sympathetic tilt. "Aw, so soon?"

"Yeah, I know," I say, frowning slightly at the sudden pang of missing my sister. "Next time she's in town, I'll let you know. I'm sure she'd love to catch up again."

"Sure, that sounds like fun," he answers. He turns when a man calls his name from Pour Toujours's door, waving at him to come back inside. "Hey, if you ever want to hang out or get drinks, text me," he adds, facing me again.

"Okay," I say softly.

We hear his name being called again, this time more urgently and with the telltale sign of irritation. "I gotta go," he says apologetically as he points a thumb behind him.

"Oh yeah," I answer awkwardly in contrast to Hayden's natural confidence. "I'll see you around."

"See ya," he calls as he jogs back toward the restaurant. I watch as the man who was calling his name swats the back of Hayden's head before he walks through the door.

"Who was that?" José's voice is full of curiosity and insinuation. "And why haven't I met him before?"

"We went to high school together. I haven't talked to him since we graduated, and I ran into him on Friday," I answer, resuming my steps toward Las Tres Vientos. "My sister invited him when she had her little party on Friday."

"He's *cuuute*," he exclaims, dragging the last word as he quirks his brows.

I roll my eyes at him as we round the corner. My stomach rumbles once again when my eyes land on the mauve sign embellished with a margarita glass and a cactus. I think about salty tortilla chips and spicy salsa while pushing away the thoughts of Hayden's attractiveness and our second run-in in less than a week.

6

Hayden

senior year

MY FINGER SKIMS over the jumble of words on the thin sheets of paper in my mom's cookbook. I study the measurements for brown sugar and flour before scooping both from the respective containers and dumping them into the glass bowl on the kitchen counter. Just as I'm holding up a measuring spoon at eye level, carefully pouring out the exact amount of vanilla extract the recipe calls for, my mom enters the kitchen.

"What's going on in here?" she asks, looking at the scattered mess on her kitchen counter.

"I had a sudden hankering for your oatmeal chocolate chip cookies," I explain, adding the vanilla to my wet ingredients. "I promise I'll clean all this up once I'm finished."

"Do you need any help?" she asks, rolling up her sleeves.

"No, I'm good," I answer, my attention still focused on the measuring spoon and bottle of vanilla extract that looks too small in my large hands.

She lifts a small bottle of a spice that isn't normally used in her recipe. "What's this?"

I look at the bottle held in her hand, peering between the hair hanging off my forehead. "I looked up online that if you use nutmeg, it brings out the warm, nutty flavor in the oats. I thought I'd try it out."

Her brows rise with a silent nod of approval. "Make sure to bring me some when you're done," she says, turning to leave the kitchen. "It's going to need to pass my taste test."

"I will, Mom," I answer, letting out a small chuckle.

As I return to mixing all the ingredients using my mom's KitchenAid mixer, the lingering scent of warm vanilla wafts into the air, reminding me why I had that sudden hankering for my mom's cookies in the first place. It had a little less to do with an actual craving for something sweet and a lot more to do with someone where our dynamic went beyond a simple "how did you do on the protein synthesis test" question or an "I should have taken an art class" rant.

The kitchen starts to warm, the sweet smell from the oven filling our home. And for a moment, I forget about everything that surrounds my life, full of everything that I'm so unsure of. And instead of focusing on this undecided future, I wrap myself in my past. A past of freshly baked cookies and Xbox marathons. A past of middle school hallways, crowded with people that I didn't know would mean so much to me.

present

"Stop dicking around, kid," Pat teases as I walk past him. His hand lightly taps the back of my head at the same time I duck, breezing past him.

As I enter the dining room, I'm welcomed by the sudden boom of Chef DuPont's voice entering the kitchen through the back door. His angry voice can be heard clearly all the way from the hostess desk.

Chef DuPont once held the torch as New York City's visionary for French cuisine, earning Michelin stars for various restaurants throughout the city. He was an amazing chef. Keyword: *was*. During his heyday in the early 2000s, he was an artist. A maestro in the creation of culinary art. But all of that fizzled when his consistently raving reviews dwindled into mediocre ones while he shoved those Michelin stars down every food critic's throat.

Pat hired him three years ago for his experience and knowledge. What Pat didn't know was that he was bringing into his kitchen an egotistical asshole who treated his kitchen staff like sewer rats, me included. Not long after I met Chef DuPont, Pat confessed to me that he needed a new sous chef because the previous two refused to work with him after seeing the kind of kitchen he ran. One that thrived on uncomfortable tension and irrationally fueled blowouts.

I know I need to suck it up for however long necessary so that I can gain the experience and knowledge I need, all in the name of opening my own restaurant one day. Still, the past few months working under Chef DuPont have been torture.

Chef DuPont is here, hours ahead of the dinner rush, to discuss our dinner menu and the lack of zest it carries. Pat, Chef DuPont, and I settle in the far corner of the fairly empty restaurant with a tablecloth spread underneath the mock menus and a tray of bite-sized appetizer samples.

"We need something that will wow the customers," Chef DuPont claims. "I'm tired of hearing that my work is second-rate and passable."

"Gus, we changed the menu barely a month ago," Pat says. He runs a hand through his thinning hair, frustrated with how difficult it is to keep an artist of Chef DuPont's expectations satisfied. "I don't know how else we can change things unless we do an entire menu revamp."

"Then that's what we'll have to do." Chef DuPont came into this meeting determined. I'm realizing that now. He doesn't want to merely discuss subtle changes that are feasible. He wants to jazz up this menu to what he thinks will be mind-blowing. But the thing is that he no longer holds that sort of prestige. He lost his touch, and he should be thankful that he still holds a place as head chef anywhere.

"We discussed this during that last revision." Pat is starting to turn red with frustration. I sit between them, my eyes ping-ponging back and forth as I play a silent bet on who'll win. "I can't keep making changes like this. While I support our menu evolving, I need some sort of consistency."

It's one thing Pat and I have always agreed on: consistency. During the last menu revision, the three of us decided that this was it. We made the changes we needed to, and we were going to stick with them for this season, making small adjustments as we went along. Nothing big or transformative, just changes that allow us to keep up with industry standards.

"Hayden?"

I turn as one of our hostesses, Hailey, faces me.

"I'm so sorry to interrupt but a shipment just came in, and they need you to sign off on the produce."

I turn to look at Pat, who nods, excusing me from the meeting.

I suppress a sigh of relief before walking back into the kitchen. A bright light streams in through the back door that's propped open for this week's shipment. As I sign the list, ticking off items as they come off the delivery truck, I let the tension ease off my shoulders knowing I don't have to sit through the rest of the meeting in the dining room. I'm thankful that Pat includes me in decisions that revolve around restaurant logistics but sometimes, I prefer being left on the sidelines. Especially if it comes with having to deal with Chef DuPont.

As I stock the walk-in fridge with our weekly produce, my mind wanders back to running into Natalia just before we sat down for our meeting. If I hadn't been going over the wine list with Hailey at the bar, I wouldn't have seen her. And if I hadn't looked up as Natalia's laugh echoed off the windows and she threw her head back with eyes twinkling in amusement, I wouldn't have gone after her.

She's no longer that reserved girl who hides behind her random books and color coordinated highlighters. Instead, she's shifted into a brighter, more confident version of that girl, finally growing comfortable in her own skin. Her voice rings like an upbeat song instead of a whispering mumble when she talks. And her laugh. She hardly laughed when we were seventeen, not that either one of us had much reason to in biology class, but I somehow know she didn't laugh like that in the five years we spent together going to the same schools. All bright and buoyant while using every expressive muscle in her face.

Like the ones that form the little wrinkles down her nose and the corners of her eyes, or the ones that make her forehead crease as the laughter makes her weak.

Suddenly, I feel this urge to embrace Natalia's return into my life. To bring back memories of us growing closer in the span of our senior year, reminding me what she meant to me back then while trying to rewrite everything that could have been. Of what I've been missing for the past eight years.

7

Natalia

senior year

"SINE, COSINE, TANGENT," I huff. "It all sounds the same!"

Carmen chuckles, her head propped up against the wall on the side of my bed as she's sprawled across my comforter. She hasn't been back home for more than one hour, visiting for a long weekend during a break in her residency program, and I've already bombarded her with my trigonometry homework.

"Don't give up, Nat," she encourages. "Just remember the mnemonic I taught you: 'Oscar Has A Hold On Angie.'"

I cringe. "It sounds so aggressive. You don't have one a little more passive? Something like 'Never Eat Sour Watermelon?'" I huff into my textbook, scribbling along in my notebook as she turns back to the book she's reading. "How do you even remember this stuff? It's been, like, ten years since you've even stepped foot in a trigonometry class."

She shrugs. "Maybe something told me I should hold on to it so I can teach it to my little sister."

I smirk, repeating the mnemonic in my head and bobbing along as I recite it in small whispers, when my laptop chimes. I look to see an alert for Facebook Messenger pop up. When I hover over the message, Hayden Marshall's name appears, bold and indicating a new message.

My brow furrows, my head jerking back in confusion.

"What?"

I look up at Carmen, her fingers twisting through her hair as she watches me. "Oh, nothing," I answer, feigning nonchalance. "Just a message from my lab partner." My gaze returns back to my screen as I open the message where Hayden's small picture accompanies it.

She nods, standing from her semi-lying position as she starts to walk out of my room. "I'm going to pick up some pizza for dinner. You want to come?"

I look up at her apologetically as I gesture toward the strewn-out papers and textbooks. "I should really catch up on this."

"Okay," she answers. She walks out the door and hollers Lucy's name in the direction of her room.

I click open Hayden's message.

Hayden: Hey, Lab Partner.

I wait, wondering if there's more. When there isn't, I type out a response.

Me: Hi, Hayden.

My attention veers back toward trigonometry, finding a spiral-bound notebook as I point my pencil toward the light blue lines running across it.

"Oscar... Has... A..."

My laptop pings again.

Hayden: So I was thinking, do you think the effectiveness of mouthwash is questionable if our cheek stains showed that much bacteria? Should we write a letter to the president of Listerine?

I smirk.

Me: I feel like that's a personal problem. Although Mr. Khan may appreciate your gusto. Some extra credit points may be in order.

Hayden: Then it's worth a shot.

There's a pause in our back and forth. I've all but abandoned trigonometry. I barely remember the mnemonic that Carmen taught me, and I know I'll have to ask her again once she comes back from the pizza shop.

Hayden: Any fun plans for this raging Friday night?

Me: Just some trig homework and pizza.

Hayden: Trig? On a weekend? You need to get out, Marquez. The world is your oyster!

Me: Are your plans significantly better?

Hayden: A Nightmare on Elm Street marathon and microwaved bean burritos.

Me: You one upped me with the movies. Enjoy your night, Hayden.

Hayden: You too, Nat. Don't forget: A squared plus B squared equals C squared.

present

It isn't called hump day for no reason. With the first half of the week behind me and the second half ahead, I feel exhausted, with no relief of the weekend in sight. The only bright side is that I'm past my weekend hangover and am finally able to look at the half-empty bottle of tequila on the counter without gagging.

I've already gotten a text message from Carmen telling me that she's left for her night shift at the hospital. It's her first of the week and will take her well into the weekend. I most likely won't see her until Sunday. I sigh, placing my laptop bag and purse on the counter, right next to my empty coffee mug from the morning and a pile of mail that Carmen brought in today. My stomach protests loudly, demanding I make a decision between leftover Chinese food or ordering take out, just as I notice a cream-colored envelope haphazardly tucked under an uneven stack of ads for furniture sales and Duane Reade coupons. It catches my attention because in the center of the envelope, my name is written in neatly handwritten cursive.

Miss Natalia Marquez

On the return address: *Mr. and Mrs. Oscar Valiente.* Matteo's parents. It's his wedding invitation.

My fingers run over the bumpy calligraphy as if I were to handle it any more roughly, it would tear apart in my hands. It doesn't matter though because it comes apart in my hands anyway. My fingers tear through it, shredding the rough paper and holding in my trembling fingers the light peach-colored invitation, along with Matteo's name and his bride to be, Jacinda Sutton. I have no idea who she is or how they met, but the simple fact is that Matteo is getting married.

He's getting *married*.

I always imagined it would be me, my name alongside Matteo's on an invitation a little bit classier as we added items to our gift registry and planned a honeymoon somewhere tropical. Did I ever really stop imagining that future? Maybe that dream started to fade when I realized he moved on and the news of his engagement made it all the way to my own sensitive ears. Or maybe it disappeared altogether the moment I tore into the invitation still trembling in my hands. Or maybe, even worse, I'm still clinging onto the vanished hope that he'll come back to me, telling me he was wrong and that he changed his mind on his own pending nuptials.

I wish Carmen were home. She would know what to say, how to soothe me before cracking open a bottle of chilled vodka as we drown ourselves in alcohol, cheddar popcorn, and *New Girl* reruns. But she's working tonight. I'm completely alone when my heart feels like it's shattered to a million pieces and the single thread of hope I clung to finally snapped.

I reach into my fridge to find the Chinese takeout container and pop it into the microwave without transferring its contents onto a plate. As I lean against the counter, the whirring of the microwave fills the silence. I start to nibble on the edge of my thumb, seconds from going crazy.

I feel like finishing the rest of the tequila on the counter, knowing that it'll waste my insides, unlike vodka, and leave me heaving into the toilet. I feel like running into the streets, screaming at a figurative

Matteo standing in front of me, lashing out my anger in efficient strides. But most of all, I want to talk to someone. Someone to listen and tell me that I'm better than this. To make me realize that this isn't the end-all, be-all and that I need to learn to move on. I want someone to hold my hand while I burn the invitation to a wedding that I sure as hell am *not* going to attend. Or, *probably not* going to attend. I mean, it would be rude to his parents, especially his mom, who has always been so kind and gentle with me. And even to Matteo, who might actually be looking forward to seeing me.

God, I'm so pathetic.

I pick up my phone just as the shrill beeping emits from the microwave, landing on José's number. I press the green call icon and impatiently bring the phone to my ear, hoping he'll answer and let me cry over something he'll claim is as trivial as spilled milk. I can almost hear his soothing voice telling me to meet him for drinks while scolding me on my wasted tears and my lost childbearing years on someone who, according to him, is definitely *not* worth my time.

My heart drops when my call goes to voicemail. My fingers tap against the counter before I scroll through my phone again. I finally land on Hayden's phone number, one that feels so new in my contact list as my thumb hovers over it. With my hesitance lingering over me, I tap out a quick message instead of calling.

> Me: Hey

After I text Hayden, I set my phone down, opening the microwave to remove my food as the aroma of the sweet and sour pork fills the air. My phone beeps just as I wince from the hot steam burning my fingertips.

> Hayden: Hey you.

> Me: What are you up to?

> Hayden: I'm just getting in from work. You?

> **Me:** Alone and in need of a stiff drink. You up for it?

There's a small pause in our back and forth. And what I find most interesting is that he doesn't question why I'm texting him on a random Wednesday or why I've become a regular occurrence in his life since we ran into each other last week. Instead, he answers my question as if we've done this dozens of times. As if we've adjusted to this new norm in a way that makes me wonder if he should have been a presence in my life this whole time, regardless of time or circumstance.

> **Hayden:** Sure. You know Butter? It's near your place.

I do, in fact. It's a couple of blocks over and perfect for a night of wallowing in self-pity and heartbreak.

> **Me:** Be there in 15?

> **Hayden:** Give me about 30. It'll take me some time to get there.

> **Me:** I'll save a seat for you.

With that, I grab my keys, leaving my still steamy Chinese food on the counter, and walk out of my apartment.

8

Hayden

senior year

I HUFF as I round the corner into fifth period, still annoyed that Jenny was yelling at me, throwing her hands in front of my face while accusing me of...I don't even know what she was accusing me of.

She saw me and Tina laughing over some stupid joke about Madame Martin and how annoying her fake French accent sounded describing our homework assignment on verb conjugation. Once she got a glimpse of us impersonating the way Madame Martin flung her hands in the air when she added an extra flair to the word "chapeau," Jenny started accusingly asking me if I thought Tina was cute, even though she's one of her closest friends, while demanding to know why I was talking to her in the first place. Apparently, I'm not allowed to talk to girls, even if it's school related.

This whole thing with Jenny is so pointless. I don't even know how I ended up in this situation. With a girl who boldly assigned herself as my girlfriend and is now scolding me like my mom whenever I so much as look at another girl.

God, why are high school girls so fucking dramatic? When I slump my backpack onto the counter, Natalia jumps before she reaches up to remove her earphones.

"Sorry," I mumble.

Her brows rise as she coils her earphones into a neat lasso. "Trouble in paradise?"

I turn toward her, the scowl on my face deepening.

"I saw you two arguing outside," she adds, her attention focused on the front pouch of her backpack as she stows away her earphones.

"It's nothing," I answer, roughly flipping through the textbook in front of me while the pages flick in sharp whips from my angry hands.

"If you ever want to talk about it…" she offers, her voice trailing off as she lifts a shoulder. "I'm a vault."

When I turn my scowl toward her, she mimes the motion of locking her lips with an imaginary key and tosses it over the edge of our table, along with a purse-lipped smile implying trust. My frown loosens, and the wound-up muscles of my jaw relax into a smile.

"We have a pop quiz, people." Mr. Khan's voice cuts through the class. His announcement is followed by collective groans and the shuffling of papers as Mr. Khan passes his quiz down the class.

"Thanks," I whisper.

Her tight smile softens, and I lightly tap her arm with my pinky as Mr. Khan walks by, giving us a warning cough.

present

When I walk through the doors of Butter, I spot Natalia quickly. She's slouched over the bar, a red-tinged drink already in her hand as she stares down at her phone. She's still dressed in what looks like her work clothes, a slim pencil skirt with a collared blouse neatly tucked in high at her waist. Her hair is tied up in a high ponytail, purposefully curled at the edges as it wisps around her nape with a thick strand of hair around the base securing her hair in a tight knot.

I don't know why she texted me, taking me up on my offer for a friendly drink, but I'm thankful she did. It's been a rough week, even though it's only Wednesday, and I need something to get my mind off things. Personal things that I most likely won't tell Natalia about but things I need to drown in alcohol, nonetheless.

"Is this seat taken?" I whisper, low and close to Natalia's ear. She jumps suddenly as she turns to face me. And before she locks her phone and tucks it away into her purse, I can't help but notice the shiny image of her and another man splayed across the screen. I pretend not to notice and flag down the bartender instead.

"Saved it just for you," she says, her voice weary. She still manages to tap the round leather stool with a smile before I slide onto it and tuck my legs beneath the sticky bar top.

The bartender stops in front of me, nodding his head, silently requesting my order.

"I'll have a Blue Moon," I say before turning to Natalia. "What are you having?"

"Vodka with cranberry."

I turn back toward the bartender. "And a vodka cranberry," I add, placing my phone that's in my hand on the countertop.

He turns away, making drinks as the clinking of glass and thin metal from the cocktail shaker already in his hands keep him busy.

"What have you been up to?" I ask, my hands leaning against the edge of the bar.

She shrugs. "Nothing, just busy with work." She pauses, taking a small sip of her drink. "Carmen's working the night shift, so I thought I could use some company."

"Does she usually not?"

"No. She took on some extra shifts cause they're short-staffed at the hospital," she answers with a small sigh. "It gets a little lonely at home by myself. And not to mention, a little scary."

I smirk, teasingly raising a brow. "Scared of the dark, are we?"

"Yes," she says, omitting an obvious *duh* with her answer. "You never know what's lurking behind the shadows."

We're interrupted by the arrival of our drinks as the bartender places them on top of small cocktail napkins in front of us. Natalia slurps her drink in her hand, the straw sucking up the rest of the contents and leaving behind melting ice cubes before she moves on to the fresh one in front of her.

I tilt my head back, glugging my beer as I keep my eyes on Natalia. She smiles at me. A smile that doesn't reach her eyes before it shifts, widening as she leans in toward me. And then I see it, that little dip her nose does when her smile grows bigger.

"You smell like pastries."

Her observation draws a small chuckle out of me. "I spent most of the day making fruit tarts and chocolate mousse."

She hums softly. "That sounds like heaven." And then she narrows her eyes and chews on her lower lip, as if she's holding back a secret or an unexpected thought.

"What?" I ask, taking another quick swig of my beer.

"I remember you baking in high school."

"Oh," I huff awkwardly.

"And now you do it for a living."

I nod, feeling suddenly shy while remembering those moments filling the small kitchen in my home. "Yeah," I finally whisper.

"Do you ever want to open your own restaurant?"

I bob my head between my shoulders while my fingers toy with the neck of my beer bottle. "Eventually," I answer. "But I gotta work my way up. It's part of my five-year plan."

My phone pings on the bar top, interrupting our conversation as the loud twanging of a taut string on a bow rings loudly and the image of a cupid silhouette fills the icon box next to the alert. I move quickly to lock the screen and shove my phone into my pocket. Natalia's brows rise in curious amusement when I glance over at her, and I know what's coming next.

"What was that?"

I hesitate, embarrassed that the level of my singleness is about to be so open and clear. "A Cupid's Bet alert."

"Cupid's Bet?" she repeats.

I nod.

"Is that like...a hook-up app?"

I grimace slightly. "A *dating* app," I correct her.

Her eyes widen with a suppressed smile. "Oh, I'm sorry to offend you. A 'dating app,'" she retorts, sarcasm dripping through her words.

"Hey," I argue. "Don't judge me on my dating life."

"I'm not judging," she says innocently. "I just didn't think you'd be the dating app type of guy. What, the ladies don't flock to you with your perfect smile and pretty eyes?"

"You think my eyes are pretty?"

"You *know* your eyes are pretty, Hayden." She nudges me with her elbow. "So how does it work? You ever-so-slyly slide into the DMs of every eligible hottie?"

"If only it were that simple," I say a little too wistfully.

"Oh, so they play hard to get." Her grin holds a devilish edge, her eyebrows bouncing up and down as she continues her tease. "I heard some men like the chase. Helps them to feel masculine, like they're feeding their caveman instincts." Her fist rises in the air, stamping her point.

"What I meant was," I say, poking her side as she flinches away, "it's hard to get past the initial talking stage. It usually just ends up being a long string of one-night stands."

She slightly cringes. "So? Are you going to check that?" she says, eyeing my phone in my back pocket. "Maybe this might be 'the one.'"

I shake my head, ignoring her and chugging my beer instead.

"Come on, Marshall," she urges. "I want to know what these women are saying to you." Her hands lift up between us. Her palms face upward, with her lower lip jutted out in a small pout.

I give, looking down at her as her smile teases through her fake frown, and I can't help but let out a small laugh. As if her making that face, pleading in that playful way, will always get her what she wants out of me. I reach into my pocket and unlock my phone before placing it gently into her open hands.

Her eyes light up against the lit screen as her lips pull between her teeth and the corners of her mouth lift with amusement. Her eyes search the screen, looking like she's solving some sexy crossword puzzle in a jumble of words like "spank" or "foreplay" meshed together in black and white blocks.

Her fingers finally stop scrolling through the long list of messages.

"This one's good. She's got a nice smile," she states, clearing her throat to read the message out loud. "'Hey there, cutie.'"

Unoriginal and bland. Natalia must agree because her mouth scrunches in disapproval before she looks at me.

"Maybe not," she says, continuing her search. "So they just message you and you message them back?"

"Well, there's a little more to it than that," I explain. "The app itself sends you potential matches through an algorithm. And I just tap on the little cupid's bow if I like them, and if she likes me back, we message each other."

"Ah," she says through a smile. "The gods doing what they're born to do: manage an online dating app." Her eyes continue to roam, lighting up as her fingers tap on the screen. And then she gasps.

"What?"

She holds the phone a little higher, and her smile spreads wider as she reads the text. "'You have a cute face. It would look even better if I sat on it.'" Her mouth gapes open in shock. "That's not real."

I peek down at the screen to see who the message is from. "Oh, Sara is very real."

"You responded to her?"

"I went on a date with her two weeks ago," I answer.

"Did...she sit on your face?"

She did. In fact, she did a little more than that, but I don't want to share that bit of information to Natalia. So instead, I give the most generalized answer as close to pleading the fifth.

"I can neither confirm nor deny that, ma'am."

"Maybe it's better you don't answer that question."

We both simultaneously take a sip of our drinks. When Natalia sets her drink back down, she taps the back of my hand with her index finger. "You really are living a lively single life there, Marshall."

I chuckle, taking my phone and securing it back in my pocket. "Are you seeing anyone?" I ask, curious, as we've rather deeply broached the topic of my own glaring singleness.

Her shoulders slouch forward, much like they used to in high school when she sat on the hard stool that tucked perfectly under our lab table in bio class. And when she doesn't answer, I get the hint that maybe she doesn't want to talk about it.

"No, I'm not," she finally says. Her voice sounds low, a tightness seeping through as if she's trying to hold back tears.

"Okay," I respond, not really knowing how or if I should ask further.

Then she turns her face toward me with her eyes downturned and brows pinched together in what looks like agony. Her forced smile falters into a sad little frown before her hands move to her face, covering her eyes as she sighs deeply.

As if surrendering to my silent curiosity, she swivels her entire body and grips my arm for support. "So, my boyfriend broke up with me six months ago," she starts, her voice showing how badly this breakup is affecting her. "We'd been together for four years. We lived together and everything. And when I brought up our future, stuff like if he saw anything beyond our boyfriend and girlfriend status, he broke up with me. So I had to pack up my things and move in with Carmen."

When her protruding lower lip begins trembling, I want to hug her. And when the hand she has gripped on my arm starts to slacken, I want to take it back and hold it between mine to let her know that this breakup doesn't determine her worth.

"Anyway," she continues, waving off her brimming emotions. "I found out last week that he's getting married."

"What?!" I shout. I realize a little too loudly when a couple of heads turn in our direction.

"And...I just got the invitation to the wedding tonight."

"Hold up." I stop her, my palms facing her. "So this asshole dumped you and found some other girl to marry. And he invited you to the wedding?"

"He's not an asshole," she weakly argues.

"Natalia," I scold. *How can she still defend him?*

"And technically, it wasn't him that invited me. It was his parents," she explains. "His mom and my mom got pretty close while we were dating so...I guess they feel some sort of obligation to stay close with my family. I don't really know..."

"You aren't going, are you?"

She scrunches her eyes closed as if to blink away the pain. When she looks at me again, she shrugs before saying, "It would be rude not to go, right?"

"Who gives a shit, Nat?"

She doesn't say anything. Instead, she smiles weakly as if to say that she knows she shouldn't go but isn't going to be able to stay away.

"Is that why you texted me?" I finally ask. "'Cause you didn't want to be alone tonight?"

She nods. "Yeah," she whispers. "Sorry I can't be better company." She looks up at me through an apologetic smile.

"What are you talking about?" I tease. "This is the best conversation I've had all week."

She chuckles lightly.

"It's a hell of a lot better than sitting through another random date," I assure. "I can only ask, 'What's your favorite color?' so many times before realizing how much I don't care."

"Mine's orange, by the way," she offers with a slight tilt in her head.

"Whose favorite color is orange?" I ask, not even bothering to hide the disgust in her choice.

"Me," she defends. "It reminds me of fall."

I poke her side again before she gives me a small giggle.

9

Hayden

senior year

I'M SITTING on the carpeted living room floor. My French textbook, a messy pile of flashcards, and a cold bowl of chocolate ice cream sit scattered in front of me. I push my glasses up the bridge of my nose for what feels like the hundredth time since I've taken out my contacts after I came home from football practice. This is why I hate wearing these gaudy things. One would think after being prescribed them in fifth grade, I'd be used to them by now.

The TV is playing in the background with the sound of my mom and dad occasionally shouting out random letters and words to fill the final vowels to the Wheel of Fortune game on the screen.

"The promised band!" my mom shouts at the same time I look at the screen to see if she's right.

"Land, Marsha," my dad corrects. "The promised land."

My mom rolls her eyes at my dad before huffing a sigh. "They don't give enough clues."

I laugh, returning my attention to my French vocabulary words.

"Have you heard back from Penn State yet?"

I look up at my dad, a little taken aback by the sudden change in topic. My mom's eyes move from the TV to my dad, then to me as she waits for me to answer his question.

"I got in," I answer, pushing my glasses up with my index finger once again. I don't bother adding that I got the acceptance letter a couple of weeks ago and shoved it into my desk drawer the second I saw the "Congratulations!" greeting below the letterhead.

"Good," he replies. "Have you picked a major?"

"No, not yet."

"Well, I assume you aren't going to play football."

"Greg," my mom warns.

"What? I just want to make sure he knows what he's doing when he leaves for college—"

"I haven't decided yet," I interrupt, attempting to mediate their disagreement before it turns into an argument.

"Well, you should decide soon. You don't want to be one of those undeclared kids and end up majoring in art or some bullcrap." I don't mean to, but I roll my eyes at his ignorance before I hear him grumble, "Hayden, I don't know why you can't just go with something safe like accounting or finance. You know you'll always have a job."

Not this again. This vicious cycle of what direction my life should lead, what my future should look like. I'm so tired of it.

I start to lose focus on the image of a cartoon swimming pool along with the word "la piscine" in front of me. I shuffle my index cards, lining up the edges to make them stack perfectly, before stuffing them into the crease of my textbook.

"What if that's not what I want? What if I don't even know if I want to go to college?"

"What do you mean? Hayden, you're going to college." The grip my dad has on the armrest of the couch tightens. I can see his fingers press into the rough fabric as his eyes narrow down on me.

"Maybe I don't want to."

"No, that is absolutely out of the question. You're going to college. You aren't going to throw away your future." He stands, leaving my mom looking up at him with disapproving eyes. "I'm getting more ice cream," he announces gruffly. He stalks off into the kitchen and I hear the fridge door being pried open.

"Hayden," my mom's voice calls. I look up at her, and a soft smile peeks through the concern in her eyes.

"I'm sorry, Mom." I move the bowl of melted chocolate ice cream from the floor to the coffee table.

"Why didn't you tell us you got in?" she asks, ignoring my apology.

"Oh," I whisper. "I don't know…"

"That's a big deal."

"I know," I say, unable to help the proud smile lifting the corners of my mouth. "I guess…I just didn't know what I was going to do, so…"

She nods. "Dad's just worried about your future. I know it doesn't seem like it, but he wants what's best for you." She pauses, giving me an encouraging smile. "We'll talk to him when things blow over a bit."

"Yeah," I answer, knowing there is no talking to my dad. And there's no point in arguing this fact with my mom. We both know how it would play out. We sit in silence, the clink of ceramic bowls coming from the kitchen intertwining with Pat Sajak's enlivened voice coming off the TV. "I'm going to finish my homework in my room."

I stand to leave the living room, a room that was calm and relaxing just minutes ago. I walk back to my room feeling all too defeated and tired from this continuous back and forth that never seems to end between me and my dad.

For the record, you would look absolutely ridiculous in an orange fro wig and a red ball nose.

The image of Natalia coaxing my worries free, replacing them with jokes, causes an unwilling smile to spread across my face. I slump back on my bed as I glance at my laptop screen nestled atop the sheets. My fingers hover over the Facebook icon on my search bar. I look through my previous messages and find Natalia's name before I type out a new message.

> Me: On a scale of one to ten, how bad would it be if I decided to join the circus? Maybe clown college wouldn't be so bad. Balloon animal design sounds like a promising major.

It's almost instant when I get a response.

> Natalia: Maybe a solid six. While taking off with only the wind behind you sounds obscurely enigmatic, I think you'd get bored once you master a sword balloon. There's only so much one can do with a foot long piece of rubber.

> Me: I guess you're right. So I should stick with regular person college?

> Natalia: Sounds like the safer option.

There's a pause in our back and forth before she sends me another message.

> Natalia: Just promise that you'll learn how to make an orange balloon poodle. Those are my favorite.

I chuckle a little to myself, not even bothering to resist the smile spreading across my face as I stare at my lit-up laptop screen. The ball of frustration that was wound up so tightly has now dissolved into this warm gooeyness melting my insides.

> Me: And how do you suggest I do that if I'm giving up my dreams to go to Jester's University?

> Natalia: Uh, YouTube? Duh...

> Hayden: I don't know. I'm pretty busy with football practice and those lab assignments you desperately need my help with. I don't know when I'll find the time.

> Natalia: How about a deal? I'll give you until, say...Thanksgiving to master balloon animals, and I'll promise to visit you when we're back home.

> Me: You would visit me?

Natalia: Of course. Who else would I share war stories with about the trenches of Coolidge View High? We're barely going to make it out of AP Bio alive.

Me: It's a deal then.

She responds with a smiley face, a colon mark and the closing side of a parenthesis, and I stare at it with a smile that matches the animated grin on the screen. I haven't really thought about after graduation, whether or not we would stay in touch, but suddenly, I can't imagine us not. How can I *not* look forward to seeing her annoyed yet amused smile as she peers over at me in her seat in class? Or the pensive look she has when she stares at the reading assignment for photosynthesis and cellular respiration? How can I go the year after high school without talking to her about whatever aspirations that I have to bury deep in order to avoid conflict with my dad? Relief pours over me, realizing that maybe I'm not going to have to wonder that at all.

Maybe it's one goodbye I won't have to say.

present

"Enough about me and my tragic love life. How about you? Anything ailing your heart at the moment?"

I smirk, taking a sip of my beer before shaking my head. Not to answer her question but to find a way to get out of talking about everything wrong in my life.

"Come on, Marshall," she says, lightly punching my arm. "Give me something so I don't feel like such a loser."

"You're not a loser," I dispute.

She raises her brows and pinches her lips in a small smile, waiting for me to give her something.

I smirk again, half amused and half surrendering. "No heartbreak or crappy ex-girlfriend to cry over."

"Obviously." She gestures toward my phone.

"What's that supposed to mean?"

"With a roster like that? I can't imagine any woman breaking through that playboy bravado of yours."

I frown as I turn away from her.

"But…" she encourages.

My frown deepens, and her face mirrors mine, her smile slipping. With her empathetic eyes and soft face, she encourages me to share. All without feeling ashamed or misguided. So I spill my heart out, every qualm resting on my shoulders ready to be lifted just an inch.

"I haven't talked to my dad in almost two years." The words sort of tumble out from my lips. When I don't say anything else, she doesn't prod. Instead, she patiently waits while her fingers lightly bob the cocktail straw from the glass tumbler in her hand.

"When I quit school and moved to France, my dad was…upset, to say the least. We already had so many differences before I left for college, like whether or not college was even in the cards for me or what major I should choose, and then I laid a bombshell on him when I decided to quit school. So I stayed away from home because of that, moved to Chicago and only visited for holidays and stuff. And two years ago, on Thanksgiving, things kind of blew up. We yelled, said things to each other…and I haven't talked to him since."

"And your mom?"

"She's kind of caught in the middle," I explain. "She supported my decision but doesn't want to take sides. But she helped me through culinary school, sending me money and paying most of my tuition."

"That's good," she says softly, focusing on the positive. She swivels on the barstool, turning to face her whole body toward me once again, her way of giving me her undivided attention. "You know, your happiness isn't a price you should pay to please anyone," she says softly. "Even if it is your parents."

I smirk. "I'm going to assume your parents love you?"

Her face drops as she hears me question my parents' affection toward me. "You know your parents love you too, Hayden," she says before averting her gaze toward the bar top and angling her body away from me. "But yes, they do love me. And my sisters."

"Don't need to rub it in." I lightly nudge her shoulder, bumping it with my elbow as her lips twist in thought.

"They've always been supportive, so I can't understand how any parent could expect anything from their child aside from their own happiness," she explains.

I let out a frustrated, close-mouthed sigh, wishing my life were that simple.

"I'm just saying," she adds. "This isn't your problem, it's theirs. It's something that they need to work through and realize you're happy with where you are in life."

"Those are some wise words, Marquez." She tilts her shoulder up in a bashful way as she tucks her chin downward. "I wish I could say something as reassuring about that shitty ex of yours."

"I guess…calling him shitty is a good start."

"Leaving already?"

I pull my pants past my hips, looking for the shirt that I had tossed haphazardly on the floor. When I peek over my shoulder at the rumpled bed, I watch as Caitlyn with a *y* lazily stretches her arms above her, exposing the top half of her naked body while she suppresses a yawn.

"I have an early day," I explain.

She turns to me, pulling the thin sheet up to her chest and tucking it into her armpits as she rests her head on the heel of her hand. "Well, I had fun tonight."

I nod, reaching for my shirt that somehow found itself under her bed. I stand, pulling it over my head and reaching for the doorknob.

"I guess I'll call you." My offer sounds more like a question than any real future plans to see her.

She flicks her blond hair, the silky ringlets bouncing as they settle onto the pillow below her, while looking at me through hooded eyes. "Looking forward to it."

I walk out of Caitlyn's apartment and into the night. It's already past midnight, as I didn't make it to Caitlyn's until after my drink with Natalia. When we parted ways, I responded to the waiting Cupid's Bet alert, only to see that I had a new message from Caitlyn. After some back and forth and a scout's salute to confirm that I wasn't an axe murderer, I met Caitlyn at a bar on my side of the bridge. Which was perfect since I really did have an early day, regardless of whether she believed me or not.

When we went back to her place, I found myself in a rut of routine. Lifting her shirt while she undid my jeans, pulling back her covers while she lowered the lights to a dim glow. Even rolling a condom on felt...like a chore. Something I needed to do so I didn't grow restless or weary. To quench that part of me that sought intimacy. I mean, that's the whole reason I still keep the app that screams *I'm single* sitting in my phone with its cheesy cupid icon, always begging for my attention as if it could fulfill this empty gaping hole that's grown deeper and wider over time.

Once I enter my apartment where it's quiet and empty, as I'm sure Dexter fell asleep hours ago, I search my fridge for a beer before settling onto my couch. My body sags against the cushions as I blow out a deep sigh.

Tonight felt like a breath of fresh air. Something to pull me out of my rutted routine of work and home that I've unremarkably settled into since I moved to the city. Everything about my life has been mundane, dull, and bland. Yet today felt different. And I know it has everything to do with Natalia and her welcomed text message to meet her for drinks.

Every time I close my eyes, I catch images of Natalia's broken heart, reminding me of how I felt about her in high school. Our friendship back then grew like a plant, nourished with inside jokes and common interests instead of sunlight and water. I confided in her so many things that I wouldn't have told a soul when my life felt so unsure.

My phone pings in my back pocket, and I pull it out to see a new message from Caitlyn. Her still naked body covered with her sheets, hiding parts of her for minimal discretion, fills my phone screen. I don't send anything back, like a tasteless dick pic. Instead, I look for Natalia's number.

> Me: Hey, just wanted to make sure you got home safe.

I don't expect a response this late, so I'm surprised when she texts me right back.

> Natalia: I did.

> Me: Good.

> Natalia: Hey.

> Me: What's up?

> Natalia: I had fun tonight. It was nice catching up with you.

> Natalia: And I really needed a friend. So thanks.

I smirk. The same words that Caitlyn said to me, sated from our postcoital bliss, feel different coming from Natalia.

> Me: Anytime, Marquez.

10

Natalia

senior year

"DID you hear the big gossip going around school?" I whisper as I slide onto my stool. Hayden looks up from his notebook. The eraser end of his pencil lightly taps the college-ruled spiral bound as he plays along with my guessing game.

"That Ben and Tina hooked up in the back of her Civic?"

"Ew, no."

He shrugs. "Well, that's the big gossip going around school."

"Yes, but we're talking about me."

"Okay, what's this big gossip going around about you?" He drops his pencil and faces me, looking at my beaming smile with curiosity.

"I got into NYU."

Hayden's eyes widen as his lips spread into a grin. "That's amazing! Congratulations!"

"I know." I sheepishly smile. "My parents are taking me to tour the campus next month."

"Wow, you're finally leaving the nest, huh, Marquez? Spreading your wings and whatnot."

74

I cringe. "You sound like my dad," I say. "Did you hear back from Penn State?"

I'm waiting for his answer while pulling out my bio class necessities. Notebook, pencil, highlighters, etcetera. When Hayden doesn't answer, I look at him. His gaze is narrowed on the desktop in front of him, not really focusing on anything aside from avoiding my question.

"Uh, yeah. Like a month ago," he finally answers. "I got in."

"And you're going?"

"I don't know."

"Well, congratulations," I still offer. "It's still a pretty big deal that you got in."

He turns to face me with a small smile, one that's close lipped and full of so many silent words that he's keeping to himself, spread across his face as he nods. I smile back, squeezing his forearm as we silently look into each other's eyes. The bustling noise of fellow biology class students starts to surround us as the classroom fills, along with our future and its inevitable plans.

present

The following weeks go by like gusts of winds interrupting a calm breeze. My days continue with the constant current of meetings, conference calls, and emails. Enough to keep my mind occupied. Then, without warning, like a squall unanchoring my feet off the ground, I'm reminded of the five-by-seven-inch cardstock sitting in my kitchen drawer, poking at the pieces of my heart that are far from being put back together.

Why can't I just move on? Matteo obviously has.

When I showed up at Carmen's house post tragic breakup, my tear-stained face already telling her everything she needed to know about my change in living situation, she told me everything happens for a reason.

At the time, my response was to stuff my face into her couch cushions and drown myself in my own tears. I took what she said with a grain of salt. Not because I didn't believe it to be true, but because the ache splintering my heart in two was too painful to view my situation with anything other than a glass-half-empty pessimism.

But now, as I figuratively point my fists to the sky as I scream "why" from the top of my lungs, I can't help but wonder this "why." Why Matteo felt it was okay for us to stay in a relationship for four years, one that wasn't necessarily perfect, but I assumed we were both content in. But when the topic of marriage was broached, he broke up with me. Why this rejection not only tore our relationship apart but left me feeling as if I'm not good enough.

I'm in the middle of simultaneously deciding the best way to destroy Matteo's wedding invitation, barrel fire sitting at the top of my list, while attaching a SpongeBob GIF in an email to José when my cell phone buzzes on my desk with a new alert. I pick it up to see Carmen's name pop up with a new text message.

> Carmen: Just confirming, we're still going apple picking this weekend?

I sigh. It's an annual tradition that we started with Matteo and David, the four of us piling into David's Subaru and driving the two-hour drive outside of the city to spend the day eating carnival-style foods and picking bushels of apples. Carmen looks forward to it every year. I had all but forgotten about it until Carmen reminded me in passing a couple of weeks ago. It's one of the few times in the year that she plans her schedule around so she can get a day off and enjoy our little double date. Well, now a trio with me being the third wheel.

> Me: Of course.

She texts back immediately with a smiley face emoji. As I'm frowning at my phone screen, I'm interrupted by the low growl coming from my hungry stomach, reminding me that lunchtime is approaching. I stand from my chair and walk the short trek to José's office, looking for something to distract me from this weekend's wistful getaway. When I walk through his open office door, he looks up from his monitor, not at all surprised by this usual interaction between us.

"What are we doing for lunch today?" I ask, silently hoping he's in the mood to make the trek to SoHo for spam musubi and pineapple coleslaw.

"Oh," José says, his voice deflated. "Jason's taking me out. He's showing a brownstone to a client in the area so he's meeting me after."

"Aw," I respond, not bothering to hide my disappointment.

"Sorry, *mami*," he says with a wink. "I'll make it up to you tomorrow."

I give an understanding nod in José's direction before walking back to my office. I guess I could have a solo lunch ordered in today...But with the slight damper this weekend's plans put on my mood, I need something to lift my spirits.

When the sudden hankering for something sweet and tarty and lemony hits in the deep pockets of my hippocampus—something Carmen informed me one random night about cravings and brain chemistry—I know where I'm going for lunch.

When I walk through the doors at Pour Toujours, I'm greeted by a hostess. She moves efficiently, reaching for a menu with a polite smile as I tell her it'll be a party for one. Once I'm shown to my seat, I turn to face her before sitting on the long, cushioned bench against the wall.

"Um, is Hayden here?"

She pauses for a second and smiles wider as she watches me slink into my seat. "He is. I'll let him know he has a visitor."

"Oh," I protest. "If he's busy, it's okay."

She nods one last time before walking away. I'm scanning the menu, glancing over the words in French with added flourishes, when I'm interrupted by the scraping of a chair against the hard floor. When I look up, I see Hayden's face. His smile is so wide and bright, telling me just how happy he is to see me, as he takes the open seat in front of me.

"You're alive," he says through his smile.

"Of course I am," I say, shyly hunching forward in my seat as I lower the menu.

"Well," he says, linking his fingers together on top of the covered tabletop. "I haven't heard so much as a whisper from you since the bar, so I thought maybe you were abducted by aliens."

"Not yet, but keeping my fingers crossed." I raise a hand with my index and middle fingers overlapping each other. "So what's good here? I hear the chef is pretty good at his day job," I tease, leaning slightly forward. Hayden inches closer, mirroring my movements. Instead of answering my question, he plucks the menu from my hands and stands from his seat.

"I gotchu," he says, winking with a knowing smile before he walks away. I smile back and wait patiently, leaning against the wall behind me. My fingertips graze against the glass goblet filled with water, the condensation already wrapping around the clear surface.

The restaurant isn't too busy, but there's the usual lunch rush traffic. People eating in pairs, much like José and I do on a regular basis, chatting work talk over a quick meal that includes warm bread and hard butter.

When I finally see Hayden's eyes meet mine through the saloon-style swinging doors, his face lights up with an eager smile. He walks through careful steps while balancing two plates in his hand. When he approaches my table at the same time I'm draping my napkin on my lap, he lowers the plates with a look that's blended between pride and modesty.

"Coq au vin and ratatouille," he claims as he watches me eye the food in awe. "And I have dessert coming your way once you're finished."

"This looks amazing," I say softly as a pool of saliva collects on the inside of my cheeks. "So...ratatouille is a real thing?" I ask, my curiosity trumping the need to ask such a silly question.

"Of course it is."

I smile bashfully, shrugging a shoulder as I lower my face. "I just thought that it was a made-up thing that cartoon rat made in the movie."

He laughs, and his shoulders bounce. "Enjoy your lunch," he says, the laughter in his eyes twinkling as he turns to walk away.

Fifteen minutes later, I'm halfway through one of the most delicious creations of braised chicken I've ever had, alongside a large, heaped serving of warm, summery vegetables to perfectly balance the whole meal. I can't believe I've gone this long thinking that ratatouille was a made-up dish. The way the savory juices squeeze out of each bite makes me crave the next time I get to enjoy a meal cooked by Hayden.

I'm polishing off the last of my meal while making a mental note to visit Hayden's restaurant more often when he reappears from behind the kitchen doors. I've been devouring my food so hungrily that I've all but forgotten that Hayden is still in the same building. The only thing present in my existence is the food I just inhaled. And now, the lemon tarts that brought me into the restaurant in the first place as Hayden places a neatly cut slice in front of me.

"I honestly cannot have another bite but you're making it so hard to say no," I say with a deep breath.

He pulls out the seat in front of me as he makes himself comfortable and places two forks between us. He picks one up and pierces the lemon tart, then takes a bite before I realize that he's staying to keep me company.

"You don't have to get back there?" I ask, gesturing toward the kitchen.

He shakes his head. "The lunch rush is dying down a bit, so I have a minute."

So we sit, enjoying each other's company while falling into a rhythm of comfortable silence and my occasional hum of satisfaction over my new favorite dessert. I giggle as I shoo his fork away from the crumbly crust, and he subtly nudges the plate a little closer to me before placing his fork down on the tabletop.

Hayden watches me squeeze the fork through my lips. I make sure I get every last smear of custard while fully aware of Hayden's narrowing gaze.

"What?" I ask through a half-full mouth. I laugh, suddenly shy that

I've become the center of attention in the small bubble that wrapped around us.

"Nothing," he answers, shaking his head. My teeth clamp down on my lower lip, the muscles around my chin tightening as I suppress a smile. And Hayden does the same, one corner of his mouth lifting as the same dimple I've memorized presses into his cheek. His eyes flit to my mouth before trailing back to my eyes, and I feel my lips tense, then relax as a weird flutter spreads across my chest. A darkness casts over his eyes as his pupils fill the shades of jade and whiskey. We silently establish this staring contest, both refusing to break away as the iron grip I have on my fork slackens. It suddenly slips from my fingers, landing on the plate with a clatter. Whatever trance crackled between us breaks, pulling us both back down to our cushioned seats and to reality.

A sudden flush crawls up my chest and to my neck. I can feel the heat travel to my ears, and I nervously bring my hand to cover my flustered state, brushing over the side of my neck and hovering over my left ear.

Why do I suddenly feel like I'm sitting on a stage under a bright spotlight, beaming with pressure and heat? Like I'm the center of attention and being noticed for the first time.

I look at Hayden again, smiling shyly. And he does the same, huffing a short laugh before coughing into his fist.

"Uh, so, you doing anything fun this weekend?" Hayden asks, his voice sounding uncertain with his gaze settled on the fork haphazardly teetering off the plate between us.

"Oh. I, um...I'm going apple picking with Carmen and David on Sunday." I tell my plans rather glumly, and Hayden catches on quickly.

"Is that a bad thing?"

"I used to go apple picking with Matteo—my ex—every year, our way of celebrating fall and whatnot," I explain. "We always went with Carmen and David, and it's become sort of a tradition."

"Oh," he says as if finally realizing why I sound so defeated about my plans.

"Yeah," I answer. "Anyway, this is the first time I'm going without Matteo, and I'm a little worried I'll feel like the third wheel."

"You can't bail?" he asks, his fingertips running over the white tablecloth.

"No," I say softly. "Carmen's been so excited about going. I don't have the heart to tell her no." We sit in a short silence, the clinks of metal utensils to ceramic plates filtering around us.

"I'll go with you."

"What?" I ask, slightly confused.

"I'll go with you," he repeats.

"Apple picking?"

He nods.

I shake my head. "No, Hayden. You don't need to do that."

"I want to." His serious eyes, ones that don't carry a hint of hesitation, look at me as if silently telling me it's okay that I accept his offer. His brows rise and lips curve into a sincere smile. "I'm off on Sunday, and it sounds kinda fun."

"Are you sure?" I ask rather timidly. I mull over Hayden's offer, thinking how *good* it would feel to accept it. A sudden reassuring calm takes over me, knowing I could enjoy a day with my sister while breaking this vicious cycle of heartbreak and tears. All because I would have Hayden by my side to loosen the tightness in my chest that I've become all too familiar with.

"Yes," he answers assuredly. "If you want me to be there, I'll be there."

I still hesitate, even with his unwavering confidence that doesn't show a speck of doubt. "Okay."

"Okay," he parrots.

11

Natalia

senior year

"WHAT IS THIS?"

I turned my head to see Hayden picking up a book that had fallen out of my backpack and onto the small space between my binder and his half-empty Glacier Freeze Gatorade.

When I don't answer, he turns it over in his hand.

"The Perks of Being a Wallflower," he reads out loud. "Is this for a class?"

"No," I answer, slightly distracted by the vocabulary terms in front of me that are on today's quiz. "My sister told me about it. Said I would probably like it."

He nods before placing the book on my binder. He then reaches for his drink, twisting off the cap before taking a loud gulp.

"You want to read it?" I offer, peeling my attention away from memorizing the word "abiogenesis" and its definition.

He grimaces as he recaps his drink. "I'm not much of a reader."

"Everyone's a reader," I argue. "You just haven't found the right book."

He shakes his head. "Well, I am not a reader."

"Give it a try," I encourage, nudging the book an inch closer to him. When I don't look away, silently urging him to accept my offering, he smirks.

"This isn't one of those mannequin romance novels, is it?"

I stifle a laugh. "Harlequin," I correct him, shoving my hand into his arm as a loose set of giggles causes me to wobble off the edge of my stool. "Ah!" I gasp just as Hayden reaches to grip my arm to fix my balance and help me upright.

"Making fun of me, Marquez?" He pokes my side, making me laugh even harder. "I guess I won't be reading your filthy romance novel."

"Nooo," I protest, not even caring that I sound a little whiny. "It's not a romance novel." I pick up the book and place it in his hands, poking a finger onto the cover. "See, no half-naked men with their hair blowing with the wind."

He raises a suspicious brow at me, and I grin, refusing to take no as an answer. "Fine. I guess I'll give it a shot."

"You never know," I say, turning back to face the table. "This might be 'the one.'"

"'The one?'"

I nod. "Yeah," I answer. "The right book that finally came your way to show you how much you love reading."

"Love is a strong word."

"Fine then," I say, a small eye roll hiding my smile. "No longer dislike."

He smirks. "We'll just have to wait and see."

present

"Hey, Nat," David's warm voice greets me as soon as I walk through the door.

"Hey, David," I answer, tired but glad to return to a home filled with noise instead of frigid quiet. "Is Carmen home?"

He points his thumb toward Carmen's room. "She's getting dressed."

I nod, placing my belongings on a chair facing the kitchen counter before walking to Carmen's room and knocking lightly on her door.

"Come in." I hear in a soft and muffled voice from the other side. When I walk in, I find Carmen sifting through her closet.

"Hey," I call out.

"Hey, Nat," she answers when she finally looks up. Her smile warmly greets me. "I'm going out to dinner with David. You want to join us?"

I shake my head. "You two enjoy your date. I'm tired anyway."

She doesn't go back to looking through her closet or simply nod at my answer. She looks at me as if waiting for me to tell her something.

"What?" I say.

I see her hesitate, opening her mouth before closing it. She turns back to her closet, briefly examining a dress she flicked off a hanger before looking back at me again.

"I know you're a big girl, and I know you're going to talk to me about it when you're ready…"

"You finally saw the invitation?"

The inner corners of her brows turn up, and she nods. "Are you okay?"

"I guess I should've found a better hiding spot." I sigh, slumping into the soft, cushy chair in the corner of her room while trying to avoid sitting on her clean bed in my work clothes. When Carmen's attentive gaze urges for an answer, I smile weakly. "I will be," I finally say.

"Are you sure?" she questions, stepping into her dress underneath her robe. "We can talk if you want."

I shake my head and rest my chin on the back of the chair as I consider her offer. My lips twist as I attempt to smile through the constriction in my throat.

"I'm okay," I answer softly.

"Nat, you don't have to act like you're fine," she asserts. "We can talk about it. I can get some of that weird tasting sweet potato ice cream you like, and we can veg out on the couch."

My smile widens, and a small giggle makes my face lift. "I'm fine, really."

She rounds her bed and sits at the edge closest to me. "Nat..."

"I talked to Hayden," I finally say when her persistence doesn't seem to relent.

Her face twists into a disapproving hint of confusion, apparently thrown off that I didn't turn to her when I normally would have. "Hayden?"

"Yeah, the guy that was at our party when Lucy was here?" I elaborate.

"The one you two went to high school with?"

I nod. "You were at work when I got the invitation, and I really didn't have anyone to talk to so I had some drinks with him," I say, explaining to her so she understands my desperation for seeking consolation elsewhere.

She tilts her head. "Like a date?"

"No," I refute. "Just a friend listening to me about my crappy love life."

She gives an understanding nod. "Well, I'm glad he was there to talk to. And I'm sorry I wasn't."

"It's okay," I assure her, even though I had deeply wished she was home that night. Still, having that time with Hayden, huddled over chilled vodka and beer while skimming over the briefly mentioned hurt that Hayden somehow knew not to dive too deeply into made me realize how thankful I am for our reunion. If not for the introduction to French cuisine, then definitely for the much-needed company a mere text message away.

She rests a hand on my arm before standing to finish dressing. She pulls her dress up all the way and removes her robe. Her hands run down the polyester material, plum colored and cut below her knees, as it accentuates her curves, stuffing away the images of her in frumpy surgical scrubs. I pick at a loose thread coming off the chair as I think about Hayden and his own set of personal woes.

"Did you ever feel like Mom and Dad pressured us into our life choices?"

Carmen stands in front of her dresser. She leans forward while hooking in her earrings as she looks at me through the reflection. "What do you mean?"

"Like, did you ever feel like you wanted to be something else besides a doctor but couldn't because Mom and Dad might not approve?"

"Of course not," she answers before turning to face me. "Do *you* feel like that?"

"No, not at all," I say to the ground, examining the chipped white toenail polish on my big toe and mentally reminding myself to get a pedicure. "I was just wondering."

She walks toward me and kneels in front of me before she places a hand on my lap. "Nat, you know that no matter what you do, Mom, Dad, and I, and even Lucy, will support you."

I furrow my brow. Of course I know that. I've known that my whole life. And knowing what Hayden has been through since his stint in college makes me feel like I've taken my family's support for granted. "I know."

"Is this about Matteo? That maybe you should have stayed with him?"

"He dumped me, remember?" I look at her with a sad smile of defeat. "I didn't really have a say in the situation."

"You could have told his mom," she suggests, smirking at the thought of me tattling as if Matteo and I were children. "I'm sure she would have forced him to marry you."

"A shotgun wedding without the pregnancy," I joke. "Every girl's dream." While the sarcasm in my voice is obvious, it doesn't hide the glum tone laced with the bitterness.

"Are you sure you don't want to go with us to dinner?" she asks again, her voice a little more encouraging this time. "David won't mind."

"I know he won't." I smile. "But I'm honestly tired. I had a long day at work."

She gives me an earnest look before hooking her shoes on her feet as she walks out of her bedroom. I follow, ready to spend the night in front of my laptop screen with a loop of whatever I decide on Netflix and any and all of the junk food I can scrounge up.

"Do you want us to pick up some takeout? We're getting Italian," David offers, looping Carmen's jacket through her arms.

"Sure," I oblige, looking at the sympathetic look that never left Carmen's face while appeasing her need to big sister me. David must know about the invitation too because he's wearing the same look of concern as Carmen.

Carmen reaches for me and wraps me in her arms. "Love you, baby sister."

I sink into her arms, and my throat tightens as she holds me in her embrace. "Love you, too."

Once Carmen and David leave for their date, I change into the oversized cashmere sweater I splurged on during my most recent trip to Bloomingdale's and settle into the couch with my laptop propped on a pillow and a bowl of cheddar popcorn nestled between the cushions. I'm flipping through my Netflix selections with my phone resting loosely in my hands when my fingers land on Hayden's number, thinking about my lunch hour spent with him and the lingering thoughts of his own personal woes that contrast vastly from mine yet are somehow relatable.

> Me: Hey, Marshall.

His response is almost instant, as if he's been waiting eagerly for me to text him.

> Hayden: Marquez.

> Me: Thanks for lunch today.

> Hayden: Anytime.

There's a pause in our back and forth. And just as I assume our conversation is over, my phone vibrates with a new message.

> Hayden: Thanks for keeping me company. It was nice to see a friendly face.

I pause, gnawing on the inside of my cheek. I haven't even thought of how lonely he must feel until now, even after he made it abundantly clear. How his day-to-day must feel tiresome, surrounded by people that don't know about his past the way I do. It makes me wonder if he's ever told his friends, like Dexter, about his parents or his life before moving to the city.

> Me: Well, if you're ever in need of a lunch date or someone to make that rat dish for, I'm just a text message away.

I end the sentence with a small smiley face emoji. And Hayden responds with a thumbs-up emoji, naturally ending our conversation before I wedge my phone between the cushions of my couch. I roll to my side and place my laptop on the coffee table for better viewing. I finally pick the perfect distraction of twinkly vampires and horse-sized werewolves as I start my *Twilight* marathon with the image of Matteo's wedding invitation burning a hole in my head, hoping to replace it with future lunch dates with a reunited friend instead.

12

Natalia

senior year

I'M REPEATING the mnemonic that Carmen taught me in my head, chanting along the words in a light whisper to study for my trig test next period when I'm interrupted by the sudden drop of a small sandwich bag in front of me. When I look up to peer at my side, Hayden looks at me with a proud smile.

"Cookies?" I ask, holding up the bag containing about four or five cookies that smell amazing even through the plastic seal.

"I baked them," he answers.

"You?" I ask, genuinely surprised. "You baked these?"

He shrugs. "I made some of my mom's oatmeal cookies not too long ago, and the baking bug bit me."

"What kind are these?" I ask, ripping open the bag and inhaling the warm scent of cinnamon and vanilla.

"Snickerdoodle."

My mouth spreads into a gleeful grin as I take a large bite out of a cookie, leaving behind teeth marks that rival the Cookie Monster's. The flavors dance on my tongue. Everything that reminds me of fall and warmth and sugar is mixed together to make me take another large bite.

"These are amazing, Hayden."

I reach out to offer him one, but he refuses.

"Those are yours," he says. "I have plenty at home."

"Oh good," I say through a full mouth. "'Cause I didn't really feel like sharing."

He laughs as he watches me eat greedily.

"Seriously, Hayden. I can't believe you made these."

"Well, believe it, lab partner." He turns to reach into his backpack for his binder. "I added ground ginger to the recipe. I read somewhere that it makes the flavors pop."

I silently nod while I listen. I practically inhale the rest of the cookie while the crumbs fall onto my open notebook.

"I'm thinking of making a vanilla cake next. At least, once I can hunt down this rare vanilla bean that's only sold in specialty stores."

My eyes widen as I push down a rough swallow. "Oh my god, Hayden. If you do, please let me try some. I promise I will be the best taste tester in the world."

He chuckles. "I'll make sure to save you a piece," he says, just as Mr. Khan closes the door to our classroom to signal the start of class. I brush the crumbs off my hands and carefully tuck the rest of the cookies into my backpack.

Hayden's gaze lingers on my hand as I pat the puffed pouch of the front pocket, securing them safely so I can enjoy them later. A light smirk presses the shallow dip in his dimple before he turns to face the front of the classroom.

"I'm glad you like them, Marquez," he whispers over the droning of Mr. Khan's voice calling over our classroom for roll call.

present

Fall has always been my favorite season. The leaves start to become a palette of colors as the air becomes crisp, and the scent of everything pumpkin and cinnamon wafts into the air. Or at least the storefronts of every Starbucks nestled within the streets of New York City. This is my eighth fall in Manhattan, and it's by far the best place to experience it. But aside from the change in temperature, it's the air of expectancy that I love the most. Each passing week means I'm that much closer to the usual holiday festivities that bring me and my sisters back home, like presents on Christmas morning and champagne flutes of sparkling cider on New Year's Eve.

My sisters and I grew up partaking in various seasonal activities. Painting eggs on Easter, lighting fireworks on Fourth of July, shopping for a real tree the second week of December. And now that we're adults, we've established our own set of traditions.

When Matteo first introduced me to apple picking, it was by accident. His colleague brought it up at work and when he mentioned it to me, I thought it would be fun, inviting Carmen along with us. After that, we went every year, adding to the list of holiday-themed traditions we've collected since we were children.

Today's the day of our apple picking feat, and I just received a text from Hayden fifteen minutes ago letting me know that he's on his way. I'm finishing getting ready, dressing myself in a warm, cream-colored sherpa sweater, fitted jeans, and my ever-so-trusty Doc Martens when I text him back with a simple *okay*. I took the time to braid my hair into two long pigtails, Dutch braiding them to lightly trail down my shoulders. After tying up the tough laces of my boots, I walk into the living room just as David buzzes Hayden up.

I open our front door, timing the minutes it takes to get there from the bottom floor to the elevator and through the narrow hallway, just as Hayden rounds the corner to my right.

"Hey, lab partner," he calls, coming to a stop at the doorway. His gaze drops, his eyes fixed on my feet for a few seconds before traveling back up.

"You want to come in for a minute?" I offer.

"Yeah." His voice sounds quiet, his answer coming out as a deep sigh in place of his usual composed response. He closes the door behind him, and his hand cups the back of his neck at the same time he shakes his head.

"Is everything okay?" I ask.

He looks at me, a small smile dancing at the corners of his eyes before it travels to the twist of his lips. "Yeah, everything's perfect."

We linger for a moment near the doorway before Carmen enters the living room.

"Ready?" Carmen calls, draping her jacket over her arm.

"Let's get this show on the road," David announces from his spot next on the couch.

Carmen and David lead the way out the door as Hayden stays by my side, waiting for me to lock the door behind me.

"I hope you're ready for all the pumpkin spice and everything nice," I say with a wide grin.

He grimaces. "Ugh, did you just rhyme?"

"I sure did."

Carmen and David stand in front of the elevator with their backs to us, discussing snack options for our guaranteed post-apple-picking hunger pang as we wait for the elevator. I feel Hayden's warmth skate over me as he stands close with his arm brushing mine through the thick layers of our clothes.

"I thought we were picking apples, not pumpkins."

"Okay, then. Apple spice and everything nice."

He cringes slightly in disapproval. "You're going to have to give me a heads-up if you keep rhyming like Dr. Seuss."

"There's no warning," I joke. "Sometimes I don't even know it's happening until I say words like 'jive' and 'hive.'"

Hayden reaches his hand to cover my mouth before I slap it away. The elevator dings as I pinch the fleshy part of his upper arm. Hayden winces at the same time Carmen looks at us over her shoulder, and I nuzzle my face into Hayden's arm. We lean toward each other, hiding our fit of giggles as Carmen eyes us with a wary look.

The drive is long, making the four of us restless. We sit while making the occasional conversation. We finally decide that we're going to have hot dogs and apple cider for lunch while listening to the music playlist that Carmen took over.

David finally pulls into the gravel parking lot of the apple orchard, and I lean my head toward the front of the car, hooking my hands on the headrest behind Carmen.

"We're here!" I beam in a quiet, singsongy voice, smiling at Hayden sitting next to me.

The four of us exit in unison, the slamming of the car doors creating a symphonic beat of low thuds. When Hayden rounds the trunk of the car, coming to my side, he smiles.

"Thanks for bringing me."

"Thanks for coming," I counter. I loop my hand around his arm, directing us to the small kiosk hut that holds stacks of baskets and wagons for people to use.

Carmen and David lead the way, her steps skipping as David smiles endearingly at her. I watch as he smoothes her hair and links his fingers through hers, kissing her temple before handing her her own basket.

I realize then that I'm more than grateful Hayden is here with me. I'm vastly relieved.

I love Carmen and David. But coming here only brings on an onslaught of memories that I have to relive as I remember what it felt like when I was happy with Matteo. And I hate that I have to relive them, even if it makes my sister happy that we're here. Because the pain that follows doesn't seem worth it. Remembering what it felt like to have Matteo hold my wooden basket as I filled it with apples or eat funnel cake with him only sharpens the dull pain, making the muddled memories come back with a fresh wave of heartbreak.

"Hey," Hayden calls.

I don't even notice when I stop walking, but he's multiple steps ahead of me. His voice is soft and gentle as he calls for my attention. When I look at him, his smile is as soft as his voice. He tilts his head toward the entrance to the orchard as his hand reaches to clasp mine, then enveloping it and reminding me that he isn't going anywhere, at least for the hours we're spending away from the city.

"Let's go," he whispers, tugging at my hand.

I nod, following his steps and reaching my other hand to wrap around his arm. Suddenly, I didn't feel so utterly and completely lonely.

"Most people like the Honeycrisp," I say, holding a ripe MacIntosh in my hand. "But I prefer these babies." I wave it in front of Hayden before taking a deep bite, savoring the tarty juices.

He smirks, setting down the half-full basket and closing the distance between us with two long strides. "I think you can give up your profession in tech to become an apple connoisseur."

"And live out here in the countryside?!" I exclaim in agreement with wide eyes. "I could even get a baby goat and a couple of chickens!"

He laughs. "Yeah, but you'd miss the city. I mean, where else can you get cheap, greasy Chinese food at two a.m.?"

I shrug. "True."

He takes my hand, the same one holding the apple with my teeth marks indented into it, and turns it to the other side before taking a large bite. The juices spritz off and land on my wrist.

"But you're right," he agrees through crunchy bites of apple. "This is pretty good."

His hand is still on mine, covering it as the juices from the apple start to coat my palm. I can see when he swallows, his throat rolling up and down as he looks at me with his light hazel eyes focused and narrowed.

"You still wear those boots," he says, his voice low and raspy.

"What?" I say, breathing out the question.

"The same ones you used to wear in high school." He takes a step back, letting go of my hand. We both look down, staring at my worn boots, now stained with a small smearing of dirt from the orchard path. When we both look back up at each other, Hayden smiles. "Like you're ready to go to war."

I swat his arm, the bitten apple falling between us. "I love these boots!"

He reaches to pinch my side, making me squeal before he runs from me. When I catch up to him, he dips his shoulder, angling it toward my stomach before scooping me up and draping me over him.

"Hayden!" I pound on his back, hitting him lightly to get his attention, but he ignores me and walks toward our basket instead. When he finally sets me down, my feet landing with a bounce on the soft ground, I giggle uncontrollably.

"I swear, you're a literal child," I scold through my laughter. He laughs at me, watching as I smooth my hair down and adjust my sweater after it rode up to my waist.

"I like your boots," he says through his laugh. And then he stops, his smile shifting into something softer, more contemplative and saccharine. "It's very much you." He tugs on one of my braids, making me slap his hand away.

"I hope that's a good thing."

"You're always a good thing, Nat."

13

Hayden

senior year

THE COMBINED students of Mr. Khan's and Mrs. Morgan's biology classes are lining up single file as we board a yellow school bus. It's time for our annual field trip to the Ladera Water Treatment Facility to learn about water waste and our city's sewage system. Totally gross, but it gets us out of the classroom for the day.

I board the bus, following behind the long line of students, trudging up the steps while searching over the sea of people for a seat. I stop about midway, spotting Natalia looking out the window. Her hair is half up today, a braided crown wrapped around the top of her head with a gold butterfly clipped to the back above a tumble of waves.

I silently slide into the empty seat next to her.

"So I finished the book," I say, unraveling a set of headphones from my pocket.

She turns to face me as I kick the rubber sole of my Jack Purcells against her black army boots, the same ones that she wears every day except when she opts for her canvased Vans. I hook an earpiece into the ear facing away from her as she peers at me with curious yet cautious eyes.

"Finally," she says, sitting up from her seat to face me. "Thoughts?" Her voice is low, almost as if she's worried that I may have disliked the book. But I didn't. And I shove away that impulse to tell her she was right all along, that the right book was waiting to present itself to me before I found out I actually do like reading.

"It was amazing," I say a little too earnestly. "I mean, it's so honest and raw. And I feel like all of us can relate to Charlie. Even a little bit."

Her eyes light up, and she smiles so wide that I can't help the tug of happiness in my chest knowing she shared this little piece of herself with me. Something that now feels like a personal connection between me and her, like a secret or a coveted memory. "I know what you mean. When I finished it, I felt like Charlie had been writing those letters to me the whole time," she agrees excitedly, squeezing my forearm before tucking her hand back between her thighs.

"Exactly!" I exclaim, patting my hand on her knee.

I slump back in my seat, facing the front of the bus, hooking the other earpiece into my ear as we sit quietly. The bus begins vibrating below us as it accelerates out of the school parking lot. When I notice that she does the same, minus the earphones, I remove one of mine and offer it to her.

She stares at it, the single earbud resting between my fingertips in the small space between us. Our fingers graze lightly as she takes it, smiling shyly before fitting it into her ear. As we both settle comfortably into our seats, my thumb scrolls through the round dial on my silver iPod.

"I didn't know people still used iPods," she comments, gesturing toward my hand.

"Yeah," I say. "I can't really seem to part with it."

She smirks.

The music starts to fill the cords leading up to our ears, my left and her right. My thumb finally stops on the next song on my playlist, Imagine Dragon's "Radioactive." As the music continues to play, Natalia leans further away. Her forehead presses against the cool window, forcing me to scoot closer toward her so the cord doesn't grow taut between us. As soon as our arms brush against each other, I smell a hint of vanilla.

We stay quiet, our conversation having transitioned to a comfortable silence while the chatter of fellow students surrounds us. We've somehow wrapped ourselves in a bubble of alternative rock, muffling the sounds around us like we're the only two people on the bus.

present

We drive back to the city, sitting in silence as we pass through rows and rows of charming scenic views. I watch Natalia looking out the window with her head leaned up against the window as the day starts to fade into a haze of orange and purple. Trying not to disturb the quiet, I pull out my AirPods and tap Natalia's shoulder. When she looks at me, I outstretch my hand to offer her an earpiece. The smile that spreads across her face makes my heart thaw. Not in the sense that it was frozen or hard in the first place. But in the way that her warmth spreads through to all the neglected ridges that I'm not even aware of.

This is the Natalia I remember. Calm and thoughtful. Not full of pain and memories of her heartache. Seeing her like this makes me want to see more glimpses of her. Whether it's the teenage version that I've almost forgotten about or the one that's grown into a woman that carried bits and pieces of my past in her heart, I want more of her.

She takes the earpiece and nestles it in her ear. The sounds of Neon Trees start to drift between us. I pretend not to notice the tap of Natalia's index finger against the cushioned seat in the space between us. Or how I'm realizing her presence in my life is one that I look forward to more often than not.

"You want a beer?" Natalia calls from her kitchen. I'm sitting on her couch with my feet propped up on her coffee table as she looks at me over her shoulder.

"Sure," I answer. I hear the refrigerator door close before she walks back to me to hand me my beer and plops herself on the other side of the couch.

"You sure you don't want anything to eat? Carmen's getting food anyway."

"Nah." I shake my head. "I should head out in a bit."

She nods, tilting her own beer back as she relaxes into the soft cushions. "I had fun today," she comments, smiling as she turns to face me.

"I did too."

"You make a pretty good date," she adds, poking her sock-covered foot against my ankle.

"You too, Marquez."

We sit in silence for a minute, relaxing after a long day on our feet while we wait for Carmen and David to return with takeout. Natalia suddenly shifts her whole body to face me, sitting up to rest her butt on the soles of her feet.

"Can I say something? And maybe you not judge me for being a pathetic ex-girlfriend?"

My brow furrows. "Why would I judge you?"

"Just…" She reaches a hand out as if to stop me, knowing that whatever reaction I have to her next words will be far from judgment but a forewarning is necessary for her to be transparent. I gesture for her to continue.

"I miss him," she finally says, her shoulders slumping a little as she says out loud what she's been trying to bury deep. "I really do. But I miss him the most when I'm lonely. Like when I have to eat dinner alone or when I have to sleep by myself at night. Or when I have no one to do things with. Like today."

My face softens as she shifts in her seat. Her face drops, and her fingers tug on one of her braids. She twirls it around her finger, and it reminds me too much of how she used to play with the ends of her hair when we were kids.

"Is there more than that? Than just missing him?" I ask.

She shrugs. Not because she doesn't know the answer to my question but because she doesn't want to say.

"I guess...if I weren't so lonely," she answers, her voice low and shy, "I could get over this breakup a lot easier." She looks back at me with an apologetic look on her face, and she shakes her head. "I know, it's pathetic."

"Nat, it's not pathetic," I assure her. She rolls her eyes and drinks her beer, avoiding my eyes. "Nat," I call to get her attention. "Being lonely is a breakup's worst enemy. It makes you do stupid things."

"Like calling him in the middle of the night drunk off vodka?" she says sheepishly.

"Did you do that?"

"Maybe..."

"Nat." My voice grows lower. The way it does when what I'm about to say is meant to be taken seriously. I scoot toward her, closing most of the space between us. "If you ever have the inkling to call your ex in the middle of the night, call me instead. In fact, if you ever feel like you're lonely and want to be with someone, even if it's to grab dinner or watch a movie, call me."

She sighs. "Hayden, I can't do that to you. You have your life to live. I don't want to cut into your life like that."

"You're not cutting into my life."

"It's fine." She takes a deep breath, the kind that's meant to be cleansing, and looks at me with determination set in her eyes. "I just need time."

I'm about to tell her that she doesn't need to depend on time, that I can be around to help mend those wounds, when we're interrupted by the front door clicking open.

"I come bearing gifts," Carmen calls as she walks through the door, a plastic bag holding multiple Styrofoam containers dangling from her fingers.

Our eyes shift back to each other, a lingering silence settling between us with the scattered words I want to say still held on my tongue. Instead of letting those words spill, I lightly squeeze Natalia's arm, to which she gives a sad smile.

"I'm going to get going," I announce, standing from the couch.

Natalia follows, walking me to the door as I wave a quick goodbye to Carmen and David.

When we reach the door, I turn to Natalia as she braces a hand along the doorframe.

"Thanks again for coming today," she says with a smile that's replaced all the apprehension she carried while we sat on the couch.

I nod. "Remember what I told you."

Her brow furrows and her lips twist in confusion.

"To call me if you ever feel lonely," I almost whisper. "And...maybe I'll do the same." Before she can question me and ask me about my own bouts of loneliness, I turn to leave.

14

Hayden

senior year

I HOVER over Natalia as she holds the scalpel over the pinned down frog in the metal tray. I'm seconds away from gagging with the pungent scent of formalin filling my nostrils when Natalia slices into the grayish skin of the frog's belly. As soon as her scalpel lifts, she smiles at me proudly.

"Did you name it?" I ask, swallowing the saliva pooled in the inside of my cheeks.

Her smile drops to a frown. "We were supposed to name it?"

I nod. "Or else it's bad luck." I don't know if it's true, but I'll say anything to put off our disgusting little lab assignment for as long as possible.

"How about Frogothy?" she says with a suppressed giggle.

"Frogothy?"

"Yeah." She shrugs. "Like Timothy, but with Frog."

I laugh. "Or Frogathan?"

She snorts loudly. The back of her hand comes up to cover her mouth as her eyes twinkle with laughter. A couple of heads turn our way and when I look up, I see Alex Spencer smiling in our direction with his eyes focused on Natalia. I nod in his direction, to which he nods back before cutting into his own frog.

"I think Spencer's checking you out," I whisper low to Natalia's ear as she uses forceps to pull back the frog's skin. I stop another gag that forces its way onto the back of my tongue.

She looks back to where Alex is sitting, and his smile widens when they meet eyes. She looks at me once again before ducking her head closer to examine the frog.

"Not interested, I see."

Her face deadpans. "How about helping me with this surgery instead of digging into something that isn't any of your business?"

"I think it's considered more of an autopsy at this point."

She rolls her eyes as she shoves the forceps into my hand.

present

"Hayden!"

I walk into my apartment with the lingering thoughts of Natalia and apple picking in my mind, greeted by the sound of my name. When I look, I find Ashton Park sitting comfortably on my couch. He stands, walking to greet me with open arms and a rough hug.

"Carly finally gave you a break from all the wedding planning?" I tease as I pull away.

Ashton, Dexter, and I met during our first year at Penn State. While I stayed in contact through the occasional Skype call and emails from different time zones and cities, Dexter and Ashton remained close all throughout college. Ashton and his fiancée, Carly, are getting married in a couple of weeks. The wedding and all the tedious details that involve it are consuming every minute of his life, making him eager to get away as much as he can.

"He had to make a break for it when Carly started making center-pieces," Dexter jokes, rounding the couch from the kitchen with an unopened bottle of beer in his hand.

Ashton shakes his head, picking up his own bottle off the coffee table. "If you two ever decide to get married, suggest Vegas right off the bat. Just make it easy and elope."

"Aw, come on," I offer. "It can't be that bad."

"Carly lectured me for an hour last week because I couldn't tell the difference between roses and peonies."

Dexter guffaws, his head thrown back against the couch as Ashton glares at him. "It's not funny!" he defends. "I finally gave in and told her to get whatever flowers she wanted. Roses, peonies, the whole damn florist. Whatever she wants so she can have her dream wedding."

I smirk.

"I have to admit," Ashton adds. "She's doing a pretty good job. If I did those centerpieces, it would look like I made them with my feet."

"So what brings you to this side of the bridge? I thought the slums of Brooklyn were below your tax bracket," I ask, poking fun of the fact that he used to be Dexter's old roommate in this same apartment until he traded it all in for his fancy Upper East Side penthouse.

He smirks. "Carly's parents are in town for the weekend, and I needed to get out of the house for a bit. I told her I had a wedding errand to run."

"And she bought it?"

"What are you talking about?" Ashton asks teasingly. "I'm here on official wedding business."

"Huh?" I ask, confused.

"You two never RSVP'd."

Dexter rolls his eyes. "Who RSVPs nowadays?"

"Literally everyone except you two," he deadpans. "You guys are going to be there, right?"

"Of course," Dexter and I answer in unison.

Ashton nods, draining the rest of his beer. "Oh," he says, turning to me, "Jacky's been asking about you."

"Ugh," I groan lightly. I hear Dexter snicker from his seat on the couch.

Jacky is a friend of Carly's. She's also a member of the wedding party that I met during a Fourth of July gathering Carly and Ashton had at their penthouse rooftop. We hit it off after a round of beer pong and when I walked her home at the end of the night, she invited me in. Before we moved on to the actual hooking-up stage of the night, I explained to her that I wasn't looking for anything serious. To which she said the word "same" before continuing to remove the rest of my clothes. But apparently, all of that changed when morning came, and she asked if I ever thought about having kids and my opinion on destination weddings. I've been avoiding her since.

"I thought you liked her," Ashton says. "What happened?"

I shrug my shoulders. "It wasn't supposed to be anything more than a hook-up. I told her that."

"I guess she got a taste of the appetizer and didn't get her fill," Dexter teases. "She wanted the whole Hayden main course."

I cringe. "You sound like a perv when you talk about sex in metaphors."

Ashton laughs. "Well, she asked if you were going to be at the wedding...and if you were bringing a date."

"You know, she's going to be all over you if you show up alone," Dexter adds.

I haven't even thought of bringing a date, or my dilemma with Jacky.

"I guess I'll bring a date," I say with a defeated sigh.

"I don't mean to find joy in your misery, but this is going to be quite entertaining," Dexter says through an evil grin.

Hours later, after Ashton's time with us ran out and he had to go back home to Carly, I settle into my room, ready to go to bed. As I pull the sheets back, my phone pings on my nightstand.

It's Caitlyn. Her number pops up on my screen with a quick *hey* bubble under the string of previous text messages. I can answer with a mimicking *hey* which will most likely result in another night of meaningless sex and the empty feeling of loneliness that Natalia was so apt to describe. Or...but that's the thing. There is no or. There's only Caitlyn. Or Jessica or Whitney. Or whichever woman, age ranging from twenty-one to thirty-five within a fifteen-mile radius, happens to match with me at the same time I match with her.

I don't answer Caitlyn. Or go on to Cupid's Bet, scrolling through messages from various women I've matched with in the past. Instead, I call Natalia, already missing the sound of her voice.

"Hey, Marshall," she answers. "Miss me already?"

"Something like that." I chuckle. "I was actually thinking about what I said," I say and stay silent.

"About?" she asks when I don't elaborate.

"You know." I clear my throat. "About calling me when you're lonely."

"Oh."

"Yeah," I answer, my voice low. "And I meant it when I said I would do the same. If you're okay with it."

"Of course, Hayden," she says. Her voice sounds so welcoming. So comforting that I can't even feel bad about taking advantage of this offer I laid on the table, knowing that it's a thousand times better than texting Caitlyn back.

"Okay…" My voice trails off, sounding a bit unsure.

"Okay."

We stay on the line, remaining quiet and not giving any indication of wanting to hang up.

"Are you…feeling lonely right now?" she finally asks.

"A little."

"Okay then," she answers, "tell me your deepest darkest secret."

"Whoa, I thought we would warm up to that kind of stuff. Maybe start with how you take your coffee," I joke.

"Or if I say cara-mel or car-mul?"

"It's obviously car-mul."

"In what universe?"

"Everyone's!"

And we stay on the phone for two hours before I realize that I don't feel so lonely anymore.

15

Natalia

senior year

"MARQUEZ?"

I look up from my book with a green straw hanging from the corner of my mouth while slurping the last bits of my matcha crème Frappuccino when I hear my name in the crowded Starbucks.

Hayden is standing in front of the entrance, having just entered the coffee house, with a wide grin on his face.

"Funny running into you here," he comments, sliding into the seat in front of me.

"My sister's at the mall, shopping. And I have official chauffeur duties," I explain, pointing to the large building across the street with the red Macy's logo facing us. I turn the book on the table, placing it downward with the spine facing up as I put my drink down next to it. "What are you doing here?"

"Just picking up some coffee," he says, tilting his head toward the counter. "Jenny likes her mocha fraps on the weekends."

"What a doting boyfriend you are," I comment with a small smirk.

He chuckles. "So," he says, leaning back in his chair and crossing his ankles underneath the table as if he plans to stay long, "you all ready for your visit to NYU next week?"

I nod enthusiastically. "My dad's already on a hunt for a 'Proud NYU Parent' bumper sticker."

My visit to tour the campus has been all I can think about as of late. But aside from touring the campus, I'm also excited to explore the city. This will be my first time in New York City, and I've been jittery from the excitement.

He chuckles, running his fingertips along the table's edge. "What are you majoring in when you leave Beavercreek for fancy ol' NYU?"

"I'm leaning toward communications," I answer shyly, fidgeting with the worn edges of my book.

"Leaning?" he asks, curiously questioning my indecisiveness. "You haven't decided?"

I lean forward, crossing my arms in front of me. "Can I be honest with you?"

He mirrors my movements, leaning toward me until we're inches apart. The light streaming through the window reflects off his bright eyes, making them look more green than brown as he narrows his gaze on me.

"You're really joining the circus?"

I lightly poke his arm. When I tell him the truth, my honest answer, I pause before sharing the small chunk of me that I don't share with most. "I don't really care what I study as long as I get out of here."

His smile falters, and his brow furrows. When he stays quiet, I continue.

"I'm probably going to major in communications just so I have a lot of opportunities when I graduate, but my goal is to leave this place. I want to move to the city and see what's out there."

He doesn't say anything, but he smirks, his smile calm yet surprised in a way that shows he didn't expect my answer.

"At least, that's what I hope," I finish, leaning back in my own chair. "Unless I chicken out or something."

"You will." I look up at Hayden, his eyes serious, his voice full of conviction. "You're going to get out there and see the world."

I smile, a flushed heat spreading across my neck. "Thank you for your vote of confidence. Now if you can carry the same tenacity when it comes to dissecting frogs," I joke, shifting the attention away from Hayden's surety in my future despite my lack thereof, "I wouldn't have to do all the work."

"I'll leave the cutting into dead animals to you, Marquez," he quips. "I mean, what are lab partners for if not to do the dirty work?"

I smile sincerely at his joke, realizing how different he is from the first day of class. When he was so abashed by his lack of preparation for our lab assignment and now, he's more than willing for me to take the grunt work, knowing I won't judge him.

Instead of getting up to get Jenny's coffee, Hayden stays. We talk about Manhattan in the fall, our favorite places to eat in Beavercreek, and our speculations on why the north side of campus, where the foreign language classes are located, smells like stale prune juice and moldy bread.

We sit and talk for the next two hours until I get a text from Lucy to meet her outside. For that short moment, I forget all about the scary future ahead of us. Instead, I focus on how Hayden and I have somehow fallen into this pattern of conversation and laughter as if we've been doing it for years.

present

"This. Is. Delicious," I groan. "You have to try some."

I turn to face José. He's sitting on the other side of the wrought iron table where our hamburgers and fries are scattered. I've just taken a long sip of the most delicious pickle lemonade that I've ever had, and the disgusted look on José's face is his silent answer to my offer.

"I don't think I've ever seen a more disgusting combination of flavors in one cup," he comments, taking a sip of his much safer blueberry lemonade.

We're on an extended lunch break. The weather outside is clear after raining most of the week, and the crisp air that's warmed from the bright sun felt too good to pass up on. So we settled for Lemon Patty, an over-the-top hipster burger joint about eight blocks from our office that specializes in various flavors of lemonade along with gourmet burgers. And now, with the discovery of pickle lemonade, my new favorite lunch spot.

"There was something I wanted to...throw out there," José says, interrupting the unintentional humming sound I'm making in the midst of my heavy slurping.

I stop, curious but a little apprehensive. The last time he looked at me the way he's looking at me right now, suggestive and insistent, I sat through a blind coffee date with a man who thought diva cups were a special type of chalice meant for "boss ladies."

"I feel like I should be nervous, but go on." I gesture toward him to continue.

"I want to set you up," he finally says.

"That's what I thought." I sigh. "No."

"Nah-taliaa," he whines, elongating the vowels as his almost nonexistent accent becomes thicker.

I hold up my hand. "Did you not learn from the last time?"

"That was a mistake," he confesses. "I should have known the moment he compared himself to Dwayne 'The Rock' Johnson."

I focus my attention on cleaning up our trash, hurriedly standing from our table while collecting various wax wrappings and paper boxes. José gathers his own trash and follows.

"My cousin Shawn just moved to Manhattan," he explains as his urgent steps catch up with mine. "He's in desperate need of a woman. A companion."

"Then get him a dog," I say briskly.

"I showed him your picture."

I side-eye him.

"He's interested."

I roll my eyes.

"And he's a good person, Natalia."

"Then why is he so desperate?"

"Well, he's not really 'desperate,'" he says, using air quotes. "He's just lonely."

My face softens. *Boy, do I know what* that *feels like.* Just as the inconvenience of being set up draws up an imaginative shield, I lower it, feeling sorry for this lonely cousin.

Breaking under José's over exaggerated pout, I throw my hands up in surrender. "Fine. I'll think about it."

He squeals and wraps his arms around me. "And I promise he isn't some creep or serial killer."

"If he is, then you're buying lunch every single day until I retire. *If* I'm not chopped into tiny human chunks and fed to the seagulls." I finally smile before playfully shrugging him off my shoulders as we continue our walk back to the office.

I guess misery really does love company. Who would have thought the one thing to convince me to go on a blind date would be my loneliness? Sympathizing for another lonely soul in New York City. And then I realize I haven't felt as lonely as of late. As much as those bouts of loneliness waver in and out, the last time I felt truly lonely was before Hayden came along. Ever since we came to the decision, much to Hayden's persistence, to call each other when we were lonely, it's as if I've been filling that void with him. With memories of him, memories of *us.* That empty hole Matteo left behind is now being filled with my past.

The smirk that creeps up on my face as I think about my long-stretched phone call with Hayden while we talked about everything and nothing comes out of nowhere. While I reminded him of his aversion to dead animal carcasses, he reminded me of my obsession with pastel gel pens and color-coordinated highlighters. As I teased him about his teeny-tiny fixation on Emma Stone and her stunning red hair, he reminded me of my own addiction to Swedish Fish, voicing his disgust for the snack I used to sneak in small bites when Mr. Khan had his back turned to us.

José and I are walking on the semi-crowded sidewalk bustling with other nine-to-fivers on their lunch break when we walk past a small bookstore. I peek inside through the glass display window, peering at the shelves lining the walls and small tables full of best sellers and sales.

"Can we go in for a second?" I ask José, who's busy with his nose buried in his phone.

He looks up as his gaze lifts toward the storefront. "Sure," he answers.

When we enter the shop, the copper bell chimes, welcoming us, as well as the scent of old, dusty books. I can practically feel the coarse pages rubbing between my fingers and the spines splitting as they're cracked open for the first time. My fingers trace over the shelves as I leisurely walk the aisles, recognizing titles from John Green and Danielle Steel before I land on a copy of *The Perks of Being a Wallflower*. The smile that spreads across my face transitions into a full giggle. I'm still laughing to myself when I remove it off the shelf. And before I know it, I'm clutching it against my chest, spreading my warmth through it. As if transferring my memories into the tightly bound pages so I can physically hold it in my hands.

"What's so funny?" José asks from behind me.

I shake my head, tucking my chin toward my chest as if sharing a silent inside joke with myself and the book.

"Nothing." I turn to face him with the laughter still dancing around the corners of my mouth. "Are you ready to go?" I ask, my hold on my newest treasure growing tighter.

16

Hayden

senior year

"TAKE five and meet back at the line of scrimmage," Coach Burns announces as he huddles together with our offensive and defensive coaches on the field. A collective sigh leaves every member of the team, all tired with still an hour left of practice.

We all trudge to the sidelines, our helmets held loosely in our hands, where we reach for our water bottles. I see Tyler kick up his steps as he practically skips to the bleachers, his dopey grin all wide and bright for his "not-girlfriend" Yuri Kim. I watch as she leans down on the metal railing with her long dark hair blowing in the wind. Behind Yuri, on the bench closest to the railing, I see Natalia, smiling along as Tyler and Yuri flirt with playful giggles and excessively touchy hands.

I'm surprised Natalia is here. When I last talked to her in bio class today, she told me her flight would be leaving early for New York tomorrow morning. I thought she would have been at home already, readying for her trip. But seeing her warm smile and laugh that I can hear without actually hearing, I'm glad she hasn't gone home for the day. I'm glad she's here, her heart still in our hometown instead of a city hundreds of miles away.

I glance back at our coaches. They're still deep in conversation with their hands on their hips and brows furrowed, so I jog over to where Tyler's standing.

"Hey, Nat," I call, nodding my head in her direction. She stands, smiling even brighter than before as she leans against the railing, mirroring Yuri's stance.

I half expect her to greet me with the shy side of her. The side that I've grown accustomed to, as it's the only side she's trusted me with so far. I don't expect her to be so…open. Almost as if she's as happy to see me as I'm to see her. In fact, ever since our run-in at Starbucks, it seems that this side of Natalia has been pulled to the surface, front and center. Smiling more, willing to fork out more pieces of her without me having to coax them out. I'm beginning to feel myself getting comfortable with Natalia and her finally acknowledging us as actual friends instead of just lab partners.

"Hey, Hayden," she calls. She rests her chin on the heel of her hand, and the tip of her nose does that little dip before she scrunches it.

"I thought you'd be halfway to the airport by now," I tease, flicking my shaggy hair, wet from the sweat soaking the dark strands.

"Caught me about fourteen hours too early," she answers.

"So you decided to ogle the football team instead," I joke, nudging my helmet in her direction. "Got those priorities in order, I see."

She rolls her eyes, smiling as she looks away. Her long hair, straightened and looking longer than when she has it curled or crimped, billows against the wind as she lets a light giggle escape through her lips.

"She came to keep me company," Yuri answers, linking her arm through Natalia's. The two share a quick look, one that says more secrets than answers, before they both face me and Tyler.

"Line up!" Coach Burns calls from the field.

"That's our cue," Tyler says, raising his helmet over his head. He flashes a quick wink at Yuri before he jogs toward the field.

I look at Natalia, her eyes still twinkling with her grin.

"Make sure to bring back a souvenir for me," I call, following Tyler.

Before my cleats step onto the field, I turn back one more time. I see Natalia still watching me, still smiling, still beaming. I bring my hand up to wave at her before she waves back. And a feeling starts to bubble in my chest. Something that feels like warmth and sweetness and home.

present

My thumb runs along the slick glass covered in frosty condensation, the tumbler holding my drink growing more and more appetizing as this conversation drags on. I'm on my second glass of whiskey, and the conversation hasn't grown any more interesting than it was when I first sat down in this dingy bar. It especially doesn't help when the person I'm having that conversation with refuses to talk about anything else besides rescue kittens or *The Vampire Diaries*.

"All I'm saying is, if everyone got their pets spayed or neutered, we would have fewer on the streets."

I nod, unable to disagree.

Her name is Lena. Twenty-seven, born and raised in Jersey, and works in PR. Oh, and has a little bit of a problem with her roommate who's allergic to cats but should suck it up because it's "not life or death." Lena messaged me on Cupid's Bet. When I responded, she eagerly messaged me back asking if I was free for drinks tonight. And I obliged. My other option to assuage the lingering loneliness that settled over me was to answer the text message I received from Jacky this morning. It was almost as if her ears were burning with smoke signals as she asked me in her message if I had a date to Ashton's wedding.

Ugh, Ashton's wedding. Maybe I can ask Lena?

I revert my attention back to Lena, her voice, a little too high-pitched and nasally, droning on and on about her cat's botched surgery when she had him neutered.

No, never mind.

"So, uh, how many cats do you have?" I ask, attempting to carry on this conversation.

"Five," she answers proudly. "My newest rescue just found his forever home with me two weeks ago. I named him Klaus."

"Oh, that's unique," I comment, slightly surprised that she would think of such a strong name for a cat. "Is it a German breed?"

Her brow furrows in disapproval. "You don't know Klaus? The original hybrid? He's half vampire, half werewolf."

I shrug in a way that's meant to apologize for my lack of vampire-slash-werewolf knowledge, but it comes off as an *I couldn't give two shits* kind of shrug.

She waves a hand at me. "Anyway, he's been having some trouble adjusting with all of his brothers and sisters."

"All four of them," I add matter-of-factly while trying my best to keep the sarcastic tone out of my voice. And if it accidentally slips, she doesn't notice.

"Yes!" she exclaims. "You see why he's having so much trouble adjusting?"

I nod, adding an uncomfortably forced smile. My gaze lands on the raised bar top where our drinks left behind wet rings on the wooden surface. Her small hand reaches mine, gently wrapping around my fingers as I still clutch my drink as if it were my lifeline.

"Did you want another?" she asks, her blue eyes peering at me through her lashes. It's getting late. And even though I don't really need to be up early tomorrow since my shift at the restaurant doesn't start until close to noon, I've already grown weary from this date.

"I actually have to be up early," I lie, taking a cursory glance at my watch.

"Oh," she says softly. "That's too bad." She adds a suggestive brow raise and a squeeze to my hand before leaning closer. "I thought you might want to come over."

She's bold, I'll give her that.

"Maybe next time."

I wave the waitress over to close our tab. Once that's settled, we both exit the bar and exchange awkward hugs before Lena heads home toward Midtown and I walk to the subway station to cross the bridge.

Just as I set my eyes on the green rails and concrete steps leading down to the train platform, my phone buzzes in my pocket.

The smile that splits my mouth in two hits me like a warm vanilla cake, spongy with a bounce light enough to lift my sourest of moods and so cozy it can heat my insides during the chilliest of Ohio winters.

It's Natalia.

"Isn't it past your bedtime, Marquez?"

"I didn't know you were keeping tabs on my bedtime," she calls through the phone.

"I keep tabs on a lot of things about you," I quip. "Like how many drinks it takes for your neck to turn pink or that you have the weirdest taste buds of anyone in the tri-state area."

"I do not!"

"Says the person who once offered me a bag of butter popcorn flavored Jelly Bellys."

"You remember that?"

"How could I not? They were disgusting."

She giggles.

"So, to what do I owe this late-night call?"

She pauses. "It's nothing."

I'm halfway down the stairs before I stop. "Nat, what is it?"

"I just…I guess…" She pauses before letting out a light hum. As if by doing that, she can hide the underlying reason she called me.

I wait patiently, knowing that pushing Natalia isn't the way to get her to open up. She says what she says and does what she does on her own terms. Not because she's stubborn but more because she's shy and reserved. That's how she was in high school, and she's still the same way now, uncovering layers of herself according to her own comfort level while peeling them back as she grows more assured and less vulnerable.

"I was just feeling a little…lonely," she finally says, breathing out the last word as if she doesn't want to use the full force of her voice to make it lack its certainty. And it isn't that she's not actually lonely. It's that she doesn't want to fully admit it.

Without thinking, I change direction. I walk back up the stairs, taking two at a time while finding it oddly coincidental that I'm at the station closest to her apartment.

"Well, then," I call a little breathlessly as I pick up my steps. "I'm glad you're holding up your end of the deal."

"I guess I am," she answers quietly.

"Are you hungry?" I ask, evening my breaths as I round the corner to where Natalia's brownstone sits. The sidewalks are thankfully empty, making it easier to maneuver around.

"It's ten o'clock at night," she answers.

"Actually, it's 10:27," I say, checking the time while remembering the lie I told Lena about my early morning. "But people get hungry at all hours of the day. And night."

I finally reach her apartment, coming to a stop at the steps leading up to her door.

"I guess you have a point," she says. "In that case, I'm starving."

I look up at the fourth floor. The window looking into her apartment is lit. A small shadow of light cascades out onto the fire escape surrounding the windows. I can't see her, but I can practically picture her up there, messy hair and swimming in an oversized sweater.

"Good. Cause I am too."

"How is that a good thing? You're all the way across the bridge."

"Or I'm downstairs."

17

Hayden

present

WHEN I HEAR the click of Natalia's door, the heavy double doors leading up to her building creaking and straining, I see Natalia walk through. She's exactly how I imagined. The mess of her wavy hair is piled on top of her head, with a fringe of curls trailing down her nape. Her small body is practically enveloped by the oversized hoodie she's wearing with a tweed coat draped over her shoulders. She sticks her arms through the sleeves as she carefully walks down the steps before coming to a stop with a light hop in front of me.

While I expect some sharp, witty comment to leave her mouth, something about how my late-night escapades resulted in this impromptu snack hankering, she doesn't say anything. Instead, she smiles sheepishly as she wiggles her fingers in front of her.

"Hi," she whispers shyly, which I find completely adorable.

"Hey," I say back. And then, she full-on laughs. "What's so funny?"

"Just that…you're here." Her hand, half covered by the sleeve of her jacket, comes up to cover her mouth.

"Well, you called."

"I didn't think you'd show up," she says through her smile, and her nose does that little dip again.

"You know the tip of your nose twitches when you smile?"

"It does?" Her eyes cross, trying to look at her nose.

"Yeah." I laugh and pinch her nose between my fingers. "It always has."

She pulls my hand away and tugs on my thumb. "What are you even doing here?"

"I, uh…" My voice trails, and I awkwardly shuffle my feet. "I had a date. At a bar a couple of blocks down," I confess.

Her smile fades almost instantly. She leans backward in a way that looks as though she's examining me, stretching her neck to the side to get a better look at my face as her hands grip my shoulders. Her cold fingers move to my chin, tugging it side to side before a hum of disapproval purrs through her closed mouth.

"What?"

Her lips form a firm line as she squints her eyes. "I'm checking to make sure that your date cleaned up her seat properly after using it."

My hands move to grip her sides just as she squeals to get away from me.

"Hayden! Stop!" she screams when my fingers start digging into her ribcage. Her hands claw at mine, failing at her attempt to pry them off of her. "*STOP!*"

"Take it back," I threaten. I try to keep a straight face, but I fail miserably when I laugh at the way the redness in her face travels all the way to the tips of her ears.

"No!" She wriggles against me, squirming in my arms.

She turns her back to me in an effort to get away, but it only gives me the advantage to wrap my arms around her, forcing her to seek mercy.

"Take it back," I demand.

She stays quiet, but her entire body trembles with laughter as she shakes her head against my chin. My fingers dig deeper into her waist, and her body jerks against mine.

"*OKAY!*" she finally shrieks. Her shrill voice echoes off the walls and sidewalk. "Okay! I take it back!"

My hold on her doesn't release right away. Instead, it slackens just the tiniest bit. I don't mean to, but when that comforting scent of warm vanilla hits my senses, I don't want to let go. My fingers skim over the rough material of her coat as she turns to face me before I reluctantly let her go. She playfully shoves her hands into my stomach, pushing me and forcing me to stumble a step backward.

"Come on," she says, laughing and turning to walk away. "I'm craving fried pickles."

"Fried pickles? Where are we going to find fried pickles?"

She smirks over her shoulder. "I have my connections."

I smirk back and follow willingly, falling in step with her. With Natalia on my left and the occasional buzzing of cars on the street to my right, this moment feels too surreal. Almost as if time has stood still and nothing has changed between us.

And while almost everything in the past eight years of our lives has changed to a great degree, some things remain the same. Like the warm vanilla Natalia's carried with her this whole time.

Natalia is clutching on to my arm, desperately hanging on as she grasps her chest with her other hand. We're both stumbling out of the small restaurant, our stomachs full of fried pickles and milkshakes, ube flavored for Natalia and chocolate flavored for me.

"You seriously have to watch your mouth when you're in public!"

"Hey," I defend. "It is way past that kid's bedtime. That was *not* my fault!"

"Di—did you see the mom's face?" she says in between whimpered breaths.

"'Mommy, what's a dirty sanchez?'" I mock in a high-pitched tone.

Natalia's laugh turns into a long, winded gasp. She turns red, and the muscles on her neck pull taut as she waves a hand at me, pleading for me to stop. "Stop! My stomach hurts!"

I'm laughing just as hard, cowering forward as Natalia leans her body against the nearest lamppost.

"I still can't believe your mom thought it was a cocktail!"

"The bartender turned red to keep himself from laughing! And then we had to explain to her what it was!"

Our laughter comes back tenfold as we remember my story about the time Pat and I took my mom to a bar during one of my trips back home. It wasn't long after I passed the legal drinking age, and she attempted to order a "dirty sanchez," thinking it was some exotic flavored margarita while claiming she heard about it somewhere on Facebook.

As our laughter dwindles, Natalia sighs, making a happy, contented sound as we continue to walk back in the direction of her apartment.

"I don't remember the last time I laughed that hard," she comments, wiping the corner of her eye and bumping her arm against mine.

"I don't either," I agree, grinning like a fool while realizing I sincerely can't remember the last time I had this much fun.

"Are you going to catch a cab home?" she asks, her hands stuffed into her pockets. She looks so comfortable, so content. And I realize that the thought I had during the moment outside on the fire escape at her apartment, when I thought she would look just as carefree and beautiful dressed down in something two sizes too big for her, is confirmed.

I shake my head. "I'll just take the subway. But I'll walk you home first," I offer, our steps growing lazier. I watch as she flips her hair back, now loose from the bun she had it wrapped in, smiling and shaking her head as if recalling our run-in with an overly curious child and equally curious mother overhearing our very not-child-friendly conversation.

She leads the way through the chilly night as the both of us wrap our arms inward in an attempt to stay warm. And before I know it, we're at the steps of her apartment. But before we say our goodbyes, Natalia turns to face me.

"So I have a confession to make," she says, a smile spreading across her face. "I called for another reason."

"So you weren't lonely?"

She tucks her chin down. "Not exactly." She rummages into her coat, reaching into the deep pockets before retracting her hand, her grip on something small and rectangular. "I was at the bookstore, and I found this. It made me think of you."

When her hands open between us, I see a fresh copy of *The Perks of Being a Wallflower* sitting in front of me. The fuzzy warmth that spreads through my chest reduces my heart to a gooey puddle. I take the book from her outstretched hand, turning it over as I let the memories wash over me.

"Do you remember?" she asks, her small voice so eager and endearing.

I nod, my throat tight, at a complete loss for words. "I can't believe you found this," I say hoarsely.

"Consider it a thank you. For the lemon tarts. And that rat dish. And apple picking."

"Thank you," I say a little breathlessly. My fingers run over the glossy surface, and a small huff of laughter slips through my lips, still surprised by this small gesture.

When I finally tear my eyes away from the book, I look at Natalia. She smiles shyly, tucking her chin toward her chest before she turns to walk up the stairs.

"Good night, Hayden," she calls softly.

A sudden panic sets in me. Not the desperate, hysteric kind but more of an urgent kind. I need to see Natalia again. Not because I'm lonely but because I want to. I want to spend my time with her, laughing and joking and reminiscing.

Grasping at whatever excuse I can find to spend more time with her, I finally find one: Ashton's wedding. It's the perfect excuse, along with a legitimate reason to spend time with her. Aside from the fact that I desperately need a date, we would have fun together. Making each other laugh with no awkward lulls in our conversation, no unnecessarily filling the silence with talks about the weather or pop culture trivia. In fact, none of our conversations have been unnecessary or stiff, veering more toward personalized and comforting instead.

"Hey," I call, forcing her to turn around. "I had a small favor to ask."

"Sure," she answers as she walks down the two steps she already took. She answers calmly before knowing what my favor is, naturally making me smile in response.

"I have this wedding to go to next Saturday, and I was wondering if you would be willing to go with me."

"Like a date?" she asks warily.

I tilt my head. "Like a friend accompanying another friend to a social event."

"Uh, yeah. Sure, I don't have any plans."

I sigh, relief plied into my breath, realizing how worried I've been about going to this wedding solo. "Thanks."

She nods, turning toward her building. "I'll see you later, Marshall."

I do a half salute that turns into an awkward bow. "Marquez," I answer before turning around. The last thing I hear before my trek to the subway station is the sound of Natalia's light giggle and the door closing behind her.

18

Natalia

senior year

"MARQUEZ."

Hayden greets me as his index and middle fingers come up to his forehead in a small salute. I dangle the small souvenir I brought all the way from New York City on my fingers in front of him.

"What's this?" he asks.

"A little gift from the Big Apple," I say as he takes the keychain with the shiny I Love NY written in the middle encased in cheap plastic. "Per your request."

He turns it over, examining the gift in his large hands with an appreciative smile.

"You got this for me?" he asks, looking at me with bright eyes.

I nod. "Don't feel too special," I add. "I got one for Mr. Khan too."

We both eye our teacher sitting at his desk at the front of the classroom picking his teeth using the end of a mechanical pencil. We both grimace and turn back to each other.

"No, you didn't," Hayden teases.

"You're right. I didn't," I confess.

He shakes his head, reaching for his backpack and taking the zipper of the front pocket in his hand. He uses his fingers to separate the ring on the keychain to thread it through the pull tab before letting it dangle. He smiles proudly, grinning before setting his backpack on the floor.

"Thanks, Marquez," he says softly, his smile never faltering.

"You're welcome."

"You better be careful, or I'm going to think you actually like me," he says, leaning toward me while speaking in a low voice.

I give an audible *pshh* sound. "Never."

Hayden nudges my arm with his elbow as Mr. Khan places his pencil on his desk and stands in front of the classroom.

present

"So it's either the cartoon hamster or the cartoon rabbit."

My brows cinch together, my lips pursing as I consider my choices. I look from my computer screen back to José, who's waiting patiently for my answer.

"Why does it have to be a cartoon anything?"

He sighs. "Because the developer wants the design to match her brand," he answers, defeated.

We've spent the last hour deciding on an appropriate logo for a computer hardware company that manufactures hardware geared toward women in the gaming industry. While a lot of the equipment screams cute and feminine with pink keyboards, headsets with cat ears, and RGB backlit monitors, it feels a little out of place to use a cartoon animal as the selling point for the entire marketing approach. Not to mention the sexist appeal to it. What, just because it's cute and fuzzy looking, only women will buy this stuff? I feel like they need to branch into different colors and designs to cater to every woman's taste. But that's José's job to discuss those discrepancies with the developer while addressing their marketing angle.

I throw my hands in the air, defeated. "I guess I'll go with the hamster then. It's less distracting. The rabbit's ears are way too obnoxious."

He nods. "Oh, by the way, Mark set up a meeting tomorrow morning with Kirby-Barton Tech about the new DDR5 RAM prototype they're developing. I guess they have a big presentation, and Mark wants both me and you to be there."

"Okay," I say, slightly distracted with a new email in my inbox.

"I'll get the coffee if you get the bagels in the morning," he suggests, an eager tone replacing the serious one we had talking shop about meetings and tech.

"Sure," I say. I smile at him as he exits my office before turning back to my monitor. When I look back at my inbox, I see the new email that caught my attention.

My eyes land on the familiar name attached to the email.

From: Hayden Marshall <hmarsh08@gmail.com>
To: Natalia Marquez <nmarquez@derntechsolutions.com>

Subject: Wedding Venue

Hey Marquez,
Just thought you might want some info on the wedding venue. I attached a link and the wedding website for Ashton and Carly.

Hayden

A quick smile quirks my lips. How did Hayden even get my work email? And a wedding website? What the hell is that?

From: Natalia Marquez <nmarquez@derntechsolutions.com>
To: Hayden Marshall <hmarsh08@gmail.com>

Subject: Re: Wedding Venue

Should I be concerned as to what a wedding website is? And just as equally concerned about your stalker abilities considering the stealth involved in finding my email address.

Natalia Marquez
Dern Tech Solutions, Inc.

His response is instant.

To: Natalia Marquez <nmarquez@derntechsolutions.com>
From: Hayden Marshall <hmarsh08@gmail.com>

Subject: Re: Wedding Venue

The bride and groom are a little intense. But the website should answer any questions about the wedding, if you have any. Like dress code and location.

And don't be too impressed. It's nothing but a quick directory search and remembering that your last name ends with a Z not an S.

Hayden

I scroll up to his previous email and click the link to the website. My office fills with the shrill music of "Chapel of Love" by The Dixie Cups with a montage of a very happy and attractive couple filling the screen. I quickly lower the volume before glancing over the links categorized in alphabetical order on the left, all lined with everything from dress code to hotel options to gift registries. Hayden wasn't kidding when he said his friends were intense. I click on the link for attire: black tie. Oh god, I don't even have an outfit that would fit the bill.

To: Hayden Marshall <hmarsh08@gmail.com>
From: Natalia Marquez <nmarquez@derntechsolutions.com>

Subject: Re: Wedding Venue

I guess I should put away my playboy bunny costume since it's black tie. Should I ask the butler to fetch the fine jewelry instead?

Natalia Marquez
Dern Tech Solutions, Inc.

To: Natalia Marquez <nmarquez@derntechsolutions.com>
From: Hayden Marshall <hmarsh08@gmail.com>

Subject: Re: Wedding Venue

YOU HAVE A PLAYBOY BUNNY COSTUME?! Fuck black tie, wear the costume. In fact, fuck the wedding. We'll have our own party. Amazon Prime ships next day if I order my captain's hat and silk robe within the next two hours and thirty-nine minutes.

Hayden

I giggle. Martha, Mark's secretary stationed right outside my opened office door, turns her head toward me. When I glance up at her, she gives a soft, polite smile and returns to clacking at her keyboard.

To: Hayden Marshall <hmarsh08@gmail.com>
From: Natalia Marquez <nmarquez@derntechsolutions.com>

Subject: Re: Wedding Venue

While I would love to see your friends ridicule you for the rest of your life for showing up to a formal event with a playboy bunny on your arm, I think I should save the costume for another night. I think Halloween might be a tad bit more appropriate.

Thanks for the heads-up. I'll make sure to dress for the occasion.

Natalia Marquez
Dern Tech Solutions, Inc.

I return my focus to my work. A new email from Mark pops up on my screen with the subject: Kirby-Barton Meeting. I open it, reading over the details and taking notes to prepare for the meeting tomorrow morning. I'm going over the meeting's itinerary and counting down the last hour until I leave the office when my phone buzzes on my desk. When I check my screen, I see Hayden's name light up on it.

"No, Hayden," I answer with a smile. "I will not wear the Playboy bunny costume for you."

I peer up and see Martha still at her desk. She glances at me but doesn't smile this time. Instead, her lips purse together as she eyes me with one brow cocked. I stand and close the door to my office before walking back to my chair.

"Oh no," he answers. "I smothered those dreams the second I realized how ridiculous I would look in a captain's hat. I think Hef was the only man in the world that could pull that look off."

"Referring to one of the world's biggest misogynists as 'Hef,'" I comment sarcastically. "That sounds promising."

He chuckles lightly from the other end. "Actually, I was calling to ask a favor."

"Another? Marshall, you better make it worth my while," I tease.

"More lemon tarts?" he asks, a pouty plea trickling through his offer.

"I'll do anything," I offer, feigning desperation. "I'll wear the damn bunny costume to the wedding."

Another chuckle. "I was wondering if you could go with me to pick out a wedding gift."

"Oh," I say.

"Yeah. I mean, I could go off the wedding registry, but I thought it would be more fun if I got them something personal."

"I thought the whole idea of a wedding registry was to pick out a gift the couple wants," I say, nudging my phone between my ear and shoulder as I distractedly scan over Mark's email.

"I had another idea." There's a small pause in our back and forth. "Do you have any plans after work?"

"A bag of teriyaki beef jerky and season four of New Girl, which I've seen about eleven times."

"So you're free?"

"I'm free."

"Great," he answers. "I'll meet you in front of your building at five."

19

Hayden

senior year

I NUDGE TOBY'S ARM, urging him to slide over a few inches on the cafeteria bench to make room for me. As I sit, I look up to see Alex Spencer sitting next to Natalia at her table, surrounded by her friends. They're facing each other, with his hands moving wildly in front of him before his movements pause and Natalia shakes her head. Her lips mouth an "I'm sorry" before his shoulders slump and he squeezes her shoulder. His hand lingers on her arm longer than necessary before sliding over her hand.

I smirk. He doesn't stand a chance. A girl like Natalia needs someone complex, not superficial and dull like Alex. She needs someone who understands her witty sarcasm and dry humor. Most of all, she needs someone who understands that underneath all of that, there's someone who is sweet and caring and thoughtful. While Natalia gives off the illusion of someone that doesn't give a shit about all the frills and drama of high school, she still cares. She cares about the people important to her, like her friends and her family, especially her sisters. She cares about books and learning what the stories are trying to tell. And even though she's rolled her eyes at me enough times to cause them to permanently remain in the back of her head, she cares about me too. She cares enough to make me smile when I need it, to listen to me when I need someone to talk to. She's the only person in this whole school that knows about the situation with my dad, and yet she hasn't judged me for my lack of will to fight for my future.

My eyes stay on Natalia, watching as Alex inches closer to her and offers her half of his Snickers bar before she takes a bite. I'm taken by surprise when Jenny approaches me. Her gaze follows mine to see me watching Natalia and Alex a little too closely.

"Natalia's your lab partner, isn't she?" she asks, more of a statement of fact than a question. Her tone carries the telltale signs of irritation as her eyes ping-pong from Natalia back to me. "She's kind of cute, no?"

I shrug. "I guess."

Jenny crosses her arms in front of her. "So you think she's cute?"

I finally look away from Natalia and land my eyes on Jenny. Her arms remain crossed, her right foot sitting just a couple of inches in front of her left with her hip jutted outwards. Her brows curve upward, waiting for my answer.

"No," I say, annoyed that the conversation has somehow shifted to my questioned attraction toward Natalia. "That's not what I meant."

Instead of questioning me further, she turns and stomps off.

"Jenny," I call, hopping off the table and going after her.

present

My and Natalia's eyes are level with the showcase of various bobbleheads, each figure dressed in different themes ranging from cartoon characters to superheroes.

"So tell me again why we're here?"

I round the end of an aisle lined with *Star Wars* bobbleheads, a Princess Leia in a gold bikini smiling at me as I meet Natalia. Her eyes track me up and down. Her gaze lingers on the slim-fitting Henley I paired with my faded jeans on my day off, different from the chef's uniforms I'm sure she's grown accustomed to.

"Ashton and Carly are both huge *Game of Thrones* fans, and I found out that this place does custom bobbleheads with character themes."

"So you're going to get them custom made Khaleesi and Khal Drogo bobbleheads?"

She holds up a bobblehead dressed in a Playboy bunny costume. Her smile beams with recognition, and her fingers toy with the figure, tracing over the bright colors and fragile lines before she carefully places it back on the shelf.

"That's exactly it," I answer. My attention piques, discovering that Natalia's pop culture knowledge on *Game of Thrones* may be more extensive than I thought if she's able to tick off character names without a quick Google search.

"Sounds better than a toaster," she says with an approving nod. "But why did you need my help? It sounds like you've pretty much settled on the gift."

I walk over to stand beside her. Our gazes face a shelf with over a dozen different variations of Khaleesi and Khal Drogo. "They have too many options."

"Oh Mylanta," she says breathlessly, her eyes scanning the selection.

"Yup."

"You know," she says with a soft voice, "maybe I should have picked my beef jerky over this."

I wink in her direction. "I'll get you something better."

"How about an eeny, meeny, miny, moe pick?" she suggests. "And no backsies."

"What did I tell you about rhyming?" I warn.

"It's an involuntary tic," she defends, shrugging her shoulders in feigned innocence.

"Fine," I agree. "It's better than my way."

"What was your way?" she asks.

"Buying them all," I joke, silently confessing the fact that I didn't really come here with a game plan. She rolls her eyes at me before turning her attention back to the figures.

I watch as her fingers pluck along the selection of figures. Her mouth silently moves along as she finally lands on a Khaleesi figure with a blue dress and a miniature dragon perched on her shoulder. She smiles proudly at me with her selection nestled in her hands.

"Nice one," I say, smiling down at her and watching the corners of her eyes crinkle. And then it's my turn. I mimic her, hovering my fingers over the figures. I land on Khal Drogo holding a curved machete with war paint smeared across his face and chest.

"I think we have our winners."

After providing pictures of Ashton and Carly at the register so that the bobbleheads look identical to the bride and groom with instructions on when to pick up the final product, we exit the store.

When we step outside, the sky is transitioning from the orangey-purple haze to a dark night sky. The air feels crisp, the remnants of summer blowing away with the incoming fall breeze, evident by the changing leaves feathering the backdrop as we slowly walk through the busy sidewalk. I fully expect Natalia to call it a night and head home, but then she peeks at me over her shoulder. Her lashes bat at me in an adorable way that comes off as playful and not flirty as she reaches for my forearm, pulling me toward her.

"Looks like the perfect night for some avocado froyo."

Thirty minutes later, we're back outside. We're each holding a cup of froyo in our hands, avocado flavored for Natalia and salted caramel for me.

"Whoever invented avocado-flavored dessert should be committed," I say, disgustingly eyeing the small cup in her hand as she hums with pleasure from her first bites.

"Hey, don't yuck my yum," she says, defending her dessert choice. "As if your *car-mul* flavored froyo is better."

"At least it's sweet," I argue. "And don't yuck your yum? Who talks like that?"

She scoops a small spoonful and points it toward me. "Here."

Jeannie Choe

I turn my head. "No thanks."

"Come on, Hayden. You can't knock it till you try it."

I give in when Natalia's brows bounce, her toothy grin, the type where her top teeth and her bottom teeth are equally exposed, urging me to sample a bite. When I pull the spoon between my lips, I taste all the hints of avocado that shouldn't be in a dessert, mixed with cream and cold, along with the trace of chocolate drizzled on top.

"That was interesting," I say, finding the combination of flavors mixing together too conflicting to say that it's bad.

She then places the same spoon she just fed me with into her own mouth, sucking off the remaining cream coating the smooth surface. "See? It's good, right?"

My eyes linger on the creases of her lips as she dips back into her cup, scooping another healthy serving. "It's interesting," I assure.

We continue our steps, walking in a lazy, comfortable pace with no direction yet having no intention of going our separate ways.

"So Dexter's renting a car for the wedding, so we don't have to worry about taking a train or a rideshare. Hopefully there won't be too much traffic leaving the city," I say, filling her in on our travel plans.

Natalia nods. "The venue looked really beautiful," she says a little wistfully. "And the bride and groom look really happy together."

She looks at me with a sad smile. The kind where her lower lip pokes out a little more than her upper and her jaw muscles tighten, causing those firm lines around her mouth to form like a parenthesis. It suddenly occurs to me that going to a wedding, one with a beautiful venue and a couple that truly loves each other, would only remind her how much she lacks those things. Those dreams were swiped out from underneath her like a rug when her ex-boyfriend dumped her.

"Are you okay?" I ask, thinking that maybe I shouldn't have asked her to go with me.

She nods, and her smile changes, the corners of her mouth quirking upward as her smile spreads toward her eyes. My smile mirrors hers, and we continue to walk in silence.

Once our dessert cups are empty, we toss them into the nearest trash bin while wiping our hands with the rough napkins it came with. I barely notice when Natalia's steps are no longer in line with mine.

When I finally do, I look back to see her with her mouth gaping and eyes wide before I walk back to her side.

"Nat, is everything okay?" She doesn't answer. "Nat?"

"Huh?" She whips her head toward me as if she forgot I was with her.

"What's wrong?"

She turns her face to look in the direction we're walking, her eyes focused on a couple walking toward us. They're happy, smiling, with their hands linked together between them, swinging and gleeful. The man leans down to kiss the woman on the cheek, which she accepts with a contented smile.

"Nothing," Natalia finally answers, her voice harsh and urgent. "Let's get out of here." Her hand, now frigid from the cold air and the dessert we just finished, grips mine as she hurriedly tries to leave our current spot.

Then it finally clicks.

"Is that…" My question trails off, watching as her worried eyes ping-pong back and forth from me to the couple in front of us, all while looking as if she's hoping the ground will swallow her whole.

It's her ex-boyfriend, Matteo. It has to be. And the woman he's holding hands with, looking blissfully happy as one half of an engaged couple. It's her ex-boyfriend *with* his fiancée.

Oh god, this is bad. I quickly glance at Natalia to see her face is still shock-ridden.

I don't know what makes me do what I do next. Maybe it's the fact that if I saw my ex-girlfriend in the arms of another man, I'd be fuming, no matter how much I claim I'm over her. Or maybe it's to let this ex-boyfriend know that Natalia is over him, no longer spending her nights in tears over the loss of their relationship, regardless of how far from the truth that is.

I pull Natalia to me, lowering my face to her. One arm wraps around her back as my other hand moves to the curve of her jaw, letting the rough pad of my thumb pull gently at her chin. I expect her to swat my hand away or screech, *What the hell are you doing?!* but she doesn't. She doesn't even bat an eye when I lean in closer, inching toward her in slow, deliberate movements.

Jeannie Choe

And I kiss her.

Her soft, warm lips slowly open up to mine as our teeth graze against each other and our tongues tangle somewhat awkwardly. Like we're trying to figure out how the other moves. And it doesn't take long because as soon as we find our rhythm, it feels like a song. One that'll play in the background of my life forever. And I'll never grow tired of it. Instead, I'll build my life around it, weaving my future and my past as I discover what forever feels like.

Kisses like this don't exist. There's no way a kiss could leave someone this feather light, like they're floating in air while feeling like complete mush at the same time. No, this kind of kiss only exists in fairy tales and at the end of cheesy rom-coms. *Right?*

Her body, tense and rigid from the shock of our kiss, falls pliant as our kiss deepens. I feel her grow heavy in my arms, making me want to take advantage of this moment while poking at the thought that I shouldn't be enjoying this. That this kiss has a purpose.

When I pull away with my hand still wrapped around her back, her closed eyes pop open. They search mine with an urgency full of questions. Questions that both of us have. Like why I did what I just did. Why my hands are still clinging to her body, the same way her hands are clinging to mine. Or how I've spent the last eight years of my life without her in it. And how in the *hell* I'm supposed to go back to living a life where I didn't spend my time kissing her.

We stand there, seconds passing as she peers up at me with a look of flustered shock, her chest rising and falling against mine. And suddenly, my heart starts to pound in my chest, thinking of a time when she looked at me the same way, eyes full of fear and confusion.

This was a bad idea.

"Hay—"

"Natalia?"

Whatever breathless words Natalia is about to whisper are cut off as we're interrupted by the sound of her name.

"Matteo!" she gasps, confirming my assumptions. She finally pushes me away, her hands fumbling with her purse strap as it slides off her shoulder. "Hi!" she screeches awkwardly.

138

"It's so good to see you," he says, grinning at Natalia with his head held high.

Natalia stands to my side. Her arms cross her chest, then her hands come together, one fist twisting into the other hand before she drops them to her side. Her feet shift below her, and she creates a small inch of space between us before quickly peering up at me. All before turning back to smiling back at him. She's so flustered and worried. And I wish I could take her away from this. I wish we could simply say "no, thank you" to whatever's going to happen next and leave.

But instead, I stay by Natalia's side and take in this guy, this shitty ex-boyfriend, to see who the fuck broke her heart to the point of hopelessness. His dress shirt, the color of day-old coffee and hanging a bit too loosely off his shoulders, looks awkward and tawdry. And a layer of stubble lines his chin, something that I assume is meant to make him look broody or suave but comes off as unkempt. I inwardly smirk, thinking how much better Natalia could do, knowing that this guy isn't worth whatever heartache is still ailing her.

As I'm thinking all this, marking his flaws and pointing them out in my mind, he leans forward to embrace Natalia. I watch her close her eyes and nuzzle her nose into his shoulder as if everything around them disappeared. A quick flash of pain deepens the crease between her brows before she pulls away, causing something in me to twist as my hate for Matteo grows.

"It's good to see you too," she whispers. She looks down at her feet, and everything about her shrinks into a meek mess of sorrow.

"I'm Hayden." I smile smugly, looking at Matteo while extending my hand toward him.

He shakes my hand, completely oblivious to the effect he's having on Natalia, with a smile and a smirk I almost imagine.

"This is my fiancée, Jacinda." He proudly wraps his arm around Jacinda, pulling her close to him. Jacinda looks at me and Natalia with a friendly smile, looking completely clueless to the awkwardness in the air.

Natalia slowly lifts her head, her sad smile barely lifting her lips as her hunched shoulders keep her from faking her way through this introduction. I reach for her and bring her closer to me, squeezing her small, limp hand to remind her that I'm right here. Matteo's gaze lands on our connected hands.

"Is this your friend?" Matteo asks, eyeing the way I tuck Natalia closer to me.

"Boyfriend, actually," I answer for Natalia when she stays quiet.

His eyes narrow, and he tilts his chin up, barely nodding to acknowledge my answer, almost as if gauging the truth in Natalia's new relationship status.

"My parents said they sent you an invitation to the wedding," he says, his voice tight and uncomfortable. "I hope you'll be there, Natalia."

"Sure," Natalia says softly with that same sad smile I want to wipe off her face.

I tug on her hand again, pulling her attention and causing her to look up at me. When she does, a sudden switch turns on, making her realize that I'm still by her side, not letting go. Her free hand reaches to wrap around my forearm, and she finally smiles at me. A real smile. Not a fake one or a pained one, but one that slowly brightens up her face.

I lean down, brushing my lips close to her ear.

"I gotchu," I whisper quietly. I quickly peck the top of her head, and I question myself whether it too is for show or if it's to appease the twisting ache in her heart that I know is there.

I turn back to Matteo. "We actually have somewhere to be." I release her hand and wrap my arm around her shoulders, pressing her against my side.

"Oh, of course," he says, a crease forming between his brows as he watches Natalia lean herself into me. "It was good running into you, Natalia. And it was nice meeting you, Hardin."

"Hayden," I correct him. My eyes narrow, catching the way he purposely mispronounced my name. And there's no missing the smirk he makes this time when I catch an obvious eye roll and annoyed head shake.

"Right," he answers flatly. He then turns to Jacinda, looking exasperated and angry. "Let's go, baby."

20

Natalia

senior year

"ARE YOU GOING TO PROM?" Yuri asks as I pick at the large bag of barbecue Lay's sitting between us at the lunch table. Her slender fingers reach into the bag for a fresh chip before popping it into her mouth with one quick sweep.

Yuri Kim is a senior like me. We've been friends through most of high school, spending a lot of our time together on after-school Starbucks runs and weekend trips to the movies or to hunt for the latest fashion trends filling our local Forever 21. It feels almost surreal that we're talking about end-of-year celebrations like prom and graduation now. The last four years flew by without either one of us realizing how quickly they did.

I shrug. "I don't know," I answer. I haven't really given it a second thought. The entire task of finding a date, then finding a dress, feels a bit daunting.

"You don't know what?" a breathless voice asks. I turn to see Lucy sliding in the seat next to mine, her hand reaching to get her own share of potato chips as she opens a cold strawberry kiwi Snapple. She gently lays the black Canon camera on the table, on loan to her from the yearbook department to catch candid shots of football practice and debate team meetings.

"I don't know if I'm going to prom," I answer her. "I'd rather stay at home and binge watch K-dramas." My brows wiggle, facing Yuri. "We could both skip prom and watch 'The Heirs.'"

Her face scrunches. "You know I don't really watch K-dramas."

"But they're so good!" I argue.

She shrugs a shoulder. "I'd much rather spend a night binge watching 'Teen Wolf' and drool over Dylan O'Brian. It doesn't really matter though," she adds. "I'm already going to prom with Tyler."

My face drops, realizing that my prospects for finding a prom date of my own are slim to none.

"You know, Mom's going to make you go," Lucy butts in, an apologetic yet smug face telling me what I already knew.

"Your mom makes you guys go to prom?" Yuri asks.

"She's going to make Nat go," Lucy explains. "She did the same to our older sister, Carmen, her senior year."

"Well," Yuri offers, "at least it'll be an excuse to shop for a pretty dress." She flicks her long hair to one side of her shoulders, her chin resting on the heels of her hands as she smiles somewhat sympathetically.

"Silver linings," I mutter, making a mental count of prospective prom dates.

present

My brain feels like a storm is raging through it while my heart rattles in my chest, telling me to decide on one single emotion and focus on that. I'm feeling too many things at once. While those different emotions become a torrent in every nerve ending of my body, I realize I'm panicking. My entire body starts to shake as a memory I've buried deep starts to resurface. And that memory, along with the reality of

Matteo's engagement, causes all of those emotions to start clustering into a ball in my throat, making it hard for me to breathe.

Hayden kissed me.

Matteo's getting married.

"Are you okay?"

I look to see Hayden's worried eyes looking at mine while understanding that the answer to his question may be no. Instead of answering, I step into Hayden, wrapping my arms around his waist while my entire body trembles against him.

"Nat," he whispers into my hair. "I'm sorry." He doesn't say anything else. He stays silent as he runs his hand up and down my back.

Why is this happening? This tightness in my chest that I can't seem to loosen.

Why does it feel like the world is crumbling from underneath me?

I breathe in Hayden's scent, feeling safe wrapped in his warmth. He is my safe place right now, just like when we were kids, and I don't know if I want to leave his side just yet, if ever. I close my eyes and shudder, finally letting Hayden go and reluctantly stepping away from him.

"You think—"

"How 'bout—"

Hayden and I speak at the same time. We look at each other and huff an awkward laugh.

"You first," he says, gesturing toward me with a sympathetic smile.

"I don't think I'm ready to go home just yet," I confess.

He tilts his head, giving me that same sympathetic smile as his head angles in the opposite direction from where we came from.

"I know a place." He suddenly grabs my hand, almost sprinting through the busy sidewalk. I stumble after him, tripping over my feet.

"Marshall, my legs are about half the length of yours. You're going to have to slow down or you're going to be dragging me behind you like a rag doll," I call breathlessly behind him.

"Keep up, Marquez!"

After multiple turns and sprints across intersections, we land in front of a bar with tinted windows and neon signs decorating the front in bright blue and pink lit-up words saying "half off mai tais" and "karaoke night."

I turn to face Hayden. "What is this?"

"Better warm up those vocal cords," he says, his hands rubbing together in front of him with that devilish grin I know only comes out when he's got something hidden up his sleeve. "'Cause I'm about to out drink you *and* out sing you."

"Hayden, I'm not doing karaoke." My mouth dries, and my palms start getting clammy. I'm definitely not doing *drunken* karaoke, let alone karaoke.

"Yes, you are."

He latches on to my wrist and yanks me toward the door, dragging me along as I uselessly resist. Once inside, Hayden plops me onto a barstool lined against a small table and walks toward the stage area, where a binder and a mic sit at the edge of a stage. He grips a pencil before he furiously scribbles his request on a clipboard.

I start toying with my fingers under the table, hunching my back forward as I try to disappear in the room slowly filling with those ending their day with a drink to take the edge off, most still in their loosened work clothes.

"So, I thought we would ease into it with a little bit of Carly Rae Jepsen and Vanessa Carlton. And then end it with a bang with a Carrie Underwood number," Hayden says, returning to our table.

When he smiles at me, his grin widens enough to cause a giggle to slip through the pile of nerves settled in my stomach.

"Wait here," he orders. "I'll grab us a few drinks."

Before I can protest, he takes off, rushing toward the bar at the other end of the stage.

As I patiently wait, I scan the room, my eyes landing on a couple sitting nearby under a low light situated in a secluded corner, acting as if they were the only two people in the world. They look into each other's eyes, their fingers tangled and ankles overlapping each other, as I watch a little too wistfully. The tears that rim my eyes appear out of nowhere, just as the tugging ache pulling at my heart becomes too much to bear.

Up until now, I've been able to pretend that Matteo isn't actually getting married. That the invitation isn't real instead of sitting in my kitchen drawer where Carmen strategically placed it under a growing pile of junk.

But now, I've seen her. I've seen him *with* her. Her dark wavy hair tumbling down in every direction. Down her shoulders to her arms, down her chest as it curved along her face and figure. Her blue eyes shined and looked at Matteo the way I used to, proud and blissful. She would make a stunning bride.

A sudden sob breaks from my chest as I quickly wipe the tears that fall before Hayden returns to his seat across from me.

"It's almost our turn," he whispers with a smile that falls as soon as he sees my face.

"Yeah," I manage before looking up at him. I gnaw on my lower lip as I force a smile through the wiped away tears.

Hayden opens his mouth but whatever words of encouragement or insult he set aside for Matteo dies on the tip of his tongue when a familiar tune starts to play over the speakers. Hayden hands me one of the shot glasses he placed in front of me, clinking his own against mine.

"This better not be tequila," I question, lifting the glass.

He makes a forced *pfft* sound before saying, "Please, Marquez. Don't act like I don't know you."

I let a small smile slip before I reluctantly toss the contents of the shot glass down my throat and grimace. Hayden drinks his own glass of what I now know is vodka, confirming he really does know me, and nudges my shoulder.

"Come on," he says, turning to walk to the stage. "Let me show you how it's done."

I follow Hayden, my steps much less confident than his. He takes the mic left on a lone barstool sitting in the middle of the stage and hands it to me, gesturing at me to raise it. He firmly grips the one already on the stage nestled in a mic stand, and we both face the room. The slowly gathering crowd causes a thin layer of sweat to form down my back. I peer over at Hayden, silently glaring at him before he wiggles his eyebrows at me in response. And I laugh, throwing my head back just as the beginning beats of "Call Me

Maybe" play in a loop over the speakers, waiting for us to finally start singing.

When Hayden sings, it's loud. It's obnoxious and shrill and scratchy. He hits all of the beats at the wrong times and the notes at opposite pitches. And it's perfect. By the time the song is finished, I'm breathless. Not from singing along with him but from laughing so hard.

When we slump back into our seats, weak from our hysterical fits of laughter, I clutch onto Hayden's arm. "Please don't *ever* do that again," I beg, wiping the tears from the corner of my eyes.

"What?!" he exclaims. "We still have two more songs on the list. Plus a very promising Carrie Underwood duet. Something about a baseball bat and leather seats."

"No, no," I say, waving my hands in front of him. "You're cut off. No one should ever give you an amp."

Hayden's mouth drops open as if to say *how dare you* before he sits in the seat next to mine. Instead of squawking through more songs about breakups and revenge, we open a tab while tallying up glasses of beer and cocktails. Our lingering laughter dies down to a comfortable silence as the bar continues to fill with more people and the music grows louder.

A man appears from the crowd and takes the stage rather confidently. He starts singing the smooth tunes of "Perfect" by Ed Sheeran, sounding very close to Ed Sheeran himself with his low, sultry voice before smiling modestly toward a small table full of people cheering him on. I turn to look at Hayden, the gratitude shining off every surface of my face.

"Thanks, Hayden."

His face is turned toward the singer when I voice my appreciation. For everything he did to make me forget, even for a moment. Instead of turning to face me, he continues to stare at the singer, making me think that he didn't hear me over the music. But then he reaches over and covers my hand with his, giving it an encouraging squeeze.

21

Hayden

senior year

"I HATE HIGH SCHOOL," Natalia says with a pout.

"I'm sure I can contribute to that statement, but please elaborate," I tease.

"My mom wants me to go to prom."

"And that makes high school the worst place in the world because…"

She sighs, slumping her shoulders forward as she removes her notebook from her backpack. "I don't have a date," she mumbles.

"Oh. And you absolutely have to go?"

She rolls her eyes, her mechanical pencil clicking against the pad of her thumb. "My mom said that I should participate in as many high school experiences as possible. That includes prom and senior ditch day."

"Wait, she's actually encouraging you to ditch school?" I ask, surprised her mom would want her to partake in an illegal activity while my mom grounded me the last time I skipped seventh period.

She side-eyes me. "That's not the point, Hayden."

We stay silent as Mr. Khan claps to get the class's attention, his hands gliding across the whiteboard as he makes the poorest attempt at drawing a plant cell.

Twenty minutes into our lecture, I rip a triangle of paper off my notebook and scribble a note before sliding it across the table to Natalia. She looks down next to her elbow, reading the messily written words: *Prom? With me?* before looking up at me as if I have horns growing out the sides of my head.

When she doesn't answer and continues writing notes on her own notepad, I nudge the paper against her arm again. She then huffs a small sigh and reaches for the paper, scribbling something in response.

When I look at the paper, she's written in her neat handwriting: You already have a date. *Your girlfriend?*

In response, I shake my head. She eyes me curiously, taking the paper back.

You guys broke up?

I nod, thankful that our forced silence is keeping me from sharing the details of my and Jenny's messy—and weirdly ambiguous—breakup. Instead of accepting my initial offer like I hoped Natalia would, she returns to face the front of the classroom.

"So that's a no?" I whisper after a long stretch of silence.

"That's a no, Hayden," she answers, her voice matching my tone in whispers and discretion.

"Why not? Would my dancing embarrass you?" I whisper. I keep my eyes on her face, waiting for her answer. I watch as her eyes move off her paper and her scowl turns into an annoyed eye roll.

She finally turns to look at me. "I'm saying no because you don't want to go with me."

"Then why would I offer?"

"It's fine, Hayden. Forget I brought it up."

present

There was a time during our senior year, in the midst of the hurrah that was graduation and prom, where something shifted between me and Natalia. It was something that I buried deep, using an imaginary shovel to pat down everything that ever happened between us. And it stayed buried until recently, when she picked up that figurative shovel and encouraged me to begin digging. It was as if Natalia herself didn't want to bring it up, to resurface those events without recounting something that neither one of us wanted to mention yet managed to pull from my mind and heart.

Until now.

It started to amble along the silent moments when she caught me staring at her a little longer than deemed normal. It lingered along the curves of my own lips and the pads of my fingers as everything from our past collided into our kiss.

And it becomes glaringly harder to ignore, even as I try to drown it all in a pool of alcohol and bad karaoke.

We settle into our seats, nestled in a small corner between an unoccupied pool table and a broken jukebox, creating our own little nook. The sounds of other karaoke patrons singing, sounding much better than my own, which sounded like a goat bleating along to music rather than actual singing, drifts over us in the crowded bar. We fill our time with stories that go as far back as middle school, even pulling an uncanny impression of our biology teacher, Mr. Khan, when he destroyed a set of cell samples by spilling his coffee on them, eliciting an awkward cry of distress that sounded like a duck and a beaver were tussling in an echoing cave. We laugh and talk and laugh some more as we push away everything that hangs in the air between us, stuffing them underneath the layers of our past.

"I'm getting some water," Natalia announces, standing from her seat. "I need to hydrate, or this hangover is going to kick my ass in the morning."

"I'll get it," I say, stopping her as I stand from my own seat. I watch as she sits back on her stool, a thoughtful smile peeking through her bottom lip pinched between her teeth. Just as I step away, I turn back around, needing to say the one thing that's been nagging at my brain this whole time.

"Um…" I say hesitantly. My hand grips the table while my eyes trail my thumb tracing careful strokes along the curved edge. "I'm sorry about that kiss," I finally say.

Her smile drops slightly as the flush already spread across her neck from the alcohol deepens into a dark cherry color. She has a cocktail straw in her hands, and she starts rolling it between her fingers as the plastic ends of the straw start to twirl frantically.

"Do you regret it?" She tilts her head to the side and her lips pucker outwards as she pulls the inside of her cheek between her teeth. She peers up at me through her thick lashes and her eyes stay wide, almost like a deer in the headlights. Like she's scared.

Of all the responses I expect from her, this is the last.

"Do I regret kissing you?"

She silently nods, eyes still wide.

"No," I say immediately. Her eyes flick to my mouth before looking back at me and she lets out a shaky sigh, almost as if she's relieved.

"Then why are you apologizing?"

She knows why. At least, she *should* know why.

I clench my jaw, stopping myself from pointing out that the reason for my apology should be clear as day. And instead of saying why by reminding her that friends don't kiss the way we did and clarifying the reason behind it, I take a slow, seductive step toward her. I pen her between myself and the wall behind her.

"I'm apologizing because…" My voice trails off. My voice sounds throaty. And thick. Like I have an entire collection of words stuck in my throat. Ones that matter, ones that I should keep to myself, and ones that want to be spoken but never will be. And I'm sifting through them, making sure to pick out those I should be saying and holding on to the ones I need to keep to myself, leaving them behind to fill that thickness in my throat.

I watch as her entire body tenses. The heat radiating off me wraps around her, causing an invisible force field to enclose us in our own bubble. Every nerve ending in my body buzzes as she leans back, her breath hitching through her parted lips as she peers up at me with her dark eyes. And they're so dark. Like two hard rocks of cinder that liquefied, making my blood hot like lava as it runs through my heart in rapid beats.

"Because it was inappropriate." My voice becomes a low rumble as my breath brushes across her cheek now angled sideways. That vanilla scent that *screams* Natalia Marquez fills the space between us, causing my heart to stutter. I fill the small remaining gap between us, inching even closer to her. This time, she doesn't lean back.

"Um...did—I mean..." she stammers when our noses practically touch. Her chin tilts up and her eyelids flutter in front of me, making my breathing raspy and uneven. My eyes trail down her neck as she exposes it toward me, and I can practically see her pulse threading against her skin.

"I should have run it by you first," I say hoarsely.

She looks up at me, our faces less than an inch away from each other. "Oh," she finally whispers. "I—it's fine. We didn't really have time to..." Her warm breath brushes across my chin.

I step away, putting back that safe space between us. I nod, agreeing with her. "I guess..." I trail. "I thought that it would make your ex jealous. Or something like that..."

She nods. "I know," she says, so low I can barely hear her over the light chatter surrounding us.

"I'll get you that water," I whisper, turning away from her before I walk away.

I watch Natalia from the bar, her eyes wandering over the rumbling crowd and music tracks playing in the background of enthused karaoke singers. I wait for the crowd to thin before I order two glasses of water. My own mouth suddenly feels too dry, and I roll a lodged knot down my throat as I tear through every memory I've all but forgotten about.

All those moments where Natalia sat next to me in high school while I silently urged for her to lean closer or brush her hand against mine. They peeled back from the years we spent apart that made those memories muggy and forgotten. But now they were clear, glistening and shining right in front of me as I realized I needed to cover them back up with something. Maybe with all the doubt coursing through me. Or with the idea that Natalia would never feel the same way. Either way, I need to tuck all of those feelings away because the last time I was here, it didn't end well.

Once back at our table, Natalia drinks her water, making sure to finish the entire glass to keep whatever hangover symptoms at bay. We settle the tab and walk out onto the sidewalk where the city lights light up the dark sky.

Natalia smiles appreciatively at me, and I watch as she tucks her head down, keeping her gaze on the ground. Her smile, too shy and timid, doesn't carry the same joy she had when we were releasing our worries through out-of-tune karaoke songs and slurping up fruit-flavored mixed drinks.

A cab pulls to a stop at the edge of the sidewalk, and my hand comes down from the air. "Your chariot awaits, milady."

"Thank you for today, Hayden," she says in a soft voice.

Right there, as she looks at me with her somber eyes and small smile, I tell myself that the kiss was a one-time thing. It can't happen again. It's too precious a price to pay to test out a theory that has the possibility of breaking us apart once again and leaving too many questions suspended between us like it did when we were seventeen. Especially when her heart is the furthest thing from exploring something new.

My hand pulls at the back of my neck as I smirk. "You're welcome, Natalia," I finally say.

I have a sudden need to be close to her. To assure her that we won't change. And that this friendship we restamped in such a short time isn't going anywhere. I lean down toward her, being careful not to pull her toward me so she can accept my embrace rather than give in to it. Her hands move up my back as she sinks into me, turning her cheek to press into my chest.

"Your ex didn't deserve you," I say clearly into her hair.

"You mean Matteo," she muffles into my shirt.

"Whatever his name is," I lie, pretending not to know his name while finally pulling away from her. "You deserve better."

She lowers her face, a sad little pout poking out her lower lip. "You know, Carmen tells me the same thing."

I tuck my curved index finger under her chin to bring her face up, and I look into her eyes, not caring that this feels too intimate even though I should.

"Then it must be true," I say, willing every bit of truth into my voice.

Her smile finally spreads wider. My eyes flick to the tip of her nose, where it dips for a fraction of a second, and then further down to her lips before trailing back to her eyes.

"Thank you, Hayden."

She doesn't sound as defeated as before, almost as if she finally believes her worth and she hears me when I say she can do better than this Matteo guy. Because that's the honest truth. Her bright spirit that seemed to dull when she stood in front of him should be sheltered. Saved for those that earn it and work for it. Not thrown around callously for it to be shut down with a simple hit at her heart.

"Anytime, Nat," I say in a low voice through a forced smile.

She steps into the cab, and I close the door behind her. She peers out the window, waving at me one last time as the cab drives off into the night. And for a second, just a second, I remember what my life felt like when I was seventeen. When I said goodbye to her the first time.

22

Natalia

senior year

"I KIND OF LIKE the blue one," I say to Yuri. "The one with all the pretty rhinestones on it."

Yuri holds up the dress I'm talking about against the plain black one she's already wearing, admiring the sparkly beadwork with a forlorn look on her face. "I know," she says a little wistfully. "It's Tyler's favorite color."

I nod, encouraging her to pick the one she's obviously favoring.

She sighs. "But my mom would never let me wear a dress with a neckline that low."

"You know he's going to love whatever you wear," I say, watching as Yuri, with her long hair that runs down to her lower back all swept up in a loose ponytail, admires the dress she really wants. She holds it up to her chest as she swivels side to side in front of the mirror.

"What about you?" Yuri asks, stepping behind the heavy curtain of the dressing room to change back into her street clothes. "Did you find a dress you like?"

"I think I should worry about finding a prom date before shopping for a dress," I answer, flicking through a small rack of dresses in the open area of the dressing room.

"I say you go solo," she calls from behind the curtain. "It's 2014. We girls don't need a boy to have a good time. Plus, you'll have me there."

I smile. I hadn't really considered going alone. Maybe it won't be so bad. Certainly better than accepting a pity date, like the one from Hayden. Why he thought asking me would be *a* good idea was beyond me. Even if he's no longer with Jenny, I'm sure he has girls within his social circle that would be a more appropriate date.

"Maybe that's not such a bad idea," I muse. "It won't—"

I'm interrupted by a high-pitched squeal. "Jenny! That dress looks amazing on you!"

Yuri steps out of the dressing room, her too-simple black dress draped over her forearm. Her gaze lands on Jenny and Tina behind me with their excited smiles following their equally excited squeals as Jenny runs her hand down the length of her dress. The same dress that Yuri just hung back up, along with her dreams of looking like a fairy tale princess. Yuri looks back at me, her brows raised with a small smirk before we step out toward the sales floor.

"Natalia!" Jenny exclaims as she notices me walk by, a hint of annoyance hidden beneath the faux excitement. "Are you guys shopping for prom? Aren't the dresses here so pretty?" She runs her hand down her sides, gliding her fingers along her hips as she waits for my answer.

"Yeah, they look amazing," I answer, my eyes landing on the lights reflecting off her gown. "But I'm still sort of looking."

She nods, her fake smile mirroring Tina's as the two of them continue to look at Yuri and me with a level of disdain that I'm not too comfortable with.

"You know," she starts just as I'm about to step away. "I didn't know you and Hayden were so close."

I take a quick glance at Yuri, the two of us sharing a confused expression, before looking back at Jenny. "We aren't," I say matter-of-factly. "We're just lab partners."

"Uh-huh," she answers, obviously dubious of my explanation. "Hayden's mentioned you a bit. Said you like to read and stuff." She says the word "read" an octave higher than the rest of the words in her sentence, as if it should carry the obvious quotation marks around it.

"Uh, yeah," I answer, incredibly uncomfortable with the direction this conversation has suddenly taken. "I guess I lent him a book once."

"We should get go—" Yuri says before being interrupted.

"Well, I'm pretty sure we're going to get back together after prom," Jenny adds. She swivels her body to face the opposite direction, right into the mirror as she admires her dress. As if she's grown bored of our conversation and is dismissing me altogether.

"You guys are going to prom together?" I blurt out, too thrown off by this bit of information to refrain from asking, knowing that I probably shouldn't dip my nose in Hayden or Jenny's personal business.

"Of course," she answers with an aggravated scowl, turning around to face me while hovering into my personal space. Her closed fists move to her hips as she scoffs before saying, "Why wouldn't we?"

"That's great," I say, hiding the sudden pang of affliction I didn't know I would feel confirming the fact that Hayden's offer to take me to prom was in fact a pity date offer. It makes sense, especially when he obviously has Jenny to go with, no matter their relationship status. "Hayden's a great guy."

Jenny's eyes narrow, her lips pursing together in a firm line. "He is, isn't he?" she says, turning back to face the mirror again, not really asking to get an answer but more to make a point. Her pressed-together lips part, revealing a sneer of a smile.

I feel Yuri's hand on my forearm. I face her, her impatient smile rescuing me from Jenny's scrutiny. "Have fun at prom," I say to Jenny.

Jenny doesn't answer. Instead, her narrowed eyes curve into a forged smile before Tina pulls Jenny's attention toward a shimmering black dress pinched between her fingers. Yuri and I both walk away as the sounds of Tina and Jenny prattling on about their prom plans echo in the dressing room.

present

Shit!

I scramble with the set of bobby pins, parting them with my teeth and scraping them into my scalp to secure the braid wrapped around the crown of my head. The loose curls that tumble down the length of my hair cascade past my shoulders, wisping around the sweetheart neckline of my dress.

Realizing that I didn't have anything to wear to the wedding, I went shopping on my lunch break the day before, dragging José with me to hunt down the perfect dress. When our eyes landed on a dress colored "dusty green," according to the salesperson, I knew I found the one. The lace trim lining the bodice and the tulle skirt that ran the length of my legs to my calves made me feel like a princess.

But I spent too much time on my makeup, making sure the blended colors of my eyeshadow didn't cross the small threshold between intense and underwhelming. So I'm rushing now, spending the next five minutes applying blush and highlighter before doing a once-over and texting Hayden that I'll be waiting outside.

My shoes are barely on with the straps loosely threaded through the buckles as I carefully walk down the steps leading to the sidewalk. Just as I'm securing my shoes, my body bent at an angle while balancing myself on one foot, I hear the light slamming of a car door. When I look up, I see Hayden walking toward me. His fingers toy with the front lapels of his suit jacket as he pulls the buttons through the buttonholes.

His shaggy hair is freshly cut, the sides down to a near buzz cut and fading upward to a neatly combed bed of dark chestnut waves. His gaze is focused on the ground, so it gives me the smallest of seconds to watch him. How his body, no longer boy but all man, moves with confidence as his long legs lead the way on the hard pavement. How his hands move deliberately across his suit jacket, smoothing out the material and adjusting the creases. When he finally looks up and sees me, his face lights up. I see it in every shift of his expression, from his eyes that change from cautious to eager, to his mouth cracking wide open to expose his perfect teeth and happy smile.

"You clean up pretty nice, Marshall."

He smirks, extending his hands out in front of him with a light tilt of his head. I giggle, taking his hand when he offers it to me. He brings it above my head and twirls me like a miniature ballerina in a music box, making my dress fan around me.

"I think we both clean up pretty nice, Marquez," he says in a low voice. "I feel like I should have brought a corsage."

With my hand still in his, I half expect him to bring it to his lips. Instead, he taps the tip of my nose before turning toward the car, where Dexter sits at the driver's seat and a blonde woman with a polite smile to his right.

"Come on, kids! The cake isn't going to eat itself."

We pull to a stop in front of a large chapel, stone, brick, and stained glass all nestled in its own arrangement of trees. Trees that still hold the fullness of leaves and haven't fallen to the ground just yet, ranging in color from forest green to canary yellow and marigold orange. I feel a gratifying rush float through my lungs with the deep exhale that takes every bit of affliction and doubt I've felt since Matteo and I broke up, and in the short time since Hayden reentered my life. Suddenly, it's all been replaced with expectancy. And I don't even know for what.

But for some reason, I can't help but connect my kiss with Hayden to it. While I knew why Hayden kissed me, I can't shut down how tender and soft it felt. How it was as if I had been kissing Hayden my whole life and I couldn't remember my life before it. Did my lips always feel this empty without him? Did my body crave his hands gripping my waist and tugging at my chin before I knew what his touch felt like?

I tried to forget all those thoughts and the fire that still lined my skin where he touched me as soon as I returned home from our day of karaoke and drinking. I tried but failed miserably. Instead, a jittery set of nerves settled in my stomach anticipating today. And now, being here with him, it's bringing back the feeling of being wrapped up in his arms all over again, feeling like I've come up for air. Like life is being breathed into me, lighting something fierce and unforgettable.

The four of us exit the car and stand on the long gravel pathway leading up the steps of the church with guests slowly trickling in, wearing bright smiles and fitted formal attire. As I smooth down the tulle material of my skirt, I feel a warm hand lightly press into the small of my back.

"You ready?" Hayden asks, the box holding his gift in his large hands.

I turn to face him. I quickly tuck my jeweled clutch under my arm and bring my hands up toward the neatly tied knot of Hayden's tie, adjusting it so it sits straight rather than at an angle.

His Adam's apple bobs as his eyes light up, and he smiles down at me. My eyes flit to his mouth, thinking about how the swollen pout of his lower lip pulled my own into him when he kissed me. How the rough pad of his thumb tugged at the curve of my jaw, opening me up to him as I tasted him in a way that I didn't think possible. He tasted like caramel and sweet cream and a tender warmth that was somehow inviting but flustering at the same time.

"All set," I say, turning my head in the subtlest of shakes while lightly patting his chest.

But we don't move. Instead, we stay, facing each other, looking into each other's eyes as the sounds of happy chatter and crunched footsteps muffle around us. Hayden brushes a lock of my hair off my shoulder, moving it so that it rests across my shoulder blade rather than my chest. When he does this, his fingertips graze the sensitive skin of my collarbone. And without even thinking about it, my eyes flutter. He must see it, my lids falling heavy and my breathing hitching, because his fingers don't leave my skin. Instead, his hand roams from the base of my neck to my shoulders, trailing a pathway of static down my arm to my hand, where it finally rests.

Our fingers tickle each other, and we're sitting in limbo where we question what to do next. Do I take his hand in mine? Do we continue this dance, this push and pull of electricity between us?

"Let's head in, guys," Dexter calls, interrupting whatever unspoken questions I'm coaxing answers for, causing Hayden to drop his hand to his side.

I don't miss the way my hand feels empty, completely vacant and bare, when Hayden turns away from me. And I also don't miss the clenched tic of his jaw as his eyes narrow, his gaze falling to my hand.

My heart starts to pound in my chest, banging against my ribcage, protesting this overwhelming feeling where every vulnerable and weak cleft of my heart feels exposed. I can't do this again. I can't risk getting my heart broken again and having to pick up those shattered pieces only to glue them back together haphazardly. And while if it were anyone else, someone where the risks aren't as high and it would be something to consider venturing into, it wouldn't be the case with Hayden. Because if things don't work out, I wouldn't only be losing someone that I had a memorable yet fleeting kiss with; I would be losing the closest thing to a best friend I've ever had.

Hayden clears his throat, gently placing a hand on my lower back again, where it feels safer. I muster a smile, one that wipes away our kiss from my memory and replaces it with all of the moments that wouldn't be there if Hayden weren't in my life.

"Come on," he says in a strained voice.

23

Hayden

senior year

"SO, how goes the prom date search?" I ask as Natalia adjusts her safety goggles, moving her neatly knotted French braid down one shoulder to avoid it from getting in the way of our lab samples.

She groans. "Ugh, don't ask."

"I find it hard to believe that not a single person has asked you."

"No, I've been asked. I just…" She looks at me, her shoulders dropping as if defeated in this whole search for the perfect prom date. "There's really no one I want to go with."

"Oh, so you have options," I tease.

"Hayden," she whines, silently begging me to stop.

"My offer's still on the table. You could save yourself from all this drama and go with the future prom king of 2014." My brows waggle at her as her mouth scrunches into an angry pout.

"Aren't you going with Jenny?"

"Who told you?"

"Jenny."

I shake my head. While Jenny and I had indeed set plans to go to prom together before we broke up, I assumed I was the last person she wanted to go to prom with. Especially when her parting words after I told her things weren't working out were: "You're a real grade-A asshole, Hayden."

"I didn't know you two were friends," I comment.

"Trust me," she says, her eyes wide as her hand comes up between us, her palm facing me to deny what even I can't believe, "we aren't. She just mentioned it in passing."

"I don't know. We talked about going before we broke up, so I guess she just assumed we were still going." I clear my throat, taking the pipette that's sitting next to her and squeezing iodine into the cell sample.

"Maybe I should just skip the whole thing," she says. "Tell my mom I got the flu at the last minute or something."

"I don't know why you won't go with me," I tease. "I may have to tweak some of my break-dancing skills, but it can't be that bad."

"Hayden," she huffs, placing her own pipette down. "I'm glad that you find my drama so amusing, but I don't need a pity date. Plus, if you're going with Jenny, how's that going to work out? We each take an arm?"

"That actually doesn't sound too bad," I joke.

She snarls in response, and I laugh. "I'm messing with you, Marquez. Come on—"

Just then, we both look up to see Alex approach our table. Alex Spencer, known for being the rich boy on campus. Everything handed to him was done so by his daddy, like his silver BMW and expensive shoes. I honestly don't think he's ever heard the word "no."

"Hey, Nat," he calls before nodding a greeting to me. "'Sup, Marshall."

"Hi, Alex," she answers, pulling her gaze away with a last second warning glare in my direction.

Alex looks at me again and then back at Natalia before we both set down our equipment, giving him our attention.

"Uh, so I was wondering…" he says, his voice cracking. He coughs into his fist, causing a few heads to turn in our direction. "If you didn't have a date for prom yet, I was thinking maybe you would want to go with me."

I smirk as Natalia looks at me. Her eyes peer up through the scratched goggles as she purses her lips together, her brows scrunching her face into a cute scowl. Then she turns to face Alex, her mouth shifting into a fake smile before saying, "Sure." She pauses, quickly glancing at me again before smiling even wider at Alex. "I'd love to go with you."

Alex smiles proudly. "Great," he says before lightly punching my arm and walking away.

"Problem solved," I whisper, unable to hide the little bit of resentful snark seeping through my voice.

Really? Alex Spencer? She couldn't have picked a more mismatched prom date for her if she had randomly plucked one out from the cafeteria with her eyes closed.

She ignores my comment, focusing her attention on our lab project instead.

I nudge a little closer, causing her arm to slip and accidentally squeeze out an extra drop of iodine. She finally looks at me, practically glaring.

"Great," she deadpans. "Now I have to prepare my sample all over again."

But I don't apologize or make some kind of annoying joke. Instead, I keep my eyes on her.

"What?" she asks, wiping the iodine that dripped on the tabletop before grabbing a new slide. She raises her goggles and looks up at me.

I shrug. "Don't forget to save me a dance," I say as nonchalantly as possible. "You know, when Alex disappoints you with his embarrassing dance moves."

Our movements synchronize, our heads lifting to look in the direction that Alex walked to. He pops the collar of his too-white polo shirt that fits a little loosely on his thin frame before rounding the corner back to his table where his own lab partner waits. He makes some quipped joke, to which his lab partner giggles with her hand covering her mouth.

I scoff, looking back at Natalia, watching her hands move across her neatly organized side of the lab table while I stand nearby, taking on the role as doting assistant. "I'm holding you to that dance."

Her eyes glare through an eye roll. And yet her lips tell a different story, one that says, *Test me, Marshall. I dare you.* I see it in the way one corner of her mouth twists while the other suppresses a smile, fighting what she wants to hide but can't.

I feel a small, challenging fire light through me, suddenly unable to wait to hit the dance floor just to prove to her that I would have been the better date to prom over Alex.

"I'll take that as a 'Yes, Hayden. Please save me from Alex when he embarrasses me and steps on my toes until they're bloody,'" I mock in a high-pitched tone meant to imitate hers. My voice rings a little loudly, and I know people are looking, including Alex. She pinches my side, causing my body to bow. "Ah!" I flinch.

"You're going to get us into trouble!" she hisses, her face turning a shade of crimson, the tips of her ears redder than the rest of her face. She turns to face the table again, adjusting her goggles so they sit squarely on her face. But even from her feigned annoyance to her stern scolding, I can see that twist of a smile around the apples of her cheeks as she shakes her head.

present

"So what did you do after that?" Natalia asks, engrossed in Dexter's story.

Dexter shrugs. "I asked her for her number," he says nonchalantly as if there's no other option besides asking the woman you publicly humiliate on a date.

"After you explained to me the dangers of going for a run in the park in broad daylight," Molly, Dexter's date, adds to Dexter's recount of their meet-cute while rolling her eyes.

I shake my head, remembering the day when I joined Dexter and a group of his friends in the park for a friendly game of touch football. Dexter overthrew the ball only to hit Molly square on the head, knocking her off her feet.

"But he made it up to me," Molly says softly while placing a hand on Dexter's forearm. "After he picked me up off the ground, he bought me ice cream."

"That's hardly a fair trade," I comment.

"Well," Dexter says, smirking in Molly's direction, "we did other stuff too."

Molly slaps Dexter's arm as his smile widens. Natalia looks at me with a face using every expressive muscle. From her scrunched-up nose and pressed lips suppressing a laugh, to the wrinkles in her forehead lifting her brows and widening her eyes, she looks so damn cute.

My hand moves to Natalia's back, pressing lightly to the bare space between her shoulder blades. When she feels me touch her, she smiles wider. She smiles in a way that doesn't feel forced or synthetic. It's the exact same smile I remember too deeply from what seems like an entirely different life. And that pang I felt when I realized I could never risk whatever this is that we have, whatever small thread of friendship and nostalgia we've been clinging to, returns. It reminds me of how it felt like when I lost her the first time and how I can't go through that again.

I'm about to lean toward her to pointedly ask what "other stuff" she thinks Dexter is referring to when her eyes lock on something behind me. Or rather, someone.

"Hayden?"

I look over my shoulder to find Jacky dressed in a navy-blue dress, matching the other members of the wedding party, with her hair piled on top of her head. I don't mean to, but I can't help but compare her to Natalia. Bright and beaming in her light green dress, looking like she stepped out of a fairy tale in contrast to Jacky's dull bridesmaid attire. The looks of every other male dressed in a suit similar to mine lingering on Natalia long enough for them to realize that she didn't come alone don't go unnoticed either.

Jacky smiles expectantly at me, her hands clasped in front of her as she waits for me to greet her.

"Hi," she says when I stay quiet. "It's good to see you."

I stand, the legs of the chair scraping against the wood as the back of my legs push it out from beneath me.

"Hi, Jacky," I finally say.

My voice sounds strained. Too formal and awkward. I hear Dexter snicker from the table. When I turn to look back at Natalia, she smiles politely, her eyes moving from me to Jacky and then back to me.

"This is Natalia," I say a little too loudly and abruptly.

"Hi," Jacky says, her face barely turning enough to get a quick glimpse of Natalia. "So listen," she continues, sidling herself up to me and grazing her hand along the inside of my arm. "I've been trying to get a hold of you since the Fourth of July."

"Uh...um..." I stutter. "Yeah. Sorry about that. I've just been really busy."

"Well," she continues, oblivious to my hesitance, "when you get back to the city, give me a call. We can catch up."

She stares up at me, playing this one-sided game of seduction as if unaware that we're in front of an audience and that I didn't come alone.

"We were just about to have a dance," I announce, reaching for Natalia's hand and pulling her to stand next to me as her heels lightly clack against the wood floor. Natalia's brow furrows, showing her confusion from the sudden shift in our conversation.

"Oh," Jacky says, taking a small step back. Her eyes narrow, her gaze moving to Natalia in the small space between us that seems to be growing smaller and smaller by the second.

"It was nice seeing you," I say quickly. I practically drag Natalia to the dance floor, with her hurried steps following behind me. Once we stop on the glossy wood floor full of wedding guests moving to the music, I pull Natalia closer to me.

"What the hell was that?" she finally asks, her left hand resting on my bicep.

"What?"

Her face deadpans.

I sigh. "Someone I hooked up with over the summer."

"And why are we running away from her?"

"I've been kind of avoiding her," I confess. "Not returning her calls and stuff like that."

"Why?"

I shrug as my hand on Natalia's lower back pushes us closer together to avoid stepping on an overactive flower girl twirling with her small wicker basket worn over her head like a hat. "It was just a one-time thing. I wasn't looking for anything serious. I thought *she* wasn't either."

She makes this little *tsk* sound that's meant to be scolding but comes off as playful instead. "Is that why you brought me? To avoid her?"

Instead of answering, I smile sheepishly.

"Hayden," she scolds.

"I know!" I finally cave, the strain of guilt and apology spreading across my face. "I know. It was a shitty thing to do. But it just kind of happened. I mean, we were all just drinking and having a good night. And one thing led to another."

Her right hand releases my left, gripping my shoulders as she gives me a small shake and a firm squeeze. My free hand moves to her waist as we both continue to dance, the music moving us rather than our own feet.

"So…" Her voice trails. "It wasn't serious?"

Her question doesn't hold the expected deride I thought it would, her finding humor in the fact that my active single lifestyle finally caught up to me. Instead, it carries the hint of caution and something familiar. Like the light pang of tenderness that seeps through her aloofness when she brings up my random dates with the women I meet on Cupid's Bet.

"No," I answer earnestly. "It wasn't. And it's been a couple of months since I actually spoke to her."

She nods. "It sounds like that roster of yours is growing in length, Marshall," she says, a lightness lifting her voice to make it sound playful. "Those Cupid's Bet girls have some competition. Maybe you should petition for your own season of *The Bachelor*."

"Cupid's Bet girls?" I ask, a single brow curved upward in amusement. I try to suppress the smile I can't help when I see the small flush of pink rise from her collarbone, like a horizon of cherry sorbet brushing across her delicate skin.

She lightly shrugs, her flush disappearing almost instantly. "I gave

Jeannie Choe

up keeping track of all your conquests. I've decided to call your groupies 'Cupid's Bet girls' from here on out. It's just easier."

"And you're not one of those groupies?"

She gnaws on her lower lip, the deep color on her lips contrasting against her white teeth. Her mouth twitches with a smile that forces its way through before she says, "You haven't wooed me yet, Marshall."

"I guess I need to improve my efforts," I whisper, lowering my head so my cheek grazes against her temple. I don't mean for my voice to grow low, the need to pull her as close to me as possible seeping through the disguised want in my voice, but it does.

With her cheek turned toward my shoulder and her body shaking in a playful giggle, I chuckle. My hand spreads the length of her flank as my thumb grazes the sensitive spot along her ribcage. My face turns so our foreheads are almost touching, and Natalia looks up at me with her hands hooked around my neck and my arms cinching around her waist. Our bodies continue to move to their own accord, swaying to the music as we develop a rhythm that's ours.

As the groom, Ashton had a couple of conditions to his wedding. Such as a red velvet-flavored cake, an open bar, and a wedding singer with a live band to play popular covers in place of a tacky DJ. That last one was one Carly couldn't even disagree with. And right now, as the wedding singer's smooth, velvety voice sings Elvis Presley's "Can't Help Falling in Love" while strumming along to a guitar hanging around her neck and a low violin playing alongside by a member of her band, I understand the appeal. A DJ wouldn't have provided this cloistered bubble expanding large enough to fit only me and Natalia. It wouldn't have sliced off this moment in time where I feel as if everything around us has vanished, leaving only us two swaying in the middle of the dance floor. And my heart wouldn't have this single moment where it hopes, just for a second, for more.

"Natalia," I whisper into the small space between us. It's only inches from my lips to hers. That nagging thought, the musing that keeps popping in my head, making me wonder if our kiss was just a fluke or if every kiss with Natalia would leave me practically ethereal, causes me to lower my head an inch closer.

I feel Natalia's hand grip me tighter, and it causes my heart to stutter. It actually feels like it skips a beat as I remember a moment from our past that's been brought to us, front and center. It's as if someone took a knife and cut out the edges of that specific memory, only to prove to us not to venture down this path. And just as quickly, the urge to kiss her disappears as I realize I'm not ready to risk losing her again.

"Thank you," I finish as her round brown eyes look up at me. "Thanks for coming tonight." I thank her instead of saying what I really want to say: *I'm falling for you all over again.*

24

Hayden

senior year

"I HEARD Ben brought some weed! He's passing it around in the parking lot!" Jenny calls over the blaring music. My gaze shifts across the banquet hall at the Dayton Country Club, the twinkling lights and bluish hue painted across the room looking so typically fitting for our 2014 Starry Night prom theme.

I look down at Jenny, her hand linked through my arm as she smiles up at me, her dark makeup smeared across her lids with lips painted in a deep maroon color. I nod when she continues to look at me, waiting for an answer. Just as we continue our steps into the banquet hall, we're interrupted by Tina approaching Jenny, tugging at her arm and pulling her toward the direction we came in from.

"Come on!" she calls to me, her smile stretching across her face as she follows Tina willingly.

Just as I turn to go with her, I catch a glimpse of someone I've been eager to see since I stepped into my rented tux. "You guys go ahead," I call over the music. "I'll catch up with you guys in a bit."

Jenny giggles, already running after Tina as they disappear into the parking lot, toward a night that requires fewer brain cells and a collective trip to Taco Bell.

I turn back to see Natalia standing in the middle of the dance floor, smiling and laughing, surrounded by her friends, with Alex close by. I take a moment to watch her and laugh when she starts to flail her arms in the air in beat with the music. She's singing along to whatever's playing over the sound system, clutching her chest and pointing to her friends dancing with her in equal zeal. Her lavender dress, glittering in silk and subtle rhinestones, swishes around her while her dark hair weaves in a tumble of curls down her back, a halo of baby's breath neatly tucked into the braid wrapped around her crown. I stand back as Alex leans down to say something close to her ear and walks away before she turns her attention back to her friends. Without Alex by her side, this is my chance.

I want to be near her. I want to say hello, tell her how beautiful she looks with the subtle flowers in her hair and soft makeup that makes her features that much sweeter. I want her to look and smile at me the way she is right now, so bright and radiant.

I walk toward the dance floor, my strides deliberate and calculated, and I stop right when the song transitions into something less upbeat and more measured with the strides of a slow strumming guitar and unhurried piano keys. Natalia stops dancing and instead begins searching the room.

"Looking for a dance partner, Marquez?" I say low into Natalia's ear as I come to a stop behind her.

She turns slowly to look at me, her smile dropping as she sees my face. "Hayden."

"Expecting someone else?" I wrap my arm around her waist and pull her close to me, more than ready to swoop in the place of her prom date.

She relaxes in my arms. One of her hands moves up to gently rest on the collar of my shirt while the other lightly grips my bicep. "I was holding out for Prince Charming, but I guess you'll do."

"I'm just here for that dance you promised."

We sway lightly as I move her closer toward the middle of the dance floor where the crowd is thicker.

"So where's Spencer?" I ask. "He ditch you already?"

Her lips purse as her eyes roll into her signature expression, somehow smiling even though she wants to tell me how annoying I am. "He went outside with Tyler and Ben."

I nod. "Leaving his date to get high. So honorable."

She smacks my arm. "He's not getting high."

I shrug, not bothering to correct her. Our bodies continue to move under the scattered spotlight glittering over us, the twinkling disco ball reflecting dim flickers of light that seem to make Natalia's face glow even brighter.

"I'm going to miss you, Marshall," she quips with a shy smile. "You actually made AP Bio kinda fun." Her delicate fingers start toying with my boutonniere, the soft petals brushing against the pads of her fingers.

"You aren't getting rid of me just yet," I answer. "We still have five weeks left of the school year." I'm grinning like a damn fool from the pride bursting through me. *She's going to miss me.*

Her smile fades, a misty wave of nostalgia passing through her as her brow furrows.

"And then we're real adults," she says, her voice carrying the undertones of worry and apprehension.

One of the loose curls from her hair falls from the braided crown. When I see it kiss her temple, I brush it out of her face. She sighs against my touch as my thumb runs across her soft cheek.

It feels as if time is warping all around us. People are still chatting and dancing and laughing, but we're moving in slow motion. The music is still playing, but it's become hushed and muted, almost as if that too has warped into a completely different tempo. Without a second thought, I lean down and let my lips hover close to hers. Her warm breath skirts across my lips as we share the air between us. And I feel like I imagine it, but her chin tilts toward me, as if encouraging me to move even closer.

I kiss her, turning everything wrong in my life right side up so it no longer feels blundering or reckless. As if holding Natalia in my arms and realizing that I want more than a few shared laughs and playful shoves makes me feel like I can finally breathe.

Natalia pushes back, her hands bracing my arms, now rigid and trembling. Her eyes turn into saucers, and I can see her breathing kick up.

"Hayden," she gasps. "We can't—I mean, you're with Jenny and…"

"Nat," I start to say.

Her hands start to push mine off her and for a second, I don't want to let go, even though she's giving me no choice.

"I–I have to go find Alex." She takes off, her heels clicking against the hard floor, and she disappears into the crowd.

present

When I walk into work Monday afternoon, I'm greeted by Hailey at the hostess counter. I'm still coming off the high of the wedding. Romantic lights, festive music, good food, and the chocolatey red velvet cake that Ashton wouldn't stop raving about. And Natalia. We dropped Natalia off, her feet bare and her heels hooked on her fingers as she walked the quick trek from the car to her apartment. I watched as she waved goodbye, her small hand coming up as she wiggled her fingers at me. She disappeared, taking away every resurfaced feeling that I buried deep, making me realize how little had changed in the eight years since I said goodbye to her.

"Boss is waiting for you in his office." Hailey points a thumb behind her toward the back of the kitchen where Pat's office sits. I nod, ready to spend the day busying myself in the kitchen and distracting my thoughts from what all of these reverted feelings mean, and stalk past her.

I rap lightly on the door sitting ajar as I peek inside and see Pat hunched over his desk, his reading glasses on and forehead creased.

"Come in," he calls without looking up from his desk. He looks up as I step through the threshold, and he gestures for me to have a seat.

"You wanted to talk to me, Pat?"

"Yes." He closes the binder he was flipping through, removing his glasses and placing them gently on his desk. "Have a seat."

I eye him. He's never spoken to me like this, all formal and businesslike. Putting aside the uncle-nephew relationship and putting in place the employee-employer one. "Is everything okay?"

"Yeah," he answers. His voice is hoarse and tired. He clears his throat. "I just wanted to talk to you about some changes I want to make around here."

"Oh," I say, finally understanding. "Is Chef going to be here too then?"

He shakes his head, leaning back in his chair and crossing his arms over his chest. "Listen, you know it's been a little tough with Chef and his ego."

I scoff. To say I understand the wrath of Chef DuPont would be an understatement. I live under his constant scrutiny and his anger toward me, claiming I only got the sous chef position through the small push of nepotism. I've never told Pat this, but I would have been long gone had it not been Pat who hired me.

"I want him to resign," Pat finally says.

I push my face toward him, angling my head to the side with a twisted face of confusion to make sure I've heard him correctly. "So you won't have a head chef?"

He clears his throat again. "I was thinking you could take over."

"Me?" I squeak.

"You're the only one I know who's qualified."

"Pat, I–I don't know...I mean..." I stutter. "You don't want to hire someone new? Someone with more experience?"

"You've had plenty back in Chicago," he argues. "It's time you run your own kitchen."

Head chef. It's a position I've dreamed of stepping into since I returned stateside from France. A medium before I eventually have the courage and experience to open my own restaurant like I've always wanted. It's one more milestone closer to having my name on the building as people seek out my food.

But it's a huge responsibility. One small mistake, and the whole restaurant is at stake. I don't want to let Pat down. I don't want to let the whole restaurant down.

I shift in my seat, the air suddenly feeling too hot and stuffy. "Can I think about it?"

"Of course." His voice is calm and understanding. I nod, leaving Pat's office while muddling over this offer.

I spend the rest of the day in the busy kitchen. Chef DuPont comes, makes his rounds, and continues his wrath while stalking the kitchen floor, keeping the rest of the staff on their toes. We have one incident of him reducing our saucier to tears and almost firing a busboy when he nearly walks into Chef DuPont, carrying a tray full of dirty dishes. It's actually a good day considering the last time Chef DuPont completely lost his temper, one of our newly hired waitresses got caught in the crossfire between him and a plate he threw against the wall. Pat had no choice but to send her home after she spent a good hour trembling in the service area.

I can't help asking myself, will that be me? Angry with anyone trying to do their job and fearing me in the process. Hurting people just so that I can prove myself. I don't want to be that person. But what if Chef DuPont was a kind, timid sous chef like me at some point? And over the years, he became this ball of anger out of necessity rather than by choice. As badly as I want to be a head chef, I don't know if I'm ready to take on that role and not turn into an asshole in an attempt to prove myself.

But now, watching every integral member of this team, I see how they respect me. They don't fear me or turn the other way with resentment for making their lives hell. They come to me for help or advice. They share their thoughts so that our kitchen and this restaurant can be successful. We all manage to turn the gears in unison and keep them grinding despite Chef DuPont's glaring presence.

I work through the rest of the dinner rush, Chef DuPont's early departure a godsend after he saw that the dinner service was moving along without a hitch, something he does quite frequently now as he relinquishes some of his control to me. I fall into a comfortable routine, one that allows me to imagine how it would feel if I didn't have Chef DuPont breathing down my back. All of the doubt and insecurities fogging my judgment disperse, like a sea of hesitance that parts, creating a path that I finally feel confident I can take. I see a future where I'll be running my own kitchen. One that I want to embrace.

With the kitchen scrubbed and cleaned, the stainless-steel counter-tops shining against the dimmed fluorescent lights that veil over the now empty kitchen, I walk into the dining area.

"Hey, Pat?"

He's lining up wineglasses behind the bar, carefully inspecting them for chips, scrapes, and water spots. He looks up when I call him, an expectant look on his face as a warm smile spreads.

"I'll take it," I say, my voice still wavering between confidence and doubt. "The job. I'll take it."

His smile widens, his teeth exposed as he grins ear to ear. "You're going to be a great boss, kid," he says, extending his hand toward me.

I take his offering, gripping firmly as we seal the deal.

"Your parents are going to be proud of you."

I nod, my throat tightening at the mention of my parents. "Thanks for the opportunity, Pat."

I wish what he said were true. That my parents, especially my dad, would be happy to know that my aching decision to choose my own path in life turned out to be the best decision I ever made. I wish this was enough for him, whatever was enough for me. And maybe it's the idea of holding on to the false hope that I can eventually repair the broken relationship I have with my dad, but I continue to tell myself it's all worth it. To come to this exact moment and work for a dream I never realized I wanted until I discovered something my hands already knew. Something that lay hidden under the dim lights on the granite countertops in my mom's kitchen or the low whirring of the bright red mixer I learned to use on my own. And it all started with the warm scent of home that gradually shifted into a reminiscent memory I hid for eight years.

Beer, *South Park* reruns, and pork rinds are my vices. I give into them when I feel like I've earned it. And today, it feels like I have. I walked out of Pour Toujours last week with a lightness in my step, knowing that my life wasn't as dead-ended as I thought. So I settle into my couch tonight after a day of going over managerial logistics with Pat, like when I would be taking Chef DuPont's place and how the transition of my position would happen. As expected, Chef DuPont's rage flooded through the entire kitchen when Pat delivered the news, claiming the restaurant would burn to the ground without him. It was the stubborn Band-Aid that Pat had to finally rip off. And with Chef DuPont's final anger-filled threat to sue Pat and every busboy, server, and/or bartender that ever crossed his path at Pour Toujours, Pat was able to finally let the entire staff know how things would shift now that I would be head chef. All of it was welcomed with cheers and relieved smiles.

I've stripped down to my boxers and an undershirt, lazing into my vices. In the middle of Kenny's muffled voice responding to yet another vulgar statement made by Cartman, my phone rings. I smile when I see Natalia's name on the screen.

I just saw her today when she visited my restaurant, bringing José with her during their lunch hour, the two laughing and chatting animatedly in our crowded dining room while I watched from afar. Watching her like that, when she didn't think anyone was looking, it caused a twinge to twist in my chest as I realized the things I felt about her. Feelings I couldn't believe were consuming my mind.

I haven't yet told her about my promotion. I want to blame it on the fact that I haven't had a chance but in reality, every time I want to tell her, my feelings overshadow the words caught in my throat. I need to keep things light, surface deep and casual. Telling her something that she'll undoubtedly be ecstatic for me about feels like peeling back more layers of me, forcing me to expose my feelings for her when I should be hiding them.

"You better not be hassling me for more pastries, Marquez," I tease through the phone.

"And if I am?"

"I would have to tell you that the whole tri-state area has run out of sugar and can no longer fulfill your incessant demands."

She giggles.

"To what do I owe the pleasure?" I ask.

"I, uh…"

Somewhere deep within my gut, during the moment her giggles dissolve and a cheesy smile creeps up on my face, I stagger toward her. My entire body leans toward the sound of her careful voice, wanting to envelope myself in everything about her. And that staggering, that hitch in my heartbeat, makes me realize what this feeling is.

I *miss* her. I miss her as if I haven't seen her for days, weeks, or even months.

But then she stays quiet, causing me to tuck away that staggering flop of my heart as she clears her throat, her silence shifting into unease.

"Nat?"

"Um," she continues, the hesitancy felt even through the phone. "So I know it's not technically the holidays yet, but I was wondering if you wanted to come over this Saturday and watch holiday movies with me and eat a bunch of junk food."

My brow furrows. Her hesitation confuses me. It doesn't sound like something she should feel reluctant to ask me, but she does. For some reason, it feels like she's worried I'll say no.

When I don't answer, she sighs. "You know," she says softly. "In case I might feel lonely."

"Uh, yeah. That actually sounds like fun."

"Yeah?" she says in an eagerly sweet voice that causes me to picture the smile on her face. "You aren't working?"

"It must be your lucky day because the restaurant has a special event that day," I explain. "I think a bridal shower or something in the evening. It's mainly catered stuff that I'll take care of pretty early, and the staff will manage the rest during the party. So I should be free from the kitchen after that's done."

She lets out a small sigh before whispering a defeated, "Okay."

"Okay," I answer back, sounding more resolute than her.

"I'll see you then," she calls quietly.

We hang up, and I can't help but think whether or not there's an underlying reason for Natalia calling me. We agreed that we would call each other if either one feels lonely, but it feels like this loneliness she's anticipating is more than just a simple bout of melancholy.

My phone rings again and I smile, expecting it to be Natalia and hoping I can cheer her up after her voice sounded so somber. I prepare myself for some quipped remark, something to change the subject and veer her mind off whatever is withering away at her heart, when I pick up the phone without even checking to see who's calling.

"I don't know what your movie choices are, but I think I'm going to have to throw *The Santa Clause* in there. It's a classic."

But instead of Natalia's soft voice, I hear a throat clear on the other side, rough and low. "Uh, it's Dad."

I sit up straighter, fumbling with the beer bottle in my hand to place it on the coffee table.

"Dad." It doesn't sound like a question or even a statement. More like an acknowledgment, as if I'm answering a yes or no question.

"Hi, Hayden."

There's a long stretch of silence after he says my name. As if he hasn't said it in so long that it feels foreign to him and he has to readjust to the feeling of it rolling off his tongue. I don't say anything else but keep the silence ringing loud and clear between us. What am I supposed to say? Tell him that I'm sorry? That I made the wrong choices and I should have been seeking his approval this whole time? Is that what he wants to hear after all this time?

"I..." His voice sounds stiff, like he's trying to find the right words even though it was he who called me. "I talked to Pat. He said you're doing some great things over there."

"Oh," I answer.

"I just called to say that...we're proud of you. Your mom and I."

I hear shuffling on the other end, muffled voices and whispers that sound like my mom encouraging him to say more.

"I know I haven't been supportive of your choices in the past," he continues. "But I wanted to tell you that I'm sorry. Pat seems to think that, anyway. That I was wrong. And that I was being an asshole

179

father." His words come out stuttered and rushed as if to fill the awkwardness with words.

"Uh…" I finally say after I'm left speechless. Utterly speechless. I've thought about this moment for years. My dad, finally realizing that his support is all I need. And that resentment, that built-up anger toward everything wrong in my life, starts to dissolve. Those layers of hurt and shame start to peel back, and I feel this weight of relief replace the guilt on my shoulders. "Thanks, Dad. It means a lot to hear you say that. Not that you're an asshole dad, but that you're proud of me."

He chuckles. "Anyway, the holidays are coming up. We'd be really happy if you could visit. I know you're going to be pretty busy with this new promotion and all, but Pat said he would give you some time off for Thanksgiving."

His voice trails with the last word as if remembering the last Thanksgiving I was back home. "Sure, Dad. I'll be there."

"Okay," he huffs, his voice lighter than the start of the conversation. "We'll talk again soon."

"Yeah," I answer, my own voice mirroring his as the weight of worry lifts off of it. "We'll talk soon."

25

Natalia

senior year

"IS EVERYTHING OKAY?"

I look to my left, Alex's concerned eyes coaxing an answer from me, before realizing how this must look. Me, rushing to him after Hayden kissed me, only to find that Hayden was actually correct—Alex was getting high in the parking lot—before I pleaded with him to leave the dance early. Maybe I was being too dramatic; maybe it was nothing, barely a kiss. But...I don't know. I feel so flustered and confused and scared.

I realize Alex is still waiting for me to answer, so I smile, giving a small nod in response with my fingers twisting on my lap. "I'm sorry we had to leave so early."

He smiles. "It's fine," he answers. "I still had fun."

I smile a little wider this time, tilting my face toward him while thinking how glad I am he didn't make a scene, demanding that we stay or that I find a ride home on my own. I reach out *to graze my hand against his arm, not realizing how intimate the act may seem while wanting him to know that he surprisingly made a pretty decent prom date.*

He takes my hand into his, gently stroking his thumb over my knuckles as

Jeannie Choe

he looks at me. A warm smile spreads across his face, almost in a luring gaze, as his eyes flit to my mouth.

A sudden realization hits me: Hayden kissed me. He kissed *me.* Why? We're friends, lab partners. That's supposed to be the extent of our friendship. So what are all of these swirling thoughts making everything so confusing and scary?

With my thoughts consumed with what happened between me and Hayden, Alex leans closer, bringing his face closer to mine. His hand, the one that isn't gripping my hand, moves up to cup the back of my head before he closes the space between us.

It was Alex who I should have kissed...right? I mean, he's the one that brought me to prom. He's the one who spent the night making sure I stayed warm with his suit jacket draped over my shoulders and thought long enough to make sure my corsage matched the lavender tones of my dress. But when I can't push away the gentleness of Hayden's hands or the playful smile that lit up his face, I realize how wrong this kiss feels.

What happens next feels like two tidal waves crashing into each other. Like the currents fighting at the same time without realizing what they're fighting. I start to retract my hand from Alex's grip at the same time he pulls it toward him, crushing it against his crotch. I feel the fingertips of his hands threading through my hair push into my head harder, the hard points of pressure causing discomfort and pain.

"Alex," I croak.

He must have taken it as some mixed sign of pleasure because when I say his name, he moves more aggressively, his tongue pushing into my mouth. My free hand moves to his chest, failing at any attempt to push him away. When his hand frees mine, I think, *He's finally stopping.* But then his hand moves to my knees, grazing his fingers along the hem of my dress and lifting it so it bunches along my thighs before he grips my knee.

"Alex, please," I cry. My hands start to claw at his chest, wanting him to stop but scared to tell him to because I don't want to upset him, while the words start to pile up in my throat. *Just tell him no! Tell him to stop!*

"Alex. NO!"

He stops just then, looking at me confusedly with a hint of annoyance evident in the way his brow furrows and his jaw clenches. "What do you mean, no?"

"I–I don't...I—"

His hand moves to cup my chin, and my entire body grows stiff. "Nat, I just thought since we had such a good time, we could make tonight even more memorable."

I look away, lowering my gaze and turning away from him.

"I promise I'll be gentle," he whispers, a half laugh leaving his lips before he leans forward to kiss me again.

But this time, he kisses me more aggressively, suffocating the air around me. A thundering fear starts to roar through me. All I feel are his hands moving across my skin and over my dress. Down to my nape, shoving my lips closer to him. Gripping my thigh, squeezing the soft flesh, pinching it to sear this memory into my mind forever.

"You don't have to be such a tease," he whispers in a low, authoritative voice. My skin begins to crawl, wanting nothing more than to wipe away his hot breath brushing against my lips. His finger tucks under the strap of my dress and in my attempt to pull away from him, the fabric snaps at the seam, leaving my shoulder completely bare.

In a panic, my hand reaches for the door, fumbling with the handle before it clicks open. A gush of fresh air enters the car, making Alex realize that I'm escaping his grips. His hand reaches for my waist, his fingers slipping against the silky material of my dress before I turn to leave with barely enough time and thought to reach for my purse before closing the door behind me.

I don't look back. Not even when I hear him call after me. Instead, my feet drag against the pavement as sob after sob heaves from my chest. I start to hobble, lowering myself to the ground just as I hear Alex's BMW drive off behind me. The shaky breaths and cries I can't seem to stop keep coming, wave after wave, as I cover my mouth to silence the cries.

When my tears stop long enough for me to stand from the cold walkway, I walk into my house. I wave a half good night to my parents watching TV in the living room, careful to keep my voice calm and steady before I trudge upstairs to my room. I somehow gather the strength to change out of my dress, my beautiful dress now tainted with the memory of tonight, and climb underneath the covers and fall into another fit of silent sobs and heart-shattering betrayal.

present

October 22nd.

It's a date I've remembered and looked forward to for the past five years. Five years ago on this day, Matteo took me to dinner at Momofuku and after a ten-course meal that ended in a mouthwatering rum cake, he asked me to be his girlfriend.

This is the first time in five years I'll be spending that day alone, without Matteo. Minus the anniversary he completely forgot two years ago and went to a Knicks game with his friends instead.

I didn't know how I was going to handle it. I didn't know if I was going to stay in my pajamas all day with my face covered in cheese puffs or if I was going to go to every bar in Manhattan to drown my sorrows in cosmopolitans and obnoxious jukebox music well into the night. But calling Hayden and having him be by my side sounded like a safer option.

When Saturday morning rolls around, I go to the nearest bakery and stock up on cupcakes, donut holes, and a whole cheesecake with the excuse that it's Carmen's favorite, tucking away a large slice for her to enjoy when she gets home from work the following morning. I spent the latter part of the previous day distracted by the looming heartache that I was sure to surface when day broke, but it never happened. While I haven't necessarily been the embodiment of what a happy single woman should be, I'm not necessarily as mournful as I thought I would be.

So I bury myself in preparation for my movie night with Hayden, hoping that staying distracted will keep those thoughts away. I flick through all the streaming services Carmen and I share and narrow down our choices to every sappy, chick flick holiday movie I can find.

As I move about my apartment, flitting around while fluffing pillows that have already been fluffed and wiping surfaces that are already squeaky clean, I can't help but think that maybe the reason I have yet to feel the pang in my heart I so highly expected is all because of Hayden.

Ever since the wedding, he's been more attentive, texting randomly throughout the day as if to remind me that I'm on his mind. I even spent my lunch hour at his restaurant more than once this week, bringing José along so that we could indulge, just a little bit, on the now-familiar French dishes that Hayden spoils me with. A small smile lifts the corners of my mouth as I think about the number of times I had a lemon tart this week, a box of extras always held in my hands on my way back to the office after a food coma inducing lunch.

It's so nice to feel like I'm being taken care of instead of neglected. To feel like I matter enough for someone to consider me.

Once I've neatly organized all our dessert choices and an extra-large cheese pizza on my kitchen counter, my intercom buzzes loudly. I press the button to buzz Hayden in and open the door to him dressed in the most casual attire a single man in his midtwenties could wear: gray sweatpants, a stark white hoodie, and a Cincinnati Reds baseball cap, all topped with black-rimmed glasses. He looks dressed for a night in.

My own attire matches Hayden's level of leisure as I chose comfort over aesthetics today, not caring much what I look like. That meant I gravitated toward my usual lazy weekend outfit: an oversized sweater, spandex shorts that are hidden under the tent of said oversized sweater, and warm, fuzzy socks pulled up the length of my calves. All of it, quite literally, topped off with a messy bun and a makeup-free face.

"You look dressed for the occasion," I comment, opening the door wider for him to enter.

"You said movie night," he answers, swiveling on his feet to face me as he steps into my living room before extending a small white to-go container toward me. "I came prepared."

"Since when do you wear glasses?" I ask as I take the container in my hands while eyeing him curiously.

He laughs. "Since forever. I just wear contacts."

"How did I not know that about you?" I open the box to peek inside, only to find the most delicious smelling moist cake with cocoa powder dusted on top.

He shrugs before gesturing to the box. "We ran out of lemon tarts, but I had a few slices of tiramisu left."

"Thank you," I say softly, clutching the box to my chest.

He nods before turning to face my kitchen counter. He peruses what I left out as his hands brace the counter.

"Are we celebrating something?"

I shrug a shoulder. "No."

"So a diabetic coma is just some…" He pauses, his hands waving over the array of goods. "Lifelong achievement you've been striving for?"

I giggle. "Something like that."

I bound toward my couch with Hayden's offering in my hand as Hayden plucks the bowl of popcorn from the counter before joining me.

"I feel like you're lying," I say, flicking my finger against the rim of his glasses. "Are these even real?"

He dodges my hand. "Why the hell would I wear fake glasses?"

I reach toward his face, removing his glasses and settling them over the bridge of my nose. I regret it when my vision distorts, making me nauseous almost instantly. "Ugh." I grimace, handing him his glasses back. "Never mind, you definitely aren't lying."

He rolls his eyes before settling his glasses back on his face. "So can you explain to me why we're watching holiday movies in October?"

I shrug. "Because I like them," I answer, trying to sound as apathetic as possible so he doesn't pry deeper before adding, "and I'm in the mood for something happy."

He gives me a wary look with one brow curved higher than the other. When I respond to his silent curiosity with an unsuspecting smile, his lips purse together into a firm line before he nods as if opting not to ask further. "What did you decide on?"

"I thought we could start strong with a Halloween movie since it's October, but a non-scary one, and then move on to a Christmas one."

My hand grips the remote as I gently place the box on the coffee table and plop on the couch.

"What!" he argues incredulously, standing above me in front of the couch. "How can you do a non-scary Halloween movie?"

"Ever heard of Casper the Friendly Ghost?" I pat the cushions, motioning for him to sit.

He rolls his eyes, throwing a loose popcorn kernel at me before he sinks into his side of the couch. "Fine," he surrenders. "But I get to choose the Christmas movie."

"As long as it's a chick-flicky, Hallmark Channel type one."

"All right," he announces, setting the popcorn bowl on my coffee table. "I'm out of here."

I lunge for his arm, grasping onto his wrist as I tug him back toward the couch. "Okay! Okay, you pick."

I cling to his arm as he tries to shake me off. He laughs as my grip on his arm tightens, making me look like a little koala bear on a tree branch.

"Okay, Marquez!" he exclaims. "I'll stay."

I let out a small squeal as I link my arm through his and lean into him.

"Wow, you really are a brat," he says as we both face the TV.

"No, I'm not," I pout.

He reaches up to my face, pinching my cheek between his index finger and thumb. I reach up to flick the lip of his hat, making it tumble off his head. He smirks at my antics, his lips twisting into a small smile.

"It's okay," he says, his hands moving to pinch my cheek again before I slap it away. "You're still cute."

Halfway into *Home Alone 2: Lost in New York*, I shift to face Hayden.

"I don't understand the appeal for humor based on other people's pain." My voice filters over the sounds of Marv Murchins's high-pitched screams.

"Here," Hayden says, running his hand through his mussed-up hat hair. "You pick." He lazily extends the remote in my direction. As I tentatively take it from him, he stretches his hands above his head, raising the bottom hem of his sweatshirt and exposing a sliver of a happy trail down the center of his stomach.

"I thought I wasn't allowed to pick."

"It's fine," he answers through a yawn.

I sit up, tucking my feet under my butt as I face the TV to make my selection. As I'm scrolling through my options, my mind made up on watching *Love Actually* before Hayden protests, Hayden clears his throat.

"I talked to my dad."

"You what?" I know I look dumbfounded, my mouth slacked open and my eyes wide with confusion, but I can't believe what he just told me. He finally talked to his dad.

"Uh...yeah." He picks at a loose thread coming off his sweatpants and flicks at it, avoiding my eyes. "Pat called him because of my promotion, and he called to tell me he's proud of me. And he mentioned he wanted me home for Thanksgiving."

"Hayden," I whisper, a smile cutting into the shock on my face. "That's amazing."

When he finally looks up at me, he smiles. His eyes curve and brighten, and his whole face softens, filling him with pride and hope. "Yeah," he whispers through a breathy laugh.

I lift off the couch and rest on my knees, wrapping my arms around his neck and clutching to his shoulders as his warm arms welcome me. I feel his nose nuzzle into my neck, sending a trail of goose bumps down my back.

I take in Hayden as he is right now. Not the seventeen-year-old boy who knew a past version of me most weren't aware of but the one who's had to fight for every bit of his worth. As the weight of everything melts off him while in my arms, I realize just how badly this strained relationship with his dad was wearing him down. And without that added weight, I see him shift into someone more confident and prouder. Someone who doesn't need to doubt himself but can bask in every bit of his success.

As our embrace tows into a comfort wrapped in warmth and soft-ness and his hand runs up and down my back, my mind replays another tidbit of information Hayden just told me.

"Wait a minute," I say, pulling away from him. "Did you say promotion?"

"Oh yeah," he says as his arms slowly slide down my side. "Pat's promoting me to head chef."

"Oh my god! Hayden!" I exclaim, slapping his chest. "Why didn't you tell me sooner?"

He shrugs, his smile growing wider as the corners of his mouth pull apart, exposing his teeth.

"We have to celebrate," I say, determined to mark this new mile-stone in Hayden's career.

I bound off the couch, skipping to the kitchen to grab the only chocolate cupcake I purchased. After rummaging through one of the drawers for a candle, I finally find one, a single number three candle that I used for Carmen's thirty-sixth birthday back in May. I light it before carefully walking it over to Hayden, my cupped hand cautiously blocking the breeze. I gently perch at the edge of the couch next to him, lowering my hand and revealing the flickering flame.

"It was the only candle I had," I explain. He shakes his head through a playful eye roll before sitting up from his seat and facing me. "To celebrate your promotion and becoming a real adult, despite what I thought of you in high school." I throw an overly exaggerated wink along with a wide grin as I watch Hayden break out into a light laugh. "Here," I urge, lifting the cupcake to his face. "Make a wish."

"You know, it's not my birthday," he answers as he looks at me over the warm glow of the candle.

"Just make a wish, party pooper."

He closes his eyes for a fraction of a second and opens them before lightly blowing out the candle.

"I have some bad news," I say, removing the candle and sucking off the frosting coating the bottom half. "You're going to have to share because it's the only chocolate one I've got."

"Well then, ladies first."

My already wide grin spreads wider before I peel back the liner and clamp my eager teeth onto the moist cake and creamy frosting, making sure to get an even ratio of both.

"Save some for me, Marquez," he calls when I let out a loud moan.

"I don't hear you," I muffle through a full mouth in a sing-songy voice, sprinkling crumbs of chocolate cake onto my lap.

He reaches across me at the same time I lean back. My hand holds the chocolate ball of heaven hostage as I extend my arm back toward the opposite end of the couch. His body presses against me as I chew to prevent an outpouring of chocolate crumbs. When he looks down at me, now lying flat against the couch cushions, I feel a warm flush spread through my cheeks while unable to control the tightening in my stomach as I convulse through my laughter.

"Marquez," he scolds. "You're going to have to share."

I silently shake my head, my cheeks hurting and hindering my ability to swallow. His large hand grips my bare thigh, my legs feeling like they're on fire from the heat lining his palm. He gives a tight squeeze, causing me to yelp.

"Hayden!" I scream. "I'm ticklish!"

"Yeah," he agrees, his laughter, just as warm as his touch, vibrating against me. "That's kind of the point."

When I don't surrender, he gives another firm squeeze, making me squeal even louder.

"Marqu—"

I cut him off, shoving the remaining half of the cupcake into his mouth at the same time he turns his face away to avoid the blow.

"Oh!" he howls.

While I thought my attack would force him off of me, he does the opposite. He smashes his face into mine, smearing chocolate all over my cheek while I struggle under his weight. Before I know it, I'm covered in crumbs and frosting.

"Hayden!" I scream.

He pulls away, caging me underneath him with his hands braced on the couch to my sides. I reach up to his hair hanging off his forehead, removing a large chunk of frosting from the dark strands.

"You've made a big mess," I finally say.

"I believe you started that."

He doesn't get off of me. Instead, his body sinks into mine a little deeper as I realize the position we're in. My legs parted, straddling his hips, while his hard chest brushes against mine. His hips rock the slightest bit, something that I don't think he means to do, causing me to gasp. His gaze travels down my face, trailing the residue of chocolate cake before landing on my lips, then down to my neck. It suddenly feels hot, too hot, and I feel the heat travel up my back and to my face.

"So what did you wish for?" I ask breathlessly. It's then Hayden finally climbs off me to reach for a Kleenex while handing me one.

He looks at me as if considering telling me, making me wonder if I already know what his wish is. Until he finally says, "If I tell you, it won't come true." He takes a long, slow sweep of his tissue across his chin to his cheek, making the act look more seductive than intended.

I look away and roll my eyes. The heat and air that felt too tight finally dissipates back into the lighter mood that filled the room before I innocently, so I thought, smashed cake and frosting into Hayden's face.

"That's not even remotely true."

"Still," he responds. "I'm not going to tell you."

"Fine. It wouldn't do you any good to tell me anyway," I tell him, dusting off the mess that made its way into my sweater and the couch.

"Why's that?"

"It's not like I can make it come true," I tell him, trying to ignore the low raspiness of his voice and the darkness filling his eyes.

26

Hayden

present

I KNOW I told myself this wouldn't turn into something complicated, something risky. But *fuck*...with her body underneath mine, all supple and trusting, I couldn't even bother to remember why I told myself that in the first place. Or why I shouldn't tell her that what I wished for had everything to do with wanting to act on an impulse that I should be ignoring while making me question what the hell I'm doing torturing myself like this.

She's starting to consume me, making me wonder things about her that I shouldn't be giving a second thought about. I want to know what it feels like to hold Natalia, to drink in her scent and let my heart swell with the idea of us. I want to learn things about her besides her preference for odd-tasting snacks or that she has a talent to shape and transfigure her hair to look different every day.

I want to know what type of kiss makes her breathless, or how she would react to my fingertips roaming over her body. To study her curves and the planes of her soft skin that are hidden from the rest of the world. I want to know whether she would moan or squirm when I nibble on the sensitive spot behind her knee. Or how badly she would writhe the first time my tongue tastes her, her hands threading into my hair as she whispers my name.

"Um." I clear my throat, settling back into the couch. "What movie did you decide on?"

She peers up at me shyly, her fingers grasping on to her remote a little tighter as her face ducks into the collar of her sweater.

"*Love Actually*," she says sheepishly.

I roll my eyes, my body still hyperaware of how close we were a minute ago as I surrender to her choice.

"Fine," I say, slowly realizing that I can't really ever say no to her.

Hayden, make me more lemon tarts.

Hayden, watch boring chick flicks with me.

Hayden, walk over hot coals and shards of glass for me.

The answer would always be, *When and where, babe?*

She wiggles her shoulders, smiling wide and shifting into the deep cushions as she cocoons herself around everything soft and plush. Her hand reaches over the back of the couch for a fuzzy throw blanket, and she drapes it over herself as she clicks the movie to start.

I avert my eyes away from her, focusing on the TV screen as the beginning credits of *Love Actually* play, people embracing in a crowded airport with Hugh Grant's calming voice filling the room.

"You know," she announces from under her covers, "I don't think it would hurt for you to expand your exposure to chick flicks."

I lift a brow, peeking at her over the rough plane of her blanket. "And how would I do that?"

"I don't know," she says in a muffled voice. "Maybe not be so repulsed by a light-hearted rom-com."

"Right," I answer, my voice monotone. "Because a guy pining for his best friend's girl is the exact scenario I want to live."

Her head lifts. "You've seen this?"

"Shh," I answer, pretending to maintain my focus on the screen. "I can't hear." I vaguely point toward the screen as I smirk.

I hear her scoff. "What are you going to tell me next? That *The Devil Wears Prada* is the best movie of all time and your favorite part is the fashion montage?"

"How did you know?" I peer over at her, my hand draped over the couch in her direction.

She rolls her eyes, poking her sock-covered toe at my thigh. "You've been holding out on me, Marshall."

She sinks deeper, her head resting on a small throw pillow as her eyes heavily blink through the flashes of light coming off the screen.

With my hand hovering over her, resting against the thick cushions, it itches. It burns with the need to run along the valley where her waist dips and roam under the covered area hidden beneath her clothes only to confirm how warm and soft her bare skin is. My body vibrates with restraint while my hand stays fixed to the cushions as I sit quietly in my seat. Her on one end and me on the other, attempting to create as much space as I can on the couch that feels like a cramped cocoon rather than a love seat.

When the credits roll, putting an end to the nostalgic holiday movie that I watched multiple times with my mom, I peer over at Natalia. She's fallen into a deep sleep. I can hear the light rumble of a snore every time she exhales through her nose with her hand resting under her cheek. It's not too late, but it's late enough that I should call it a night.

"Nat," I whisper, gently rubbing her shoulder.

She stirs, her hand moving to bring the cover up to her closer, causing her to hide underneath it.

I smile. *How is she this freaking adorable even when she's sleeping?* "Nat," I whisper again.

"Hmm," she groans.

"I'm going to go," I say, my voice low and soothing.

She finally lowers the blanket, her sleep-ridden face and mussed hair peeking from the frayed edges. Her hooded eyes peer at me through her lashes and hair that's come across her face like a sheer curtain. And I can't help it. I move my hand to brush the hair out of her face while staring down at her. Her eyes blink open multiple times before she slowly rises, my hand still lightly resting on the side of her head before I pull away.

"Sorry," she says, her hands coming to her cheeks to squish them together, causing her lips to pucker together like a fish.

"For what?"

"For falling asleep."

I shake my head, refusing her apology. "It's fine," I answer hoarsely.

Because it was more than just fine, it was ideal. I'm slowly learning that I need these moments where she has her guard completely down, letting me know that her trust in me won't waver. It's the only thing I can cling to when I'm unsure of so much between us.

She sits up, the blanket dropping as she brings her hands above her head, stretching while working through a full yawn. "What time is it?"

"About ten past eleven," I answer. "It's not that late."

She nods, shifting in her seat as she focuses her gaze downward on her fuzzy socks and starts chewing on her lower lip.

"Is everything okay?" I ask, noticing her sudden hesitance.

"Yeah," she answers somewhat unconvincingly.

"What is it?" I ask, gently coaxing the truth from her.

She sighs, followed by a small smile that isn't really a smile at all, as it never reaches her eyes or her cheeks. "There was a reason I asked you to come over today."

"Oh?"

"Yeah," she answers, looking up at me as her eyes downturn even further. "Today is Matteo's and my anniversary." She pauses, twisting her fingers and gnawing on her lower lip.

"Oh," I repeat myself, this time pouring more understanding than curiosity into my voice while cringing at the mention of her ex. "Are you okay?"

She nods, her head bobbing up and down through a tight-lipped smile. "I thought I would be really, *really* bad, but I'm actually handling it better than I thought."

I smile back, mirroring the up and down of her head as her smile warms.

"I guess…the reason I'm telling you is to say thank you."

"Thank me? For what?" I ask, my brows bridging together, confused.

"I feel like the reason I'm okay today is partly because of you." She reaches her hand toward me, grazing against my covered arm as she tilts her head to the side. "Not just today but a lot of the days. I think I'm okay because of you."

I shake my head, brushing off her gratitude with something between a smirk and a scoff, enough for her to know she doesn't need to thank me.

"Nat," I say softly. "You know you can call me. Anytime, anywhere. I'll always be there for you."

She looks at me, the hesitancy that causes her to avoid my eyes now spreading through her hunched shoulders. While she doesn't say anything, she nods. She nods in a way that shows any situation where I can be more than just a name on her contact list would be tentative. I wouldn't be the one who would come to her rescue, the first person she thought of when she had to call someone. But I need to be. I *need* to be that person to her.

"I mean it, Nat," I push.

She nods again, her head bobbing a bit more assertively, with a smile that peeks through her teeth pressed into her lower lip.

I clear my throat, standing from the couch as I smooth my hands down my sweatpants, making sure I have everything before I leave. I move silently, replacing the cushion that I distorted while leaning against it and smoothing out the extra throw blanket I used. Natalia stands as well, slowly following my steps as she walks me to the door.

"Are you glad we did this?" She lowers her head, looking down at her fingers twisting at the hem of her sweater again as I turn my back against the front door. "This whole 'calling each other when we're lonely.' Are you glad we did it?"

When she looks back up at me, she has doubt written all over her face. Her small smile is the only appeasement from the apprehension she's oozing.

"Why do you say it like that? Like I would say no?" I ask.

She shrugs. "I just want to make sure that you're not doing this because you feel sorry for me."

My brow furrows. "Nat, why would you think that?"

"Because of my breakup," she explains, her shoulders dropping as the inner corners of her brows turn up. "I don't want you to do this because I'm some heartbroken mess that you think you need to fix. Even if we have fun."

I reach for her hands, placing my much larger one over her two that are overlapping each other. My thumb runs over her pinky as I attempt to console her. To make her realize that nothing about the time we spend together is out of pity. It's actually the furthest thing from it.

"I don't feel sorry for you," I say softly. Maybe a little too softly that she doesn't believe me. "I think you're incredibly strong for not letting Matteo shatter your world. And I think that even though you believe you're fragile and so close to giving up on love, you aren't."

"I'm not?" Her eyes twinkle as they look at me, so full of hope and expectancy.

My head shakes side to side, just enough for her to know that I disagree with this idea of herself. This perception that she's broken, closed off from true love. Because that couldn't be further from the truth.

"You shine, Nat," I whisper. "You glow so brightly, and you don't even realize it."

Her presence lights every room, every dull place she walks into. Like the sun peeking through the clouds at sunset, when you can appreciate its beauty without it being overwhelming. That's the thing with Natalia's light; it's subtle. You only see it when you learn to appreciate it hidden under her layers. In a way that she reserves that light for those that earn it. But when you do earn it, learning how to peel back those layers, it becomes the light that guides all of the warmth coursing through your body.

She leans in to hug me. A heavy, almost outspoken sigh exhales from deep within her chest. I reach my arms around her, unable to resist her embrace. I pull her to me, burying my face into her messy hair and loose clothing, not even ashamed at how much I love holding her in my arms.

"Can I tell you something?" she says into my shoulder.

"Always."

"You're my best friend," she says. I can only see the top of her head, the knotted locks crisscrossing under my chin.

I chuckle, unable to stop the warmth spreading through my chest, causing me to laugh in a way that feels comforting. A light giggle rolls through her too, causing her shoulders to shake in my arms.

She pulls away from me, looking up through her round eyes that twinkle in the low light near her entryway and that smile that lights up the small space between us. "Thank you, Hayden," she says.

"You're welcome."

27

Hayden

senior year

WHEN I GET to school on Monday morning, the buzz about how "sick" prom was starts spreading through the hallways. Everyone is talking about their weekend hookups and binge drinking escapades. I, on the other hand, spent the weekend worried that when I kissed Natalia, I pushed her away completely. I had this sudden fear thinking she would be angry at me for assuming something that was clearly one-sided. Or worse, that she wouldn't even acknowledge me when I saw her in class.

When I walk into bio class and sit in my usual seat, Natalia already in hers with her head slouched between her shoulders, I can't help but notice the grim expression on her face. Her eyes stay focused on the textbook in front of her, her teeth gnawing on her lower lip as her brow furrows and her hands are clenched in tight fists. I start thinking to myself that this is how it's going to be between us from now on. Her sitting in her seat and me in mine, without a single word passing between us.

"Um, Nat," I say in a low voice.

But she doesn't look up. I sigh, regretting everything. How stupid I was to think that she actually wanted me to kiss her and how I interpreted everything so wrong.

I want to tell her that I'm sorry. I don't want this to be how our friendship ends. I lift my hand to her shoulder. And instead of turning to face me, she flinches. She recoils as if my hand were a hot brand.

A cold shiver runs through me. I take my hand off her shoulder but every inch of my skin crawls, coming up with a hundred different scenarios where Natalia has been hurt. "Nat, what happened?"

She shakes her head. "It's nothing."

"Natalia." The classroom begins filling with students, a sign that the bell is about to ring and that class is going to start.

"He kissed me, and he didn't stop when I asked him to," she finally says in a low voice.

My brow furrows in confusion. "What do you mean?"

Natalia sighs, her hands coming to her face as her trembling chin peeks through the slits of her fingers.

"We were in front of my house, and we sat in Alex's car for a minute. And he turned to kiss me. At first, I let him and when it got kind of uncomfortable, I tried to stop him, but he wouldn't."

My jaw clenches as I shove my fist under the desk. "Did he hurt you?"

Her eyes peek through her hands as she finally faces me, and I see the tears rimming her eyes. Her chin trembles even harder, but she shakes her head.

"No, but..." she manages through a strangled voice. I see a lone tear spill down her cheek before she turns the other way.

She's not physically hurt, but he still touched her. He still did something she clearly didn't want him to do.

I rest my hand on her back, running my fingers over her sweater. She keeps her face turned away from me, and I feel the tension in her shoulders slacken at the same time a broken sob breaks through her. I'm so thankful, so relieved that she didn't flinch from my touch like she did the first time.

The bell rings before I can say anything else. Mr. Khan stands from behind his desk and turns his projector on, instructing us where we're picking up in our textbooks. I barely hear any of it. Instead, my hard gaze is narrowed on Alex Spencer sitting on the other side of the room. He's laughing at something his lab partner said, completely oblivious to the effect his actions had on Natalia's prom night. My blood begins to boil. It simmers in my gut as I think about running the hard knuckles lining my fist through that smug mouth of his.

A light sniffle brings my attention back to Natalia. The lines of her notebook remain blank, unlike other times when they're filled with long scribbles of biology terms and haphazardly drawn images of neurons or a DNA helicase. Her body leans into my touch, and that fire that makes me seethe cools. I start to focus on consoling her until the knot that's at the root of her displaced shame loosens. I keep my hand on her back, silently letting her know that I'm still here by her side while wishing I could hold her in my arms instead.

present

I slump onto the sofa in my living room as soon as I walk through the front door, physically restless but emotionally drained. I drop the six-pack of beer I picked up on the way home on the coffee table before kicking off my shoes and letting my head fall back against the soft cushions. My gaze lingers on a small chocolate stain on my sleeve and I can't decide if the memory of that stain makes me happy or sad.

"Hey," Dexter calls when he walks out of his room. "You're home early."

I look at the clock hanging above the TV. It's close to midnight. "This is early?"

He looks like he's about to go out, dressed in a casual dress shirt with the top two buttons undone and fitted jeans.

"I'm going to get some drinks with some work people. You want to come?"

I sigh. The way I see it, I have two choices. Sit at home, drinking alone and wallowing in my newfound realization that I'm falling for the closest thing to a best friend I've ever had. Or go out and drink with people to distract myself from the wallowing I'm going to do regardless.

I stand from the couch. "Sure," I answer through a light groan, eyeing the loose, relaxed clothes that I wore to Natalia's. "Let me just change."

Once I'm dressed in something more fitting for a night of drinking, not to lighten my mood but rather to numb the sour state of it, Dexter and I leave our apartment.

"I think you might have some fun tonight." He grins at me.

I eye him curiously as he locks our door, and I pull my arms through the sleeves of my jacket.

The walk to the bar is quick, taking us no more than fifteen minutes. It's loud inside. And sticky. Everywhere I step, it seems to take an extra ounce of strength to peel my feet off the floor. But Dexter's friends are nice. Welcoming and energetic as they order a round of drinks. We all surround a small table in the middle of the bar, the noise and bustling chatter distracting my thoughts.

I turn away from the group and walk the three steps it takes to reach the bar to order another drink. Something stronger than the two beers I downed within the half hour since we'd arrived. I see Dexter approach me as I take a sip of the fresh glass of whiskey I ordered, his face already flushed and a half-empty tumbler carrying something clear and fizzy in his hand.

"This is Brittany," Dexter shouts over the noise, the same grin he gave me before we walked out of our apartment plastered across his face. "We work together."

Next to him, a young blonde woman that I would normally talk to and flirt shamelessly with stands expectantly. She shouldered her way through the crowd behind Dexter, settling herself beside him. Her flirty smile exposing teeth that are too white flickers as she looks at me, then at Dexter when I don't say anything.

I clear my throat before realizing that I'm being rude and extend my hand toward her. "Nice to meet you," I say.

She giggles loudly enough that I can hear it over the noise, sounding like a high-strung bird chirping at the crack of dawn. Not necessarily shrill but difficult to stomach. Or maybe it's that I've gotten used to Natalia's sweet, buoyant laughter. The one that I can feel even when I can't hear it, seeing it bounce off her eyes and her cheeks, gleaming from her lips as they curve upward, deepening the creases between her nose and around her mouth. It's the kind of laugh that lights up her whole face. The only kind of laugh that I ever want to hear.

Dexter steps away and leaves me and Brittany alone, clinking his drink to mine as he leaves. The awkwardness bounces off the both of us as I refuse to make eye contact with her.

After the third sip of my whiskey and the tenth time she's twirled her finger around a lock of her hair, she finally says, "I'm going to talk to my friend over there."

She points to someone behind me, and I nod, not even looking in the direction she's referring to. She steps away, her brows raised in obvious disappointment as she scurries toward a more welcoming audience.

And then I see him.

Matteo.

He's standing at the other side of the bar, his arm around a blonde woman, looking very comfortable and relaxed. As if he was out on a date. Only I know it's not his fiancée. Because his fiancée looks a lot like Natalia. Like a second-rate carbon copy he settled for once he real-ized he made a mistake.

My glaring eyes stare at him, knowing that not only did he break Natalia's heart, but he's also a sleazeball probably cheating on his fiancée. When he looks up, he sees me blatantly staring. He drops his arm that was draped around the woman's shoulders and takes a small step away from her. As if to hide the fact that the woman next to him isn't the one he's engaged to. He lifts his chin toward me. And when I don't respond with either a wave hello or a nod of acknowledgment, he stalks toward me.

"Henry, right?" he asks when he reaches me.

I openly smirk, but it comes off as more like a scoff. "Hayden."

"Sure." He smirks back. "Listen, this"—he swivels his thumb between himself and the blond—"it's nothing. I'm just out having drinks with some friends."

I raise my brows, indifference radiating off my refusal to answer him as I tilt my drink back instead.

"So," he continues carefully, "it would be great if you didn't mention it to anyone, like Natalia or her parents. With Jacinda being pregnant, it's been a bit tense at home. To put it lightly."

My eyes narrow. So that's why they're getting married. It's a shotgun wedding, and he's staring down the barrel of the gun while out gallivanting with another woman.

I don't answer him. I look away and continue to sip my drink, finishing it off with a long tilt back.

"Anyway," he says, a little too confidently considering everything he just told me. "How's my Natty doing?"

My Natty. The possessiveness in his voice makes my blood simmer. As if she could ever be *his* Natty.

"She's great," I answer. My voice is strained, restraint barely holding back the urge to punch the smug smile on his face.

"That's good to hear." His smile grows wider. He's completely ignorant, thinking that he's making Natalia's boyfriend jealous. But even though I'm not her actual boyfriend, the overprotective impulse makes my body tingle in an effort to defend her. To stand up for her and let this asshole know that Natalia isn't wasting a single moment thinking about him, not even on their anniversary, which I assume he doesn't even remember.

"You know, I do miss that little minx from time to time," he says, placing a hand on my shoulder and squeezing it. "She knew how to get parts of me excited in ways I'm sure you're aware of."

The crack of my fist hitting his jaw is all I hear. The rumble of people gasping and clamoring comes next before Dexter rushes to my side, his splayed hand grazing my waist. I watch Matteo stumble to the ground, taking a stool or two with him as he grasps for something to catch his fall. I can almost see the stars circling above his head as he stands, all clumsy and staggered.

Dexter's hands are still on me, ready to hold me back in case a second swing is in order. Matteo wipes the blood leaking from the corner of his mouth before he scoffs and looks at me. My hand vibrates at my side, numb from the adrenaline forcing the pain at bay. As I stand there, watching Matteo gather his bearings, it starts to burn. My knuckles start to throb, but my focus is on Matteo, the anger cutting through his flared nostrils and glaring eyes.

"This isn't fucking worth it," he grumbles. He starts to walk away, storming past me toward the exit, but stops when he's inches away from my face. "You can have my sloppy seconds."

I struggle against Dexter's now firm grip, ready to bury another fist into his nose, but stop myself. What good is this going to do? Pummeling his face into the ground to…what? To threaten him and tell him to stay away from my *girlfriend*?

"What's going on over here?" Both Dexter and I turn to face the bar, where the bartender stands in front of us with his arms crossed over his chest.

"Nothing!" Dexter answers. "That guy just bumped into us and tripped over the chairs. Probably too drunk or something."

He nods before walking away, and Dexter turns to face me.

"Who was that?" he asks.

"Nat's ex."

"Why were you punching him?"

I wince from the pain that's starting to shoot up my arm now that the adrenaline has abated. I look down and notice the redness and swelling that's starting to puff up my knuckles. I shake my head, my face grim and angry. So *fucking* angry. "It's nothing."

28

Natalia

senior year

"IF YOU WANT, I can rough him up a bit," Tyler offers, half joking, half serious, with his arm loosely wrapped around Yuri's shoulders. Yuri sits across from me, a large bag of sour cream and onions Lay's Potato Chips sitting between us.

I finally told both of them what happened after prom when Alex dropped me back at home. I was hesitant, not wanting to draw any unnecessary attention. But when all I could think of was Alex's rough hands gripping my knees open a little too forcibly and his tongue pushing its way into my mouth after I had firmly pursed them closed, I needed to tell someone. Someone that I could trust.

While I knew that Yuri would have held my hand through the whole ordeal, I didn't expect Tyler, Alex's friend, to take my side, even offering to use physical aggression to scare him.

"It's fine," I say, attempting to reassure them both. I'm starting to move on, relieved that all that came out of it was the gradually fading memory of the incident and the yellowing bruises on my thigh. What bothers me the most, but shouldn't, are the rumors that Alex is spreading around school calling me a cock tease and that I'm hiding a chastity belt under my clothes. Tina and a small group of her friends didn't even bother to hide their snicker when they approached me in the girl's bathroom, asking how I was going to use the toilet without a key to unlock my "celibacy contraption." I shudder, thinking about the encounter when I scurried off as their laughter echoed off the tiled walls.

"Are you sure?" Yuri asks, her eyes concerned. "I mean, not about Tyler beating him up but maybe talking to someone else about it? Like the police?"

"No!" I gasp. "That's so unnecessary. Really, I'm over it."

Yuri's eyes downturn even further.

"Or...I will. Get over it. Eventually," I add. Eventually...but for now, I'm making myself sick thinking about those acute details I've tried to erase from my mind.

Yuri opens her mouth to say something when Lucy sinks into the seat next to me. She starts opening one of the two frosty Coke cans she brought with her, the aluminum seal letting out a sharp crack as she lifts the tab.

"Oh! We got sour cream and onions today?" Lucy squeals. She giddily reaches for a handful of chips as I eye Yuri not to say anything, my silent plea moving on to Tyler as I give him the same look. So instead of carrying on our conversation, Yuri and Tyler turn to face each other, their doe eyes holding a far-off look as they smile and whisper something I can't hear over Lucy's loud chewing and even louder gulping.

I look across the cafeteria and see Hayden walk in, his backpack slung on one shoulder and Jenny following close behind. She struggles to keep up while he doesn't even bother to look back to make sure she's still there. His face looks tense, tight, as his eyes level over the crowded room. He sits in his seat along the long bench surrounded by other members of the football team, Jenny still trailing him like a puppy dog as he settles with his backpack on the table.

His deep scowl and clenched jaw remind me of when I told him about Alex in bio class. I didn't mean to tell him, but it slipped when he kept looking at me with his worried eyes. He coaxed the truth out of me without prodding too deeply, and it felt good to finally tell someone. But then he looked livid, like he was ready to trash the entire classroom. Every fiber in his body tensed right next to me, and I could feel the hardness radiating from his body. We never even brought up our kiss. It was as if what happened between us took a back seat when I told him about Alex, and all I could focus on was the way he consoled me with his warm hands and even gentler touch.

Maybe I shouldn't have told him. The fewer people who know, the better. But then he got angry for the sake of my well-being. And it warmed me. It stirred a level of safety in my gut knowing that not every guy out there would be like Alex, too eager and reckless. There would be guys out there like Hayden, protective and funny and caring. Ones who wouldn't push if I pulled away.

I continue to watch Hayden, stealing glances of him rummaging through his backpack and retrieving a bottle of Gatorade. When he smiles at his friends, he does so politely, the irate frown never fully leaving his face. And then his eyes meet mine. The grim frown that set his mouth in a firm line shifts into a relaxed smile, almost as if seeing me, safe and in one piece, is enough to wash away whatever angered him at the moment. I smile back before turning to open the second Coke can that Lucy brought, thanking her as she slides it toward me.

Maybe I should have gone to prom with Hayden.

present

"Do you think I shine?"

"What?" José looks at me as if I just asked if the sky was turning purple.

"Like, do I make—am I a happy person?"

José smiles. "Of course you are, Natalia. Why do you ask?"

I shrug. "Just asking…"

I stop to walk through the doors of Pour Toujours as a gust of wind blows past us. José peers into the restaurant, his hand coming up to wave at a man sitting at a booth before he holds the door open for me.

"Well, make sure you're that ball of sunshine right now because Shawn is already here."

Once I walked into work on Monday, José's relentlessness followed me around all morning. Apparently, he set up a lunch date for me and his cousin, Shawn, that José would be joining to supervise. Without me knowing, he already decided on holding this impromptu setup at Hayden's restaurant.

Shawn looks exactly like José described. Dirty-blond hair, full beard, and blue eyes that look like someone dipped a ladle into the ocean and poured it right into his irises. He's a bit older than me. He just got out of an eight-year relationship and moved to the city for a fresh start. He stands as we approach the table and awkwardly brings his hands together in front of him, shifting on his feet as he greets us.

"Natalia, this is Shawn," José introduces us.

"Hi," I say sincerely, my smile widening as I look up at him. "Nice to meet you."

"Likewise." He waits for me to sit before sitting back down. A gesture I don't miss and one that makes me catalog him into the gentleman category of New York City's most eligible bachelors.

"So," I start, my eyes lightly roaming over the menu, "you two are cousins? You guys look nothing alike."

Shawn chuckles. "I got the blond hair and blue eyes from my mom's side."

José rolls his eyes and swats a hand in Shawn's direction. "I asked my mom every day why Shawn gets to have those pretty baby blues while my eyes look like *caca*."

The three of us share a laugh as José looks on approvingly.

"Nat?"

I turn to look and see Hayden standing near the bar. "Hayden!" I walk toward him to greet him. "We're just having lunch."

I hook my arm through his and guide him back to my table just a couple of feet away to make introductions.

"Hi, Hayden," José calls, already comfortable and on a first-name basis with Hayden. "This is my cousin, Shawn." José gestures toward Shawn, who waves at Hayden with a polite smile.

"Nice to meet you," he calls, returning the same polite smile. I look down at his right hand and notice that it's red. And swollen. When he sees me inspecting it, he moves to cover it with his other hand.

"What's wrong with your hand?" I whisper.

"Nothing," he whispers back.

His face is serious, his jaw tight and eyes narrow, and he gives me nothing. My smile falters as I continue to look at him, silently willing him to give me answers. Or at least to smile back at me with that easy, relaxed smile that never makes me question a single thing between us.

"It was nice to see you guys," he says to José and Shawn. He turns to face me. "I have to get back to the kitchen."

He smiles softly at me, his warm hand gently squeezing my forearm before he breaks free of my grasp and turns to walk away, leaving me to face his backside.

"Is that a friend of yours?" Shawn asks, looking up from the menu once I settle back in my seat.

"Yeah, we went to high school together."

"Oh," he exclaims, surprised. "That's great you two have kept in touch all this time."

I stay quiet, considering correcting him but not wanting to confirm the inaccuracy in his observation. We continue our lunch as I steal glances toward the kitchen, hoping to see Hayden again. He looked so upset, and it worries me. I wonder if something happened. Maybe something with his parents or here at work. But when we spoke, just briefly, he gave nothing away, leaving the gnawing feeling that I want to right whatever wrong caused the tightness radiating off of him.

José's sharp elbow to my side brings me back to the table, the mouthwatering scent of bouillabaisse and croque monsieur drifting into the space between us as Shawn's courteous expression sits across from me. He lets out a short huff of laughter, more from embarrassment rather than something actually being funny.

"I was just asking how long you and José have known each other."

"Oh!" I exclaim a little too loudly. "Um, we've been working together for about…three years now?" I turn to José for confirmation.

José nods, agreeing. "And I've been trying to get her laid since her feo ass ex-boyfriend dumped her."

"José!" I hiss as my face turns hot with embarrassment. Even if he threw in a tacky insult meant for Matteo in an attempt to defend me, this man I just met doesn't need to know my history of past relationships.

But Shawn politely chuckles, more laughing with José than at me. "It's fine," he answers. "I just got out of a long-term relationship, so I get it."

I smile at him before glaring at José. Unaffected by my silent threat to trash his office and mold his stapler in Jell-O, he smiles proudly. I suppress the urge to flick his forehead and turn my attention back to Shawn instead.

He's very handsome, just like José said. He's also very kind and polite. And funny in the way that he knows when to say the punchline and how to gauge the conversation to slip in a witty yet inoffensive joke. He's perfect. Yet I can't bring myself to show interest.

Even as we settle our bill after our short lunch, having to make it back to the office before a meeting with Mark, I don't give into José's glare urging me to offer my number or a possibility for a future meeting. For some reason, I can't shake the lingering guilt that settled in the pit of my stomach as José keeps pushing me to go on a date with Shawn.

As we walk out of the restaurant behind Shawn as he hurries back to his office in the Financial District, not too far from our own, I turn back to look for Hayden. I can't help but wonder if this pang of hesitance has anything to do with him. The reason he remains a constant in my life, only a press of a button to wash away my loneliness, is because we're both actually lonely. Take that away and there would be no reason for me to call him in the middle of the night to discuss why we both equally adore Winston Schmidt but can't stand Nick Miller. Or if it was worth it to trudge out of our warm beds and into the late New York City night just so we could meet up over a cup of hot chocolate and fresh donuts. I would have to give all of that up, and I don't know if I'm ready to let go of my best friend. To let go of the one person that never once thought that I was "too much."

When I was with Matteo, I did a lot of tiptoeing, always feeling as if I was too much. And maybe having Hayden by my side, reminding me that I would never be too much to him, is the reason I'm finally able to see how preoccupied I was in my relationship.

There were so many things that I masked through the blindness of love when I was with Matteo. When I would laugh a little too loudly, he would roll his eyes and turn the other way out of embarrassment. When I would skip or dance because something excited me, he would tell me to calm down. When I reached out to him affectionately, requesting to hold hands or a kiss out in public, he would deny me. As if my overabundance of affection was out of place for an adult. Now, as I look at the rubble of our relationship from the outside in, I feel freed from being that embarrassed girl who felt shunned from being too happy or excited.

When Hayden told me I shined, I realized that I really did. Without Matteo's narrowed eyes and pursed lips looking at me, wishing I were different, I turned into someone who didn't have to hide under a shadow. I don't have to look over my shoulder when I feel every single emotion course through me, worried that I may be too expressive, too eager. Because Hayden doesn't force me to stow away that side of me. Instead, he encouraged me to be me.

When I laugh too loudly, he piles on to the jokes, making my laughter ring even louder and longer. When I skip, he joins me. And when I do things that Matteo would normally turn away from like forcing him to blow out a candle when it wasn't even his birthday or trying avocado-flavored frozen yogurt, he does so willingly. With a smile and words that make me feel like I'm not too much. As if I'm exactly the person he needs in his life.

I'm not ready to let all of that go.

"Natalia," José scolds when we walk back into our office building. We're standing in front of a closed elevator door, waiting patiently for it to take us back to the buzz of the workday. "Please say yes if the man asks you to dinner."

I sigh. "José—"

"Just hear me out," he interrupts. "No pressure. Just a dinner to get to know each other. You two don't even have to call it a date."

I throw my hands in the air, giving in. "Fine."

José squeals, clasping his hands in front of him just as the elevator ding announces its arrival. "I'll give him your number."

29

Hayden

senior year

I PULLED into the school parking lot Thursday morning with Jenny sitting in the passenger seat. She texted me the night before, asking if I wouldn't mind picking her up since her car was in the shop. While that may have been true, it was obvious she wanted to make a point by coming to me instead of one of her friends.

"I have to meet Tina before first period," she announces, her door opening a few inches before she starts to exit the car. "She wanted to talk about something."

I nod, my gaze narrowed in on a familiar silver BMW parked a couple of rows over.

"Is everything okay?" Jenny asks.

I don't turn to face her. Instead, I silently nod again, reaching for my backpack in the back seat before exiting the car. I don't check to see if Jenny's following. Instead, I stalk toward the car I've been eyeing, checking to see if the driver is still anywhere nearby.

When I round a row of cars, I see Alex Spencer. He's leaned up against the hood of his car, a small group of people gathered around him, all smiles with the low rumble of chitter chatter before the first bell.

Prom should have been remembered as a benchmark for every memorable moment of our senior year, right alongside graduation and the last day of school. It should have been something that I, along with everyone who attended, remembered and reminisced about. But I can't. Not anymore. Knowing how it ended for Natalia, knowing that she was all alone with Alex *fucking* Spencer to grope her, made me so fucking angry. I've become a ball of fury ever since Natalia told me what happened. Whenever I close my eyes, all I can think of is beating the shit out of Alex. And that extremely fine line that borders between me being a friend for Natalia, one that she turned to when the pain from that night became too much to bear, and me acting on every simmer of hate that I have toward Alex, begins to blur.

"Hey, Spencer!" I call. I don't even bother trying to hide the anger seeping through my voice. My blood feels like it's actually boiling, bubbling up inside me, making my entire body shake with rage.

When he hears his name, he looks up to face me, a stupid grin plastered on his face as if he didn't even give what he did to Natalia a second thought. I drop my bag on the asphalt before taking my final step, stopping a few feet from his face with my hand gripped into a tight fist.

"Hey, Marshall," he answers, tilting his chin toward me.

And before I know it, my fist hits him square in the face. The impact makes him stumble, bracing his palms against his own car before staggering to the floor. I know it's a low blow, sucker punching him when he least expects it, but I don't even care. Every time I think about Natalia with her head ducked low and flinching when I moved a little too close to her, it makes me furious. I want to pound his face into the ground until he can't smile that smug-ass grin, until he knows that I know what he did.

Everyone starts to gather around us. Alex sits on the ground, wiping the trickle of blood oozing from his nose.

"What the fuck, Hayden!" he shrieks.

"I swear to God, if you touch Natalia again...if you even look at her, I will come after you," I growl, my fist still clenched and wound so tight that my nails dig into my palms.

Just as the words leave my mouth, I feel someone jerk my arm. I turn to see Jenny looking up at me, confused and angry.

"Hayden!" she shouts.

I don't say anything to her. I don't fucking care anymore. So she walks away. I watch as she does, not even bothering to go after her.

"Okay, people! That's enough!"

We're interrupted as Mr. Walton stands between me and Alex, instructing the crowd to disperse. He turns to face me.

"You," he says, pointing at me. "In my office. Now."

I take one last look at Alex, his dumbfounded face not even bothering to fight me back. Instead, he keeps his gaze on the ground, wiping his nose again as the blood continues to trickle.

I pick up my backpack and follow Mr. Walton to his office.

present

I know being alone with Natalia is starting to become reckless. The more time we spend just the two of us, I feel this pull toward her. This current that seems to thicken when she wraps her hand around my arm or when she smiles up at me, her eyes twinkling as her nose crinkles in the most adorable way.

But that doesn't stop me from wanting to be near her. To bathe in the presence of her, drinking in her infectious laugh. It's what keeps me going. To call her when I'm feeling lonely. Or when she's the only one that makes me feel like I'm *not* lonely. Regardless, I'm looking for ways to be around her while maintaining that length that extends from my shoulders to the tips of my fingers, knowing it probably isn't the smartest thing to be doing.

"So," I say as casually as possible through my phone, "I was wondering if you were planning on feeling lonely this Friday."

I called Natalia, finding any excuse to talk to her or see her. Dexter snagged an invitation to a Halloween party at some hot club that was exclusively guest list only, and it felt like the perfect excuse to call Natalia. Any excuse to see her without having to be all alone with her, feeling like the room is closing in on us.

"Service!" Stephan, my new sous chef who was promoted from his position as the chef de partie, calls from the service line, naturally ushering me out of the busy kitchen into the quieter walk-in refrigerator.

"Are you at work?" she asks through the phone.

"Yeah," I answer, talking over the low hum of the motor fan while hunching forward to stay warm. "But it's dying down out there. I had a minute to myself."

"Perks of being the boss?"

I chuckle. "Something like that."

I can hear her smile, a small breath filtering through the phone as I imagine that smile spreading across her face. "Um, so what did you have planned for Friday?" she asks.

I hear the opening of her door followed by her shoes clacking, most likely being kicked off as soon as she walks through her door. It's late, nearing nine p.m., and she's barely making it home from work. She sighs, following the clanking of her keys hitting her kitchen counter.

"Dexter invited me to this party. I guess one of his coworkers rented out a club to throw some big costume bash, so he asked if I wanted to come," I say, my voice cautious. "And I got the night off so..."

"Oh, so it's a Halloween party?"

"Yeah," I answer.

"Well, it's a good thing that I have my Playboy bunny costume hidden in the back of my closet," she answers through a breathy laugh. I chuckle too, waiting for her answer. "Oh, but Carmen's off that night. I think she wanted to do something."

"Bring her," I offer. "And David too," I add.

"Really?"

"Yeah," I assure. "Dexter's got a hand in the guest list, so I think we could invite my entire extended family and yours and get away with it."

She giggles from the other side. "Okay," she answers through a yawn that ends in a deep sigh.

"You sound tired."

"I am." Her voice stretches through another yawn. "My boss wanted to get started on this big project for a prospective client, and we had to stay late working on a pitch for the morning."

"I..." I want to offer to come over to her house as soon as I get off work. To prop her feet on my lap while I rub out all the calloused tension. To bring her takeout while I silently listen to her talk about this big project that I'm sure she's going to kick ass in.

But I don't, of course. "I'll talk to you later then. So you can get some rest."

"Yep," she answers through another yawn. "I'll see you Friday, Marshall."

"See you Friday, Marquez."

Friday night comes and I'm sitting at home, anxiously waiting for Natalia to arrive with Carmen and David. Dexter is in his room, getting ready, while I stand in front of our kitchen counter, already dressed and ready to go an hour ago.

After some minor back and forth with Natalia, we settled on a matching-slash-couple's themed costume. Something so that the other wouldn't feel so out of place. We finally decided on the most relevant and allusive costume for us two: Hugh Hefner and a Playboy bunny. And while she confessed that she didn't actually have a Playboy bunny costume, I'm looking forward to this party and seeing her in what will further deepen my attraction to her. I mean, I *am* still a member of male species with typical heterosexual tendencies.

I sigh, shake my head, and roll my eyes in one sweep. *Great*. What a way to set myself up.

I open the fridge for a bottle of water and then change my mind. I open the cupboard where I thought I had a stash of Reese's peanut butter cups. When I come up empty-handed, I go back to the fridge for a beer. I'm restless. My fingers mindlessly tap on the counter, strumming along to the seconds ticking on the clock. When Dexter walks in, dressed in a flight suit jumper and aviators tucked into his collar, he sees me pacing the small area connecting our kitchen to our living room.

"What's with you?"

"Huh?" I jump, swiveling to face him.

"Whoa," he replies. "Easy there, big guy."

My body slumps, leaning against the counter, and I drink the cold beer gripped in my hand. "What are you supposed to be?"

He straightens, smoothing out the material running down his chest. "Maverick. *Top Gun*?"

I nod, wrapping my robe over my bare chest a little tighter.

"Do these ants in your pants have anything to do with how ridiculous you look in a silk robe? Or is it about Nat coming out with us tonight?" he asks, referring to my costume while flicking at the captain's hat sitting on the top of my head.

I side-eye him, almost slamming the amber-colored bottle onto the counter.

"It is, isn't it!"

"No, Dex. It isn't," I deadpan.

"I knew it!" he exclaims, punching his fist into his opposite hand, completely ignoring my denial. "That's why you got all pissed off when you ran into her ex the other night."

"Dexter," I scold. "Can you keep your mouth shut? I beg you."

"I—"

He's interrupted by a soft knock at the door. I look at the clock on our microwave, glowing neon green and forever running two minutes ahead. It's just past ten p.m., and Natalia is a little early.

"Just," I say, turning back to Dexter, "don't say anything stupid."

He responds by grinning as if holding back a big secret. And I glance at him one more time before rounding the corner to our door, giving him another silent warning.

When I open the door, Natalia is standing there alone. Her body is wrapped in a large trench coat, the belt bound tightly around her small waist. Large bunny ears rest on her head, all lopsided and adorable.

"It's just you?" I ask, peering over her shoulder.

"Yeah. Carmen and David are going to meet us there."

I step aside to let her in. When I close the door and face her, her apprehension is clear on her face. For a second, I think that she's feeling the same tension that's oozing out of every pore of my body. But then she starts fidgeting with the thick belt wrapped around her waist, and I realize that she's shy about her costume. And just like that, all of the tension wrapped around the nerves settled in my chest dissipated.

"Are you going to show me your costume?" I ask, a playful smile dancing on my lips.

She smiles through pursed lips and shakes her head.

"What?!" I practically shriek. "I put on this ridiculous thing," I say, gesturing to my silk robe. "You have to give me a peek at what you look like."

She rolls her eyes, slowly undoing the ties of her belt. And then she peels back her coat, slowly revealing what's underneath.

When we discussed costumes, we skimmed over various options from matching banana suits to superhero leotards. I knew what she was going to wear tonight would border that fine line between the Natalia I've grown all too familiar with and the Natalia burning through my most coveted fantasies.

I have to practically clamp my teeth into my fist because *holy fuck*. Each one of her legs is wrapped in fishnet stockings, all the way up to the creased curves of her hips. The skintight bodysuit she's wearing cinches her waist and stops far below her neckline, only outlining the perfect cleavage that rounds the top of her breasts. She topped off the entire ensemble with a white collar and black bowtie wrapped around her delicate neck. And her pouty lips are painted a cherry red, matching the smoky-eye makeup that makes her brown eyes pop against the charcoal hues.

"Don't laugh at me," she demands with a small scowl when she sees the struggle on my face. Me? Laugh? What could I possibly find funny when all I can think about is slinging her over my shoulder and dragging her to my room?

I clear my throat. "It looks good on you," I comment, my voice thick and low. And I don't mean to, but I stalk toward her, all slow and authoritative, not even caring that I look as pained as I feel not being able to touch her how I want. My steps are deliberate and calculated as I come to a stop inches in front of her. My fingers start playing with the front flaps of her coat, flicking them open a little wider. The pads of my index and middle finger start brushing along the covered parts of her stomach when Dexter steps into the living room to greet Natalia.

"*Hellooo*," Dexter calls, too eager and loud. Natalia smiles politely, her hand coming up to wave at Dexter as she turns to face him. "Wow, Nat," he exclaims, looking her up and down. "You are wearing that costume." He stoops down to hug her, lifting her off her feet as she giggles against his shoulder. He groans a little too enthusiastically while swinging her body side to side.

"Nice to see you too, Dex," she says as her eyes curve and the apples of her cheeks round.

"All right, you two," I say, stepping in between them. "Let's break it up."

Dexter finally places Natalia back on solid ground before nudging my ribs with his elbow, giving me a mischievous bounce of his brows. "So how's that beautiful sister of yours?"

"Carmen?" Natalia asks, a little confused.

"Lucia!" he corrects.

"Oh, Lucy. She's good." She looks at me, a confused furrow between her brows deepening as if asking me what the hell *that* was about. I give a light shrug, continuing our silent back and forth as she takes a small step closer to me.

Dexter nods, licking his lips before reaching for his keys by the door. "Well, tell her I said hi." He turns to face me, his movements slightly rushed as if he's late as he heads toward the door. "I've got to stop by somewhere on the way. I'll see you guys there."

"Oh," I answer, unaware that our plans have changed. "So we're going to meet you there instead?"

He nods. "Just let them know you're on my guest list. You shouldn't have to wait in the line."

I nod back.

"Natalia." He lowers his head. "I will see you and a shot of tequila with your name on it later tonight," Dexter says as he tips an imaginary hat and walks out the door, leaving me and Natalia. Alone.

I clear my throat, the sudden noise cutting through the silence.

"It's a little early," I announce. "You want a drink before we go?"

"Sure," Natalia says softly. "So this is the fancy ol' bachelor pad, huh?" She shifts her feet, moving to walk through the semi-cluttered living room as she follows me to the kitchen.

"Yep," I answer, my back turned to her as I talk to her over my shoulder. "We hide the blow-up dolls and lava lamps when guests come over. We don't want people knowing how provocative our single lifestyles really are."

She giggles as I walk to the fridge to retrieve a beer. I open it with the edge of the counter by slapping my palm against the metal bottle cap, causing a ribbon of mist to float out the top from the broken pressure.

"Thank you," she whispers softly with a small smile. An awkward silence lingers as she drinks her beer, the glugging of it leaving the bottle sounding louder than it actually is. "So..." she says meekly, her fingers twiddling in front of her. "I have some news."

"Oh?"

Her lips press together in a firm line. "I may have an impending date...in the near future."

Those words feel like a punch to my gut, the force from it hitting me like a wrecking ball. Demolishing all the senseless daydreaming I've been doing, imagining how it would feel like to *be* with Natalia.

"It's with Shawn. That guy who was at lunch with me and José the other day? At your restaurant."

"Oh," I answer softly.

She nods. "He hasn't asked me out or anything, but José's been so persistent that I entertain the idea and at least go on one date with him. But I don't know."

There's a strain of annoyance in her voice, and I believe her. She looks so hesitant, equivocating between going and not going on this possible date. So I do the one thing that I don't want to do. The one thing that any supportive and caring friend would do.

"I think you should go." My voice sounds forced. As if I don't want to say the words and I'm holding them back as far as I can because I know it would be wrong. Because that isn't what friends do. "I mean, you know, when he asks you on a date."

"You do?" She lifts her face and her eyes round, giving her a full puppy dog effect with the added twinkle from the kitchen lights. *No, I don't*, I think.

"Yeah," I answer, failing in an attempt to sound convincing. "He seemed nice."

"You mean in the two seconds that you met him?" she teases.

"No, I–I mean," I stutter, huffing a laugh at how much difficulty I'm having just trying to convince Natalia to do something I don't want her to do. "It wouldn't hurt to give it a shot. You know, get out there and meet someone."

"What if it's horrible? Like, he ends up being some weird stalker or worse..." She lowers her voice in a hushed tone, bringing the sideways plane of her hand against her mouth as if she were telling me a secret before saying, "He's a mama's boy."

I chuckle as I watch what little humor she has about the looming possible date trickling through her jokes. "Are you scared?" I finally ask.

"No. I mean...I don't know, Hayden." She lightly brings her hand to her face, avoiding her eyes to prevent smudging her makeup. "I guess I'm just looking for excuses to get out of it."

"Nat," I say softly. My whole body softens, not just my voice. My face, my posture, even my hands as they move to lightly grip her shoulders. "Just go and see what happens."

She looks up at me, smiling sadly with downturned eyes. Instead of fighting me like I wish she would, she gives a sad nod.

"Best case scenario, your kids would have pretty blue eyes."

She rolls her eyes, pushing me away. "Oh my god, Hayden. I don't need that kind of pressure."

I chuckle. "Come on," I say, taking the beer bottle from her hand. "We have a party to get to."

30

Hayden

senior year

I ROUGHLY JOG down the stairs, taking them two at a time as I run to answer the doorbell that just rang. It's the second day of my three-day suspension for punching Alex. While his dad came to Mr. Walton, threatening to sue the school and press charges, Alex stopped him, requesting that his dad drop it and move on. So after Mr. Walton delivered my sentence, my parents grounded me for two weeks, in addition to my suspension.

When I open my front door, I see Jenny standing on our front porch. She's fumbling with her car keys between her hands as she looks at me with her bottom lip drawn between her teeth.

"Can we talk?" she asks, looking much less the scrappy Jenny that I'm used to, now replaced by a more reserved version.

I look over my shoulder, checking the time on the clock hung above our fireplace. My parents are getting off work and are due home any minute. If they see that Jenny's over, they'll probably ground me an extra week for breaking the rules. "Yeah, sure," I answer. "I have a couple minutes before my parents get home."

I close the door, stepping out onto the porch instead of inviting her inside, and we both sit on the front steps.

We stay silent for a moment too long, waiting for the other to speak first. I don't really have anything to say to her, but I know she's here to ask questions about the fight, most likely wanting to know how Natalia was involved. And to be completely honest, she's the last person I want to explain the situation to. Luckily, she breaks the awkward silence first.

"I don't know what's going on with you and Natalia," she says, a waver in her voice that I've never heard. "But I swear to God, if you're cheating on me—"

"No," I cut her off. "It's nothing like that."

She sighs. "Then what the fuck was that?" Her hand is outstretched in front of her, referring to the exact situation that got me grounded.

"First of all," I start, a little annoyed, "we aren't together. So even if I *were* seeing someone else, I wouldn't be cheating on you. And second, something happened, and Alex needed to know that he fucked up. That's all."

She stands, throwing her hands in the air before yelling, "I don't even know what that means!"

I suppress the urge to roll my eyes. "Look, Jenny." I stand and face my front door, already ready for this conversation to be over. "We had a good time at prom, and I like you…as a friend. But I don't think we should see each other anymore."

When I look at her, I see the tears welling up in her eyes. "I can't believe you're dumping me for Natalia Marquez."

I groan, frustrated that she didn't hear a single word that I said. But this is such typical behavior of her. It's why I broke up with her in the first place. "I told you, that's not it. There's nothing going on with me and Natalia."

"Whatever," she huffs, turning to walk away, wiping the tears now streaming down her cheeks. "Do whatever you want. Date her, screw her over like you've screwed me over. I don't care. I'm so fucking done with you!"

I sigh, unsure if it's from relief or annoyance, as she walks away into her Toyota Camry and drives off.

I walk back into my house, thankful that my parents didn't walk in on Jenny's outburst. Why does this keep happening with us, with me and Jenny? This surplus of drama that she seems to create out of nothing feels so exhausting, and I want nothing more than to just walk away from it. And the fact that she claimed I've been cheating on her with Natalia. The thought itself sounds completely outrageous.

I'm sure by now Natalia knows I've been suspended. She might not know why or the details of the fight that left Alex bruised and bloodied, but I hope that she would at least notice my absence. And maybe even miss me the way I've missed her.

And *fuck*, do I miss her.

It's been five days since I've seen her, including the weekend, and I miss sitting in class next to her, passing each other looks and whispering jokes that result in secret smiles. It took five days for a divot-sized dent in my heart to turn into a decent-sized crater thinking about how much I'll miss Natalia even more when the school year ends. I'm left wondering how much bigger that hole will grow over the summer. And after the summer passes, that hole will continue to grow, the distance between me and her spreading longer and wider. That ache I felt, when I held Natalia in my arms while we danced in the low twinkling lights surrounded by everything romantic and enchanting, returns as I think about how, if I could, I would go back to that moment time and time again. But I wouldn't kiss her. Instead, I would hold on to her and wish for time to stand still. If I had the choice, I would never let her go.

present

Natalia's hand falls into mine once we approach the crowded entrance of the club.

"Natalia!"

We both turn to the sound of Natalia's name and see Carmen and David walking toward us. Carmen is dressed in a mermaid costume while David is rocking a pirate hat and eye patch, all topped off with a fake beard. Natalia's arm extends out, causing me to grip her hand more firmly. I look down at our hands, the point where our bodies are joined together, and I can't help but feel a pang in my chest knowing how good this feels. Wishing that I could hold Natalia's hand whenever I want.

"Carmen!" she calls, her other hand gesturing toward Carmen to break off from the long line behind us and join our side.

We all wave simple hellos, the crowd urging us to either enter the club or get out of the way. The four of us greet the attendant, giving Dexter's name, and the red velvet rope drops to let us in.

We're welcomed by the vibrating thrum of the music and the flashing lights bouncing off the walls. I can barely hear over the noise, let alone speak, so I use my hands to signal the direction of the main bar before everyone nods in agreement.

I stop once we reach the bar, which is equally crowded with other costume-clad patrons and bartenders scrambling on the other side. Cups, bottles, and shakers all move in a blur among men and women in their own costumes fit for the occasion.

I lean down toward Natalia. "You guys want a drink?" I speak as loudly as I can over the music.

She turns to Carmen and David and signals the universal drinking sign, miming an imaginary cup tilted back, and they both nod. I order a round, something strong and sure to evoke shivers, and pass it around. We all toss each glass back, Natalia practically gagging as she brings the glass back down.

She tilts up on her toes, a hand gripping my shoulder as she speaks into my ear. "I'm going to regret this in the morning, aren't I?" she shouts over the music.

Not answering her rhetorical question, I clink my own empty glass to hers instead. It draws the response I want: a sincere eye roll and smile, followed by a playful shove to my half-bare chest.

And maybe it's the crowd, making us feel like we're the only two people in the room while being surrounded by hundreds of sweaty bodies, or the fact that I haven't stopped thinking about her since I left her apartment after our movie night, but my hand moves to cover hers resting lightly over my heart. I press it into me, letting her feel the rampant beating against my chest as I look down at her. She peers up at me through her lashes, her eyes round and lips parted. I dwell on the fact that she hasn't pulled away. Her hand hasn't lifted, forcing me to press it down harder. Instead, she follows the lead of her hand and shifts closer to me.

I could stay in this moment forever. Looking into her eyes, my hand covering hers and our bodies leaning toward this thick, vacant space between us.

Natalia turns away when Carmen's hand moves to her shoulder to get her attention. They exchange a quick word before Carmen and David walk away toward the cramped dance floor.

"I think I want another," Natalia announces, her voice strained and laced with something that hints at unease.

My brows lift. "You sure?"

Her throat bobs before she nods.

"What about regretting it in the morning?"

She shrugs, only one shoulder lifting as she smiles coyly, her eyes never leaving mine.

It's loud, the bass vibrating the house music off the floors and the lights flashing all around us. Natalia's skin glows, a sheen of sweat coating her skin as she flips her hair over one shoulder, fanning her neck. She's finally ditched the coat she was hiding under and is now moving in all the glory of her costume, even proudly showing me her backside to reveal the cutest little cotton ball of a bunny tail.

Her smile becomes lazy with only one corner curving upward, and her eyes are hooded as she zones in on my lips. I smirk at her as she sways toward me.

"I hope your dancing skills are better than your ability to hide the fact that you like chick flicks," she says, her voice low but somehow loud enough to ring clearly through my ears.

Every nerve ending in my body buzzes with electricity. She pushes her body against mine as the crowd ushers her toward me. My hand moves to her waist, my thumb tracing lazy strokes over the fabric lining her stomach. Her hands glide up my chest and wrap around my neck, comfortably resting on my shoulders as her hips continue to sway side to side.

I bite back whatever snarky remark I have at the tip of my tongue, watching as her drunken haze lowers her inhibitions. I don't want her to realize that this is probably not what we should be doing. Because I don't care. I don't care that if she remembers this moment tomorrow, she would be embarrassed, regretting every step that brought her to this intoxicated buzz. I don't care that I shouldn't be enjoying the fact that her body pressing into mine makes me notice how her cleavage rises up and down. I lower my head down to her as her fingertips press into my neck and graze higher into my scalp, forcing me to suppress a moan.

She brushes her lips against my ear. "What would you say right now to those Cupid's Bet girls you can't seem to get enough of?"

I stiffen. I don't want to talk to her like some random girl that I hook up with, filling her mind with degrading words meant to seduce her. That isn't what I want to do with Natalia. I want to tell her that I care about her. I want to laugh and sing with her until our cheeks hurt and we're a giggling mess of breathless mirth. But that's not what this is.

"I think at this point…" I start as she pulls away and looks up at me. Her eyes are clear, none of the drunken haze obscuring them as she waits for my answer. "I would suggest we go back to my place and hope that you're not drunk enough to regret your choices."

"Brazen for you to assume that the possibility of regret would stop me from making stupid decisions."

My brow curves up, entertained by the meaning of her suggestive and unsubtle words. "You wouldn't regret coming home with me?"

She lifts a bare shoulder, tilting her head to the side as she bites her lip through a very flirtatious smile. She doesn't answer me, her gaze growing darker and darker. She must feel the apprehension and edge leech off of me because the smile slips. Her hand moves down my now bare chest and grazes down my stomach, resting at my waist. I feel her hand lightly press against the muscle lining my hips, the tips of her fingers running purposeful strokes over the ridges through my robe. Her mouth parts as her chest heaves, making it damn near impossible to look away from those alluring cherry lips.

I want to fucking kiss her. It's all I can think about. Having her lips against mine, my tongue slipping through them as it brushes along the smooth terrain of her mouth. I imagine my hands roaming all over her body. Through her hair, down her back, between her thighs.

Suddenly, my heart feels like it's rattling in my chest as a small rise of panic makes me lean away from her. And then I remember the last time we were placed in this spot, when I thought she wanted me to kiss her but pushed me away instead. When I acted on something that felt just as right as it does now and instead, it backfired so heavily that I regretted it.

I clear my throat. "You want some water?" I have to yell over the music, but my voice still sounds weak and unsure.

She nods, her round eyes looking too serious. I notice her hand still on my waist. I notice the heat that flames across my skin where her fingers feel like hot brands. And I notice the way her mouth angles toward mine, urging me to do the one thing I shouldn't.

31

Natalia

senior year

TOMORROW'S the last day of school. The last day of my grade school career, where I will end it with the ceremonious packing of my lifelong belongings into multiple suitcases and boxes after the graduation that I've been waiting all year for. I've collected some of the belongings from my locker in my backpack, making it heavier than it normally is, leaving the rest for the following day.

I'm lugging the heavy bag over my shoulder to my car all alone because Lucy ditched me to hang out with her friends after school. With the school year coming to an end and her yearbook duties finally over, Lucy's time in school has shifted from her studies to the mall's food court for corn dogs and lemonade.

As I slowly approach my car, my focus more on the straps digging into my shoulders rather than what's in front of me, I see Hayden leaned up against my car. I come to a stop a few feet away, finally dropping my heavy bag to the floor with a deep thud.

"Hey, Nat," he calls as he sees me approach.

"Hi, Hayden," I say. "Get lost on the way to your car?"

He pulls his hands away from behind his back, revealing a small disposable Tupperware container. He holds it up between us as I step closer, a small smile replacing the pained look on his face that I've been seeing more of.

"Happy last day of school," he says, pointing the container at my chest.

"It isn't the last day of school yet," I say, taking the box from him.

He shrugs. "Close enough."

I peel back the lid, peeking to see what's inside.

"It's vanilla cake," he says. When I look up at him, I grin. So wide that I feel the stretch of my smile cutting into my cheeks.

"You made this for me?" I ask as a joke because he couldn't have possibly made this for me. If anything, he's merely keeping his end of the bargain: to let me taste test his next line of baked goods. But instead of denying it, he nods.

"I did," he answers, a grim smile cutting across his face. "The vanilla reminded me of you."

"Oh," I whisper. "Well, thank you."

I don't mean to, but I stare at him a little longer than I expect to. I see the shadow that casts over his face as his jaw flexes and the creases that line the space between his brows deepen. I see the knot roll down the center of his throat before he reaches to give my arm a light squeeze. I see the Hayden that I normally see in class, the one that filled the boring time teasing me and making sarcastic jokes, fold inside him as that version of him is slowly replaced by the Hayden in front of me now. One who looks too uncertain of the future, of a life where our daily interactions will no longer exist. One who's silently whispering his goodbyes to me.

"Yeah," he finally answers, pushing himself off my car and walking away. "I'll see you at graduation."

I clutch the container in my hands, wrapping my fingers around it like a treasure. "I'll see you at graduation."

present

"Paging Dr. Garcia to ER, bed four. Dr. Garcia to ER, bed four."

My fingers fidget with the handles of the brown paper bag containing two orders of warm chicken shawarma and a fresh batch of chocolate chip cookies.

After a lazy weekend of lounging at home and working through some emails to distract myself, Carmen called me from the hospital, begging me to bring her lunch after a grueling end to her shift that blended into another eight hours into the morning. Something about being short-staffed and having to work an ungodly amount of overtime.

After nursing a quick hangover, thanks to Hayden forcing liquids to hydrate me and a greasy burrito delivered to my doorstep, I collected my bearings and replayed every image etched into my mind, all of it blurred a little by alcohol. Flashes of Hayden brushing his hand against my waist, looking at me like his mind was at war, his smile twitching as if each personal thought he carried had some insinuation.

How am I back here? How are *we* back here? It's like we've both unwillingly stepped into a time machine that led right back to that dance floor at prom, the last eight years not making either one of us an ounce wiser. Instead, we're still those confused seventeen-year-olds, still so unsure about our feelings.

Maybe I'm looking too far into it, but I can't stop thinking about the way Hayden touched me. Running his hands over my body through the thin material of my costume, causing a prickling that felt akin to pins and needles coursing over my skin. And the way he looked at me, so grim and searing.

I shake my head, almost as if I'm trying to shake the image of his piercing eyes out of my mind. I know I'm looking too much into this, whatever *this* is. And I need to let it go. All these lingering thoughts that are causing me to think that the way Hayden looked at me meant more, I need to let that all go.

I look up just in time to see Carmen walking toward me wearing navy-blue scrubs and a white doctor's coat. I stand to greet her.

She sighs as she smiles, embracing me in her arms. "Thank God you're here. I'm starving."

"I have just the remedy," I say, holding up our lunch between us. I force a smile, shifting my thoughts from Hayden to being present as I see how my frazzled sister needs some extra support to get her through the last hours of her shift.

"Are you okay?" she asks, her brows drawn together with concern.

I nod, my smile widening in an effort to convince her. "Yeah, I'm just hungry too."

"Come on. We'll eat in the cafeteria."

Carmen is eating her second cookie, the wax wrapper that once held her shawarma sitting on the table in front of her when she looks at me.

"So," she starts.

My brow furrows, waiting for what this "so" is insinuating. "So…"

"What's going on with you and Hayden?"

I let out a nervous laugh with an unconvincing smile. "What are you talking about?"

Her smile grows, her eyes focusing on a loose chocolate chip hanging off the edge of her cookie. "I saw the way he looked at you."

I lower my face, staring a little too hard at the crumpled napkins in front of me. When I don't say anything, Carmen continues. "Actually, David noticed how he looked at you. Said you two make a cute couple."

"Nothing's going on, Carmen," I deny rather begrudgingly, not helping my argument. "We're just friends."

"Okay." She shrugs, popping the remains of her cookie in her mouth. "If you say so." She doesn't sound the least bit convinced. If anything, her words sound like an appeasement to my denial.

I sigh deeply, and that gets Carmen's attention.

"You can talk to me, you know," Carmen says softly.

Her hand reaches across the table and covers mine. I can feel the roughness of the cookie crumbs on the pads of her fingers rubbing into the back of my hand. When I finally look up at her, I groan, bringing my face to the hard table. My shoulders slump along with my head, and I hear Carmen lightly chuckle at my dramatics. "That bad, huh?"

"Carmen," I whine. "I don't even know what's going on."

She places her hands back in front of her, intertwining her fingers and patiently waiting for me to continue. And so I do. I tell her everything. Our agreement, our unspoken past that either one of us refuses to bring up, Hayden's mild obsession with random hookups and a specific dating app that seems to haunt me. And my broken heart that seems not as broken as before. In fact, the temporary Band-Aids are starting to wear thin and unnecessary. The wounds are healing and leaving behind healthy scars, a distinct reminder that I'm stronger now. And it's all thanks to Hayden.

When I finish, Carmen whistles. "Nat, that sounds kind of complicated."

"It really shouldn't be, right?"

Carmen shrugs. "I mean, yeah. It shouldn't be."

I lay my palms on the table, determined to move on from this. Intent on reverting back to what all of this is: two friends helping each other.

"Maybe you two should talk about it," Carmen suggests in a soft, cautious voice. "Before it becomes even more complicated."

I nod, shifting my gaze from my splayed-out hands to the unanswered questions of what all this means scattered around me. My phone rings, the light buzzing interrupting my wallowing. When I extract it from my purse, I see Hayden's name flash on the screen.

Speak of the devil. The devil with a flirty smile and warm hands.

"Hello?" There's no answer on the other side, just the soft ruffle of movement and background city noise. "Hayden? Are you there?"

Still no response.

"Hayden?"

"Nat," he finally calls. His rough voice is weak, devoid of energy or life. "I, uh…my dad…" His voice trails off. I stand to walk away from Carmen and the clamor within the busy cafeteria. I stop short of a glass wall displaying a grassy lawn which I find so peculiar in the middle of the city.

"Hayden, what happened?"

"My dad's…He's—" A muffled sob cuts off his sentence. "He died this morning."

Everything seems to stop around me. Utensils held mid-air as they make their way into the mouths of hungry hospital workers. Kitchen doors that swing open but stay stuck, giving me a glimpse of the hectic kitchen. And my heart. It feels numb. Like it actually stopped beating and is sitting in my chest as a hardened muscle while I process Hayden's words.

His dad died.

"Hayden, are you at home?" I manage.

He sniffles before answering. "I'm at work, but I'm going home right now."

"Okay, I'll meet you there."

32

Hayden

senior year

"LOOK AT THE BIRDIE!" my mom calls as my dad and I face the camera with his rough hand resting on my shoulder. The camera flashes as I hear my dad elongate a high-pitched "cheeese" through his teeth. "Okay, me next," my mom says, shooing away my dad from my side while shoving her camera in his hand.

Before she turns to face the camera my dad has angled toward us, she peers up at me with her twinkling eyes that continue to repeatedly mist over every time she looks at me in my cap and gown. She lifts her hand to flick the tassel dangling in front of my face. "Oh," she cries before looking away, wiping the tear off her cheek that slipped away.

"Marsha," my dad protests. "He's graduating high school, not moving to Antarctica."

I chuckle, glancing over at my dad. While he brushes off my mom's overabundance of emotions, I can see the same mistiness coating his eyes when he takes in my freshly ironed graduation attire.

"I need to get some tissues before all these tears ruin my makeup," my mom's teary voice calls as she scurries down the hallway.

Jeannie Choe

My dad lowers the camera, clearing his throat before taking a step toward me and placing a hand on my arm.

"We're really proud of you, Hayden," he says, his gruff voice cracking as his mouth presses together in a downturned frown.

"Thanks, Dad," I say, still a little shy from all the attention that I've gotten in the last days dwindling down to graduation. I look up at the threshold to our front door where my mom taped a "Congrats Grad" banner and silver mylar balloons, all glittering against the hallway lights. And unexpectedly, my dad takes another step closer and pulls me in for a hug that lasts about four and a half seconds. He pats my back, pulling away before nodding as if silently telling himself his job is done.

It's moments like this that make me feel guilty for ever feeling any instance of anger or frustration toward my dad. For every time he nudged a little too aggressively to seek out a future he deemed appropriate, there was a moment where his emotions peeked through. Where those moments were wiped away with a pat of encouragement or a more acute focus on other things, like our shared love for fantasy football leagues and my mom's baked goods. It makes me wish that my future plans mirrored his so that I could enjoy these moments rather than focusing on those times our disagreements left lingering marks of resentment and disappointment.

"Okay," my mom calls, reentering the room with a wad of tissues held up in her hand. "I have these for emergencies."

She stops next to me, her eyes landing on my dad as she notices him wiping at his eyes. He tries to hide it, turning away to face the other direction, but then my mom offers him a tissue.

"I'm fine," he answers, waving his hand at her offer. "I just have something in my eye."

My mom smirks, rolling her eyes as she tucks herself under my arm, once again ready for our picture.

"One more and then we have to leave," my dad says, clearing his throat as he raises the camera once again.

present

When I was twelve, my dad gave me a worn copy of *The Outsiders*. It was his favorite book and one that his father passed down to him too. At that young age, I didn't understand the value of a book. I hated reading. I brought the book with me when I left home for college, finally seeing that reading may be a hobby I could dip into. I still hadn't read it, but it didn't feel right leaving it behind. So in between classes, sitting in the courtyard and in the library, I read it. First, to see what the big deal was. And then the second time, while sitting at an outdoor terrace in Place de la Comédie, it was to feel a closer connection with my dad and my grandpa while I was an entire world away. Then, the numerous times after that, I continued to read it because it brought on a sense of comfort. The feeling of being home away from home.

As soon as I walk into my apartment, still dressed in my chef's uniform, I walk to my room and straight to my dresser. I open the drawer that holds the book, shoved into the back, all crumpled and neglected. I haven't read it in over two years, since the last time I saw my dad. I can't bring myself to read it now, to open it and look at my grandfather's name written on the cover page, marking it as his. Ours. So instead, I clutch it against my chest, reminding myself how it felt to be held by my dad when I cried because I scraped my knee as a child. Or listening to his soft words calm me as he taught me to drive. Or hearing his controlled anger lecture me when I came home past curfew.

I will never be welcomed by his embrace again. Never be able to walk through the doors of my childhood home and hear his voice ring through the rooms. Never see him stand by my mom as they wave me off, driving away and reminding me to stay safe on the road. He will never watch me have a family of my own, hold his grandkids, or meet whoever I choose to spend the rest of my life with.

I will never be able to tell him that I'm sorry I was so selfish for the past two years. That I wish I would have put my anger and pride aside so that we could come to some sort of medium. A balanced agreement

Jeannie Choe

where we would both be satisfied and continue the relationship we carried as father and son. That's never going to happen.

A heart attack.

He survived a fall from our roof while putting up Christmas lights, a beer-infused fight in a crowded bar on St. Patrick's Day years before I was even born, and even a concussion when he was sixteen playing football. But he couldn't survive this.

The doctors told my mom it was so intense, so massive, that his body gave out before they rolled him on the gurney through the hospital doors.

He's gone. My entire world withered away into ashes. I just got him back, our stubbornness having pulled us apart. And just as quickly, he's been taken from me.

33

Natalia

present

WHEN I KNOCK on the door, there's no answer for a long time. No shuffling of feet, no sound of life from the other side. Until the lock slowly clicks and the knob turns gently, finally allowing me access.

I don't know what to expect. Anger, sadness, laughter, craze, or nothing at all. All I know is that Hayden needs me. And I want nothing more than to be there for him.

He stands there, one hand braced along the doorframe and his head lowered so it hangs between his shoulders, his hair sticking out in different places from his fingers raking through it. His eyes don't meet mine. They stay far off, looking at everything and nothing. He steps back, letting me follow instep as I close the door behind me. He still doesn't look at me, but I watch as the tears pool along the rims of his eyes.

"Hayden?" I call softly. He doesn't answer. So I bend my knees, lowering myself so I stand below him, forcing his eyes to meet mine. "Hayden," I call again.

It's then that he finally looks at me with sad eyes and a weak smile as if whispering the silent lie: *I'm okay.* When I don't smile back, silently letting him know that he doesn't have to be so stoic about his dad's death, I finally see the pain relent. The betrayal that life just tossed at him with the heartbreak that he will never see his dad again.

His chin quivers as a tear spills down his cheek. His face twists and turns as the reality of his dad's death crashes into him like a fresh wave, vicious and unapologetic.

When your world comes crashing down on you, you crumble with it. Nothing in your muscles or bones is enough to hold you together, so you submit to the weight of everything. That's exactly what Hayden does. He crumbles, sinking into my arms as I feel the ripple of sobs tear through him. Our legs give out as we sink to the floor with his face buried into my shoulder. I wrap my arms around him as he clings to my waist.

And I cry with him. I cry knowing that he will never be able to see his dad and welcome him back into his life like he planned to. Knowing that I will never be able to ease this aching pain cutting through his heart. That there is nothing I can do to help him.

Every mark of pain that etches into his heart etches into my own. I feel the grief he let filter through his chest and into his soul as his cries ring through the silent apartment.

"Hayden..." I whisper through my own tears. "I'm so sorry." My heart feels tight in my chest as I grieve alongside Hayden, not knowing what to do. *What do I do? How can I fix this?*

His hold on me grows tighter as he buries his face into my neck. He doesn't say anything, doesn't plead or curse. He keeps crying as I continue to whisper "I'm sorry, I'm so sorry" into his temple. And every time I say it, his hands move to a different part of my body, clawing at me to hold him close. To console him and comfort him. Because this is what he needs right now. Me, wrapping my arms around him and carrying the heaviness in his heart so that he doesn't bear the weight of it on his own.

We sit there for I don't know how long but eventually, Hayden's cries die down, and we lean against the door with his head on my shoulder. I hold his hand in my lap, squeezing it every so often to let him know that I'm still here, still feeling everything that he's feeling.

My best friend is losing a piece of himself. And the only thing I can do is hold his hand through it.

Hayden stares out the small window, neither square nor oval, watching the pearl of clouds settled over the horizon. I gently place my hand on his, now resting loosely on the armrest between us. When he feels the warmth of my hand, he slowly turns toward me. The glow of light streaming into the cabin softens his features and the pain in his eyes.

When our cries died down as we sat on the floor of his apartment, leaving us a tangle of limbs comforting each other, I helped him make travel arrangements. He called his mom, letting her know that he would be home in the morning. I emailed Mark to let him know I wouldn't be in the office for the next couple of days. Family emergency.

Because that's what this is, isn't it? Hayden is family, becoming a fixture in my life that I consider kin and familiar.

Once we settled our itinerary, I went back to my apartment just after midnight and packed a small carry-on, adding the only modestly appropriate black outfit I have. Just in case. We met in front of the airport, silent and solemn, and I took Hayden's hand and walked through La Guardia to go back home.

When I look at his face now, his tired features exhausted from the tears, he smiles weakly.

"Thank you for coming with me," he whispers. Not "you didn't have to come," not "I can do this on my own." Because it would be a lie. I do have to be here with him. If not for him, then for me. I can't let my best friend walk into this alone.

"Of course," I answer, my head resting against the seat.

When we land, we part. We both agreed it would be best that he go home alone, assess the situation with his mom and extended family, and I come over when things have settled. Or as settled as they could be.

Jeannie Choe

So I take a cab home to my parents' house.

When I walk through the doors of my childhood home, using the key that I never gave back to my parents, I'm hit in the chest with everything familiar and warm. The sounds and memories of me and my sisters listening to pop music, or my dad watching TV in his recliner and my mom incessantly scrapbooking or watering her plants.

My mom rounds the corner from the kitchen, her floral apron wrapped around her over her work clothes as she dries her hands on a thin dish towel.

"Natalia?" she asks. "What are you doing here?"

I don't answer her. Instead, I drop my luggage at my feet and walk toward her, my feet heavy against the thick carpet. I wrap my arms around her neck and sink into her warmth. And I sob. I cry knowing that I can hold her in my arms. Knowing that her physical self is here, in front of me, worried that there's something wrong with me.

"Nat, you're scaring me. What happened?"

"I love you, Mommy," I mumble into her hair.

34

Hayden

present

AS SOON AS I walk through the front door of my childhood home, I'm rushed with a greeting from every mourning relative that gathered around the living room. My aunts and uncles, cousins, and even family friends that my parents gained over the decades they've spent in Ohio, growing within this life that revolved around routine and consistency. A standard that I walked away from and now regret with everything in me. Because if I had stayed at home, listened to everything my dad asked me to do with my life, I would've been there to say goodbye. I wouldn't be carrying around this anvil of guilt making my heart heavy.

"Hayden!" my mom calls from the living room. She runs toward me, her arms wide open and eyes rimmed red. She pulls me close to her, running her hand up and down my back as she sniffles back her tears. "I'm so glad you're home."

The next hour becomes a blur. I'm ushered into the living room, extending my greeting to everyone while my aunt passes around plates of some slop she claims is casserole. My own remains on my plate, cold and uneaten, as I can't stomach a single thing.

Late into the evening, when it's just me and my mom, we sit across from each other at the kitchen island, the dim light hovering over us like a spotlight. I stay quiet while my mom fidgets with her wedding ring. I wonder to myself how long she'll wear it until I push that thought out of my head.

"We were going to visit you," she says, her quiet voice louder than it actually is over the silence. I look up at her, but her gaze is settled on her ring, the diamonds and platinum twirling around her finger. "He wanted to go and see your restaurant. Eat your food."

I sigh as I run a hand over my face, scraping against the day-old scruff settled around my jawline. When I don't say anything, she keeps going.

"He really was proud of you. When Pat called and gave him crap for being so stubborn, he changed. It sounds strange, but it was like he knew he needed to let you know how proud he was. Like he knew he was saying goodbye." The last of her words are drowned in a sob as she wipes her eyes with a napkin that's become a permanent fixture to her hand as the day has worn on.

I stand, round the counter, and wrap my arms around her to console her.

"I'm sorry, Mom," I whisper into her hair.

She turns to look at me, her soft smile peeking through the quivering of her chin. "Oh, honey. You don't have to be sorry."

I shake my head. "No, I should have just listened to him. Done what he wanted. Then at least I would've had the last two years with him."

She stands from her stool, swiveling to face me as she stands over a foot shorter than me. She holds my arms in her hands, squeezing them to get my attention. The tears start welling up as my throat constricts with the regret lodged there. *So many regrets.*

"Hayden, listen to me," she urges. When the first of my tears fall, I finally look at her. "Your father wanted what was best for you. Your future, college, everything. He just wanted what he thought was best. But he was wrong."

I become a blubbering mess as her solemn eyes look at me, convincing me that my choices aren't a mistake. Her hand reaches to move my hair out of my face and wipe my tears. Although it's point-less, as the tears don't seem to stop.

"He was stubborn, and you had to deal with the result of that stub-bornness. But don't you for a second believe that he wasn't proud of you."

I sob, lowering my head onto her shoulder as she pats my back. "I just miss him. So much."

"I know, baby. I know."

I'm sitting on a twin-size bed, decorated with yellow floral sheets and a stuffed walrus named Harold, in Natalia's childhood bedroom. My back is leaned up against the wall where Harry Styles's face is smiling directly at me. I would move further away, but then I'd be eye-to-eye with Robert Pattinson.

"You know that Edward dude was wearing a wig when he filmed *Twilight*?"

Natalia's head pops up from behind her laptop, and her brow furrows, with a scowl of disapproval on her face. "No, he wasn't. You made that up."

I shrug.

She rolls her eyes before returning her intense gaze back to her lit-up screen.

I've been back home for twenty-four hours now, and I had to get out of my house. The family members that were there when I arrived returned in a swarm the following morning, fawning over me and my mom as we assured them we didn't need more food. I needed to get some air. So I called Natalia, hoping to spend some time with her and get my mind off funeral planning. With all the arrangements jotted down by the funeral planner my mom hired, the service will take place this Friday. It's fast. Too fast. In a few days, we'll be saying our good-byes and lowering my dad's casket into the family plot where my grandparents are buried.

I want to bring Natalia back to my house, introduce her to my mom so she understands that Natalia is important to me but with the chaos that's settled in our living room, it'll have to wait.

My foot that's extended over the edge of the bed taps the bottom of Natalia's where her leg hangs over the opposite knee. She looks up at me again but this time, there's no hint of the annoyance she carried when I dissed Edward Cullen.

"You want to talk?"

I simultaneously shrug and scratch my head. "I think I'm getting a little bit of cabin fever."

She closes her laptop and gently places it on her desk, where it sits under a corkboard of pictures with her and her sisters and string lights that are turned off.

"Come on, Marshall," she says, her hand patting my thigh as she stands up from her cushy lounge chair. She reaches for the keys to her dad's minivan and turns back to face me. "I know just what you need."

After a fifteen-minute drive, we turn down multiple streets that start to look familiar. Residential areas that have warning signs for children crossing and the repetitiveness of stop signs and speed bumps. After a final turn, we come face to face with Coolidge View High. The parking lot is full of cars parked half haphazardly in assigned spots and those that are marked as student or faculty. Natalia pulls into an empty spot with the sign Visitor posted at the head.

"Aren't we a little late for biology class?" I joke as she turns the ignition off.

She smiles as she opens the door, reaching for her keys before exiting. I follow suit before I look at the large span of space ahead of us. The football field, re-turfed since we left, holds a newly designed scoreboard with a modern looking falcon painted next to the digital zeros on display. It sits empty, most likely in between classes, so we sort of dawdle toward the end of the wired fence where there's an opening leading to the bleachers.

"Isn't this trespassing?" I ask.

"I think they make some sort of exception for alumni," she answers. "I mean, come on. We should get some sort of consolation for surviving four years here."

I smirk as I climb the steps up the bleachers, walking all the way to the top, where we get an even wider view of the field. Natalia follows, her hands outstretched as she teeters side to side to maintain her balance. I reach out a hand for her as she takes the final step to the top, then drop it when she lands with a slight thud next to me.

"Wow," she gasps. We both sit, looking out toward the field. The wind blows between us, causing us to fold our arms inward.

"Does it feel smaller to you?"

She turns to look at me, giggling. "Maybe you just got bigger." She pokes at my side which makes me poke her back before we dissolve into giggles.

When our laughter dies, she leans her head against my shoulder, wrapping her hand along my forearm. She inhales deeply, breathing in the fresh air that we both forgot about when we moved to the city.

"Did you ever think you'd be back here?" she asks softly as her eyes gently close.

I shake my head. "Never in a million years."

She opens her eyes and turns to look at me. "I'm sorry you aren't here under better circumstances, Hayden."

I give a tight-lipped smile instead of shaking my head. I can agree with her. Maybe even tell her that I wish my circumstances were different and that I weren't here with her. But I can't imagine a better place than being right here, right now, with her.

"I'm glad I'm here with you," I whisper, the honesty seeping through me.

She smiles, her face lighting up as she looks at me. My hand lurches just then before fisting at my side. I stop it from moving even an inch. I stop it from cradling her face, brushing away her hair, and tucking it behind her ear.

"Nat," I start to whisper. I don't know what I want to tell her, but I need to say something. Anything to get this well of confusion to shift into something sure. But then we're interrupted by the muffled tone of a new alert on my phone in my pocket. An obnoxious twang that rings so quietly but sounds loud in the small space between us. When we both hear it, she pulls away, and her hand drops to her side before she faces the open field again.

I grimace, taking a deep breath and cursing whoever it is that interrupted us. I hate that she pulled away so quickly. Both she and I know what the telltale sounds that came from my phone mean, but it doesn't mean anything to me. I don't care who's on the other side of that message. What woman is waiting for me to respond to the Cupid's Bet message that caused us to separate. I just want to be right here with Natalia.

I clear my throat. "When are you flying back?"

"I'm staying the rest of the week," she answers. "I got a flight out Friday night."

I nod.

"I thought I would stay for the service," she adds hesitantly. "If you want me there."

I look at her, her eyes cautiously searching mine as she gauges my reaction.

"Of course I want you there," I finally say.

35

Hayden

present

"I MET Greg when I was fourteen. I was just about to enter high school, and my big sister brought home this big, burly quarterback that looked at her like she was the stars and treated our family like his own. And I knew then that he wasn't just my sister's boyfriend, but my brother as well." Uncle Pat's voice rings through the funeral home, his body raised behind a low podium next to a blown-up picture of my dad. "When I went to college, he and Marsha dropped me off at my dorms. He never treated me as an extension of Marsha but rather myself as an individual. He told me, 'Patrick, I don't care what happens with me and Marsha, I'll always be here for you.' He will always be my brother. Not a brother-in-law or an extension of my sister, but my brother."

Natalia sits next to me in the row of folded chairs, her hip brushing against mine as her hand covers my clenched fists. She looks ahead, a soft, polite smile spread on her lips as Pat continues his memories of my dad and him. Ones that didn't include my mom but were distinct to two of the most important men in her life before I came along.

After my mom takes the podium following Pat, thanking everyone for coming through a fresh wave of tears, we all stand and make our way back to my house for the reception. Natalia drives, her dad's minivan coming to a stop in front of my house as I sit in the passenger seat. Cars line the streets, people funneling toward the front door to my parents' house, and we both watch, sitting in silence as I take a moment to prepare myself.

"Ready?" Natalia's soft voice calls from the driver's seat.

I turn back to her, looking away from my house. I nod.

"Hi, Hadey." My aunt Rita greets me in the kitchen once her hands are finally free from rearranging several platters ready to be moved to the table in our formal dining room. "How you holding up?"

I nod an acknowledging nod. "Is Mom around?"

"She went into the basement to grab some tablecloths."

I nod again, a new staple in my form of non-verbal communication. "Did you need help with anything?"

She looks down at the large spread. "Maybe just bring some of these out." I reach for a large platter holding deviled eggs when she stops me. "Actually, can you grab the cooler from the garage? Pat brought in the ice so we could fill it."

"Sure," I answer, stepping away.

Natalia, who's been hovering around me, steps in. "I can take these," she says softly. Aunt Rita looks back at me, silently urging me for an introduction.

"Uh, this is my friend, Natalia."

Natalia smiles at Aunt Rita by way of greeting her with her hands full.

"I'm Rita. Nice to meet you, sweetheart. Thank you for helping."

"Of course," Natalia answers before turning to walk to the dining room.

When Natalia is out of earshot, Aunt Rita turns to me. "Is she your girlfriend?" Her eyes bounce with expectancy at the first girl that I've ever brought home.

I tilt my head. "Really? Now?"

She smiles softly, her hand reaching to stroke my arm. "She's pretty. And very sweet."

I shake my head. "So the cooler?"

She nods. "I'll keep an eye on your friend."

I raise my brows before heading toward the door leading to our garage, only to get hit in the gut with everything that represents my dad. I flip the light switch next to the doorway. The fluorescent lights flicker on and are barely bright enough to light up the workstation in one corner. When I look to the other side, I see road signs and old license plates mounted on the wall next to a flat screen. A raggedy recliner faces it, right next to a small table with coasters stacked neatly in the middle.

Everything about this space, a room in this home meant to house a car, screams Greg Marshall. Football trophies from his high school heyday sitting on a shelf, Cleveland Browns memorabilia strategically placed next to them acting like a makeshift NFL shrine.

I walk to the recliner, not sitting in it but running my hands along the soft leather. I don't want to taint this space that'll serve as a last memory of my dad. I want to preserve it as long as I can. As if I can grasp the fading memory of him before it slips through my fingers, just like the unfinished business I had with him. All the plans I laid out since his phone call to make up for the last two years we lost, all misting into thin air.

"He got that chair at a garage sale over the summer." When I look at the doorway, I see my mom's sad face watching me. "He refused to pay thousands on a La-Z-Boy, so he dragged that onto his pickup and slumped it right there. He was going to move everything down to the basement once it got colder but..."

She walks toward me, folded tablecloths resting between her hands, before she stops next to me. She reaches up to squeeze my arm, moving her hand up to pat my shoulders.

"Come on, honey. You should eat something," she whispers, her voice giving her away.

"Actually, I think I'm going to go lie down. If that's okay."

She nods, her downturned eyes looking at me with understanding.

36

Natalia

present

I RETURN to the kitchen once the last of the platters have been brought out. The kitchen island sits empty now aside from a few serving utensils and unopened soda bottles.

"Natalia, thank you so much for your help," Hayden's mom says softly from the other side.

"Of course, Mrs. Marshall. Anything I can do to help, please let me know."

"Oh, honey. Marsha, please."

A small, humorous smile twitches at my lips.

She grins back, the first I've seen since Hayden introduced me to her at the funeral home. "Marsha Marshall. I guess I should have been a bit pickier about who I married, huh?"

I smile fondly back at her. I can almost see the fresh memory of her husband returning front and center as her smile softens.

"Whew! I think that's it, Marsh." We're interrupted by Rita returning from the dining room as her hand moves to wipe the loose hairs from her forehead. "You must be hungry," she says to me. "Why don't you get something to eat? You can sit in here if you don't feel like mingling with everyone out there."

The appreciation on my face can't be more obvious. But my attention is on something else. "Actually, have you seen Hayden?"

"He went to go lie down in his room," Marsha answers with a weak smile.

"Oh."

"It's up the stairs. Second room to the right."

I lower my head, nodding as both she and Rita turn to leave the kitchen and enter the packed living room. A hint of hesitancy causes my body to pause, making me brace the countertop instead of walking out of the kitchen. Maybe Hayden wants to be alone. Maybe he doesn't need me to invade his space and instead wants to linger in his grief alone so he can do so without feeling like he has to hold back or hide. But then that doesn't feel right. It doesn't feel right to let him work through this alone, pushing aside those who offer their condolences, including his mother's warm embrace. I need to be there for him when he's ready to open the floodgates and let everything spill.

"Natalia?"

When I turn in the direction where my name was called, I come face to face with Jenny Chen. She looks like she hasn't aged a day. The only difference is the dark-haired toddler wearing a dress shirt with a teeny-tiny bow tie perched on her hip.

"Oh my god. It is you!" she exclaims. She steps toward me, pulling me into her for a quick embrace before her baby protests. Jenny looks at her baby and bends down to retrieve the pacifier that fell from his mouth. "How have you been?"

She turns toward the kitchen sink and runs the pacifier under the faucet before plopping it back into her baby's mouth.

"Good," I answer quietly, eyeing the natural and maternal way she wipes off a smear of crusties staining her baby's cheek.

"I can't believe you're here! My husband, Jack, is Greg's nephew," she explains. "How did you know Greg?"

My hand bracing the counter grips the hard surface tighter, and I start to tap my thumb along the rounded edge. "Oh, um, I didn't," I answer, looking away from her. "I'm here with Hayden."

She scoffs lightly, then smiles at me with her head tilted to one side

Jeannie Choe

as she shifts her baby from one hip to the other. "I knew he had a thing for you," she says.

"Oh no," I say, my hands coming up between us, denying her incorrect assumption. "I'm just here as a friend. There's nothing—"

She chuckles. "It's fine." She waves her hand at me. "High school was such a long time ago."

I lower my head and settle my gaze on the shiny linoleum floor.

"I didn't really dwell on it because I was so angry but when he got into that fight with Alex Spencer because of you, I knew there was something going on. No matter how much he denied it."

My brow furrows as I look up to face her. "He what?"

"He walked up to Alex and punched the daylights out of him," she explains. "It was right after prom."

I don't care that I look too curious, too eager. I lean toward her, my eyes serious and pleading for more information. "Did he say why?"

Her own brow scrunches in confusion.

"Why they got into a fight," I explain.

"Oh," she says, her hand lifting slightly. "Not really, but I think he mentioned something like Alex fu—messing up." She looks at her baby, smoothing his hair as if suddenly remembering that he's there.

I nod.

"Anyway," she continues. "We broke up after that."

"You did?"

She nods. "We were so young and so wrong for each other," she explains. "And...I didn't want to be second fiddle to anyone."

"Jenny," I say, doing my best to sound apologetic, even though I didn't know all of this happened. "Hayden and I were always just friends. There was never anything going on."

"I know." She lifts her hand to graze my arm, giving it an assuring squeeze. "But he saw you as more than that."

Her baby starts to wail just then, clawing at his mom's shoulders as he turns to bury his face into her neck. "Oop, someone's getting a little fussy," she says, nuzzling her face into her baby's hair. "I should get him down for a nap."

"Yeah," I answer. "It was nice seeing you."

"You too, Natalia."

256

37

Hayden

senior year

MY BRAIN FEELS FOGGY, slightly muddled from the alcohol. What's that age-old saying? Beer before liquor? Or is it liquor before beer? I guess it doesn't really matter at this point. I've already consumed what feels like half of the keg sitting outside Toby's parents' lake house. And I've lost track of the shots of Jack I've taken in between those Solo cups of beer.

I'm walking through the kitchen, my steps heavy and lazy, making my way toward one of the coolers lined up against the wall when I'm stopped by Jenny.

"Hayden!" she squeals. "Oh my god! I can't believe how drunk I am!"

I lean forward, risking my balance as I dig through the chips of ice for a bottle of water. I chug, emptying the entire bottle as Jenny tosses back her own red cup filled with who knows what. As soon as the refreshing water hits my stomach, I already feel better. I reach for a second and a third, extending one of them to Jenny. She takes it hastily before placing it on the counter nearest to her instead of drinking it.

"I think I want another beer," she slurs, her eyes hooded as her hand lazily runs up my stomach. "Can you get me one?" She bats her eyes at me with a crooked smile.

I nod, peering above her head in the direction of the keg sitting outside. As I walk away from Jenny, my steps are less draggy, more purposeful. As if Jenny approaching me for more than a simple request for beer brought on a moment of clarity, a moment where I needed to wear a layer of armor so I didn't fall for her advances.

Just as I approach the keg, I notice Natalia walking toward the dock out back where it's settled under an awning and overlooking the dark water behind the lake house. I step away from the keg, leaving behind Jenny and her subliminal request for more than beer. I follow Natalia's path to find that she's leaned up against the railing facing the water.

"Hey, Marquez," I call as I take the last step onto the wood planks. She turns to look over her shoulder, smiling an easy, relaxed smile. Almost as if she's been expecting me. "I didn't think you were the post-grad partying type."

"Yuri dragged me," she answers, sliding over to make room for me. I sidle up to her, brushing my arm against hers.

"So how does it feel to be an official high school graduate?" I ask, lightly nudging her.

"Outlandish," she says with a small hum. "You?"

"Underwhelming."

She chuckles. "Did you expect trumpets and fireworks when you walked off that stage?"

"I did," I jokingly admit. "So what are your plans for the summer?"

Her shoulders roll back, and her back straightens before she turns to face me. "I'm heading out to New York next month."

"Already?" I question, my smile disappearing instantly.

She nods. "My sister's already out there, so she said I could stay with her until the semester starts. Get to know the city and settle into my dorm a week or two before my first day on campus."

I smile a small smile, exhaling a smirk. "Beavercreek's going to miss you."

"Beavercreek? Or you?" She tilts her head in my direction, her cheek leaning against her turned-up shoulder as she smiles shyly at me.

"Maybe...mostly me," I say, my voice hushed and low. Her shoulder drops, her cheesy smile fading into a cautious one. My eyes land on her hand that's resting on the railing, trailing the soft skin glowing under the string lights hung above us. My fingertips graze over the back of her hand, tracing her knuckles as I swallow the ball lodged into my throat. Maybe it's the alcohol or the thought that I may never see her again, but I feel bold, causing me to say things that I wouldn't have otherwise. "I'm going to miss you a lot, Natalia."

I look into her eyes twinkling against the white glow of the moonlight. Without even thinking about it, about what would happen next if I kissed her the way I want to so badly, my hand cups her cheek. Her eyes flutter as a breeze blows between us, and a lock of her hair brushes against her lips. I reach to tuck the loose strand behind her ear, focusing my eyes on her full lips that part just enough for a small sigh to squeeze through.

A knot twists in my chest. It tightens and chokes back everything I want to tell her. I want to tell her how much I've been thinking about her over the past few months. I want to tell her that I'm so fucking scared of letting her go, no matter how much I know she isn't mine to let go in the first place. I want to tell her that what happened at prom, us kissing and never talking about it again, is something that I don't regret anymore. Even though it caused a wedge between us, leading us away from our normally uncomplicated friendship, the feeling of her lips on mine canceled out every one of those regrets, every whisper of doubt. Because kissing her was worth it.

I want to tell her that I'm falling for her. That she coaxed a side of me to break through, allowing me to face what I thought I was too cowardly to face. And I want her to tell me not to let her go. That I don't need to because she'll wait for me, whatever that means.

And then she does something that flutters a leap of hope to bloom in my aching chest. She says my name in a way that she knows all of these hopes and whims I'm thinking, wishing for them to be true.

"Hayden."

Her hand moves to grip my forearm, her delicate fingers tracing my skin, not to stop me but to encourage me. To do what it is that I want to do. Something that she won't push away this time.

My head lowers, angling toward her. But I feel so scared. Because when I'm with Natalia, fear fuels every action I make. Fear that she'll reject the idea of us because we don't make sense. The sweet, quiet girl who has dreams to see the world and make a difference alongside the scared, ill-prepared jock who doesn't know what he wants.

But still…

I brush my cheek against hers. I nuzzle into her soft skin and the vanilla that makes her smell like home. I feel her warm breath skirt against my cheek. And she whispers my name again, her breath catching as she speaks gently against my skin.

"Hayden."

Just as I'm about to turn to face her, we're interrupted by the loud splashing of water, causing me to drop my hand. When we both turn to look toward the water's edge, we see a horde of people running to the still water and breaking the surface with their excited squeals and thrashed movements. I turn back to look at Natalia, a solemn look replacing the far-off one she had a second ago.

"I'm going to miss you too, Hayden."

present

My body sinks into my twin-size bed. I'm facing the dresser sitting no more than two feet from the side of my bed. When I was fifteen, the space didn't seem so small. Now an adult that has long outgrown the growth spurt phase, I'm muddling over how I can rearrange my room so I don't have to walk sideways to get through that small space.

But why? What's the point of making plans, rearranging things to fit a life that I don't even live anymore? A life that fills me with guilt and something similar to penitence.

My fingers toy with the charcoal-toned buttons on my sleeve that shimmer like gray pearls. I realize what a poor job I did ironing my shirt this morning when I notice the creases running along the sides of my arm.

There's a soft knock on my door. Before I even look up and allow whoever's on the other side entrance, I already know who it is. I can tell by the gentleness of her knuckles against the hard wood and the cautious movements opening wider the door left ajar. And my heart lightens just the smallest bit, jumping as I anticipate seeing Natalia.

As she takes the first step through the threshold, I look up to see her sad eyes looking at me. "Can I come in?" she asks softly, her eyes trained on me as I look away.

I nod.

She walks slowly before sitting next to me on my bed. The sunken mattress groans a bit, sinking deeper as we lean against each other from the caved-in springs.

She leans her head against my shoulder. Her hand wraps around my forearm before resting in my hand. She's done this a dozen times, naturally staking her place against me as if there was never a time when she wasn't a part of my life. But instead of folding her hand into mine, clasping her fingers to wrap around my palm, she links our fingers together. They intertwine into a woven knot, spreading my fingers and nestling hers between them. My heart thumps a beat harder as the warmth from her skin settles into the grooves of my hand.

When I turn to look down at her, she lifts her head, and our mouths stop inches away from each other.

We both stay quiet, our shallow breaths warming each other's skin. I let my eyes wander down to her lips, committing every crease and wrinkle to memory while revisiting how it felt to have them on mine. How they felt so warm and sweet while reminding me of everything bright and colorful.

My hand gravitates up to cup her cheek, and her skin feels so soft, so tender. She leans into my hand, closing her eyes as I watch her body sink into my touch. My thumb runs along her cheek, stroking her skin, then running along the bottom edge of her lower lip as it moves against the pad of my thumb.

A hunger takes over me. I no longer care to hold everything back because I feel like I've given up on doing so. So I kiss her. I close the inches of space between us and open my mouth, latching onto hers as she kisses me back. Her hand moves to rest on my waist, holding on to me as I feel her fingers press into my covered skin. When she angles her face to the side and her lips open wider, letting my tongue lick the slick surface of her mouth, I taste a flavor that can only be described as *need*.

I lean forward and hover over her as I lay her down on my bed. I press into her, shifting my weight so I don't crush her, and I move her legs apart with my knee. She gives a soft moan into my mouth, and I feel her hips push into me. I respond with a deep groan of my own and she whimpers. She fucking *whimpers*, and that sound coming from her turns the concrete wall I put up to avoid this crushing feeling in my chest into rubble and dust.

My hands move from her face to her waist, urgently pulling at her simple black dress. I start lifting the low hem, skimming along the soft skin of her bent knee before riding up higher to her bare thigh. I know she can feel the urgency, from every knead of my hands to my hardening dick invading the almost nonexistent space between us, but I don't even care at this point.

This is what I want to spend the rest of my life doing. Kissing Natalia, feeling her warm skin under my fingertips and never having to think of all the regrets in my life. Like never reconciling with my dad in time to rebuild a relationship with him. Or having let go of Natalia all those years ago.

Let her go.

I can't let her go. But what if I don't have a choice? Like the first time I did. What if no matter how strong my grip holds on her, she leaves? Because we don't belong to each other. And if this doesn't work out, if *this* crumbles like so many other things in my life, how am I supposed to go on without her?

I break our kiss, her lips pulling with mine before she realizes that I'm pulling away. Her eyes, full of everything from fear to curiosity to want, search mine, twinkling against the glowing twilight streaming in from the windows.

I lower my head, our foreheads leaning against each other as I exhale a deep sigh into the space between us.

"Hayden?" she says breathlessly.

"I shouldn't have done that," I say hoarsely. The pain and willpower it took to stop that kiss fills the cracks that make my voice weak and shaky. And instead of fighting me like I want her to, she nods. "I'm sorry," I whisper.

She closes her eyes and shakes her head, our foreheads still touching and her hand gently squeezing my bicep. Removing myself off of her, I snake my arm around her waist and sit her up.

We look at each other, our emotions on our sleeves and too many questions suspended in the air between us that neither one has answers to. We stay like this, looking at each other with all of our thoughts. Everything between hesitancy to yearning. But not regret. I don't regret kissing her. Just like the first time, I can't regret it.

"Hayden," she finally whispers. "You're my best friend. I–I don't want to lose you."

I smile a sad and weak smile. "I'm not going anywhere."

38

Natalia

present

I LEFT a couple of hours after the service, catching a flight just after midnight. Hayden stayed back a couple of extra days before leaving his mom's side on Sunday night. We haven't seen each other since Hayden dropped me off at the airport. Our last exchange was a text message from me to him letting him know that I made it back to New York City in one piece and that I left my laptop charger at his house the last time I had to jump on to answer some emails.

There's been no further discussion of our kiss. What it means, if it means anything at all. But I feel more confused than ever. The look smeared across his face when he stopped our kiss scared me more than anything else. I'm scared that he regretted it. Not because he didn't want to ruin our friendship, but because he didn't want to journey down a path he wasn't sure he wanted to take. To test the waters of us only to realize it wasn't worth the trouble.

And what of our lonely hearts? This whole time, us leaning on each other through our bouts of loneliness has remained intact because we've been able to see each other as just that: a shoulder to lean on when needed. But that line seems to blur now, creating this bottomless pit of doubt and questions to linger like a promise that was never to be made.

When I walk into my office on Monday, after a quick greeting to José, I settle into the work that piled up during my week-long absence, only working from my laptop in between the memorial service and nostalgic visits to my old stomping grounds. As I'm elbow deep in emails, I'm interrupted by a ping on my phone with a new text message from an unknown number.

> Unknown Number: So, I hear my annoying cousin can be a bit of a brat around the office. Can I make it up to you? Since I am the older one.

A pause.

> Unknown Number: Dinner?

I smile at my phone screen. While his number is not yet saved on my phone as this is our first digital interaction, I finally put two and two together to realize it's Shawn who's texting me.

> Me: Ah, but if it weren't for that annoying cousin, I wouldn't be cashing in on this dinner.

> Shawn: So I guess you should be thanking him for a free meal.

> Me: Nothing a seven-course meal topped with an expensive bottle of wine can't fix.

> Shawn: Exactly how annoying is he?

I smile at my screen again, finding myself amused by his good-natured humor and confidence. But then I think of Hayden. Hayden, who I have yet to see after our kiss.

When he kissed me, it felt like he was finally coming up for air. His lips moved hungrily. Like he had spent weeks mapping how that kiss would play out. I felt every bit of need pouring out of him. I chalked it up to him processing his grief, turning to intimacy during a time when he didn't know how to handle his dad's death. But my lips still burned, tingling with the urgency to have his lips on them again. What if he never stopped it? What if we went on until we let that fire burn into our souls and ignite everything that overflowed to the surface?

And then I remind myself he *did* stop it.

I chew on the inside of my cheek, pursing my lips and worrying my brows together as I mull over my answer to Shawn. When my response never comes, he sends another message.

> Shawn: How about this Friday? Seven?

Friday night...I don't have plans. No date with another man, no invitation to mollify that spiral of loneliness. But will Hayden be calling me? To see if I'll be feeling lonely with more plans to fill our shared loneliness? Should I be waiting for that call? I hate to think that if he does call, I'll have to tell him no. To tell him that our agreement is no longer necessary as I've chosen to fill my loneliness with someone else. Another man who would definitely treat our dinner as a date. But I can't keep doing this, leaning on Hayden to fill a void that I should be filling on my own. Because doing so means our relationship will teeter further away from that line that defines our friendship. One that he made clear when he pulled away from me.

Without a second thought, I text Shawn back.

> Me: Friday sounds perfect.

"You got me into this mess. The least you can do is help me figure out what to wear," I whine. My phone is held to my ear with my shoulder, and my neck feels sore from the strained position it's been sitting in for the past twenty minutes.

"Natalia," José says in a low voice in an attempt to soothe me. "You will be fine. Just wear a sexy little dress, and he won't be able to keep his hands off of you."

I groan. "That isn't helping."

"Why are you even stressing about it now? Isn't the date on Friday?"

I sigh this time, defeated and still clueless on what to wear to a real first date. Period. Something I haven't been on since I graduated college. *Oh my god. Has it been that long?*

"I just need a distraction, I guess."

"You have nothing to worry about. That boy is already smitten with you. You just have to be your sunny little self and charm him."

A rough knock on my door interrupts our conversation.

"I still need to look nice," I answer, getting up off my bed and walking out of my room.

"Honey, you always look nice."

I smile into my phone screen before peeking into our peephole. Through it, I see a man I recognize even through the distorted glass.

"Natalia?" I hear José call through my phone.

"I have to go," I barely whisper.

"Alrighty, baby girl. I'll see you tomorrow."

I don't extend any other greeting, simply hanging up before setting my phone down.

When I open the door, Matteo stands there, looking disheveled and tired. His eyes are rimmed red, and his facial hair is growing into an almost full beard. And his eyes look at me as if he's pleading. *For what?*

"Hi, Natalia."

"Matteo, what are you doing here?" I question.

"Can we talk?"

I don't move. I don't step aside for him to come in or even answer him.

When I stay silent for too long, he speaks again. "I just wanted to talk to you for a minute."

"I don't think that's a good idea," I finally say, my voice low and barely a whisper. He ducks his head lower. To listen to my soft voice or to intimidate me, I don't know, but I lean back in response.

"Is it because of your boyfriend?"

I blink, trying to decipher what boyfriend he's talking about. Then I remember our encounter. When I stood by, completely and utterly hopeless, as he and Hayden exchanged an awkward greeting. And I realize...I no longer feel so weak and broken. When did that hopelessness fade away?

"No," I answer, shaking my head. My answer sounds curt, bordering on blunt. From my rigid posture to the white-knuckled grip I still have on my door, nothing about my appearance says that he's welcome here. "I just don't think it's a good idea that..."

What? That we just talk? I can't even place why. But I know him being here, alone and looking the way he looks, can't end well.

"Is he here? With you?" he asks.

I shake my head again. "No."

He looks down at his feet, shuffling them as his rigid posture relaxes a bit. "I'll just be a minute."

I sigh, finally loosening the grip on the door and stepping aside to open it wider. He takes the cue and walks in, circling the small space of our entryway before turning back to face me.

"This is nice, Natalia," he comments sincerely. "Looks like you're doing well."

I close the door, locking the deadbolt in place before walking toward the kitchen. He follows close behind.

"Did you want something to drink?" I offer, using any excuse to avoid looking at him.

"Uh, sure. Whatever you have is good. Thanks."

I reach into the fridge, rummaging to find that all we have is orange juice and bottled water. I choose the latter before closing the door and walking it over to him. The air is so tense. So cold and frigid as we come face to face with the remnants of our failed relationship. One that I finally want to move on from.

He loosens the plastic cap and takes a small sip, twisting the cold bottle in his hands before facing me with narrowed eyes. It's then he hits me with the reason he came here tonight. "I miss you."

This is the moment I've been waiting months for. I imagined it, time after time, but so differently. I thought I would jump for joy and into Matteo's arms, thrilled that he finally realized how much I loved him. How much we belong together. But none of that happens. Instead, my brows pinch together, my whole face tightening as I feel angry and frustrated.

"Matteo, you're getting married."

He sighs, his hands fisting together on the counter. I watch as his knuckles turn white before he runs a hand through his dark hair. "This is all so fucked up, Natalia."

I shove down every impulse to ask him what he means. As curious as I am, I don't think I'm ready for his answer. Or maybe I truly don't care enough to ask.

He rounds the counter, his movements becoming urgent and rushed as he closes the space between us and braces a hand against the countertop. "I don't think I'm getting married."

"You don't *think*?" I question, unable to hide the accusation in my tone. "Matteo, what the hell does that even mean?"

"I don't know. I keep thinking about us and—"

I give an exasperated sigh as I take a small step away from him.

When I take in the man in front of me, the same man that I was head over heels in love with, I realize how foolish I was for letting those past moments of betrayal turn into shame and doubt for myself rather than holding him accountable for our failed relationship. All of the excuses I made for him, telling myself that he still loved me when he forgot our anniversary two years ago or pushing aside the hidden resentment when he stopped telling me how beautiful I looked or how lucky he was to have me. I told myself too many times that he still cared. That he was just too tired or forgetful or had a stressful day at the office. I realize that what we had, it wasn't love. It was habitual, ordinary, routine. Something that grew over time when we became too comfortable with one another. Something that I should have walked away from a long time ago but didn't know how to.

"Matteo…"

"It's that boyfriend of yours, isn't it?" he interrupts.

I sigh.

"I knew it when I ran into him at the bar. I knew I wasn't going to get you back." He looks back down at his feet, his shoulders slackened in defeat.

"What bar?" I blurt out.

He looks up at me, head tilted in confusion. "He didn't tell you?"

My silence is my answer.

He lets out a shaky exhale. "I was out with some friends, and I ran into him. I may have said some things that might have set him off and…"

"And what, Matteo?"

"We…" He pauses, his throat bobbing before he says, "He punched me."

"What the hell?" I gasp. "When was this?"

"I don't know," he says softly, shaking his head. "A couple of weeks ago?"

I can't believe it. Whatever happened between Hayden and Matteo, it had to be because of me. I turn away, raking my hair with my fingers before fisting them in frustration. "Matteo, I think you need to go," I finally say, facing him once again.

He looks at me, a slight rise of surprise evident in his rounded eyes and panicked face. "Natalia, I made a mistake."

"It doesn't matter," I say, a strain in my voice. "We're over. You *dumped* me, remember?"

"I know," he says, flinching away from the harsh truth. "And I wish I hadn't ended things with you the way that I did. And now I feel like I'm in such a mess."

"Do you love her?" I ask.

He doesn't answer. Instead, he keeps his gaze on the countertop. And when his silence answers my question, making me feel sorry for this woman that he made an empty promise to, I shake my head. "Matteo, you need to leave," I say again. "Whatever mess you need to work through, it isn't here. You need to talk to her."

He nods, his hands coming up to his face as he rubs out the knots of tension from his temples. "Yeah," he says with a defeated sigh. "Can I just say one thing?"

I tilt my head, waiting.

"I'm sorry. It was wrong of me to end things the way that I did," he says through a rough voice. "And...I just want you to know that I didn't plan on hurting you. I was just scared."

My deep-seated sigh is the forgiveness I didn't know I was ready to give. "Whatever's going on with you and Jacinda, work it out. Marry her, don't marry, that's none of my business. That's between you two. But don't make the same mistake you did with me."

"Yeah," he concurs. And without any other parting words, he walks out of my apartment.

39

Natalia

senior year

"IT LOOKS like our choices are narrowed down to The Fault in Our Stars or Transformers."

I turn to face Yuri as her eyes scan over the movie times displayed on the marquee. "I think Ansel Elgort is always the safest choice."

She smiles at me, stepping toward the box office window to purchase our tickets. "I'll get the tickets if you get the snacks," she offers, turning to face me over her shoulder.

"Okay," I agree. It's my last weekend before leaving for New York City on Monday, and I called Yuri to see if she wanted to spend one of my last nights in Beavercreek visiting our local metroplex so we could stuff our faces with popcorn and movie theater candy.

Once our tickets are taken at the turnstile, we walk up to the concession stand, eyeing the display case while deciding between the cherry or blue raspberry Icee.

"I'm going to use the bathroom," Yuri announces. "Just get me a bag of Skittles with the popcorn."

I nod and watch her walk away, taking a step forward as the line moves ahead. As I scan the crowd filled with Saturday night patrons filling the theater on this warm summer night, I see a familiar face. Hayden is stepping out of the theater room located near the far end of the concession stand, grinning, with a bucket of popcorn held in his arms. I'm about to call his name and wave at him when I see Jenny follow his steps out of the theater, linking her hand in his.

So many things have happened between me and Hayden. So many things that we never talked about but should have. Like why he kissed me at prom. Or why he didn't kiss me at the lake house.

Our friendship should have remained insignificant, a small traffic sign in the middle of the road reminding each other of a past linked to our future. But it feels more significant than that now. It feels more like a landmark than a passable road sign. When his warm hand rested on my cheek, it felt heavier than just a light brush of his skin against mine. It felt like by saying goodbye to him, I was leaving behind a piece of myself. Right inside that small classroom where the entirety of my senior year felt bundled and placed on the table Hayden and I huddled over.

Maybe it's more than just a feeling. Maybe it's something much more tangible, more real. Something that I should have grasped rather than let slip through my fingers. Maybe the warmth that I feel flooding through my veins means that Hayden should remain more than just another Coolidge View alumnus I'm saying goodbye to. He should be something more permanent, everlasting.

"Miss?"

I face the cashier behind the concession stand waiting patiently with a polite smile. I step up to the counter just as I watch Hayden link his arm around Jenny's shoulders, and the two walk out of the building.

present

As confused as I am after Matteo stops by, I don't cancel my date with Shawn. I'm more determined than ever to move on. To use this date as

273

a starting point so I can embrace my newfound appreciation for being single without the heaviness that Matteo left behind. But I'm finding that the heaviness is replaced by the confusion I feel clouding over my head. My heart's become torn in two, and I can't help but place Hayden at the center of the two halves.

After days of planning out my outfit for my date with Shawn, I still come up empty-handed. So on Friday night, thirty minutes before meeting with Shawn at Buca's, I'm standing dressed in my underwear with two narrowed down choices lying on my bed. It's either a black dress, clingy and short while exposing enough of my shoulders and arms to look sultry and a little too appealing to the opposite sex, or a bright floral romper that looks like something I would wear on a day trip to the beach.

Going with the obvious choice, I slip on the black dress, shimmying into it and hooking the thin straps onto my shoulders. I look at the mirror, watching as the thick fabric, ruched and bunching together down my middle, lines my curves. I admire the outfit, thinking about how Hayden looked at me in my Playboy bunny costume, eyeing all of the exposed areas while making light sweeps against my skin through the thin material.

This is something Hayden would like.

I shake my head, pushing aside those thoughts just as I hear the front door click open.

"Nat!" I hear Hayden's voice from the living room.

I didn't tell him about Matteo visiting me. I didn't know how to bring it up and ask why he got into a fight with Matteo without being prepared to hear the answer. Still, curiosity gnaws at me, and hearing his voice now makes my heart kick up a beat knowing that I'm keeping this small piece of information from him.

"I'm in here!" I call from my bathroom. I haven't zipped up my dress yet. I'm fully aware of the peek of my black bra showing between the V in the back of my dress as I lean forward across my sink to put on my earrings. From the reflection, I see Hayden round the corner into my bathroom with my laptop charger gripped in his hand.

"Are you going somewhere?"

I finish putting on my earrings before answering. "I have a date."

"With who?" A light scowl cuts through his face as he eyes my backside.

I clear my throat, the sudden tension in the room making it feel like the walls are closing in on me. "Um, with Shawn."

"Oh. He finally asked you out?"

I nod, my back still turned toward him.

"And you're wearing that?"

I finally turn to face him. "This?" I ask, waving my hand in front of my dress. "No, I'm changing into a scuba suit in a minute."

He doesn't smile at my sarcasm like he usually does. He doesn't even roll his eyes. Instead, his expression turns grim as his eyes travel the length of the dress down to the short hem.

"Why, does it look bad?"

He coughs into his fist. "Uh…"

My brows rise as I turn back around to apply lipstick. "Wow. That bad, huh?"

"No, it looks good."

We look at each other through the reflection, our eyes catching as I remember how his lips felt on mine. How his kiss felt warm and inviting, everything it shouldn't have. And I feel like he's thinking about the same thing.

"Anyway," I say, my voice shaky and nervous. "Thanks for dropping that off." I tilt my chin toward the black cord sitting in his hand.

"Uh, yeah. No problem."

I reach toward the zipper running down the middle of my back. My fingers graze against the flimsy metal as I struggle to reach it.

"Here," Hayden says gently. He steps forward, placing the cable on the counter as I lower my hands and let him help me. His hand sweeps my hair to one side, exposing my neck and shoulders before moving to pull the zipper up. His other hand grips at my waist, holding on as he tugs at the zipper. I can feel it vibrating as it slowly glides through my dress, causing the material to cinch at my waist.

When my dress comes to a full close between my shoulder blades, he doesn't step away. Instead, he hovers over the dip where my neck and shoulder meet. I know I should turn, say thank you and walk away, but I can't. The heat of his body absorbing into mine is too inviting. So I tilt my head, exposing more of my neck as his hot breath blankets over my skin, begging for him to touch me. My eyes involuntarily close, and I feel the hand that's still resting on my waist grip me harder.

As my head lolls, a whisper of a moan squeezes through my lips. Hayden clears his throat. "What time is your date picking you up?"

It takes me more than a few blinks before I realize that Hayden is no longer hovering behind me. In fact, he's stepped away and has walked into my living room, already settling onto my couch.

"He's not," I answer, following his steps. "I'm meeting him."

His brows knit together. "Where?"

"Buca's. On third."

"That's, like, ten blocks from here."

"I know," I answer. I'm hooking my heels, bending over as I lean against the back of the couch. "It'll take me like fifteen minutes."

He suddenly stands, putting on the jacket that he laid neatly on the back of the sofa.

"You're going to head home?"

"I'm going to walk you to the restaurant."

"What? Why?"

"You can't go out alone in the city looking like that." He stands, looping his arms through the sleeves of his jacket as he walks up to me.

I laugh. Not necessarily because I find anything particularly funny, but the tension between us is so tight, all I can do is laugh. But Hayden's not laughing. He's not even smiling. As he inches closer to me, his face becomes even grimmer. His lips are pulled together in a tight line, and his eyes narrow. His brows come together to shield his eyes, making them dark and a little unnerving.

I roll my eyes and smile nervously. "Thanks, Dad, but I think I'll be fine." I reach for my faux leather jacket hanging off our coat rack before looping an arm through the sleeve.

He leans forward, wiping the smile off my face. "Let's go, Natalia."

"How's your mom doing?"

We walked eight blocks in absolute silence, save for my heels clicking against the hard pavement. Occasionally, the clicking would speed up to catch up with Hayden's long strides, making our silence sit even louder.

"She's doing better," he answers, bobbing his head up and down with a light scowl that hasn't left his face since we walked out of my apartment. "My aunt is staying with her for a couple of weeks. So she won't be alone."

"Oh, that's nice of her."

"Yeah, I think I'm going to visit her again after she leaves. Maybe check on her and help pack up my dad's things if she's ready."

I reach out to smooth the sleeve of his jacket and give him a reassuring squeeze. "I'm sure she would really appreciate that."

He moves his arm away to run his fingers through his hair, causing my hand to fall back to my side. He doesn't go into further detail about his mom or anything else surrounding his dad's death. We continue to walk in silence.

When we come to a stop in front of Buca's, I see Shawn through the window. He's seated at a small table that's perfect for an intimate party of two, and he's hunched over his phone.

"My date's already inside," I whisper. My hair flows sideways in the same direction as the cool breeze that blows by, somehow creating more distance between us. I tuck a loose strand of hair behind my ear and look up at him as we both pull our gazes away from the window looking in.

"Well, have fun on your *date*." His teeth grits as he enunciates the last syllable. It's such a simple sendoff, but he adds a small hint of ridicule to embarrass me. Teasing me as if anything about tonight can't possibly end in any sort of happy ending. He turns to walk away. His body sways, and his hand comes up to his forehead to salute me off.

"What was that?"

He turns his head, his body still facing away from me. "What?"

"'Have fun on your date?'"

"Was that not what I was supposed to say?"

"Hayden," I whisper with a defeated sigh.

"No, no. You're right," he says as he finally turns, stepping closer to face me. "What I meant to say was that I hope you have a horrible time tonight."

I frown, my brows knitting together as his voice turns dry, riddled with rude sarcasm. "I hope that this is the worst date you've ever had. And that he doesn't get off that fucking phone of his and he makes you pay for his dinner."

He comes so close to me, I can feel his hot breath hit my cold cheek.

Then he lowers his voice. "I hope that if for some god-awful reason you end up fucking that guy, it's the worst sex of your life."

Tears start to pool along the rims of my eyes, my throat constricting as all words leave me. My ears ring as my ragged breaths echo and vibrate through my chest.

"Was that what I was supposed to say to you?" His voice is deep, raspy, as the pain seeps through everything he wanted to tell me since I told him I was supposed to go on this stupid date.

We both stare at each other, this heat that sparked between us kindling into something confusing and unsure. And everything stands still. Nothing moves around us. Or if it does, I don't notice a single thing except his dark eyes and the thick space that stretches from me to him.

"Good night, Hayden," I finally say, my voice devoid of potency, making me sound helpless and scared. When an uneasy chill travels up my spine, I wrap my jacket inward, hoping the violent shiver is from the bitter cold rather than the overwhelming hurt coursing through me.

In response, he scoffs before saying, "Good night, Natalia." He turns to walk away, and I get a good view of his backside, where the frustration is set in his tense shoulders and his harsh steps show every ounce of anger coursing through him.

40

Natalia

present

IT TAKES ABOUT seven deep breaths and clenching and
unclenching my fists multiple times before I'm able to walk through
the restaurant doors. Tears threaten to fall, but I rein them in, trying to
erase my conversation with Hayden from my mind.

As soon as I walk in, before the hostess is able to greet me, Shawn
looks up and waves with a buoyant smile from the table, looking the
complete opposite of what I'm feeling right now. I weave between the
tables, walking my way toward Shawn as he stands to greet me. We do
a half hug, him leaning into me with one hand pressed to my back,
before we both take our seats.

"I was worried you were going to blow me off," he says.

While he's joking, there's concern written on his face as he reads
my expression. With my brow furrowed and a light frown that I can't
seem to turn up, I don't blame him. And instead of contradicting him
by laughing at his joke, I look up at him with sad eyes.

"Is everything okay?"

I don't answer. Instead, I tilt my head to the side. Just enough for
my answer to be confusing. Not a yes, not a no. Shawn clears his

throat, his smile faltering and eyes softening as he sees me on the brink of tears.

"Uh, did you…I mean, we don't have to do this."

When the first tear falls, my hand moves quickly to wipe it. I laugh, baffled that I'm crying on my first first date in years. "I'm so sorry," I say between my watered-down chuckles.

He smiles, his kind eyes void of judgment. "Do you want to talk about it?"

I shake my head and smile. "No, I'm okay."

He nods, and his eyes scan the table as he splays his hands on the white tablecloth. I don't look up at him. Instead, I fix my gaze on the pronged edges of the fork sitting at my right. My breathing starts to come out in staggered sighs, and he clears his throat.

"Natalia," he says softly. I finally look up. "We can do this another time. Or never."

I smile, the tears pooling along the edges of my eyes again.

"I would hate for the chef to think that the pasta here's so bad it made you cry."

A fresh wave of tears causes my throat to clog just as a weak huff of laughter slips through my lips. How easy would it be if this could be something? How simple would it be if we could get through this date, have dinner with a couple of good-natured laughs sprinkled in between and a long good night kiss? But that's not what this is.

I smile, the inner corners of my brows turning up with everything from appreciation to apology because Shawn doesn't deserve any of this.

"I'm so sorry," I say again.

"It's fine," he whispers, reaching for my hand. And I leave before I start crying into the still-warm bread.

I'm leaning up against the door with my hands gripping the wooden doorframe. I didn't go home like I should have. Instead, I spent the last hour trying to hail a cab and crossing the bridge to Hayden's apartment. All while boiling over my feelings for him.

Luckily, when I arrived at his apartment building, the door swung open as someone was leaving, allowing me swift access inside. I don't even know what I'm going to say to him, why I came here. But I know that I can't just go home. Not when the pent-up anger in my chest keeps telling me to confront Hayden and demand answers.

He was the one who broke our kiss. He was the one who pulled away, making me wonder if he regretted it, if he wished it never happened. Why the hell was he so upset? Was he actually jealous that I went on this date? As I ask myself these questions, coming up with dozens of possible answers that makes the confusion swirling in my head become torrent, my heart starts to flounder over the thought that maybe it all means something. Maybe the feelings I have for Hayden stirred something in my heart, and the result is anger. Confusing, frustrating anger.

The door finally swings open. Hayden stands on the other side, his glasses on and eyes bleary, dressed in a plain white undershirt and plaid boxers.

"Nat? What are you doing here?"

"I left my date at the restaurant."

There's a beat of silence as he rubs his hands over his face, his glasses lifting slightly in the process. When he doesn't say anything, the frustration inside me builds even higher.

"Did you hear me?" I grit through clenched teeth. "I ditched him before we even had a chance to order our drinks."

He sighs. "I heard you, Nat."

"And that's all you have to say? That you *heard* me?"

When he finally looks at me, his eyes look tired and weary. With the redness rimming his light eyes and the clenching tic of his jaw, a flash of fear zaps through me. What if I interpreted this all wrong? What if the way my heart pitter-patters and somehow aches at the same time whenever I'm around Hayden is all one-sided?

But then his nostrils flare and his eyes light up with anger, fueled by that fire igniting between us, instantly erasing those doubts. "What do you want me to say, Nat?" he asks. "Do you want me to congratulate you? Slap a hand on your back while I tell you to go back there and make sure to use protection with that fucking wannabe Justin Bieber reject?"

I scoff, mirroring his anger, making my face red and the tips of my ears hot. "You are such an asshole."

"Well, if that's what you think of me, I think I'll go back to sleep."

"You know what? Thank you for that bit of sound advice," I say, a sarcastic smile peeking through the hurt in my words. My arms are splayed out, and my head is lowered slightly in a small bow. "I'll make sure to pick up a box of condoms on my way back to Buca's."

I turn to walk away, my steps hobbling as the adrenaline tingles through my body. My throat starts to tighten as tears prick the corners of my eyes. The ache in my heart starts to become unbearable as I try to work through Hayden's harsh rejection.

Then, just as I start to walk away, my arm is jerked back. I crash into Hayden, and my hands come up to meet his wide chest.

His hand moves to cup the back of my head, crashing his lips to mine. Our kiss is sloppy, completely urgent and hungry. My fingers lie flat against him before tightly gripping the thin fabric of his shirt into small, wrinkled clusters.

When our mouths open, welcoming the tangle of our tongues, I moan. As soon as I let the urgency become vocal, he grips me even harder. He moves us, my feet dragging along the hard floor as he steps into his apartment and closes the door behind me. My back crashes against the closed door while my fingers trail down his hard stomach, lifting the hem of his shirt. He breaks our kiss, chucking his glasses onto the side table at the entrance before reaching over the back of his shirt collar to pull it over his head. He peels off my jacket already hanging off my bare shoulders as the warm pads of his fingers run down the length of my arms.

"Turn around," he orders, his bare chest heaving heavily.

I comply, my hands pressing against the cold, hard door and my cleavage swelling in front of me. His fingers trace along the short hem of my dress, lifting it to expose the bottom curve of my ass. He presses his free hand firmly against the door right next to my cheek.

"Tell me you didn't wear this for him," he growls into my ear. "Tell me you wore this dress for me."

I turn my head sideways, facing him over the curve of my shoulder. When I see his eyes lowered as they skirt over my body, all I see is lust. Pure, hungry, aching lust.

"It was for you."

"*Only* me, Nat."

My breath hitches, completely ragged and uncontrolled. I'm so turned on I can't even breathe correctly.

"Only you," I say breathlessly. Just as the words leave my lips, his hand glides up the inside of my thighs. So painfully slow. His rough hands stop as they meet my lacy black thong, now soaked through the sheer material. When he finds the wet heat between my legs, he groans.

"*Fuck*." His voice is low, so hoarse it almost sounds painful. "Did I make you this wet?" His finger hooks the bottom curve of my thong, teasing me in slow deliberate strokes. "I love that I do this to you… because you have no idea what you do to me." I don't hold back when a moan ripples through my throat.

My head rolls to one side, exposing my neck to him. Only this time, there's no question what I want from him. His hot tongue meets the sensitive spot behind my neck, right where it meets my ear, making me shiver as the slick heat glides across my needy skin. I feel the tug of my zipper being lowered, gradually exposing my back and reminding him of the choice of negligee that I chose to wear tonight.

"You wore this sexy little thing for me too, didn't you?" His fingers toy at the clasp that meets in the middle of my back, teasing as he calculates his next steps. My eyelids fall heavy and I suck in a sharp breath, feeling intoxicated from the desire I'm silently begging from him.

I nod, unable to form coherent words.

He finally unhooks my bra, letting it and my dress pool around my feet, around the sharp bottoms of my heels. I'm left only in my thong and stilettos.

"I'm going to fuck you so hard, you aren't going to remember a thing about what's his face back at Buca's." As the words leave his mouth, he presses his hard erection to my lower back, letting me know exactly how badly he wants this. Just as much as I do.

He flips me back around to face him. When I look down, I can see the strain of his hardness against the thin fabric of his boxers stretching to a full point.

He hoists me up, lifting me as my heels click together behind his back. His mouth lowers, enclosing it around my hard nipple, sucking and pulling, making the back of my head hit the door with unbridled pleasure.

"Hayden," I moan, my nails digging into his shoulders.

One of his hands moves between us, dipping into my thong, while the other supports my weight. His fingers stroke my clit, gliding across the slick wetness. When his fingers dig deep into me, curving toward him as he strokes a spot that makes me draw in a sharp intake of breath, I moan again, loud and vulnerable. An electric thrum vibrates through my body as my back arches into him, all while I pull and tug at the roots of his hair, inflicting more pain than I mean to. His mouth moves across my bare chest, nipping and tugging at my skin before latching on to my other nipple.

"Keep doing that," I croak, my voice strangled and weak. His finger continues to move in slow, evenly pressured strokes, his thumb circling me while rubbing against every sensitive nerve ending bundled between my legs, and the electric current continues to shoot right through me. "*Ohhh* my god, Hayden. I'm so close." My thighs tremble around his narrow waist, squeezing him tighter. When an orgasm rips through me, I lower my face into his shoulder, biting into his hot flesh as it muffles my cries while I claw at his bare back.

"Fuck, Nat," he grits. "I could listen to you say my name like that all night." A lazy smile curves at the corners of his mouth. And then he does something so carnal, so goddamn erotic. I didn't even realize how hot it would make me until I see Hayden's hungry eyes bear into my own as he brings his fingers, glistening with my orgasm, to his mouth and sucks it right off as if he's savoring the taste, licking off every last drop like I just poured sweet honey all over the rough edges of his fingertips and knuckles.

He leans forward, running his nose along my neck, and hums

against my skin. "You taste like heaven," he says with a voice that sounds so low I can practically feel the growl that comes with it at the base of his throat.

As I slump in his arms, too limp and sated, he pulls me away from the door and walks toward his room. My hands move to grip the roots of the hair at the back of his head again, tugging as I kiss him with impatience. Once inside his room, he kicks the door shut and lays me on the soft mattress of his bed. He lowers himself, hovering over me as his breath skates over my skin.

His hands graze down my hot, needy skin methodically as he hooks them along the straps of my thong to shimmy it down my hips and tug it down my legs. His lips latch onto my skin, right where my hips meet my legs, sucking as he leaves his mark on me before moving up my body, stopping to pay extra attention to the spots that make my body writhe. As his lips finally meet the dip in my collarbone, my back arched off the bed, he grinds into me.

As our lips meet again, he speaks soft words into my mouth. They spill out of him between our kisses. He breathes them into my soul as my heart longs for what I've been wanting to hear. "These lips are all I've been thinking about."

"You mean since we kissed in your room?" I ask, so damn breathless I can barely get the words out.

He shakes his head against my temple. "Since that night at the lake house eight years ago," he finally says, his admission sounding full of the pain and longing that's built up over the years. "Since we went apple picking and I saw you in those damn boots. Since prom. Since the wedding."

I pull away to look at him, my eyes searching his for answers. "Why didn't you tell me?"

"Natalia," he says, his brow furrowing slightly as he breathes against my lips. He shakes his head again. And instead of answering, he covers my lips with his own, pulling me into a crushing, hollowing kiss. It's a kiss that's separate from the passion vibrating between us. It's one that's meant to erase every question running through my mind. He's sucking them off my lips instead, allowing me a moment to be in this without demanding answers first.

My arms and legs start wrapping around him, pulling him closer to me, all while holding on to this kiss as if I were starved. He reaches behind him to remove my heels, unhooking each one, and they clack to the floor. Then his hands grip at my waist, flipping me so I hover over him. I instinctively grind against him, feeling this built-up pressure inside of me, aching for him to fill it. He shifts, lifting his hips to shimmy down his boxers, springing his erection free before reaching for his nightstand to remove a condom. He hands it to me, holding it loosely between his fingers, urging me to put it on him.

I scoot back just the tiniest bit to make room before ripping open the foil packaging. I look down at his length. My mouth practically waters from the anticipation of finally feeling him, aching to have him fill me. I glide down the thin latex, sliding it over him while gripping the base of his cock, holding him while watching him throw his head back into his pillow, moaning through the shock of pleasure merely from my firm grip.

When the condom is on, fit snugly over him, he looks at me. His hands move to my bare hips, sliding over my skin with a tight squeeze on my waist. "Ride me," he demands, lifting me over him. I brace myself against his chest, pushing into the hard muscle as I move to position myself at his tip. And I slowly lower myself, so slowly. I move inch by inch, enjoying too much the aching pain smeared across Hayden's face, becoming even more turned on as he stretches me bit by bit.

"Holy *fuck*, Nat," he grunts. "God, you're so fucking tight."

I finally lower myself into him completely, leaning forward as my body slumps from the wave of ecstasy rippling through me. And without even thinking about it, I clench myself around him.

He groans in response. "Nat, you're going to have to stop doing that," he hisses. "In fact, you're going to have to stop moving altogether. Otherwise, I'm going to come, and I don't want to just yet."

I shake my head, refusing to stop doing what my body wants. "It feels so *good*," I drawl.

Instead of lifting myself to slip in and out of him, I hover above him, gripping the wooden headboard above his head. When I do that, my breasts hang low in his face, causing him to lift his head and lick the curves that line the creases between them. I start to rock back and forth, my hips moving on their own as they chase another orgasm slowly building up inside me, living for the delicious friction I'm causing between us.

"Nat," he grits, his hands pulling at the skin at my waist. "You feel so. *Fucking. Good.*"

I continue the back and forth, rubbing into his pubic bone while discovering the even more delicious friction I'm creating there. As a steady rhythm builds, the pain etched on his face starts to fade, leaving behind a mask of pleasure through hooded eyes and an almost devilish smile.

"That's it, baby," he says in a strained voice, letting a loud moan end his sentence. "That's my girl."

I feel a ball of tingles start to gather low in my groin, making me throb. I moan. And not in a sexy, seductive way but in a way that is completely abandoned and wild.

"Hayden, I'm going to come again," I gasp. I bury my forehead into his shoulder, muffling a cry into his skin now damp with a thin layer of sweat.

"I know, baby," he mumbles into my hair, holding back his own orgasm through the tightness in his voice. "*Fuck*, you look so fucking sexy when you're about to come," his low voice rasps.

And then it hits me, the orgasm that tears through my core, causing me to yell out so loudly that it ripples against my throat. I feel the contractions grip him tighter and tighter as he buries his face into my shoulder, fisting my hair while my body levitates into nirvana where everything that surrounds me feels like some sort of spell work or sorcery.

Just as I'm coming down from my high, I'm flipped on my back. Our bodies are still connected as he adjusts himself while resting on his knees. He grips my thighs and drags me closer to him. He withdraws enough so that his tip is still inside me, teasing me as my nails dig into his arms.

"I wanted to take my time with you, Nat, but I don't think I can," he says, his eyes bearing into my soul. "I don't know how much longer I can last."

I lean forward, looking into his eyes with everything that burns between us. We burn for each other, that fire kindling and finally combusting as we tuck away every single reason we shouldn't be doing this.

I pant against him, aching for more. "Fuck me," I say, baring my teeth with each syllable. As soon as the words leave my lips, he slams into me so hard that I have absolutely no control over the desperate cries that squeeze through my lips. Each thrust thereafter comes harder and harder.

I meet every one of his thrusts. My inner thighs squeeze against his hips, caging him toward me and encouraging every shift of movement that brings him closer to the edge. Just as my thighs begin to tremble around his hips, he bucks into me faster and faster.

My moans grow louder, more frenzied, as his muscles grow taut. Everything, from the lines on his abs to the thick cords that run down his neck, bulges. Muscles that cover his torso, all hard and masculine. As if the last eight years spent off the football field didn't affect him one bit and they all remain affixed to him through muscle memory and a generally active lifestyle.

His hand wraps around my throat, grabbing hold so that his thrusts plunge into me more deliberately, more purposefully. And just as I reach to grip his forearm, further encouraging his hold, a loud groan resounds through his chest as he comes.

"*Fuuuck*," he howls.

It feels like his soul connects with mine, letting our hearts peel back from the ashes of our fire with nothing left but the glowing embers, letting me know that this is just beginning. The sparks will always be there because *this*, this burning ache, this chasm of impatient hunger… it will *never* die out.

He stills and his body slumps over mine. I feel his heart gallop in his chest as our ragged breaths sync through heavy gasps of air. "Holy shit, Nat," he says against my skin.

My breathing evens out as I eye him, my hand hovering over my forehead, trying to process what just happened between us. Neither of us had a moment to think about our actions. We didn't consider what would happen to our friendship and what we wanted out of an actual relationship.

I push those thoughts aside as a sweet, exhausted slumber begins to lull over me. Hayden moves to lie beside me after removing his condom and lazily tossing it in the direction of his wastebasket. He drapes his arm over my side as I turn to face him, both our arms tucked under our heads and our eyes searching the other's.

"Hayden," I whisper. I want to tell him that...I don't know what. But if someone asked me right then and there if I love him, if I could picture spending the rest of my life with him, imagining a future together, the answer would be yes. It would be yes a thousand times over because I can't imagine saying no. I can't imagine walking away from this with anything other than the greatest love story of my life.

Maybe these thoughts, these feelings, have been brewing in my mind since we both reentered each other's lives. Or maybe it's been there since we were seventeen, lodged into a lone crevice in my heart where I let it expand into feelings I didn't know I had until we finally exploded. We took a chance. That's what this was, us taking a shot at something great. Because we deserve it. Don't we? After all of this time, didn't we earn that road that led to all the what-ifs being answered?

But there are still so many of those what-ifs. And they begin to fester in my mind, held at the tip of my tongue as he scoots closer to me, pressing his warm body against my shivering one shaking from all the fear and uncertainties.

We stay quiet, staring at each other while somehow saying so much more than actual words. Words that may be misunderstood or misspoken if not said carefully. Instead of making mistakes, saying things when we aren't ready to, Hayden cups my cheek with his warm hand and kisses me. He kisses me as if he's unsure. As if he still has yet to figure out what all of this means.

41

Hayden

senior year

MY ARMS and legs ache from lugging the two boxes along with my oversized suitcase to my dorm room. With the elevator inconveniently out, I had no choice but to trek the two flights of stairs to the second floor.

"I think that's the last of it," my dad calls, entering my room behind me with his arms wrapped around a third box.

My mom follows close behind him. She walks in empty-handed as she examines my new home. "Well, this is cozy," she comments, eyeing the bed next to mine. It's already settled in by its occupant with navy bed sheets and a MacBook resting on the pillows.

As I turn to face my mom at the doorway, I see a friendly face enter the room as if he's in familiar territory. "You must be Hayden," he says, extending his hand toward me. "I'm Dexter."

I shake his hand. "I take it this is you?" I ask, pointing to his bed. He nods, swinging his leg around the bed to slump into the soft mattress.

"I hope you don't mind that I took this one," he says.

I shake my head. "Not at all. Either one is fine with me."

My dad clears his throat. "Well, we're going to head out. We still have to check into our hotel. And we've got a long travel day ahead of us tomorrow."

"Yeah," I answer. I follow them both down the stairs and out to the curb where my dad's truck is parked.

"Call us if you need anything," my mom says with a shaky voice. "If you ever want to come home for a long weekend, just call us. I have alerts set on my phone for flights so don't worry about the travel."

"I will," I say obligingly as she pulls me toward her. She clings to me for a few seconds too long before I turn to face my dad.

He pulls me in for a rough hug, brief yet warm, before patting my shoulder. "We'll see you for Thanksgiving if you don't visit until then."

He lets me go and walks toward the driver's seat, my mom pawing at the passenger seat window like a stray dog in the pound. I wave at them as they drive off.

When I walk back up to my dorm room, Dexter isn't there, so I have the room to myself. And instead of unpacking, I lie on my bare mattress, reaching into my pocket for my phone. I have a new text message from Jenny, most likely checking in as if we were still a couple. Instead of reading it, I open my Facebook app and scroll through my feed. I land on a collection of pictures that Natalia posted just a couple of days ago. She's in New York City, visiting all of the touristy spots. The Statue of Liberty, Times Square, Central Park, the Met.

I tap my thumb on the messenger icon, hovering over her name.

I map out a witty greeting, referencing the Big Apple and all the wonderful amenities it offers, but then I stop myself. What good will it do, reaching out to her as if I can revisit our friendship? As if nothing has changed and I would see her tomorrow afternoon in AP Bio?

But I miss her. I miss looking forward to seeing her every day, watching her giggle through her shyness and roll her eyes at every corny, cheesy joke that I make. The last time I saw her at the lake house, I wish I told her just how much I would miss her. Not something as simple as missing a friend, but more. Instead, I walked away, turning to Jenny instead because it was easier. I masked my feelings and turned to someone who felt safer, even if it was temporary.

I let Natalia go. Not that she was mine to let go in the first place, but I let go of the idea of having her in my life. As a friend, as a fellow Coolidge View alumnus. Even as a Facebook friend, only sending the occasional "congratulations" or "happy birthday" greetings. And for some reason, letting her go felt like saying goodbye to a part of me that I didn't want to let go.

I lock my phone away and tuck it back into my pocket before I stand to open the first of my boxes, relieved when I see my bedsheets on top. While I unpack, I focus on the silent goodbye I whisper in my head, the one that's meant for Natalia. I repeat it over and over again to myself as I wish I were saying hello again instead.

present

The morning glow streaming into my room shines a light on us, bringing clarity to what happened. I watch as Natalia sleeps. I watch her chest rise and fall, feeling unexpectedly calm and somber at the same time. Her mouth twitches when I run a hand through her hair to move it out of her face, and her eyes flutter in the way that I know she's going to stay asleep for longer than I would have.

I can't even regret what happened. Not when it all felt so fucking right. I felt it last night when I held her in my arms, and I felt it this morning when she was the first thing I saw as soon as I opened my eyes.

I pull the cover that slipped down to her waist before I carefully get up, pushing off my mattress with as little movement as possible. I leave the room quietly, moving slowly to minimize the creaking of my bedroom door.

When I walk into the kitchen, Dexter is already up, dressed and drinking a cup of coffee.

"Well, good morning, stud." Dexter smiles at me over the rim of his coffee mug, practically saluting me as he raises his cup in my direction.

I pull at the sweatpants hanging low at my hips as I reach up into the cabinet for a mug of my own.

"Good morning," I croak. My voice is hoarse, most likely from the screaming match I had with Natalia when she knocked on my door. And while we were having sex.

God, we had sex.

"As your roommate, may I put in a special request? Considering we share a wall?"

The steamy cup of coffee that's making its way toward my lips stops midway. My face deadpans as I wait for this request.

"Next time you decide to bring a woman home, maybe keep the noise level down to a minimum? I'm rather fond of my eardrums and would appreciate it if you could help me keep them intact."

I don't say anything. I don't even humor him with an arrogant smirk like I normally do.

"Who is she anyway? I thought you were going over to Nat's last night."

Again, I don't say anything. But when I stay quiet, he puts two and two together.

"Oh shit! Was that Nat in there?"

"Shh! She's still sleeping," I whisper sharply.

Dexter draws in a breath. "You are so fucked."

"What are you talking about?"

He takes an annoyingly loud and slow slurp of his coffee. "I'm assuming you guys haven't talked through what this means for you two."

"There's nothing to talk about."

"So, like, you two are a thing?"

"I don't know," I answer, shaking my head. "Right now, we're just friends. I guess..."

Dexter's brows rise so high, I'm actually worried they might lift off his hairline. "Last I checked, friends didn't scream each other's names while they climaxed."

I stop drinking my coffee, setting it down on the counter as I stare at the warm steam rising above it. Dexter walks out of the apartment without another word, but I don't hear him leave.

What the fuck have I done? What the fuck have *we* done?

As badly as I wanted it to happen last night, I'm fucking scared. I'm scared that while I'll do anything for this to keep happening, for us to keep progressing into something, Natalia isn't in that place. She was on a fucking date last night, for Christ's sake.

What if she isn't ready to move on? Or worse, what if she is but not with me?

Just as I groan into my hands, rubbing the heels of my palms into my eyes, I hear Natalia walk out of my room. She's fully dressed, with her purse clutched between her hands and her rumpled hair tampered down as best she could do without a mirror or hair care products.

She walks up to me as her bare feet pad along the wood floor. She moves cautiously as I stand upright to meet her.

"You want some coffee? Dexter brewed some before he left."

She keeps her gaze lowered, and her toes twiddle beneath her. "I should actually get going," she says to the floor. She's avoiding me.

"Nat," I whisper.

"Carmen worries if I'm not home on the weekends when she comes home from work so..." She turns her body toward the door.

I reach for her wrist, grasping the soft skin around her pulse point as my thumb rubs into the curve of her palm. "Nat, what are you doing?"

She looks up at me. And the agony in her face pierces through my heart. I can feel her body lurch, almost as if she wants to say something that she shouldn't. As if there's something stopping her from baring every bit of her to me when I should be the one person she should never keep anything from.

"Nat," I plead softly.

She lets out a frustrated sigh and starts to gnaw on her lower lip. "When you got suspended senior year, right after prom, was it because you got into a fight with Alex Spencer?"

I feel like I've just suffered whiplash. "What are you talking about?"

"Why did you get into a fight with Alex?" Instead of repeating her question, something that she already knows and isn't necessarily asking for confirmation, she goes to the root of it.

"I don't remember."

She huffs. "Don't lie to me. I talked to Jenny when we were at your house. She told me you guys broke up after that. Because of me."

"Nat," I start to say. Our eyes stay locked on each other, neither one of us backing down in our silent stand-off.

"Why did you get into a fight with Alex?" she finally asks.

"Because he fucking touched you!" I snap. "That fucking creep put his hands on you. And I saw the look on your face. Like you could still feel him touching you, and I wanted to kill him!"

"I wasn't yours to defend," she says in a steady voice, too calm in contrast to my angry one.

I look up at her, almost speechless. "I know that."

"If you knew that, why did you punch him?"

"Because of everything that happened at prom. And I was…"

"You were what, Hayden?"

"I was scared!" I finally throw at her. "Is that what you want to hear?"

"Why didn't you tell me!"

"How the hell was I supposed to tell you when you were leaving? You were so ready to move out here and live this life that I couldn't be a part of back then. How was I supposed to tell you those things and watch you walk away from me?"

Tears start to glisten in her eyes, and she starts biting her lower lip before taking a slow, staggered breath. "Is that why you didn't tell me about what happened between you and Matteo at the bar? Because you were scared?"

This time, I know it's whiplash. I swerve my head toward her so quickly, I feel a twinge in my neck muscles from the sudden jerk and shock. "How did you know?"

"He told me," she says flatly. "He came to my apartment earlier this week, and he told me you two got into a fight."

"Why the fuck was he at your apartment?" I grit, clearly unsettled by the fact that they were together, most likely alone.

She looks away from me. "He…told me he misses me."

"So you two are getting back together?"

"No," she answers with a conviction that's hard to deny. But it doesn't matter because the anger simmering inside me is making me irrational.

"Are you sure? Because it sounds like you're finally getting everything you want."

"What the hell is that supposed to mean?"

"Matteo. Him wanting you back. Isn't it what you've wanted all along?" I say it even though I know it's not completely true. Because the possibility of her wanting me instead is going to hurt even more if I find out that it isn't true either. Because her rejection is something I won't be able to bear if I find out that I'm the furthest thing from what she wants.

She huffs, turning away from me. "You have no idea what I want."

You want me.

That's what I want to say. Because I want it to be the truth with every fiber of my body. I want her to want me more than I need air to breathe or the sunlight to warm me. I want it more than how badly I want her. Because I could live my life wanting her, always finding a way to have her in my life even if she would never be mine. But her deciding that I'm not what she wants, what she needs? I don't know if I could survive that.

"Hayden," she pleads. She doesn't say please, but I feel it leak from her quivering lips. When I look at her, her eyes look on the brink of tears. The tremble in her chin and the involuntary frown that turns the corners of her mouth downward urge me to tell her.

I want you, Natalia. All of you.

And it's there, ready to pour from my heart. "Nat," I start. "I—"

Our conversation is cut short by the obnoxious twang boinging on my phone. Our eyes travel to the countertop where my phone is sitting. The screen is lit up with the cupid silhouette sitting dead center on my screen. My hands brace the countertop, the muscles in my arms straining against my grip. Why the fuck do I have to get a Cupid's Bet alert right *fucking* now?

She looks back up at me one more time as if gauging my next move. As if figuring out if there's a choice to make between what lies on the counter and her standing in front of me.

"I'll talk to you later, Hayden," she finally says, discreetly wiping her cheek as she turns to walk away. She stops at the door, hooking on her heels in silence. I watch as my body numbs and stiffens, refusing to listen to my silent demands to stop her.

My chest starts to feel tight. *I'm losing her.*

All of the panic that set in on the last day of school comes rushing back. A day that should've been spent deciding which graduation party to hit up or who would be the designated driver. Instead, all I was able to think about back then was the small smile on Natalia's face when we said our goodbyes. How the scraping of the metal chairs against the linoleum floors and the collective hoots and cheers from the rest of the class overpowered any goodbyes I had reserved for Natalia. Instead, I watched her walk away from me. And it's happening all over again.

Just as it was then, I can't do anything except watch.

42

Natalia

present

"THAT'S IT." The remote held loosely in my hand is snatched away, forcing me to break my gaze away from the screen in front of me. Carmen stands over me with her arms folded over each other and her lips formed in a straight line of disapproval. "Nat," she says softly, her tone not matching the sternness in her face. "What happened?"

It's been a full thirty hours since I left Hayden's apartment and in those thirty hours, I've spent about twenty of them crying and the other ten either stuffing my face with slices of the large pizza I had delivered or watching trashy reality television. Carmen saw me when she came home this morning surrounded by a moat of used tissues, throw blankets, a half-empty bag of potato chips, and an entirely empty tub of matcha ice cream.

She slumps onto the couch next to me, meeting me at eye level as she waits for my answer. Instead of answering her, I bring my arms up to my face, covering my eyes so she doesn't see the tears forming while my trembling chin peeks from under my elbows.

"Nat," she says my name again. But instead of probing further, she pulls me into a deep hug.

"Everything is so messed up," I whimper through my tears. Carmen pries my arms away from my face, revealing the stream of tears pouring down my cheeks and the trail of snot peeking from my nose.

"What happened?" she asks again. She reaches toward the coffee table for a Kleenex and hands it to me.

I blow my nose, the shrill trumpet noise vibrating between us before I tell her everything. From the date that didn't happen with Shawn, something she was looking forward to as part of the get-over-Matteo plan she established when I moved in, to me sleeping with Hayden. Even the gritty details of our anger-filled words ending with the loud twang interrupting our rough-edged argument. Everything about it was filled with unanswered questions and unspoken words.

My heart twists into a knot, pulling even tighter as flashing images of Hayden filter through my mind. I felt so pathetic standing in front of him, tears spilling while I silently begged him to choose me. To choose us. All the while he stood there, refusing to look at me, letting me walk away instead.

"It sounds like he needs to figure things out," she says softly, more to herself than to me.

I turn away, blubbering incoherent words as I finish off my literal sob story with an unintelligible "whatever."

What hurts the most about this whole situation, and what keeps the fresh wave of tears constantly flowing, is how much it reminds me of Matteo. I'm never going to be enough. Never going to be worth committing a life to. Never going to be worth giving up a life of single-dom. No matter what, I won't fulfill whatever need or yearning Hayden or Matteo or anyone else has to settle down. I'm not *ever* going to be enough for someone to finally *choose me*.

I can't believe I'm back here. All of those months spent crying over Matteo felt as if they were for nothing. I did all of that wallowing only to be back to where I was when Matteo tossed me aside. And for some reason, Hayden not choosing me hurts more than when Matteo dumped me. Maybe it's the burned down hope that things were different with Hayden. Or maybe it's that with Hayden, I didn't just lose some guy, I also lost my best friend.

The single thought of having lost my best friend makes my chin tremble harder while the deep ache in my chest starts to pull at those knots that have grown thicker and tighter. And even though everything confusing about us is what causes my heart to ache, he's the one that I want to go to and talk about it. I want to run to him and pour my heart out to him because he would know exactly what to do to make that ache stop. He would know exactly what to say to make me whole again.

I love him. So much.

But I lost him. And there's nothing I can do about it.

"I'm sorry we don't have a fancier Thanksgiving dinner," I say apologetically to Lucy from across my kitchen counter.

She shrugs. "Don't worry about it," she answers, her fork poking at the shrimp chow mein on her plate. "It's better than staying in an empty apartment and having frozen mac and cheese."

While our usual plans for Thanksgiving are to go home and have a warm and fully cooked meal by our parents, this year, our parents decided to forgo holiday traditions altogether and take a cruise to Alaska. Lucy and I hid our disappointment when we got the news, while it didn't matter one bit to Carmen, who would be working anyway. So on a night that should have been spent surrounded by our childhood home, Lucy and I are sharing a meal taken out of paper to-go containers in my dimly lit kitchen with the fireplace rolling in the background.

When I stay silent a moment too long, my blank gaze zeroed in on the now cold noodles on my ceramic plate, Lucy reaches her hand toward me.

"Have you tried calling him?" she asks gently. I lower my head before giving a small shake and a firm-lipped smile, keeping the tears at bay while I try my best to stay in one piece.

"Maybe you should," she adds.

I sigh and shake my head again. A fat drop of a tear starts to accumulate and pour from the outer corner of my eye. My chin begins to tremble for what feels like the hundredth time, and I lower my face even further to hide all of the uncontrollable, overwhelming emotions that cause it all to show on my face.

I hadn't filled Lucy in on all the gritty details until she arrived at my apartment yesterday morning. After she got over the initial shock that I was "dating" Hayden *freaking* Marshall, she bad-mouthed him, calling him a selfish playboy who used me before tossing me aside. And I didn't have the energy in me to disagree with her. Mainly because I can't. While I won't go as far as claiming that I've merely become another notch on his bedpost that he's rapidly tallying up, I sure as hell feel like I don't matter enough to him to be considered otherwise. He so easily let the possibility of us slip through his fingers and let me walk away from us instead.

There it is again, that humiliating chill that runs through me every time I think about how I practically begged Hayden to want me. I can't stop picturing the way my tears and trembling chin waved every plea I was trying to hold back.

I have to stop. All this rehashing and reliving, it's making the pain unbearable.

I hear Lucy sigh. "You want to watch a movie?" she suggests with a cheerful smile. "I'll let you pick."

I lightly chuckle. "Sure."

She stands from her seat, pushing our plates to one side before rummaging through my freezer. "Oh! You have the sugar-free mango sorbet!" she squeals.

I slowly stand from my own seat to take our plates to the sink before moving to the couch. I smile at Lucy over my shoulder. I'm grateful that I'm not spending the night alone, looking forward to the pistachio-flavored froyo sitting next to the awful tasting artificially sweetened mango sorbet instead. Lucy reappears with both, stopping by the utensil drawer to grab two spoons before joining me on the couch. She hands me my own pint-sized tub and settles close to me.

"I'm glad you're here with me tonight," I say, patting her thigh.

"Me too, Nat," she says, clinking her spoon to mine, forcing a giggle to release from my lips.

43

Hayden

present

"I NEVER THOUGHT I would see the day that *I* would be helping *you* cook Thanksgiving dinner," my mom says over her shoulder as she retrieves the roasted brussels sprouts from the oven. I'm by the stove, mashing a large pot of boiled potatoes, making sure to get the perfect consistency of creamy and buttery.

"Well, believe it, Mama," I call, straining against the potato masher in my hand.

"Is dinner almost ready?" Pat calls as he leisurely walks into the kitchen. An empty wineglass sits in his hand and a look of hunger is spread across his face, evident from the way he's eyeing the turkey loosely covered in tinfoil on the kitchen island.

"You know," my mom answers, "if you're so hungry, you can help instead of asking every five minutes if dinner's ready."

Instead of actually helping, he turns to refill his wineglass. "I leave the cooking to you two," he answers matter-of-factly.

I finish with the potatoes and move on to remove the pomegranate salad from the fridge, vibrant in reds and greens against the spinach and candied pecans sprinkled on top. My mom was reluctant to stray away from her usual Thanksgiving dinner, stating pomegranates and brussels sprouts didn't say Traditional Marshall Family Thanksgiving. But Pat persuaded her, saying my cooking will be sure to surprise her. And when I brought in all the herbs and spices to flavor the turkey, along with some ingredients that she wasn't familiar with, her wary look turned into a curious one.

My mom is adding her final touches to the candied yams, something she insisted she take care of, as it has always been one of my favorites and she wanted to make something for me to enjoy. I turn toward her to slop the finished mashed potatoes onto a serving plate. Once the platters of food, too many for just three people, sit ready to be moved to the formal dining room, we make multiple trips before sitting down and digging in. We eat quietly, not because it's awkward but because we can't talk with our mouths full of warm, savory food that pairs too perfectly with the hints of sweetness in the salad and yams. By the time we're done, I'm so full. I feel like I'm going to explode out of my pants.

Once all the leftovers are transferred into Tupperware containers and the dishwasher is running with the low hum of water sloshing in the machine as it vibrates underneath the countertop, we all sit in the living room. My mom puts on *Meet Me in St. Louis* while we all enjoy a slice of store-bought pumpkin pie.

When Pat's light snoring from our recliner naturally signals the end to the night, my mom gets up from her comfortable spot on the sofa.

"I'm going to turn in," she says softly before turning down the volume to the TV. She walks toward me and gives me a light peck to the top of my head. "Thanks for dinner, Hayden."

"You're welcome, Mom."

"I'm glad you're home." I look up at her, her eyes glistening against the glare coming off the TV. She runs a hand along my shoulder and gives me a light squeeze along with a sad smile.

"I'm glad I'm home too."

She turns to walk away, and I watch her trudge up the stairs to her room. When the movie ends, I turn it off and go to my room, leaving Pat to sleep on the recliner. I'm tired, worn from the day spent in front of the stove, but my mind feels wired. Like I can't shut it off. Instead it's filled with all of the things that make my heart twinge and throb.

As soon as I walk into my room, I sit at my desk and lean back in my swivel chair before letting my fingers run over the wooden desktop. I glance quickly at my clock to check the time. It's late, close to midnight, making me wonder what Natalia's doing right now. If she's no more than fifteen miles away, in her parents' home, winding down after enjoying dinner with her family or if she's still back in the city, alone and without me.

I haven't spoken to her since she walked out of my apartment. I wanted to call her. I should have. I should have gone after her and let her know how I feel. Tell her that I didn't even bother to check who messaged me on Cupid's Bet. That instead, I deleted the app altogether, not caring what the unread message said. I wanted to tell her... no, I *should* have told her that I love her. That the reason I can't push aside all the fear and doubts is because it fuels every beat of my heart when it comes to her. And that even though I want nothing more than to spend my days by her side, I'm scared that all the things that went south in my life would happen to us too. I'm scared of losing her before she's even mine.

My eyes start to trail over the scattered yet organized mess on my desk under the soft glow of my desk lamp. Over the worn football signed by Paul Warfield sitting in the corner and the Paramore tickets I tacked to the corkboard on the wall. I open the small drawer to my right, finding it rather organized and not full of junk like I expected it to be. I start to pick at my old possessions, trying to place when I got them or when I last used them. On top, right up against the side of the handle, I see a worn leather wallet and my old mouthguard. Just as I slide out my school ID from my old wallet, I see the light reflecting off something hard and plastic in the drawer, causing me to lean forward a little further and peer inside. My fingers catch on a metal ring where an acrylic keychain hangs.

It's the old keychain that Natalia got me. All scuffed and dull with the words I Love NY encased in plastic.

A sob breaks loose in my chest. It hiccups through my throat as that twinge in my heart starts to twist. It winds and coils until my heart feels like it's snapping, breaking apart so that the pain that slices through it can be felt with every thought that crosses my mind. Every bad decision, every moment of regret, all of it making the pain spasm against my chest, begging me to make it stop.

I break down with my hand gripping the keychain as if I know it's my last thread of hope. My world feels like it's crumbling to pieces. From losing my dad and knowing that I will never be able to get the time back that I lost with him to losing Natalia too, having to say goodbye to her when I knew I wouldn't survive having to do that again.

The tears start pouring down my face as I break the dam that I held up for so long. The dam that's been weak and feeble since Natalia walked out of my apartment, since I got that call from my mom when my dad died. If I think back far enough, it's been cracking and deteriorating since the last Thanksgiving I had here at home. Or even since graduation when I said goodbye to Natalia. I've been holding myself together for that long, not realizing how much I needed to fall apart. I needed to fall apart to move on, to understand that my dad's death was an incident of circumstance and not a punishment for not reaching out to him sooner. I needed to crumble to understand how much Natalia means to me, not having realized that without her, I couldn't be put back together. I'll never be whole without her. She's my best friend, my everything. From my heart to the small voice in my head telling me that I'm destined for so much more than I give myself credit for, the ghost of her lives in and around me.

My chest starts to heave, the sobs coming in uncontrollable waves. As I become a blubbering mess of never-ending tears and snot, I slump to the floor and lean my back against the cold wall, still holding on to the one piece of Natalia that I've never had to say goodbye to.

I miss her so much.

"I got an early flight back. I'm leaving tonight," Pat announces the next morning over a cup of fresh coffee. I look at him from my cereal bowl, slurping the last remnants of milk. My eyes feel swollen and sore, having been put through the ringer before sleep finally stopped the tears from flowing. I know I look like shit. I sure as hell feel like it.

"Oh," I finally answer. "I don't know if I can get a seat on the same flight." Our flight back to the city isn't until Saturday afternoon, and I don't understand why he changed our travel arrangements.

He shakes his head. "I have some things to take care of. But you're staying."

"What are you talking about?"

"I want you to stay a couple of weeks. Maybe a month."

"Pat, I have a kitchen to run," I say. "At *your* restaurant," I remind him.

"I know. Stephan can step in," he says calmly and surely.

"I can't just leave him to run things," I argue.

"Yes, you can. That's why he's your sous chef. He and everyone else in that kitchen can manage just fine for a couple of weeks while you're here." He pauses, his hands coming to wrap around his coffee mug. "You have a good team. They've all learned a lot from you. Trust me, they'll be fine."

My brow furrows. "Why?"

"Your mom needs you. She's going to need your help to pack up your dad's things and settle into a routine that your dad isn't a part of."

I nod, silently agreeing with him.

"And...I think you could use the time off."

"Me?"

"Hayden," he says sternly. "I know it's been rough since your dad died, but you've been in a rut. I see you on autopilot every day. You come to work, do your job, and leave. Your eyes look blank, like you don't care about anything, and I'm worried about you. Your mom and I...we're both worried about you."

I look away, keeping my gaze on the bowl in front of me, staring at the leftover crumbs of cereal scattered at the bottom as they turn soggy with milk.

"I'm sorry, Hayden," he says, his voice hoarse. "I should have made you take the time off sooner. I guess things have been hard for all of us, and I lost sight of things."

The same constriction in my throat starts to ball up again as I realize how much everything has been weighing me down. He's right. From my lack of energy at work to the rutted routine that's been fueling my days as I run on fumes. I'm trudging through each shift at the restaurant. Like I'm barely surviving.

"It's fine, Pat," I say, my voice weak and scratchy.

"I already talked to your mom. She thinks it'll be good for you...for the both of you, if you stay for a while." He leans back in his chair, tilting his coffee cup back as he keeps his gaze on me, waiting for me to answer.

I finally nod. "Okay."

44

Natalia

two years ago

"HAPPY ANNIVERSARY," Matteo croons. His smile is lazy and relaxed in contrast to the harsh, cold winds blowing around us.

"Happy anniversary?" I question, pulling away with a confused smile. "Our anniversary was last month. Remember how you forgot?" I tease.

Matteo chuckles, pecking the corner of my mouth. "And this is my way of making it up to you."

"I thought this was a work trip."

"Well," he says with a shrug, draping his arm around my shoulders, "I guess we're killing two birds with one stone."

I roll my eyes, lightly shoving away from him before wrapping my scarf around me tighter, nuzzling my nose into the bright orange cashmere. When we landed at O'Hare International Airport, we didn't expect the normally cool temperatures in Chicago to be so cold this early in November. Or at least, I didn't.

"Aren't you glad you listened to me when I told you to pack warm?" Matteo says, gesturing toward my scarf.

"Hmm," I hum. "What would I do without you?"

Matteo turns away from me, linking our cold hands together as we continue our leisurely steps through Lincoln Park. We simply bask in the one day off that Matteo has before a meeting the following morning, the reason for this supposed "anniversary trip."

Suddenly, Matteo pulls his phone out of his pocket, the buzzing noise vibrating in his hand before he answers it.

"This is Matteo," he calls, his hand holding mine slackening as his steps stop. "What are you talking about? They aren't supposed to be here until tomorrow...yeah, okay. I'll be right there." He promptly hangs up and faces me. "Natalia, I'm so sorry. The investors are already at the office. I guess they want to move the meeting up to today."

I pout. "What about dinner?"

"I'll try to make it out in time for our reservations but if not, I promise I'll make it up to you tomorrow."

I continue to pout, shoving my hands into my pockets as I watch him distractedly look down at his phone.

"Do you want me to walk you back to the hotel?" he asks.

I shake my head. "It's too far, and you're in a hurry. I'll just explore a bit and head back when it gets too cold."

He nods, placing a quick kiss on my cheek before hurrying off.

I swivel on my feet, suddenly realizing that I'm in a city where I know absolutely nothing or no one. With no specific direction, I continue the steps I was walking with Matteo, hoping to find something to kill the time.

As the slowly setting sun continues to glide across the sky, I find a small French bistro close to Lincoln Park Conservatory nestled between the park and brick buildings. From the outside, I can see a large display case holding various cakes and pastries. Wanting to get out of the cold and having a sudden hankering for something sweet, I walk inside.

As soon as the warmth hits me, I unwrap my scarf, suddenly feeling too stuffy. The inside is quaint. A good-sized dining room is separated from the café side where there's a takeout counter for those that want to order from the bakery. When I get a closer look at the display case, I already know I'm going to have trouble deciding what I want with too many choices of fruit tarts, brownies, and flavors of cakes, all of which I want to sample at least once.

"Are you ready to order?" a soft voice asks as I continue my ogling. I look up at the cashier, a brunette woman with a black apron, her name, Janet, neatly embroidered across her chest.

"Um," I answer. "What do you suggest?"

She smiles wider, her eyes lighting up with kindness. "One of our pastry chefs makes the best vanilla cake. It has a rich strawberry cream cheese frosting, and it is actually heaven in your mouth."

I giggle. "I'll have that. And a cinnamon latte, please."

"Sure," she answers.

After a quick transaction and I'm handed my order, I settle into a stool along a long bar-like table facing out toward the street. I drape my scarf over the back of the stool before opening up the small to-go container holding my slice of heaven. When I take the first bite into the spongy cake, I'm hit with a sudden wave of nostalgia. I don't know how, but this cake…it tastes like home. Like bustling classrooms filled with clinking petri dishes and complicated lab assignments. Or a busy parking lot scattered with farewells and unspoken words.

Janet wasn't wrong when she said the cake was like heaven in your mouth. I finish the entire cake, taking small sips of warm cinnamon latte in between bites. As I'm clearing my trash, my phone buzzes in my purse.

"Hello?"

"Natalia," Matteo calls from the other line. "I'm heading back to the hotel. Are you there?"

"I'm on the other side, near the conservatory. Is your meeting over?"

"Yes and no," he answers. "The investors just wanted to do a meet and greet before they check into their hotel. I think it's their way of trying to catch us off guard. But that means I'll be able to make it for our reservations."

I smile, already walking out the door and ready to make the trek back to our hotel. "I'll see you back in our room."

present

The next month passes by without so much as a hiccup. I fall into a routine at work as the weather gradually shifts from the breezy fall to the biting cold that comes with the December chill. Everywhere I look, I see the holidays are gradually approaching, from the storefront windows covered in Christmas decorations to holiday music filtering through every place that has a sound system.

I've been spending the last couple of weeks gradually moving on from whatever rejection I suffered this past year. From Matteo, from Hayden, from every thought that passed through my hopeful heart thinking I was destined for something more. Instead, I bury myself in work. I spend my lunch hours inside my office, opting to have food ordered in instead of dining out. And while I repeatedly tell José that it's to avoid the chilly weather outside, in all honesty, it's to avoid the lingering thoughts of Hayden just a few blocks away. Probably busy, filling his time with work just as I am, while letting go of something that could have blossomed between us. Something that could have grown if sheltered and valued.

I briefly fill José in on the relationship that didn't happen between myself and Hayden, something he already assumed. When I appear more heartbroken than before, his persistence to mend my broken heart grows tenfold, and he urges me to call Shawn back after our failed first date.

I spent this past week preparing to travel back home for Christmas. It's the last few days in the office until the new year, and I'm finishing Christmas shopping while packing for my extended vacation. Another plus to this vacation home is that Carmen will be joining us, unlike last year, with David in tow. It'll be the first time David is meeting our parents in the three years that they've been dating, and he's been a ball of nerves ever since we booked our tickets.

Tonight, it's the night before Christmas Eve, Christmas Eve-Eve as Lucy puts it, and I have a holiday work party that I'm attending before

Jeannie Choe

taking an afternoon flight the following day while Carmen and David are to fly out on Christmas morning once she gets off work.

Dressed in a simple green dress the color of deep emeralds, all topped with my hair in loose, wavy curls swept to one side and a dark, maroon-colored lipstick, I scan the large banquet room in the fancy hotel that feels too formal for it to be considered a party and more like an extended workday instead.

"Have you tried the scallops?" José asks in hushed excitement, approaching me with a small appetizer plate full of said scallops. "They're to die for."

I peek at his plate, where a small pile of the pan seared scallops, drizzling in a savory smelling oil, sits, waiting for me to have a sample. I pluck one from the plate and pop it in my mouth, and it practically melts off my tongue.

"They also have some sliders that have applewood smoked bacon in them," he says through a full mouth. "So don't get too full off of these."

I nod, agreeing with him as I reach for a second scallop.

"Mmm!" he exclaims, waving at someone behind me. I turn and see Shawn walking our way with an easy smile. I flip around to face José again.

"What is he doing here?" I hiss.

"I invited him," he answers almost too nonchalantly. As if I don't know the tricks he has up his sleeve. "Just make nice and have a small chat."

I have enough time to roll my eyes at José with a hint of annoyance before greeting Shawn with a smile as he approaches us.

"Hey, cuz!" José greets Shawn.

"Hi," Shawn answers. I keep my gaze on my wineglass loosely held in my hands.

"I'm going to grab some of those sliders before they run out," José says before scurrying off to the food table, ignoring the accusatory glare I'm giving him. When we're left alone, Shawn finally faces me.

"Fancy seeing you here," he says as I peek up at him through an embarrassed smile.

I finally let out a nervous laugh as we work through our embarrassment. Mine more than his because it was me who walked out on our date. Me who left him behind at a nice restaurant to have sex with another man.

"Hi," I say with a voice that sounds more like I should be saying sorry.

"So I'm having a serious problem with this girl I kinda like," he starts to say. "You see, she ditched me on our first date. Maybe you can help me figure out what to do so that I can finally sweep her off her feet."

My hand moves to cover my mouth as a wide smile spreads across my face. "I'm so sorry about that," I say, my brows curving inwards as I plead my apology.

"You can make it up to me," he says, leaning a bit closer. "How about a redo?"

I sigh. "I'm not the best company as of late."

He bobs his head up and down. "That's okay," he says, understanding laced into the calmness of his voice. "We'll take things slow."

"Slow," I repeat.

"Slow."

"I can do slow."

The night continues with more appetizer-type foods like crispy coconut prawns and fried mac and cheese balls. The mood and spirits around the party liven as more alcohol is consumed. By the time I'm ready to call it a night, I feel significantly lifted. Like I have something to look forward to other than a long night wallowing alone.

"I should head out," I announce, my third glass of red wine running through me. "I have a long travel day tomorrow."

Shawn tosses back whatever remains are in the glass tumbler he's holding and checks his watch. "I should head out too," he says casually, placing his empty glass on a nearby table. He turns to me, lightly placing his hand on the small of my back. "We'll walk out together."

I nod, taking one last glance at José, his smile wide and excited, before Shawn and I walk toward the coat check and exit the building.

Once Shawn and I walk through the heavy revolving doors, the air outside is chillier than when I walked in. The clouds in the sky look menacing, even against the darkness.

"They had snow in the forecast," he announces, gently placing his hand on my back again, this time wrapping his fingers to lightly grip my waist. "It looks like we might have a white Christmas this year."

"It's been a while since Manhattan's had a white Christmas," I comment as he steps toward the curb to hail a cab. Just as I wrap my coat around myself tighter, a cab stops in front of Shawn. "It's going to be hell catching another," I add as he starts to open the back passenger door. "Why don't you go ahead and take it? I can walk."

"We'll share it." He steps aside and gestures for me to enter the car.

"But you're on the opposite side of town."

He tilts his head toward the open door, further urging me to get in and out of the bitter cold. "It's fine."

I finally budge, stepping toward the car as my heels click against the hard pavement. Once inside the warm car with the heat blasting through the vents at full power, I turn to Shawn.

"You really didn't have to share a cab," I say apologetically.

"And let you walk home all alone?" he says with an incredulous tilt of his head that naturally brings his palm toward his chest. "What kind of gentleman would that make me?"

"Well, thank you," I say with a shy huff of laughter. "It saves me from having to unthaw my feet in a warm bath when I get home."

We pull up to my apartment quickly, the hotel not being too far, and the taxi pulls to a stop on the road. Shawn turns to me.

"I'll call you," he says in a low voice, his gaze zeroing in on my lips.

I swallow the lump lodged in my throat. "Yeah," I say too quickly. My hand hooks onto the door handle, clicking it open as I shift a little closer to the exit. "Thank you for the ride," I almost whisper.

He tilts an imaginary hat. "Anytime."

I step out into the cold winter air and face the car as it drives off as Shawn waves at me from the closed window. I shift on my feet as I turn to get into the warm comfort of my home.

It's then that I see a figure stand from the steps leading up to my apartment. When he comes to a full standing position, I finally see his face. It's Hayden, walking toward me with his head hung low.

45

Hayden

two years ago

"MOM, don't worry. I'll be there," I call through the phone breathlessly to my mom on the other end.

I'm speed walking toward Au Revoir, the French bistro I've been working at as a pastry chef for the past three years, with the view of the reflective windows from the conservatory to my right.

"Okay," she answers, unconvinced. "I just know how things can be between you and your dad. I don't want you two to be all cross with each other for Thanksgiving dinner."

I sigh. While this is something that's caused a constant strain in our family dynamic, it seems pointless for her to continue to worry about something inevitable. My dad and I, we're always going to disagree. It seems to be our nature and something that's gotten worse over the years.

"I'll play nice," I offer, approaching Au Revoir. "Mom, I have to go. I'll call you later."

"Okay," she answers. "Let me know your flight details so we can pick you up at the airport."

"I will."

Jeannie Choe

As soon as I walk through the doors, glad to be out of the cold weather that seemed to have become increasingly chilly overnight, my eye catches on something bright and orange near the bakery side of the restaurant. When I look, I see a lone scarf draped over the back of a chair facing the window. I walk over, taking the scarf in my hands. It's warm and soft, as if the person wearing it left it behind only minutes ago.

I walk over to the register with the scarf in my hand just as a wave of something familiar hits my senses.

That smell...

I bring the scarf up closer to my face, realizing that the smell, like warmth and vanilla and home, is coming from the warm fibers lining the cashmere material.

Everything reminiscent and wistful hits me in the chest. My entire body feels like it's levitating, being transported back to a small classroom where inside it, I existed inside a bubble with a certain seventeen-year-old girl beside me. Everything about it reminds me of a time years ago, when so many things in my life felt unsure, there was a moment when hope bloomed and goodbyes were measured.

"Is everything okay, Hayden?" I look up to see Janet, our hostess-slash-cashier, behind the register in the bakery.

"Uh, yeah," I answer. "I guess someone left this behind." I reluctantly extend the scarf, not wanting to part with it, and Janet takes it from me.

"I'll hold on to it in case someone claims it."

"Thanks." I nod before walking into the kitchen.

present

I sat and watched. I watched as she smiled sweetly at her date, her round eyes looking at him while he looked at her with every flicker of heat that radiated through his body. I felt it coming off of him even

316

from where I was sitting. I watched as she politely stepped away, opening and closing the cab door before it drove off.

I shouldn't be here. I shouldn't fucking be here watching her come home from a date with another man. Watching as she moves on from everything that I want to share with her. But then she looks at me, her steps coming to a slow stop on the sidewalk as I walk toward her, not even bothering to fight this current that always seems to pull me closer to her.

Seeing her here now, it feels like a dream. I miss her so *fucking* much. And every second after she walked out of my apartment, I wanted so badly to tell her everything. About how I'm so scared to lose her again. How losing her when we were seventeen felt like losing a part of myself. I want more than anything to reach out to her, talk to her as if nothing has changed and the next time I would see her would be sitting in the classroom with her legs tucked underneath the lab table and her elbows resting on her opened binder.

"I—" I start to say. But then my words are cut short. Because she closes the space between us in three short strides. Her hair billows behind her as the cold wind blows past her. I hear her whimper, her breathing growing staggered as she crashes into me. Her body, so warm and so full of everything that makes her my Natalia, hits mine like her next breath depends on it.

My entire body wants to give in. To collapse to my knees while I hold her, not even bothering to tell her how I feel and letting my tears do the talking. I want to, but I know that I need to explain to her. She needs to know how I feel with words and promises. No more sitting on my feelings, letting them remain as questions that I'm too scared to answer. She needs to know how much I care about her, how much I love her.

"Nat," I rasp.

I hear her sniffle, her hold on me loosening. And just as I'm about to protest, she looks at me. Tears pool along the rims of her eyes as the tip of her nose reddens. Her lips scrunch together in a small pout, and the little crease between her brows fissures as the bubbling anger spills through her tears. What were tears of sadness and relief a second ago turn into anger and resentment. As a loose sob breaks from her lips, she starts pounding her fists into my chest.

"Where. Have. You. Been?!" she grunts between hits. I watch the tears stream down her cheeks as she continues to push me away. Her frustration causes all the hurt to spill through her words. I loosely hold her wrists in my hands before pulling her toward me, wrapping my arms around her.

"I'm sorry," I say, cradling her head. I kiss her temple, attempting to soothe her anger as I run my hand up and down her back. "I'm so sorry."

She pushes her hands into me, causing us to separate again. Her shoulders hunch forward as the anger melts into exhaustion. Her hands move to her cheeks, wiping the tears as they continue to pour. "You need to walk away if you aren't going to stick around because I can't do this. I can't..." She stops when a sob breaks loose from her lips.

I close the space between us with one quick stride. I lift my hands to reach for her before she turns away.

"You watched me walk away, Hayden. You made it so clear that you didn't want me, and I sat here completely heartbroken, wondering why I wasn't good enough!"

I cup my hands to her cheeks, frantically searching her eyes for any sliver of forgiveness she may have set aside for me. "You are more than enough for me. And I'm never letting you go."

She tries to pull away, but my hands grip her cheeks harder.

"I can't survive doing that again. I can't let you go and let another eight years pass by sitting here just thinking about you. I *can't* do that again." Everything about my voice says raw and unbridled. Because I've given up on trying to hold everything together. I don't care anymore. I don't care that she can see every bump and crevice of my heart, completely open and vulnerable. She could spend the rest of our lives holding it in her hands, memorizing all of the details that carry every ounce of love that I feel for her. And I would never expect to get it back. It belongs to her anyway.

The anger in her eyes dissolves, replaced with a face of questions.

Silent words of *what are you talking about* and *why didn't you tell me then* float between us.

"I love you so fucking much. And it...*hurts* thinking about this ending," I say, my voice cracking. I lean my forehead against hers and close my eyes, letting a warm breath plume into white mist in the space between us.

The ache in my chest forces an image into my brain. Me alone, without Natalia, never being able to hold her in my arms and knowing that she exists in this world without me. All because I let her go. As that ache turns into a knot of balled-up pain, my eyes grow wet. I realize I can never live that life. One without Natalia.

While the tears continue to trickle down her cheeks, a cry squeezes through her lips. "Hayden..." Her voice trembles and shakes as a hiccup causes her breath to hitch.

She leans her face toward me as I dip mine, our cheeks grazing against the other. I can't believe this is happening. After eight years, it's as if everything I wanted and every fear that crossed my mind canceled each other out and we're here now, trying to understand why this didn't happen so many years ago.

"I–I don't..." she whispers. She breathes a shaky sigh against my skin. "You aren't going to lose me again." She reaches for my hand, interlacing our fingers as she brings them flush against her heart. As our bodies come closer together, I can feel the heavy thumping of her heart against my hand.

"Nat," I said softly. "I know it doesn't make any sense for me to say this, especially after all this time..."

The middle corners of her brows turn up, coaxing the words out of me and allowing me to be completely honest.

"But I am so in love with you," I say, whispering the words against her lips. "A part of me feels like I've always loved you."

A loud sniffle draws in her next breath. And she nods. As if she doesn't have a single doubt, like she understands. As if I don't even need to say it out loud because she feels it. Every tenderness and throbbing of love that beats against my chest is loud enough for her to already know without me even saying it.

I bend down to kiss her. Not one that's deep or urgent but one that only skirts across the corners of her mouth. Along the lines that curve her bottom lip. Then I brush my cheek against the spots I just kissed, feeling her warm breath as it fogs in the cold air around us.

"What are you even doing here?" she asks, her voice hoarse and weak.

I take a small step back, reaching into my coat pocket and then revealing a small box for her in the middle of my palm. "I wanted to give you your Christmas present."

"You got me a present?" she asks, a small smile lifting the corners of her mouth.

I chuckle, unable to resist a smile seeing how adorable she gets at the mention of a gift.

"Open it," I urge, nudging the box closer to her.

She takes the box in her cold, delicate hands, carefully undoing the small bow that I personally tied that looks like a mangled knot of ribbon instead of a bow for presentation. When she lifts the lid, we both look to see the small plastic keychain sitting in the middle, scuffed with scratches that make the shiny surface dull from years of wear. She lifts it from the box and holds it between us.

"I got you one just like this," she whispers, the I Love NY swiveling as it moves against the metal links.

"It's the same one."

Her lips part into a surprised smile along with eyes that twinkle against the low street lights that hover over us. "You kept it this whole time?"

I nod.

"Why?"

"Because," I whisper, bringing my forehead to hers, "it's the only part of you that I got to hold on to."

Without saying anything else, her arms wrap around my neck, pulling me down to her for a kiss that makes me feel like I've come home. Full of warmth and vanilla. Full of everything that fills me with love, all of it for her.

"I'm sorry I didn't come sooner," I say. Even though she smiles at me, relief wrapped in every touch she traces on my now chilly skin, I can see that the month apart from her has caused scars to harden around her heart because I wasn't there.

"What took you so long?" she finally asks, her voice scratchy through the slight tremble in her wrinkled chin.

"I went back home."

When her brow furrows, her way of silently asking for more answers, I continue. "I went home for Thanksgiving, and Pat thought it would be good for me to take some time off."

She smiles, warming my heart as she squeezes my arm as if encouraging me to keep going.

"And..." I add. "I wanted to call you, but I...I didn't know if you would want—"

"I did," she interrupts. "I wanted you to call, to come to me. Anything."

"I thought I needed to stay away. At least until I figured out how I could be your friend without expecting more from you. But...I didn't know how to do that. I didn't know if I could..."

"That's not what I wanted," she lightly protests. "For us to be just friends. As much as I would have taken it if that's all you were going to offer me. It's not what I want." It's my turn to choke back the tightness in my throat and swallow through my trembling chin. She wants me. This whole time, she's wanted *me*.

"When I found this in my room," I continue, cupping my hand under hers, the one that's cradling the keychain, "I realized that I wasn't ready to let you go. And I wasn't willing to just be your friend or someone that you only called when you were lonely."

My thumb grazes against her lower lip when her teeth press into it. The full pout that swelled as she thoughtfully gnawed through her pain softens now as she lets my thumb run along the smooth surface of her lip.

"I want to be everything to you," I say, not even caring how my voice scratches, baring my heart to her, or how vulnerable I sound. "And I want to give you everything. My heart, the world, all the desserts and weird tasting foods."

She laughs a watery laugh, her eyes curving as her tears start to fall again. I swipe my thumb against her cheek as she leans closer to me. "I love you too, Hayden."

I let out a shaky sigh before kissing her. I kiss her as if I've been holding my breath this whole time and I've finally broken the surface. *She loves me.*

"Say it again," I whisper.

"I love you." Her hands roam all over me, pulling, gripping. "I love you, Hayden. I love you."

I didn't know I could physically feel gravity shift as the weight lifts off my entire body. Everything, from the burden of my dad's death I carried to every ounce of fear I never needed to have when it came to me and Natalia. It all becomes lighter, nonexistent, as Natalia tells me she loves me.

"*God*, I love you," I groan. My arms wrap around her waist as I feel her shiver, letting her absorb what little warmth I have left from sitting out in the cold for so long.

"Can we get you inside?" I ask, murmuring into her hair. "Get you somewhere warm."

She smiles up at me, nodding as the first snowflake falls and lands on her eyelash.

46

Hayden

present

MY HANDS ARE slick against Natalia's bare skin, damp and warm from the last hour we've spent tangled in her sheets. I run my fingers along the strands of hair matted to her forehead before trailing them down the dip in her spine. Her hooded eyes roll back as her head lolls to one side, holding on to my neck as she scrapes her nails against my bare back. Her legs are draped over mine, straddling me, as she slumps into my lap, coming down from the high of her third orgasm since I all but tore that sexy green dress off of her, exposing all of the irresistible valleys and rises of her curves underneath the soft fabric. Or was it her fourth? I lost count after the first two, unable to focus on anything besides the way her sweet pussy gripped me each time. And sweet baby Jesus, is her pussy fucking sweet. I don't want to do anything else for the rest of my life besides live buried inside her, feeling how tight she is, with her limbs wrapped around me and the rest of her body flush against my own. I will never get over the feel of her body against mine, all soft and warm and naked.

"Do you need to stop?" I ask, breathing against her hot skin, pressing light kisses along her collarbone, her neck, her ear. She moans as my teeth graze against her jaw, which makes me pull the skin at her waist, guiding her over me.

She shakes her head, answering me while working through what little energy she has left with her loose legs and almost rubberlike arms. "I just need a moment before my legs turn into absolute Jell-O."

I chuckle lightly before scooping my hand to the back of her head and fisting her hair to angle her face down toward me to kiss her. She complies, latching onto my lips and bringing her hands up to the side of my face, letting me run my tongue over the ridges of her mouth so that I can taste all of her.

"My lips are going to be chapped by tomorrow," she says into my mouth between our kisses.

"Sorry," I say through a smirk and a curved brow that says everything but sorry. "I've just missed these lips so much." My gaze lowers to her full lips, now swollen and smeared with the dark lipstick she so perfectly applied. She shifts over me, sliding in and out, causing me to hum with pleasure into our kiss. "I thought you needed a moment," I groan when she sinks deeper into me.

"Yeah, but when you talk about my lips like that, I feel like I've gained all of my energy back."

I roll over her, laying her down, and her head lazily hits the mattress. My body hovers above her before I grab both her hands and bring them above her head, pressing them into the mattress as her body stretches under me. I slowly guide myself in and out of her, loving the way she moans when I do it. It sounds so erotic, like I could get off from the mere sound of her pleasure.

"I can't believe we spent all this time *not* doing this," she says, her voice strained as her hands break free from my grip and run along my bicep.

"Tell me about it." I lower myself against her while giving me enough space to lick her along the upper curve of her breast, loving the way her soft skin feels against my tongue. "We were so fucking stupid."

She laughs, the muscles that hold me close inside her clenching around me, making my own arms turn into mush while I bury my face into her shoulder. I continue to thrust into her, building up my pace as

I watch the laughter wipe off her face, replacing it into a twisted look that skims that fine line between pain and pleasure.

Her breathing picks up, matching mine, while her legs draw up to my sides. She doesn't say anything. Instead, she lets out what sounds like a mixture of a moan and grunt, signaling the start of another orgasm building inside of her. I can tell by the way her breathing hitches and her mouth forms in a perfect O.

God, she looks so *fucking* sexy.

Just as I feel her orgasm clench around me, the sensation making me feel like my spirit has lifted out of my body and sits hovering over me until I somehow recover, I come too. I groan so loud, I have to muffle the sound against her neck, loving the way she still smells like vanilla, even through the sweat that seeps through her pores.

"*Really* fucking stupid," I say breathlessly into the sheets that surround us. We both smile against each other's skin, basking in the aftermath of the most heated sex I've ever had. That we've *both* ever had. Because I don't even need to ask her to know that it's never been like this with anyone else. Not with that weasel of an ex-boyfriend of hers or anyone else before that. *Only me.*

When we finally catch our breaths, we wrap ourselves in the blankets and watch the night sky through the large windows that line Natalia's bedroom walls. We watch as the light snowfall filters through the cold air outside, admiring it as it coasts through glowing streetlights. I pull her against me, loving the way her curved backside molds against my front, and bury my face into her hair.

My eyes start to feel heavy when I feel Natalia's body pull away from me. She reaches toward her nightstand, where my gift rests in the small box I wrapped it in. She takes it in her hand, letting the round metal ring loop through her index finger as the large charm rests in her palm. She's holding it up in front of her when she turns to face me.

"I still can't believe you kept this all these years."

My hand rests on her stomach, warm and still slightly damp, as I watch her look at the keychain in awe.

"It's the best Christmas present I could ever ask for," she whispers, holding it against her bare chest.

My brows lift with a playful smile, caressing the skin lining her stomach and waist. "Better than a box of lemon tarts?"

She nods eagerly. "Better than a whole tray."

I chuckle, nuzzling into her neck.

And then she gasps. "I didn't get you anything!"

I nuzzle deeper, my tongue poking through my lips as it runs along the curve of her neck. And I feel a low hum vibrate through her skin. "I can think of about nineteen ways you can make it up to me."

"Nineteen?!" she exclaims through a laugh. "We aren't bunnies, Marshall."

I bury my face into her neck again, finding that soft spot below her ear completely irresistible as I tremble with laughter. I pinch her side and she squirms, clawing at the sheets to get away from me. I use my strength to pull her toward me, and she yelps before a fit of laughter makes her breathless.

"*God*, I love how you feel." I kiss her deeply, and her body becomes limp in my arms. So pliable and receptive as her hand moves between us to grip my already growing erection. I groan a deep, rumbling growl as I feel her smile against my lips.

I arch a brow, bucking into her hand as I grow harder from her purposeful strokes. "Nineteen doesn't seem that high of a number now, does it?" I whisper.

Natalia's sweet laugh is the last thing I hear before she climbs back on top of me, pressing her warm, naked body against mine as I fall into a past that I dreamed into reality.

epilogue

Hayden

three years later

"HAYDEN! *The Empire Tribune* is here for the pictures!"

I look up from the bustling kitchen as Natalia scurries back out the doors leading to the now-crowded dining room. I look to my right at Johnny, my new sous chef, before he nods a quick okay to excuse me from the kitchen. When I enter the dining room, everyone turns to face me, cheering and clapping as they extend their warm congratulations. The crowd filled with friends, family, and colleagues is gathered to celebrate the biggest professional milestone I could ever achieve: opening my own restaurant.

"They're waiting outside," Natalia says, taking my hand as we walk out to the brisk spring air providing the perfect backdrop for our grand opening. A sweet smile peeks through her cherry lips matching the red sundress twirling at her waist. Her hair, wavy and half of it piled on top of her head, billows down her back as she turns to look at me over her shoulder.

Just a year and a half after working with Pat as his head chef, popularity for Pour Toujours seemed to grow overnight. I started incorporating dishes and culinary techniques that were new and bold. And it caught the attention of food crazed New Yorkers and those that traveled the trek to Manhattan to sample Pour Toujours's emergent menu. The restaurant that was already fairly busy with regulars and tourists started to grow cramped with reservations filling five to six months in advance.

When I set up announcements about my restaurant's opening, journalists, food critics, and even social media influencers reached out to me, wanting to be one of the first to try my food. So naturally, what would have been a simple grand opening turned into a frenzy of photographers, upbeat music, and good food.

I reach for the obnoxiously large gold scissors and grip the heavy handles as the photographers position themselves at the far end of the sidewalk close to the bustling street. I stand on the other side of the wide red ribbon, Natalia standing on one side of me and my mom and Pat standing on the other, my uncle extending the same support he's offered since I told him about my plans to branch out on my own. The four of us smile proudly, gleaming with glee as we face the cameras, and I slice open the blades toward the waiting ribbon.

I turn to Natalia before I squeeze the handles together. "Come on," I say, gesturing toward my ready hands. "You're doing this with me."

"Hayden, this is your day," she protests through a sweet smile, her brown eyes looking like warm pools of honey in the bright sunlight.

I lean down and quickly peck her cheek. "This is as much my day as it is yours." I say it because it's true.

Every fruit of labor that I poured into this restaurant over the past seventeen months was all with Natalia by my side. She was the one who slapped on protective goggles and gloves as she tore down drywall. She was the one who scurried all over town, choosing the right china and glassware when I was elbow deep in vendor selections and employee interviews. She was the one who stayed up with me late at night when the doubts still filtered through, reminding me that every bit of my hard work was proof that I could do this.

And it was she who inspired the name I gave our restaurant. My bright ray of sunshine that lights up everything around her, causing the air to shift into something hopeful.

Soleil. I literally could not have done this without her.

I nudge at her again, watching the way her smile widens and her eyes light up with laughter as she gently grips the scissors that are becoming heavier in my hands.

"For Soleil," Natalia whispers as she lets me guide the way.

"For Soleil," I repeat.

We look back at the cameras as the ribbon breaks between the surprisingly sharp blades, dropping to the concrete as a roar of clapping and flashes of cameras surround us.

Natalia

The dining room is empty. The floor swept clear of the littered trash and remnants of a celebration. Hayden and I are surrounded by the low glow of candlelight still lit on the tables, all now cleared and cleaned with the essential staff having gone home for the night. It's late, nearing one a.m., but we're both still high on the day. A day spent surrounded by our friends and family, all supporting Hayden while extending their true congratulations on such a successful grand opening.

"Is everything locked up?" I ask, gesturing toward the back door on the other side of the kitchen.

Hayden nods as he neatly tucks away a stack of menus behind the hostess desk at the front entrance. His chef's uniform, with the Soleil name embroidered in a golden yellow over the left side of his chest, is unbuttoned, exposing his white undershirt pulled tight over his torso. He looks so comfortable, completely in his element, as if finally finding a place where he belongs. He rummages through something else with his head ducked low behind the hostess desk.

"Was there something else that you needed to take care of?" I ask.

And instead of answering, Hayden's face reemerges with a grin and a small speaker held in his hand.

"What's that?"

He clicks on the speaker that's already connected to his phone via

Jeannie Choe

Bluetooth, and music filled with guitar strings and slow piano tunes fills the air. He saunters toward me with a hand extended my way as a small giggle leaves my lips.

"May I have this dance?" he asks, tilting his head toward me. I gently place my hand in his as he pulls me to him. His arm snakes around my waist at the same time my hand reaches for his shoulder. We start to sway, moving gently with the music as our bodies finally relax.

I hum against his warmth, letting the day melt off, finally able to enjoy my alone time with Hayden. As much as I spent most of the day by his side, I missed him. I missed being alone with him in our own little Hayden and Natalia bubble.

"Thank you for all of your help today," he whispers into my hair. "I think a nice foot massage is in order when we get home."

I nod against his chest. "I agree." I feel his body vibrate with a light laughter as his hold on me tightens, pulling me closer as his warmth spreads through me.

I can't wait to get home, our home. As soon as the grand opening for Soleil was set on paper, we hunted down an apartment for us two. Something small and affordable where we could comfortably watch Hayden's business grow. When we finally found a one-bedroom that fit our budget in Brooklyn Heights with a teeny-tiny view of the East River, we were ecstatic. No more late nights having to sleep in separate apartments with good night texts and good morning phone calls instead of extending those greetings face to face. No more tiptoeing around Dexter or Carmen when we would spend the night at each other's apartments. Since we moved in two months ago, we've been gradually furnishing our apartment and unpacking our things into an area of permanence rather than a small sock drawer in the other's bedrooms. We're making the small apartment ours, and it couldn't be more perfect.

"You did good, Hayden," I whisper, my eyes closed while letting Hayden continue leading our dance. "Your dad would have been so proud."

I pull away to look at him, peering up as he swallows a knotted ball down his throat. He nods, his brow furrowing with understanding. We both turn our heads at the same time, our gazes landing on the small table situated in the far corner of the restaurant. It sits empty, much like all the other tables, but this one will stay empty, with a framed photo hanging on the wall above it. It's an old grainy picture of Hayden and his dad. Hayden is sitting square on his dad's shoulders, both of them wearing matching football jerseys as their focus is on the football field behind the camera. Hayden told me it was taken when he was four years old at his first Cleveland Browns game. When he showed it to me, I had it framed, set aside so that we could reserve this table for his dad. So that he'll always be there. For every day the restaurant opens and every night that it closes, Greg Marshall will be there, right next to his son.

"I couldn't have done this without you," he whispers, his voice cracking as he rests his forehead against mine. "Soleil would never have happened without you by my side."

"Hayden, this is all you," I argue. Because it is. As much as he expressed his appreciation for all of my help, every bit of the hard work poured into this restaurant was because of his efforts. All of the days he spent brainstorming new flavor combinations and design options for the restaurant's interior while I was at work. All the long nights taking care of miscellaneous details or organizing shipments. All of it is evident in today's success.

He smiles, his eyes closing as he lowers his face to nuzzle his cheek against mine. "Always so modest," he says, smiling against my skin. He turns his face, letting his lips brush against mine as his hands travel up my back to my nape. He guides me toward a kiss, one that's so passionate that I feel breathless.

"I love you so much," he says, his hot breath skirting over my throbbing lips.

I sigh, my heart feeling so full, brimming with too many emotions. "I love you too."

Our bodies continue to move, no sign from either one of us wanting to separate and make the trek back home. We could stay in this moment forever, wrapped in our own bubble with no one to disturb it.

I feel Hayden's hand roam over my body, trailing light sweeps down my arm before finding my hand. He links our fingers together and brings them to the small space between us, nestling them against our hearts. We look into each other's eyes with every emotion, every feeling pulling to the surface.

I squeeze his hand a little tighter, wrapping my fingers around his to let him know that I don't ever want to let him go. I feel his breath stutter, short gasps leaving his parted lips. His eyes squint, and a small furrow deepens between his brows, almost as if he's realizing something. Some new revelation that enters his heart as his breathing kicks up and his heart beats faster against my hand.

"Marry me," Hayden whispers.

"What?"

"Marry me," he says again, a little louder than the whisper he let squeeze through his lips. I pull away, eyes wide and looking for any indication that he's joking. "I mean it."

Our bodies stop swaying, and he lets go of my hand, reaching into his pocket to reveal a small velvet envelope with a shiny metal clasp. Something so discreet I would have never noticed it.

"I got this a couple months ago, and I've been waiting for...I don't know what I was waiting for because I've known I want to marry you for a long time now. I guess I just wanted to make sure the moment felt right."

He takes a small step back, stooping down so he kneels on one knee as he peels back the flap of the envelope to expose a beautiful, sparkling ring that looks to be from a different time period. "Marry me?"

I nod, smiling as a tear trickles down my cheek. "Yes, of course I'll marry you!"

He squeals. Actually, we both do as he stands, lifting me in his arms and twirling me in the small space. When we both grow dizzy, he sets me down. His trembling hands reach for my left hand, sliding the ring onto my ring finger.

"It's vintage," he explains. "The seller said circa 1920. Art déco."

"It's beautiful," I gasp. How did he figure out something so timeless would be so perfect for me, the hopeless romantic who always dreamed of her happily ever after?

He drops my hand and cups my face before kissing me. He groans into my mouth as his hands move urgently over my body, pulling at my clothes and begging to be closer to me.

"We should get home before we end up deflowering little miss Soleil," I say breathlessly as I pull away from him. "We don't want to break a health code violation."

He laughs, nuzzling his face into my neck as he practically carries me through the restaurant. "Agreed," he murmurs against my skin, pecking featherlight kisses over my flushed cheeks.

I flit around the tables, blowing out all the candles as Hayden does a once-over, acting much like the responsible adults we've grown into. When Hayden finally locks up and we walk into the late city night, we skip as we head home.

Our home. Our future. All full of promises that we intend to keep.

a look at book two

No Place Like You

Falling for him once was a risk. Falling for him again might break her.

Lucy Marquez has always done what's expected—steady jobs, quiet sacrifices, and a selfless smile. But when an internship at a prestigious New York photography agency offers her a chance to pursue her dreams, she takes the leap, keeping one small secret: her family has no idea she's in the city.

Dexter Greer is comfortable in his Brooklyn bubble—a stable life, low-key nights, and an apartment he's finally settled into. But when Lucy, the woman who walked out of his life three years ago, turns up in his orbit, it's anything but simple.

Thrown together in the city that never sleeps, their chemistry reignites, blurring the lines between unfinished business and undeniable attraction. But with Lucy hiding her true purpose and Dexter guarding his heart, they'll have to decide if love is worth the risk—especially when there's no place like them.

AVAILABLE APRIL 2025

acknowledgments

I can't believe I'm writing this for the second time. The first time around, it felt surreal. Now, it feels like a fairy tale.

There are so many people that I need, and want, to thank for making this come true. But I need to start with the biggest support system my hopeful little heart could have conjured up: BOOK-STAGRAM.

How is it possible that this many supportive, loving, caring, and just overall amazingly wonderful number of people exist in this one little corner of the interweb? Just HOW?! I am in awe of every single one of you every day. The constant messages of support, the hyping each other up, and undying love for books that brought us all together. Every single one of you is the mirror that I should be looking into every morning. Not the one I see from across the bathroom sink, poking at every flaw and doubt I will never be rid of. It should be all of you, reminding me to love myself and to love each other. So, from the bottom of my heart, THANK YOU.

An extra special thank you to some of my bookstagram sisters: Katherine, Hazel, Kaye, Katy, Molly, Lek, Leni, Anna, Min Young, and Cleo. You ladies are my rock, my first readers that showed nothing but love for my babies. Without every word of encouragement and guidance, this book would not have been in existence. Thank you! And an especially big thanks to April. You are the PA I dreamed up, always there to be the string on my pinky when I have ten million things to juggle. To take on so many things that I will never be able to do on my own. Thank you for keeping my head on my shoulders when I feel like it's going to spin right off!

To my beloved readers... The right words can't be summoned to bundle what I feel for you guys. First off, if I try, I'll just end up crying ugly tears. But second, there is simply no way I can express the deep gratitude I have for every single one of you. Thank you for simply being you and let's all vow to never stop reading and never stop learning.

To my girls, and the ones that this book is dedicated to: Amy, Cheann, Mhelisa, and Rose. This sisterhood is the one I want to grow old with and I expect nothing less from each and every one of you.

To my amazing husband. No story I write, no book I publish will ever be in existence without you. This book is as much yours as it is mine. Thank you for being the book husband of my dreams. I love you so much.

And my babies. I do this for you. So you know to always chase your dreams. We will always be here to support your dreams, so never stop dreaming. The sky's the limit. Mommy and Daddy will always be here to help you reach it.

And, last yet certainly not least, my editor, Katie, my cover designer who managed to bring Hayden and Natalia to life, Sarah, and my amazing beta/proofreader, Anna. You ladies are wonderful at what you do. Your dedication to your craft shows in the quality of your work and I feel so honored to have each of you be a part of this process.

—Jeannie Choe

jc

JEANNIE CHOE
ROMANCE AUTHOR

Specializing in new adult contemporary romance novels, Jeannie Choe offers stories ranging from angsty and emotional to heartfelt and outright adorable. Because who doesn't love a happily ever after filled with squeal-inducing moments of romantic gestures?

Living off an endless number of paperbacks, cold brews, and 2000's rom-coms, Jeannie lives in Southern California spending her days with her family and two attention-seeking elder dachshunds.

www.jeanniechoeauthor.com

f 🅾 ⓐ ♪

www.ingramcontent.com/pod-product-compliance
Lightning Source LLC
LaVergne TN
LVHW040754300125
802365LV00022B/449